Out of the Darkness, a Sound Came to Him— a Steady Drone, a Chanting by Many Voices

He turned to flee, charging aimlessly into the blackness of the great forest. Running blindly, he stumbled and fell hard to the ground. Fear paralyzed him and an icy sweat caressed his spine. He sensed another presence.

A huge figure towered above him. Entirely naked, with a thick coil of gleaming gold at its throat, the muscular form clutched a double-bladed axe in its right hand and a heavy sword in its left.

As the axe hand slowly raised, the fallen man cried out. He clawed desperately at the earth as he struggled to flee from the savage creature. Then a hand, hot and pulsing with blood, gripped his shoulder. The drone of heathen chanting filled his skull and fetid hissing breath was on his cheek. He knew at that terrible moment that this was how it must end...

TRINITY GROVE

DAVID VANMETER SMITH

AVON BOOKS  NEW YORK

Grateful acknowledgment is made for permission to reprint the following:

Excerpt from *Angel Pavement* by J.B. Priestley; reprinted by permission of the Peters Fraser & Dunlop Group Ltd.

Excerpt from *The Masters* by C.P. Snow. Copyright © 1951 by C.P. Snow; copyright renewed © 1979. Reprinted by permission of Charles Scribner's Sons, an imprint of Macmillan Publishing Company.

TRINITY GROVE is an original publication of Avon Books. This work has never before appeared in book form. This work is a novel. Any similarity to actual persons or events is purely coincidental.

AVON BOOKS
A division of
The Hearst Corporation
105 Madison Avenue
New York, New York 10016

Copyright © 1990 by David VanMeter Smith
Front cover illustration by Gary Ruddell
Published by arrangement with the author
Library of Congress Catalog Card Number: 89-91363
ISBN: 0-380-75835-0

First Avon Books Printing: February 1990

AVON TRADEMARK REG. U.S. PAT. OFF. AND IN OTHER COUNTRIES, MARCA REGISTRADA, HECHO EN U.S.A.

Printed in the U.S.A.

RA   10   9   8   7   6   5   4   3   2   1

To my mother, Martha,
who taught me to love books
before I could even read

PROLOGUE

Midsummer Cambridge

The long-roofed chapel of
    King's College lifts
Turrets and pinnacles in
    answering files,
Extended high above a dusky grove.

> William Wordsworth (1770–1850)
> St. John's College

Seen from above, the figures hurrying across the carefully manicured grass are little more than confetti scattered across a green baize surface. But on closer inspection it can be seen that all these multicolored specks are moving in unison toward a central point near the river. A section of the gently sloping riverbank has been cordoned off by policemen's black peaked caps, and the crowd, which has been forming for some time, is pressing forward as close as it can to the scene.

Cambridge college gardeners are meticulous about the grass that is allowed to grow within the precincts of the ancient institutions they serve, and the lawn between the River Cam and King's College Chapel is a particular showplace. The brilliant expanse of green provides a perfect counterpoint to the soaring windows and spires of the huge chapel built and added to by three Henrys, kings of England. But on this morning the shadow of the west end of the magnificent building falls on dozens of students, townspeople, and tourists tracking across its carefully tended green, all drawn like a magnet by the rumor of murder.

An early morning mist rises gray and ghostly from the river, clinging to its banks like cotton to a wound. The morning sun is just breaking through an overcast charcoal sky, heavy with rain barely held in check. Nearby, black-faced sheep graze stupidly in King's Meadow across the river, their vacant chewing faces oblivious to the unusual activity around the waterway they share.

Coming closer still, two heads stand out in the crowd streaming toward the riverbank. A battered Irish tweed and a trilby, both topping earth-colored raincoats, push forward with authority. Passing police lines with a nod of glossy cap visors, the two move quickly down to a small knot of men and a lumpish black tarpaulin near the steaming river.

Detective Inspector Lewis Janeway and Detective Sergeant Church are not used to being called out of their beds so early on a Saturday. Cambridge is generally a quiet town. A town of academics and the tradesmen and servants who tend to their needs. Because the university dons generally attack one another only with the pen, homicide is a most uncommon event.

Black plastic is pulled back to reveal the body discovered washed up on the bank less than an hour before. Janeway has seen bodies before, with Scotland Yard and before that in the army, but he is not prepared for what he sees now. This is not a victim of drowning. It is a young man, foreign-looking, black hair, dark eyes open and staring, and every bone in the body appears to have been broken. Hands, arms, and neck are twisted at wild angles, and several bones protrude grotesquely through the skin. The body is naked, and its dead white flesh is literally covered with cuts, some very deep, others little more than scratches. The left leg is nearly hacked through at the calf. Worse still, causing even Sergeant Church to swallow hard, the body has been disemboweled.

Janeway orders constables to disperse the crowd or at least to push them back. Newspaper photographers and a few ghoulish tourists are snapping pictures of the scene from the bridges spanning the river nearby. Constables are dispatched to clear the bridges and cordon off both sides of the riverbank upstream while a radio call goes out for more men.

The River Cam is only the size of a small canal as it meanders around the backs of Cambridge college buildings. Just wide enough for several narrow punts, with students or tourists manning long poles at one end, to pass in midstream. The body may have been dropped into the flow upstream and carried by the current to be washed up here, where there is no wall along the low bank near King's.

While Church oversees the grisly work of the forensic team, Janeway thinks of the long hours ahead, combing the banks of the Cam for evidence and questioning students and dons whose medieval college windows overlook the river. With the crowd pushed back, police photographers are now grimacing and talking among themselves as they take their shots of the mangled corpse.

The excitement of the challenge is already making Janeway's heart beat faster. He looks up at the twin spires of the four-hundred-year-old chapel towering over the scene and asks silently for guidance. But the tall figure in the crushed tweed hat standing down among the popping flashbulbs on the riverbank gets no reply.

THE
LAST
DAY

CHAPTER 1

Four months later
Saturday, October 30
Trinity Wood

But the best I've known
Stays here, and changes, breaks, grows old, is blown
About the winds of the world, and fades from brains
Of living men, and dies.

Rupert Brooke (1887–1915)
King's College

Morning arrived in a blue haze. Soon the sun pushed its way through the mist, and then it shone so brightly that the clear sky around it showed white and only gradually turned to a deep ultramarine to the north and south. The western sky was bluest of all. Everything else within sight—grass, shrubs, hedgerows—was glistening green, illuminated by the sun's brilliance. This blue-green symmetry was broken only here and there by the scarlet red of a poppy and by the black curtain of Trinity Wood, shadowboxed by the low-hanging sun.

Once, the great Forest of Essex had stretched out across southeastern England from the Bow in London to the Cambridgeshire fens. But now only Epping Forest and a few isolated stands of woods such as this one remained uncut. Huge swatches of virgin timber had been downed to build the fleets that had beaten back the Spanish Armada and then gone on to paint the map of the world imperial red over the course of the next three centuries. During that same time farmers had pushed their fields steadily forward, out into the remaining woodlands. Later still, it had been the turn of the developers and modern town planners to have their way with what was left of the original forest lands.

This ancient stand of trees might have been cut too if it had not been the property of Trinity College. The great Cambridge college, the largest landowner in Britain after the Crown and the Church, owned so much land that this small forest plot had escaped notice and so escaped the feller's axe over the centuries.

A morning breeze blew in off the breakers of the North Sea forty miles to the east. It rustled the topmost branches and rattled the dry autumn leaves of the oaks in Trinity Wood. But deep within the heart of the wood there was silence.

No wind stirred the branches of the ancient trees of Trinity Grove. The circle of massive oaks around the clearing hidden deep inside the wood looked out impassively on the stillness. No insects rode the beams of morning sunlight in the forest clearing. No creatures moved among the fallen leaves.

All was quiet in Trinity Grove until a sudden, hollow rush of air began to climb through the trunk of the largest oak, building like a wind swirling up from the depths of the earth. It issued forth from a twisted knothole mouth in a gnarled shape like the face of a man high up on the moss green trunk. The wind rushed out, breaking the stillness of the ancient grove and carrying with it sounds of shouting and cries of pain and a faint trace of music like a hollow flute. It was almost time.

The young man stood at his window watching the woods. The scene was beautiful and full of peace in the early morning light. Insects swam around close to the ground, and thrushes noisily pursued them through the wet grass. It was the sort of morning on which adventures are begun.

Unfortunately, Nick Lombard, an American student three thousand miles from home, had not planned any adventures for this particular morning. It had been a triumph of sorts simply to drag himself out of bed. He noticed that the windows were frosted over for the first time that year. The heavy woolen robe felt good and warm in the chilly room.

After lighting the small gas fire, he left it to begin its impossible task of warming his single drafty room. Nick went out into the hallway and walked to the front door of the old house. Stepping out into the autumn freshness, he was blinded for a moment by the sun, blazing coldly in the eastern sky above Trinity Wood. The air was as wakeful as a cold shower, surrounding him with a chill vitality.

Autumn for Nick had always possessed just as much potential for new beginnings as spring. These were the two seasons for change. Summer being too hot and winter too cold for anything much greater than sitting and dreaming of what could be done in the spring or fall.

As his bare feet began to feel the cold, Nick retreated back inside the old farmhouse. Wychfield was a college hostel for graduate students. Located about a mile from the center of Cambridge, Wychfield was the property of Trinity Hall, one of the oldest of the twenty-five colleges that made up the ancient University of Cambridge.

With the influx of research students in the 1970s, the large house had been converted into nine bed-sits for students who could not be accommodated in the medieval college buildings in the town. It was a huge, rambling two-story structure with eight large brick chimneys rising from its steeply peaked roof. The college had invested in a modicum of modernization for the old house, but the solid stone foundations of Wychfield dated back at least a thousand years—before the Domesday Book, where the new Norman masters of England had carefully recorded the landholdings of its Saxon lord.

After dressing and downing a watery cup of instant coffee, Nick thought about going over his notes. Stacked beside his desk were a dozen file boxes filled with five-by-eight note cards, each with a single item of information on the subject of the origins of the Tory party.

Nick was beginning his third year of Ph.D. research, and he felt he was finally making some headway. It had taken a full six months just to narrow his subject sufficiently to begin his dissertation. In the following year and a half he had examined numerous volumes, stacks, and dusty bundles of private papers and obscure correspondence. All his efforts to date were distilled onto the five or six hundred notecards before him. After two years of research, he was sorting his notes. Soon he could actually begin to write.

But this morning he simply stood by his window looking out toward Trinity Wood. He watched a swallow chasing an insect across the lawn. It swooped and dove and then poised, hovering motionless in the air like a hummingbird for a moment before diving again to within an inch of the ground in pursuit of its prey. The chase seemed more of a game than a life-and-death struggle for survival. Nick continued to watch until the flight of the hunter and the hunted led them out of his field of vision toward the wood. Then he left the house.

Trinity Wood lay between the old farmhouse and the shortest approach to the town, Madingley Road. There was a more direct, though longer route into Cambridge along the busy Huntingdon Road, but Nick often took the pleasant shortcut through the woods along a narrow path cut by generations of farmers and woodsmen before him. To get to the woods, Nick first had to cross a field, part of Wychfield Farm, which lay between the tree line and his window.

Plunging his hands into the pockets of his jeans as he trudged across the field, Nick was aware of the shortness of the sleeves of his corduroy sports coat. He had never considered himself tall at five feet ten inches, but he had found that Americans tended to be longer in the arms and legs than the clothes sold in English shops. The wind blew his dark hair across his forehead. Nick had his father's Italian-American looks, but had inherited his mother's clear blue eyes.

He thought of Tony Lombard, retired now from the Pittsburgh glassworks and hating every minute of it. His mother had died when he was still in high school, and he was glad to have three sisters living near enough to look after his dad. He reminded himself to finish a letter home. The idea of graduate school in England had caused some dissension in his family, but his father had finally settled the matter. Nick could still picture Tony looking up from his armchair by the television and laughing, "Who knows, if the boy comes back a doctor, maybe he can cure my achin' back."

Nick noticed the quiet as soon as he entered the woods. It was like stepping into a cathedral. Oaks, elms, and holly pressed up close to the edge of the path. Overhead the branches of trees formed a natural vaulting through which Nick could hear the wind whistling softly as he walked down the long, sheltering tunnel. Damp leaves muffled his footfalls. Occasionally he passed through a golden shaft of sunlight from a gap in the overhead canopy. Once he turned sharply at what must have been the sound of a small forest animal rustling the bushes deeper in the woods. On other afternoons Nick had taken time to wander, exploring small pathways and tracks, but today he walked on.

Midway along the footpath he passed a small, overgrown turning that led toward the oldest stand of trees in this ancient woods. Located near a natural clearing at the heart of the forest was a stand of oaks known to many generations of country people as Trinity Grove. Nick knew that the existence of the old grove was not well known anymore. None of his friends had ever been there, and he had only managed to find it once himself. But the sight of the gnarled and massive oaks had been worth the effort. He remembered simply standing and staring dumbly, awed by the age and sanctity of the spot.

As he walked past the obscure side-turning, Nick promised himself that he would find the hidden grove again someday. The commonplace rustlings of the ancient woodland died in his wake as the dark-haired foreigner passed through its precincts. A choice must soon be made.

CHAPTER 2

Saturday morning
Cambridge

Rumors strange
And of unholy nature, are abroad.

Lord Byron (1788–1824)
Trinity College

The tall, erect figure of Detective Inspector Lewis Janeway strode briskly down Emmanuel Road toward the Cambridge City Police Headquarters on Parkside. His gray, military-style overcoat was buttoned against the autumn morning chill, and his battered tweed hat sat firmly on his head. Behind his back his gloved hands clasped the slim leather swagger stick that he had continued to carry after leaving the Royal Armoured Corps thirteen years before. The rest of his uniform was carefully packed away in a brass-bound trunk in his flat, but it had not seemed natural to him to part with the stick that had been an extension of his arm for so long. He had carried it during his ten years of service with Scotland Yard, and despite curious glances from some of the younger constables, he had continued to carry it during the past three years of his semiretirement with the Cambridge City Police.

It was not unusual to find him making his way to the station on a Saturday morning. Not since the murder. Janeway's enthusiasm was running at a rate he had not known since leaving the Yard. He had not realized just how much he had missed the hunt.

Lewis Janeway was used to action, and he never would have left Scotland Yard in his mid-fifties had he not suffered a stroke. After three years of carefully moderated activity, his strength had returned, but he had felt himself slipping into a certain lethargy in the quiet college town—until the murder.

Once again he went over the circumstances of the crime in his mind. It did not fit any pattern he had encountered before. The murder victim was a young Spaniard studying at one of the many small language schools in Cambridge, taking advantage of the famous name of the town. The boy had no known enemies, or friends for that matter. He had only been in the city for a month, in a summer program, and had kept to himself. Janeway had thought at first that there might be politics involved, but his inquiries with Spanish authorities and with Interpol had confirmed all the details the young man had given to the school and to British Customs about himself. He was not politically active, had no history of drug use, and no police record. He was a serious student, a practicing Roman Catholic, and was studying English in order to enter his father's small export business.

All very commendable, but it gave Janeway absolutely nothing to build on. He glanced across to Parker's Piece, where two students were energetically kicking a ball around on the grass. The dead student, Vicente Cordillo, had also been athletic. According to the few language students who had known him, Cordillo had been an enthusiastic cyclist. To keep in condition, he had bought a used ten-speed cycle and had spent most of his free time exploring the countryside around the town. On the last afternoon Cordillo was seen alive, he had left his rooming house dressed for cycling.

Janeway was sure there must be some hint of a motive he was overlooking. Jealousy? In Janeway's experience, love ranked only slightly lower than greed and distinctly above any other passion as a motive for violence. One acquaintance had informed the police that Cordillo had mentioned meeting a girl about a week before his death. The boy had casually commented on his luck in meeting a very attractive young woman, a blonde, but had said no more about her. No one had seen him with a girl, and there was no reason to believe that he had ever seen her again after that first meeting. Still, Janeway thought it odd that if she was still in Cambridge, the girl had not come forward despite the numerous appeals in the press and in student publications.

The inspector turned briskly into the modern brick building housing the Cambridge City Police Headquarters. At the front desk the duty sergeant and a uniformed constable greeted him respectfully.

"Morning, Inspector."

He touched the brim of his hat with his stick. In three years he had earned their respect, and he hoped their confidence, but he had not tried to encourage an informal familiarity with the men of the force. He had learned in the army that men were more likely to place their trust in a leader who remained something of an enigma. Soldiers didn't look for a friend in their officers. They counted on those hidden depths, whether real or imagined, to bring them through unforeseen difficulties in times of crisis.

Two weeks ago the yellow bicycle described by Vicente Cordillo's landlady had been found neatly and properly chained to a bike rack in Churchill College. Since then, police inquiries had centered on Churchill and the areas of Madingley Road and Storeys Way nearby. Janeway had read dozens of reports on the questioning of students, staff, dons, and local residents. He had spoken to many people himself, though absolutely nothing useful had been learned. Photos of the dark-haired youth had been posted all around Churchill College, but no one remembered seeing him there. Churchill was coed. He could have gone there to see a girl, but Janeway had no full description of Cordillo's reported blond acquaintance.

The inspector's upstairs office in a front corner of the building was furnished with comfortable pieces, most of which he had purchased at his own expense or brought with him. Janeway felt that if he was to spend most of his waking hours in an office, it should at least feel like home. He had rejected the functional modern furnishings provided by the city and moved in a large oak library desk and a high-backed swivel chair, as well as several overstuffed armchairs and a battered leather divan, where he had spent more than one night since the murder investigation had begun. The office was not really large, and it was overcrammed with furniture, but he liked it that way. A large window looked out on Parkside, and the first thing Janeway did on entering the room was to raise the louvered blinds.

Late morning sunlight fell on the rich colors of a Bokhara as he hung his hat and coat and habitually moved toward his desk near the window. He sat leaning back in his chair, hands behind his head, and gazed out at the park as his thoughts continued, uninterrupted by the familiar motions of beginning another working day.

Every time it seemed as though he might find some pattern or motive in the crime, he came up against the apparent irrationality of the way in which the murder must have been committed. The brutality with which the body of a strong young man had been torn apart was difficult to imagine. The autopsy report had detailed the numerous cuts and wounds on the body, in which had been found traces of soil and vegetable matter common to Cambridgeshire, as well as microscopic traces of several metals, including copper, iron, and tin, apparently from the weapon or weapons used in the attack. Janeway was convinced that the killing had not occurred on the banks of the Cam anywhere near where the body had been found. The ground and gardens on both sides of the river had been exhaustively searched without result.

Every contact and informant was being drawn upon. If a break came in this case, Janeway was sure it would come from someone who had heard or seen something on the night of the murder. From the extent of the wounds, it appeared that more than one person must surely have been involved. The angles of the blows struck seemed to bear this out. Many of the cuts and scratches on Vicente Cordillo's body were superficial and could have been caused in any number of ways: a fall from a bicycle into a roadside hedge, or running through bushes or heavy underbrush—either of which would also explain the particles of vegetation in the wounds. Other abrasions, however, were more massive than would have been made even by a knife blade. Several had cut through bone and could only have been inflicted by a heavy-bladed instrument like an axe or a butcher's cleaver wielded with considerable force.

Then there were the twisted limbs, the broken, protruding bones, the neck and collarbone snapped like a child's toy. The body almost looked as though the boy had been savaged by some huge animal. The bones had been broken, however, after death, as though the murderer or murderers had been unable to stop venting some blind fury upon their victim.

There was also the disembowelment to consider. The inspector had never before encountered that particular circumstance in a murder, and he still was not able to picture such a killing taking place. If only he could, he felt other things would begin to make sense. But the scene as it must have been was almost too bizarre, too terrible to visualize.

A knock on the office door interrupted this by now familiar

line of thought. "Come," Janeway called out, leaning forward, arms on his desk.

"Morning, sir." Detective Sergeant Colin Church trudged into the room with the weight of the world on his stocky shoulders, which was not unusual for Sergeant Church.

"Take a pew, Church." If the Sergeant noticed the word-play, it was not apparent. "Beautiful morning."

"Won't last, sir. Been a week since the new moon. Weather's changin'. Winter soon."

Colin Church was a fenman. He had been born not twenty miles from where they sat, in Fen Drayton, and except for a stint in the army, he had hardly traveled twenty miles beyond that in all his fifty-two years. He was country-bred, and still kept a small plot of land with his wife near their cottage on the Newmarket Road.

Janeway had known this sturdy yeoman stock long before meeting Colin Church. As a young lieutenant and later as a captain in the Yorkshire Dragoons, he had commanded men like this. Solidly built and strong from work in the fields, short in stature but broad-shouldered; taciturn around their officers, they were always ready with a complaint in the enlisted men's mess, but equally ready to do whatever was asked of them in action. Twenty-three years in the army had taught Janeway that he could not ask for better men beside him.

He had taken to Church from the first, but he knew that even after three years, the sergeant was still evaluating him. He was an outsider, born up north. But the two men worked well together and had been a team since the day Sergeant Church had been asked to drive the inspector newly arrived from London around the city on a tour of familiarization.

"Any new developments, Sergeant?"

"No, sir. Men are expanding the search along Madingley Road, stopping at every house."

"Good. We'll go out and join them in a bit. Why don't you get yourself a cup of tea before we do?"

Church rubbed his nose with a thick knuckle. "Aye, I think I will. Can I get you something?"

"No, Ceylon will have to survive without me. I've given it up in the mornings." Since the murder, Janeway had resumed a number of the bad habits that had led to his stroke—late nights, too much caffeine, irregular meals. He had managed to avoid cigarettes so far, but only by taking up a pipe, which

did not really suit him. But he remembered his doctor's ada-
mance about cigarettes at his last checkup. The inspector
reached for a notebook as Church left the office for the tea
urn.

No tea in the morning, Church ruminated as he followed
the row of overhead lights down the corridor. He thought he
was used to most of the inspector's peculiarities by now, but
he never knew quite what to expect. He supposed that this
latest oddity had to do with his medical problem.

The sergeant got his large mug down from the shelf and
filled it to within an inch of the rim with steaming brew. Then
he added two heaping spoons of sugar and plenty of milk,
stirring the mixture vigorously so that creamy brown liquid
spilled over, making one more wet circle on the paper mat
beneath.

Church had known gentlemen like Inspector Janeway in
the army. Tall, aristocratic, self-confident. Cavalry types, like
the inspector with his swagger stick and carefully trimmed
mustache. Church had never liked officers, but he knew
enough not to underestimate men like Lewis Janeway.

The heels of the sergeant's sturdy boots clicked on the tiled
hallway as he returned to the office, tea in hand. When he
knocked and entered, the inspector was reading from a case-
book.

"You know, Church, we have no motive, no clear modus
operandi, no murder weapon, and no suspects. By God, we
don't even have a scene of the crime."

"Yes, sir."

"Not very damned good is it?"

"No, sir." Sergeant Church tugged at a rather large ear-
lobe. "Point of fact, it might not be a murder at all." Church
paused, looking slightly embarrassed by the sound of what he
had said.

"What I mean, sir, it could have been an accident of some
kind. I've seen men chewed up pretty badly by farm machinery. Factory machines could do the same or worse. It
could have happened accidental like. Then somebody got
scared and dumped the body in the river."

There was silence for a moment. Janeway closed his notebook, and the sergeant shifted in his seat.

"I know it's pretty unlikely, but it's something to keep in
mind," Church affirmed.

"No, you're absolutely right on both counts. It is unlikely, but we have to consider every possibility. Check on factories in the area, though God knows there are few enough of them, and have your friends in the County Constabulary poke around any farms that would have large machinery."

Pleased with himself, the sergeant took a noisy swallow of his tea as Janeway continued. "What sort of weather are we in for later? Will we need our macs and wading boots?"

"Wrong sort of clouds for rain, sir," Church said confidently. "Almanac says fair today. Clear moon last night." He glanced out the window at the brightening sky. "First day of winter coming up day after tomorrow, but the cold should hold off for a bit."

Janeway leaned back in his chair. "Your predictions always amaze me, Sergeant. Sounds sort of mysterious to someone from the city."

"Nature is a mystery to most folk, sir. Change of the seasons is important to country people, though. Passed down to us that way."

"By your grandparents, I suppose."

"Further back than that. Passed down from them that was here before us, a long way back. Before the Christian Church." The sergeant paused, not used to talking so much about country ways to his superior, but he wanted to finish the thought.

"Nature was the most important thing to them. Still is for people livin' on the land. Crops to be planted and harvested, livestock to be cared for, winter stores put up. Take the last day before winter. Very important to the old folk. Samain."

"The last day of October. But what did you call it?"

"Samain." The old word had slipped out. "It's an old name for the Eve of All Saints . . . from before there was saints . . . or before people hereabouts had heard about them anyway."

"Of course, All Hallows' Eve. Halloween," the inspector laughed. "I had no idea what a fund of information you are, Sergeant. Samain. I shall have to remember that." Janeway stood and looked out at the broad green of Parker's Place.

"You know, Church, you've got me thinking now with all this new moon, Samain business. It's all a bit reminiscent of black magic." From the corner of his eye, the inspector caught Church's frown as he toyed with his empty tea mug. "You remember the Manson killings in California. There are some very strange people in this world. Do we know of any suspicious groups around Cambridge? Lord knows, we may as well look at every possibility. Farm machinery. Witchcraft."

Church scratched his chin and shifted positions in the overstuffed chair. "Well, there's that group that's taken a stall in the market. They sell all sorts of odds and sods—jewelry, leather belts, crockery, even some vegetables. Have what they call a commune, sort of a farm really, up in the Gog Magogs. Don't know where they got the money to buy the place. Used to be a fine little piece of land. They been there a few months now, I suppose."

"Since before our murder at Midsummer?"

"Aye. I remember they came in the spring. Just in time for plantin', it was. Been some strange tales about them, according to the county police. Neighboring farms have complained about music and sort of singin' or chantin' late at night. Tales of animals with their throats slit, but no one I know has actually seen one."

"Very interesting. Well, Sergeant, you speak to your friends in the County Constabulary about that, too. We may have to pay a visit to this so-called commune. Perhaps we should go up there tomorrow night if this Samain is the big event you say it is."

Another long day, Church thought. But he would enjoy the excuse to talk with his old mates in the county police. He thought of that scruffy lot in the market square, and them with their own farm up in a choice spot on the Gog Magog hills. He wasn't sure exactly what the inspector was thinking, but he wouldn't mind paying that lot a visit.

"By the way," Janeway said, "that young reporter phoned again yesterday. Terry Graham, with the *Evening News*. If he should speak to you, we have nothing more to report since finding the bicycle."

"He's an eager one, all right."

"A bit overeager. I get the impression that this is his first real story. I don't mind young Graham digging through old records, as he tells me he's doing, but if he keeps making his own inquiries, he could get in our way. Be civil, but don't encourage the boy." Janeway walked over to the rack near the door and retrieved his coat and Donegal headgear.

"Well, Sergeant, it's the field for us." He slapped his side with his stick. "You might want to go with one of the dog teams. Commune a bit with nature."

Sergeant Church looked down at his empty tea mug. He had hoped there would be time for another cup. Instead, he picked up his coat and hat and followed the inspector out the door. Aye, he said to himself, it was going to be another long, bloody weekend.

> Gowns grave, or gaudy, doctors,
>   students, streets,
> Courts, cloisters, flocks of churches,
>   gateways, towers.
>   William Wordsworth (1770—1850)
>   St. John's College

After leaving the long green nave of Trinity Wood, near the Madingley Road, Nick crossed the greenery of the Backs. A few months earlier these college gardens had been thronged with tourists, but now he passed only students as he crossed the river and entered the back gate of his college.

Trinity Hall, like all the medieval colleges of the university, was built like a fortress. The massive, iron-bound gates and high stone walls were originally erected to keep townspeople and other undesirables out. Later, during more puritanical centuries, they had served a reverse purpose by keeping students in. Now the original function had again come to the fore. Though thousands of tourists trooped through Cambridge every holiday season, these gates and walls, and the vigilant porters who guarded them, regulated that flow and discouraged random wandering by outsiders.

The exclusive nature of the design also reflected the lingering antagonism between the townspeople of Cambridge and the privileged students who studied in these walled medieval buildings. But the townspeople of Cambridge knew that the world-famous university in their midst was the main industry, source of employment, and generator of income for their sleepy Cambridgeshire market town. Nick had observed that Cambridge was in many ways like a nineteenth-century industrial town, dependent on a single industry, though without a single factory or smokestack showing. The industry was education, and everyone in the town relied in some way upon it.

Businesses flourished in the wake of a constant flow of new capital as students and dons came and went, grants washed in from the central government, and new high-technology enterprises emerged from the laboratories of the great university. At times the townsfolk resented the squawking and strutting of their golden goose, but they continued to feed it, serve it, and keep it housed in secluded comfort behind secure stone walls.

"Stand and deliver!" growled a voice emerging from around a corner of a library built when an earlier Elizabeth had sat on the throne of England.

John Blessed, Nick's oldest friend in Cambridge, joined him in walking toward the elegant white cupola above the college hall. "And where are you going without a drink in your hand, Johnny?"

"Why, having just come from the college bar, I thought I'd stroll over to the Grad Room," Blessed answered, returning to his natural Irish brogue.

A proud graduate of University College, Dublin, Blessed had already been at Trinity Hall for a year when Nick arrived, and he had taken it upon himself to show the new American the mysteries of Cambridge student life. The Irishman was doing a definitive study, so he said, on the way in which the history and the folklore of his country were intertwined. Over a glass of Jamison's he had more than once told Nick that Irish folklore was considerably more accurate than the history, which had been written and rewritten by scholars and scoundrels over the centuries. Blessed did much of his research from the customer's side of several local pubs.

Entering the main court through the covered passageway between the college hall and the kitchens, they followed the cobbled walk to the door of the Graduates' Combination Room. The room's only two occupants were silently reading the Saturday newspapers.

"What is this, a wake?" Blessed called out.

"Sorry," Tom Newell replied lightly, "some of us just don't have your joie de vivre."

"Some of us didn't spend lunchtime in the college bar," Nick added, walking to a list posted on the notice board.

"You should read a paper once in a while, Blessed John," Kebby Mlanga said, with the careful pronunciation of every word he had learned in the English School in Nairobi. "Maybe we have one here in Gaelic."

They all knew that the quiet African they liked so well would go back to his own country, after completing his law degree, to be groomed for a leading role in his government. In a few years they would be picking up their newspapers to read about good old Kebby.

A cultivated voice spoke from the doorway. "Ah, Lombard, just the chap I wanted to see." St. John Ainsley-Hay breezed into the room and dropped into one of the cushioned window seats with a copy of the *Times*. He crossed his long legs casually as he continued speaking. "About the dinner this evening. Can we manage another body? And what a body it is. She's Austrian, or Swiss or something, and she says that she will be 'vury, vury hippy' to attend. Her English leaves a bit to be desired."

John Blessed tugged at his beard. "And we all know which bit you desire."

"Bright boy. Now, Nick, about this dinner . . ."

"Well"—Nick glanced at the posted list—"it looks like we can squeeze her in."

"I shall do the squeezing in later, Lombard, but you can add her to your list."

"In the meantime, that extra place at dinner will cost you twelve quid, St. John." Nick pronounced his friend's name in the proper British manner: "Sin-jin."

"Naturally," St. John replied. "Frauline Christina will be extremely grateful to you both. She'll be the one with the large tits, saying Ja, Ja, Ja!"

"I'm off," Nick announced. "I still have to make the rounds to see the chef and the wine steward and then reserve some silver with the butler. Sherry will be here at seven. Remember, Tom, there's still an extra place."

Tom's look expressed a grievance that Nick well understood. "Finding a date in this town is like trying to squeeze blood from a turnip," he sighed, "but you never know your luck."

"No," Nick agreed, "you never know."

CHAPTER 3

Saturday afternoon London

Double whiskies in crimson-shaded
bars; smoking hot steaks and chops
and a white cloth on a little corner
table; knowing gossip, and the fine
reek of Havanas, round a club fender
and fat leather chairs.

> J. B. Priestley (1894—1984)
> Trinity Hall

J. Macvicar Swann, head porter of Trinity Hall, Cambridge,
had spent a pleasant and satisfying afternoon in London
visiting . . . well, if called upon to describe her, he would have
said an old friend. She was certainly friendly, and there was
no denying that she was getting older every year.

Swann had been calling on Miss Lacey regularly, every
fortnight for the past fifteen years, since the year after he had
lost his wife. His financial situation at that time had limited
him to shorter visits when he and Miss Lacey had initiated
their acquaintance. Of course, the price her friendship had
commanded in those days had been somewhat higher as well
—as adjusted for inflation—but over the years their mutual
demands, personal and pecuniary, had arrived at a happy me-
dium.

Swann now visited Miss Lacey in her modest lodgings for
most of an afternoon, on a Saturday or Sunday every two
weeks, rain or shine. It was part of the steady rhythm of his
life. He always phoned her in advance, and she would prepare
a small luncheon. Swann was fond of his food, and these days
a home-cooked meal was often the high point of his afternoon
visit. Today, though, she had been in rare form, and it had
been a toss-up between her bubble and squeak and her slap
and tickle for best performance of the afternoon.

It was 6:45 when British Rail delivered Swann back to

Cambridge. J. Macvicar Swann was a large man, well-upholstered, but with an erect and dignified carriage. He carried his weight well, like a badge to the community that here was a man who could be relied upon to do the right thing under any circumstances. Rather too prominent ears and a thick fringe of gray hair high up on his cheekbones, under his eyes, added to his intimidating aspect and seemed to dare anyone to make light of his rather notable appearance.

Swann sailed through the throng in the crowded rail station like a Royal Navy cutter, leaving in his wake less-determined travelers who wandered about looking at signs, checking their watches, and dragging along children and other baggage.

He would arrive back in college by 7:30. This was one of the many things Swann's regular weekend visits with Miss Lacey had taught him. He was tempted to cogitate on the more delightful lessons he had learned during those fifteen years of pleasant afternoons, but he forced his concentration onto other things. He wanted to be back in time to keep an eye on another of the graduates' infamous black-tie dinners. Nick Lombard would be involved in the festivities, he knew, and Swann felt a special responsibility toward Nick. It had been partly through his own modest efforts that the young American had entered the portals of Trinity Hall.

Sicily had been the scene of Corporal J. Macvicar Swann's first meeting with U.S. Army Private Tony Lombard. They had gone on to survive a number of close calls together while pushing the Germans back up the boot of Italy. Just after V-E Day, during one of several London pub crawls, the two former comrades-in-arms had agreed to keep in touch, and true to their word, one or the other of them had corresponded at least once every year since 1945. When Tony had written about his son's research scholarship to Cambridge, Swann had seen an opportunity to render a service to his old friend. His intercession with the dean and bursar had helped smooth the way in admitting Nick Lombard to Trinity Hall.

Swann liked his old friend's son. Too many of the young gentlemen at Cambridge today were all swagger and no substance. He pursued this familiar line of thought as the bus from the station took him to the City Center, where he disembarked and made his way on foot in the early evening dusk to the front gate of Trinity Hall.

Under the college arms, an ermine crescent on a background of sable, the yellow light of the Porter's Lodge welcomed him back like a sheltered port in a storm. Opening the door, he was disturbed to see no one in evidence behind the long counter that split the room down the center. As he entered further, he beheld an even more disturbing sight. A long, thin body in baggy tweed trousers was bending sharply at the waist and presenting its posterior aspect to the door. The figure slowly rose and turned, placing a hand at the base of a protesting spine, to reveal the upper portions of the college chaplain.

"Really, Swann," said an irritated voice in the best of accents, "how often have I asked that my pigeonhole be moved up from the bottom? I'm at an age when bending over like this could prove fatal."

"Very sorry, Chaplain. I'll see to it." Then, removing his coat and hat, he continued. "Someone should be here to get your post for you, Reverend Anglesey. Nigel is on duty this evening."

"Well, his present absence makes that fact somewhat irrelevant. In any case, Swann, I'm expecting several rather large parcels. They are very old volumes and should be handled carefully. I particularly need one volume on Druidic ritual for my talk in Norwich next month," he added more to himself than to the porter.

"Hocus-pocus?" Swann had known Dr. Anglesey for nearly twenty years, and he occasionally teased the chaplain, in a respectful way, about his interest in ancient folklore and religions. It was all magic and superstition to Swann, and such things held little practical interest for the head porter.

"What's that? I can imagine the picture you have in your mind, Swann, but there is a great deal even you could learn from your forebears."

The porter smiled as the tall, slightly stooping figure of Dr. Anglesey departed toward the cozy warmth of his college rooms.

Before that figure had entirely disappeared from view, another—also tall and rake-thin, also stoop-shouldered, but this one without the excuse of age—entered the Porter's Lodge. Sullen, downcast eyes, hidden further by drooping lids, one more so than the other, avoided the severe gaze of J. Macvicar Swann.

"And where do you propose to tell me you've been, Nigel? Out for a stroll?"

"I was just makin' my rounds, is all," the young man protested in a voice revealing a boyhood in the Cambridgeshire fens.

"Rounds is it?" Swann stopped him. "Come in here, boy." He opened the gate for the wayward underporter. "You know you lock up when you're away from the desk." The boy looked at his feet, a few scruffy strands of hair falling over his brow.

"I'm trying, really trying to give you a chance to make something of yourself, Nigel. And what do I get for my thanks? I may as well send you back to the fens to tend your pigs."

Through a haze of despair Swann recalled the difficulty he had these days in recruiting underporters, and he softened a little. "All right, boy, carry on. I'll make my rounds now."

Nigel Pinder glanced up as Swann turned to leave. What did the old bastard expect anyway? Still, it was a job. He watched the stalwart form of the head porter, hands behind his back, bowler roundly adjusted, stroll into the gloom of the main court. Nigel wondered idly if Swann and the others knew something he didn't.

J. Macvicar Swann stopped at the precise center of the main court, where two walkways crossed, splitting the courtyard into a grassy quatrefoil. There was no respect anymore among the younger servants, he reflected. No initiative. No sense of tradition or history. A chap like Nigel didn't belong in the college, but what could he do? He scratched a shaggy cheekbone and gazed up at the stars.

CHAPTER 4

Saturday evening
Trinity Hall

Gather ye rosebuds while ye may,
Old time is still a-flying.
Robert Herrick (1591 – 1674)
Trinity Hall

The sound of laughter from the Grad Room disturbed the head porter's melancholy thoughts. He glanced toward the lights there, and then over at the candlelit windows of the wood-paneled room on the opposite side of the quadrangle, known since the seventeenth century as Dr. Eden's Room.

Swann reflected on the hundreds of dinners like this one he must have witnessed in the past thirty-odd years. Of course, he had never been a guest, but it had never entered his mind that he should be. Still, he knew the ritual as well as if he had attended them all. The head porter glanced at his father's gold watch, securely chained to his waistcoat. A leisurely procession of graduates and their dinner guests should begin across the court at any moment. He decided to wait, standing his ground at the center of the square. The faces changed from year to year, but he was sure he would recognize most of them.

Before long, the door to the Graduate Combination Room swung open, spilling yellow light out onto the cobbles and grass of the main court. The head porter saw Guy Chamberlain, the graduates' president, leading the way. The little Frenchman remained a mystery to Swann. His habits, dress, and manners were more British than most old Etonians, but even black-tie dress could not disguise a classically Gallic profile and accent.

John Blessed and Ainsley-Hay were close behind their president, who was escorting Hay's date. "Good evenin' to you, Mr. Swann," boomed Mo Roper, the tall Texan walking beside Nick Lombard.

Swann wished Roper would not always "Mr." him, but he knew how bad Americans were at dealing with servants. He remembered another Yank who had called him "Swanney" for two long, irritating years.

The head porter nodded to Nick and glanced at the shadowy figures still emerging from the Grad Room before turning slowly to stroll back toward the Lodge. Not a bad lot, he thought. Not a vintage year, but all things considered, not bad.

Nick saw the round, compact form of the bursar and followed the older man's sonorous voice up the narrow flight of stairs and into the inviting candlelight and oak of the Eden Room. Nick found himself seated at the juncture of two tables. Across from him was Ainsley-Hay and the rather spectacular cleavage of Christina of Austria. A married couple, Kevin and Julie Rees, sat nearby, and as they chatted happily to each other, Nick studied their sharp-featured English profiles. He liked watching their easy relationship, but it made him think. He was twenty-five, and since coming to Cambridge two years ago, he had not been romantically involved with anyone.

Most of the town girls Nick had tried chatting to in pubs or shops had given him a clear indication that they were not interested in university types. Most were intent on finding a nice plumber or lorry driver to settle down with in a cozy little council house or suburban semidetached—preferably before they reached the age of twenty.

"A penny for them, Nicky dear," said a beautifully accented female voice on his left.

"Is that all you think they're worth these days, Samantha?"

She laughed and put her hand on his arm. Samantha Pennethorne was an outrageous flirt and the most evident of a half dozen female graduate students recently admitted to Trinity Hall after 625 years as an all-male bastion. Soon after her arrival, any number of college Fellows had contemplated withdrawing their votes for admitting women and retreating back behind their seclusive walls.

"Nick," she said quietly, "have you ever considered acting? You remind me of someone I've seen recently in an Italian film. That dark hair and those lovely blue eyes. Not to mention that gorgeously Roman nose." She touched this rather prominent feature coquettishly.

"It's Italian, all right. I don't know about Roman."

"I'm serious, Nicky. Can't you take a compliment from a lady?"

"I can, but it's rather a novel experience for me lately."

"Well, I'm surprised. You have a very photogenic face . . . with a nice Roman nose, whatever you say. Very . . . Mediterranean."

After dessert, port was decanted through muslin, and a series of toasts was followed by relaxed conversation. John Blessed, Guy, and St. John were all paying close attention to the glass belonging to Christina of Austria, ensuring that it remained well filled. Christina had drunk more than she was used to already, and her English was becoming increasingly experimental.

Nick leaned over and lit his cheroot from one of the heavy silver candelabra. "Well, it looks like a successful evening, Bursar."

"As always," the bursar answered jovially, the port having raised his mellow voice level by half an octave.

"Excuse me, Bursar," Julie Rees spoke up. "Kevin and I were talking earlier about that terrible murder last summer. We heard that the police were questioning some of the dons living in college about what they might have heard or seen."

"That is quite true, my dear." The bursar was willing to neglect his port to chat with this attractive young woman. He turned his chair to face her more squarely. "They questioned me, in fact. My rooms look out on the river. I managed to convince them, however, that it had been quite some time since I had done anyone in."

"Did you see anything suspicious?" Kevin asked.

The bursar's rosy cheeks rounded out into a smile. "No, I slept soundly through the fatal night. The chaplain and I had been comparing the diverse merits of Armagnac and Ansbach brandies, as I recalled for the police inspector. Curious fellow. Wore a tweed hat the whole time we talked, though it was a warm day in July."

"Wasn't the poor boy who was murdered a foreign student?" Julie said a bit doubtfully.

"I read that he was at one of the language schools on Station Road," Nick ventured.

"I believe he was Spanish," the bursar confirmed. "The

inspector showed me a photo. Dark hair, olive skin. Looked quite Mediterranean, poor fellow."

Nick could not tell whether the bursar's condolences were for the victim's death or his national origins. "I gather they still don't know why he was killed."

"Or how," Kevin agreed. "He was really torn to pieces. A chap I know was there by the river when they found him. Said he had never seen anything like it. Sliced up from head to foot. His insides all—"

"Kevin!" Julie interrupted. "I don't think you need to go into graphic detail."

"You brought it up, remember?"

"Evidently they haven't yet discovered where the grisly deed took place," the bursar contributed. "They haven't found his shoes or clothes, and they've gone over the riverbank with a fine-tooth comb. I should know. For days I was serenaded by the sounds of police dogs and heavy boots." With an easy grace that belied his slight stature and not so slight build, the bursar took Julie gently by the arm, leading her away in the direction of the port decanter. "Let me get you another glass of wine, my dear." Julie glanced back at her husband and winked.

Kevin smiled. "He must be taking lessons from Guy."

Nick had begun to feel the effects of the evening and the wine even before the ritual of passing the loving cup began. The remainder of the evening was something of a blur to him. Later he remembered a delicious kiss from the Austrian girl, looking up at him with dreamy eyes. He recalled the scent of Samantha's hair once again, and a clumsy embrace from another female as she tried to keep her balance with the silver cup. It all made him realize just how lonely he was.

He vaguely noticed stumbling down stairs in the dark, port stains on starched white shirtfronts, and the head porter unlocking the gate in answer to raucous knocking while stifling a huge yawn that stretched his hairy cheekbones back toward his ears.

In the lamplight of Trinity Hall Lane, Nick left his friends. Guy insisted on helping to escort Christina home, and St. John was too tired to object. Nick watched them struggle off with the pretty redhead between them, their wavering silhouette creating a strange six-legged creature against the lamplight of a narrow cobbled passage.

Taking a deep breath, Nick walked unsteadily in the opposite direction as a cold wind began to rise off the river. The shortcut through Trinity Wood would have him home in his bed ten minutes sooner.

> This same flower that smiles today,
> Tomorrow will be dying.
> > Robert Herrick (1591—1674)
> > Trinity Hall

The girl emerged from the shadow of a gray green willow and stepped into the moonlit clearing as if into a pool of pale gold water. Her slender figure was swathed in a scarlet cloak that left only her fine-featured face bare, framed by a cascade of golden hair. Green eyes stared straight ahead as she glided toward the center of the circle of moonlight. All around the clearing ancient oaks frowned down on the scene, their claw-like upper branches lost in darkness. A steady easterly wind stirred the hidden tops of trees and the shadowed tangles of shrubbery beyond the filtered light of the forest clearing.

There was music, like wind through a hollow flute, that became more distinct as the girl approached the center of the circle of honeyed light. Its sinuous cadence, at first like random wind through a rotted tree trunk, began to form a more stylized rhythm. The song that emerged was primitive, beginning slowly with subtle repetition of phrases and gradually weaving a spell that seemed to capture the natural rhythms of the earth. Alternating with it and adding percussion was another sound emerging from the darkness of the trees, a slap like skin on skin followed in a rhythmic pattern by a resounding thump, such as a stick would make on a hollow tree trunk or a crude skin drum.

The girl was aware of the music around her, and her slim body swayed gently to its magic as her red-clad figure reached the center of the clearing and turned back to face the way she had come. She looked toward the willow and the largest of the oaks beside it, a massive and ancient tree with a gnarled configuration of knotholes and distended bark halfway up its trunk forming what looked like the grotesque face of a man. She gazed wistfully at the trees before her eyes closed slowly, her head inclined toward one shoulder, then the other, in time with the music, and her rounded hips encased in scarlet cloth also rising and falling to the sinuous rhythm. Her hands were clasped over her breasts to hold the garment closed around her body as she swayed to the music in the shadowed moonlight, her fingers showing white against the red of the rough cloth.

Slowly she released her grasp and the cloak slid from her naked body to lie like a pool of blood at her feet. Her slender feet stirred its folds as her long, tapered legs moved in gentle, sleepy motions to the flute and drum. Opening her eyes after a moment, the girl stooped gracefully to grasp the ends of the scarlet cloak, which she then cast out before her like a blanket on the grass, her delicate breasts rebounding with the motion. Then she continued her dance on the ruby square in the center of the clearing, her fine hands moving over the perfect curves of her milk white body as the sensuous music increased in tempo.

Hands flat against her undulating hips, the girl swung her head in a slow arc, casting her long yellow hair like a silken net. Increasing in time with the rapidly building music, her motions took on a dizzying speed, hips rotating above bended knees, coral-tipped breasts heaving below bare swaying shoulders, head thrown around in abandonment with a shower of golden hair covering her face. Then the rising crescendo of unearthly music stopped suddenly, in midbeat, as the golden girl fell limply onto the scarlet cloak. She was face down, legs drawn up, and downy arms outstretched. Only the rapid heaving of her rib cage showed life in her collapsed form.

As her breathing slowed, the music began again, first the reedy sound of a flute soon joined by the hollow slap and thump of a skin drum. Moonlight reflected off the smooth curves of hips and buttocks as she stirred. Shoulders moved, one arm sliding up to reveal a soft thatch of white-blond hair in the cleft between the softness of underarm and even softer breast. Legs straightened and then retracted as the girl rolled over onto her back. Then she lay still under the light of the three-quartered moon, legs spread wide and arms outstretched, forming the five-pointed star of ancient human sacrifice. As if considering this delicious offering, the moon hid its face momentarily behind a gray streak of cloud, casting the night-shrouded grove and its goddess-sacrifice into darkness.

Strange music slithered through the shadows of the trees as the emerging moon touched the outstretched girl, tinging with gold the downy softness at the center of the human star and spreading from there to each golden hair on legs, stomach, forearms, and cascading in tresses across ivory shoulders and chest until her body appeared to have been dusted with a fine talc of powdered gold.

As if accepting the blessing of the moon, the girl pulled her gilded limbs in closer to her body and began to move once more to the swelling rhythms of flute and drum. She grasped an edge of the bloodred cloak and held it tightly against her as she rolled her body across it, gathering up its folds against her flesh. Her body squirmed and writhed sensually inside her scarlet cocoon as the music built to match her reverie. A gold-tinged leg emerged from the writhing red creature on the forest floor, then an arm, a breast, a face transported in a private ecstasy. Then she reversed her earlier movement, unrolling the cloak beneath her to lie once again exposed on her back, face up to the stars.

The primitive beat and swirl of the music now filling the grove matched the girl's abandoned ritual of self-pleasure. She made love to the bloodred cloak in the center of the clearing, entwining its folds around every crease and curve of her supple body. Slowly her hand reached down and grasped the corner of the cloak beneath her, drawing it slowly, sensually up between her down-flecked legs until it was caught fast at her pelvis and pulled taut toward her heaving chest. Then, her toes curling in pleasure, she slowly rubbed the tip of the rough ruby cloth against the cream white softness of her breasts, causing her nipples to redden and stiffen even more as she felt the gentle tugging against her soft inner thighs and the tenderness between them.

As the music wove its sensuous spell, the girl moved the tail of scarlet cloth away from her swollen breasts. Holding it now with both hands, she stroked it upward until a length of it stood unaided like a stiff red phallus rising up to monstrous height from between her outspread thighs. She caressed the instrument of her pleasure, stroking and pulling it toward her, tugging it tighter against her impassioned sex, writhing wetly against the bloodred cloth clasped between the softness of her thighs. Her moans and small cries of pleasure entwined with the sinuous music from the shadows of the oak grove looking down on her shameless display. White body and scarlet cloak were one being in the moonlight, lovers joined in an impossible love.

At the moment the haunting music reached its discordant crescendo, the girl cried out in her climax. Her cry, expressing an anguished longing more than passion, soon died out in the absolute stillness of the forest clearing. Still lost in a delirium of momentary fulfillment—and an eternity of unfulfilled desire—she rolled abruptly onto her stomach, legs tucked up against moon-dappled buttocks in a fetal curve. The smooth female body, so voluptuous only a moment before, took on an innocence lying now in the twilit grove, arms crossed demurely across a softly heaving breast, lips parted in a sigh. One green gold eye gazed back at the oak tree with a face, half-hidden now in shadow. A falling tear stained the cloak beneath her a darker scarlet. Before a second tear had fallen like a drop of blood, small night creatures were once again stirring and nocturnal birds gave throat to cries from the depths of Trinity Grove. The ancient ritual had again begun.

> It was a dark
> and stormy night.
> > Edward Bulwer Lytton
> > (1803–1873)
> > Trinity Hall

In the face of a stiff east wind whipping in from the North Sea, Nick slung his raincoat off his shoulder and struggled into it over his dinner jacket. He hoped the chill November air would clear his head.

Crossing Garret Hostel Bridge, he glanced down at the moon's reflection spread out on the ripples of the water like a misplaced streak of chrome yellow paint. Somewhere nearby a college clock struck twice. There was no other sound except the wind. Only a few months before, a student about his own age had been found murdered in this peaceful river. For a moment he could almost see the naked, mutilated corpse floating facedown on the gently flowing water below him. Blinking the gruesome scene away, he walked on, concentrating on the steady rhythm of his shoe soles on concrete until he reached the edge of Trinity Wood.

God, how he wanted to be home in bed. His head was spinning now despite the fresh air, and he felt nausea coming on. The light of the moon was intermittently hidden by heavy clouds, increasing the difficulty of staying on the narrow pathway once he had found it. Repeatedly cursing aloud and stumbling into more than one tree, he drunkenly navigated the long, shadowed tunnel leading toward Wychfield.

Inside the wood it was unnaturally quiet. The strong east wind that had been rustling the tops of trees all along the Madingley Road had stopped. Filtered moonlight through the trees illuminated the path ahead as he tramped forward over the soft padding of the forest floor, but each time the moon was screened behind a cloud, he was left in almost complete darkness. Trees seemed closer to the path than he remembered, their branches scraping along his shoulders. Then the wind picked up.

Nick increased his pace, but it was difficult to move faster in the blackness as the trees grew thicker overhead. Then, suddenly, he heard a sound in the uppermost branches like the noise of many thousands of insects rubbing their wings together in a frenzy. A cold wind swooped down on the forest with gale force. Nick felt the icy climate of the Russian steppes, two thousand miles due east to the Urals. The dim light of the woods faded steadily, until Nick could only see the blurred shapes of trees bending under the unnatural force of the frigid wind.

Leaves whipped against his face, and the roaring in his ears seemed louder than any natural wind. He tried to run but stumbled over a root in the darkness. With only a vague sense of direction to guide him, the young man plunged forward, desperately trying to stay on the path. A branch slammed hard into him from behind at the same time that another struck the backs of his knees, causing him to fall again. Nick knew that this was no drunken fantasy. Something strange was happening in Trinity Wood, and it seemed to be directed at him.

Nearing panic, he crossed his arms over his face against branches beating on him from all sides. The wind was caught in a steady wail now, blocking out all other sound. Nick knew that he cried out, but the feeble sound was swept away. Leafless branches clutched at his clothing and scratched at his face and hands. He tasted blood on his lip.

Roots and tendrils were everywhere underfoot, and he fell again. Then he glimpsed a circle of light. It must be the way out. But it seemed so far away. Dark moving shapes of wind-whipped branches and night black tree limbs obscured the lighted opening like dancing figures as Nick struggled toward it. Overhead the wind screamed in a banshee wail as Trinity Wood bent under the force of an unnatural storm.

SAMAIN
EVE

CHAPTER 5

Sunday, October 31
Gog Magog Farm

No persuasion on the part of devils, saints,
Or angels, now could stop the torrent.
Lord Byron (1788—1824)
Trinity College

The woman rolled onto her side in the big, old-fashioned bed. A gap in the curtains threw harsh morning light onto her face, showing lines and creases that makeup usually softened. She pulled back the curtains and swung her bare legs out onto the cool wood plank floor, her long black hair swinging free so that the light turned its streaks of gray to silver. She walked nude to the window and pulled the drapes together, glancing back to see that the man was still asleep. Her body was excellent for her age, breasts full and high, hips narrow. But she remembered it as it had been. The young man in her bed had many times explored her body in the dark; his touch knew its every curve and hollow. But now, in the cruel morning light, she slipped a black shadow of a nightgown over her nakedness before returning to the bed.

The man stirred as she settled her weight beside him on the soft mattress. She took advantage of the opportunity to study his face in its last moments of vulnerable sleep. Unruly red hair and a beard the color of fire. Striking blue eyes now closed on the world, fringed with pale orange lashes and brows. She knew those eyes well, knew the power they could exert over others. But they held no special power for her. Jan Troop was just another man. Someone to be used and eventually used up.

Eleanor Woodbridge had known many such men. Only a few had been true believers. The sleeping Dutchman was not one of them. He had his own ends and his own means of using people. Mrs. Woodbridge smiled to herself. No doubt he thought he was using her. Perhaps he thought his firm young body, fifteen years her junior, held her in thrall. The woman resisted laughing aloud. She sat up in bed, raising her arms above her head and beginning to twist her long black hair into a braid around her head. Her bosom moved voluptuously under the thin black gown as she stretched to reach the pins on the bedside table. She fastened her luxuriant hair up off her neck and shoulders in the severe braided style she always wore during daylight hours; she wondered what the others in the commune would think if they could see her at her best, hair cascading down over bare white shoulders as she leaned over her young lover.

She knew that the young man sleeping beside her was bound to her sexually, though she was always careful to preserve his egotistical illusions, pretending to swoon at his every caress and gasping passionately even at his most pitiable attempts at lovemaking. She knew all his weaknesses and told him they were strengths. Eleanor Woodbridge had long ago learned how to deceive a man. And it was all for the greater good, of that she was certain.

By her side, the nominal leader of the Pentacle Commune stirred again toward wakefulness. The woman looked at his ginger-bearded face with contempt. It was regrettable that she needed such a man, even for a time. But he could draw the people she needed, and he had supplied this isolated farm and the money it took to provide for their needs. Of course, Jan Troop had his own foul reasons for founding the commune, and she loathed him for involving her in them, though she had chosen to allow it to serve her own higher purpose. For Eleanor, the religion was everything. It justified all she had to do. To finally have a community practicing the old ways was worth it all, even if they were not all true or worthy believers. Even though this young Dutchman was using her influence to hold the group together, using the religion to frighten them, his contemptible purposes still served her own. And she served a higher power than Jan Troop could ever imagine.

Troop opened his clear blue eyes on the world. His narrow face stretched in an animal yawn, showing even white teeth, and then his sharp features relaxed into a sleepy smile. "Awake already, Eleanor? And dressed?" He rolled onto his side and reached out a pale, freckled arm to grope for her breast.

She allowed his hand to squeeze and knead her flesh like

an overripe fruit, but she spoke to prevent him going further. "Not now, dear boy," she whispered, her voice breathy with pretended desire. "I'll give you a special treat later, but now we must talk."

Reluctantly Jan Troop settled onto his back, stifling another huge yawn. "If it's about money..."

"No, it's about tonight. About the ceremony."

"Ah, yes," he said with a leer. "Samain."

"Yes, Samain. Everything is prepared. The ceremony has been explained to the group, and this evening I'll go through all the rituals with you again."

"Good, I especially like the part where I—"

"I know very well which parts you like," she interrupted, "but the ceremony must be taken seriously, Jan. Samain is the most important festival of the year in many ways...and the most dangerous."

The Dutchman's face turned serious. "I know, Eleanor. I'm sorry." He knew too that he needed her. Her and the binding force of her mad religion.

Mrs. Woodbridge watched the bedside clock as they talked about the coming evening's activities, then there was a quiet knock on the bedroom door. "Just a moment, my dear," she called out in her kind but commanding voice. Then she turned to the head of the commune. "I've chosen the sacrifice for the ceremony," she whispered. "It's a great honor, and the girl is willing, but I haven't explained to her yet all that is required."

Troop's voice was low in reply. "You're not going to tell her everything, are you?"

"Of course not. Just enough to encourage her." Eleanor Woodbridge adjusted the pillow behind her back and smoothed the robe across her midriff. "Once she's had the drugs, everything will come naturally. You will control it. I'll tell you how."

Troop rubbed his eyes. "Who did you choose?"

"Sara."

"Sara," he protested, but the woman saw the glimmer of lust in his ice blue eyes. "But she's so new. So young."

"Sara is a true believer," Eleanor said flatly. "Or at least she will be soon, and that's what matters. She has the power in her." Suppressing a desire of her own, she thought of the beautiful young girl standing patiently in the hallway. She wished that she could be there to share in the revels of Samain

Eve, but it would not be right. Her time would come later, in private.

"Come in now, Sara," she called out with the same cool, commanding tone that she always used in the commune.

Jan Troop felt a stirring in his loins gazing up at the delicate beauty of the young girl who appeared in the sunlit doorway, and thinking of the ceremony to come. Long golden hair framed her innocent features like a shimmering halo.

Eleanor could sense his lust, mingling with her own strong feelings for the girl, but her voice did not betray her. "Sit here, my dear," she smiled, motioning to the edge of the big bed nearest her as the young American girl edged nervously into the room. "Jan wants to congratulate you on being chosen to be the Samain Maiden, and then we'll explain to you a little more about the ceremony. This is going to be a very special night for us all."

> Let us have wine and women,
> mirth and laughter,
> Sermons and soda-water the day after.
> Lord Byron (1788–1824)
> Trinity College

Nick Lombard felt like the Prisoner in the Iron Mask. His skull was filled with dull throbbing, every sound reverberated, and he could not get at the aching to make it stop. It was past noon when he crawled out of bed. Outside the sun was shining on a few harmless-looking clouds as Nick turned away from his window and took a halfway clean glass to the kitchen for water. No one was in the hallway or in the big communal kitchen; probably all out enjoying a fine Sunday afternoon.

He dropped two white tablets into his water. As they dutifully fizzed away, promising relief, he shuffled back to his room and closed the door. Then he drank the frothing mixture, pinpoints of spray stinging his nose, and sank down into his only armchair to allow it to work. Thinking back painfully to the night before, he remembered very little, including how he got home. Then, suddenly, he pictured Trinity Wood bending under the force of a storm. A drunken dream? Thinking back now, it seemed incredibly violent, coming without warning and then gone again just as abruptly, leaving him to stumble home across the muddy field of Wychfield Farm.

Then it occurred to him why his leg had been hurting. He remembered falling. Quickly he looked at his palms and forearms. Welts and scratches where he remembered crossing his arms over his face in defense against wind-whipped branches blocking his path. His face. Getting up, Nick reached for the shaving mirror beside his bed and saw several red marks across his left cheek. Hell, he thought, so damn drunk he couldn't even walk home without falling into the bushes and getting himself cut up.

A noise drew Nick to the window, where he saw Wychfield's tenant farmer revving the engine of his tractor as he drove out into the field that lay between the old house and the woods. The tractor lumbered across the field, growling stupidly under its diesel breath. Huge tires cut into the sod, flinging particles of its broken and ripped surface into the air as it furrowed a jagged incision across the belly of the field. Scattering choking clouds of dust in its wake, the metal beast roamed up and down the ranks and files of the helplessly sprawling plot of ground, ironically laying down seeds of life in the gaping wounds of the earth.

Gazing across at Trinity Wood, Nick was struck by stirrings of remembrance from a dream. It was mixed in his mind with his experiences in the storm, but he was sure that the dream had followed later, after he had struggled home to fall exhausted into his bed. The memory became clearer as he stared out at the steadily prowling tractor and the sunlit woods beyond.

In his dream, Nick had been in a woods that reminded him of Trinity Wood, but had at the same time been different; much larger and thicker, with much taller trees than the little woodland he saw now. It had spread out around him in all directions endlessly like an ocean of trees. He had been making his way along an obscure track where massive trees pressed in close to him on all sides. It had been dark in the huge forest, and the ground under his feet was a soft mulch of rotting leaves and vegetation. Some trees he passed were ten or twelve feet around, towering overhead to block out the yellow light of the moon. No woodsman's axe had ever been heard in these dream woods.

Nick had sensed that he was on his way to an important meeting, and he had been in the woods before. But it was not a friendly place. Danger was close at hand. He remembered stopping beneath one of the largest trees, a massive oak with twisted roots thrusting above ground. Above eye level on its gray-scaled trunk, gnarled bumps and cavities in the bark formed the grotesque approximation of a human face. Eyes, nose, twisted grinning mouth, were all there in the distended features of the moss-covered trunk. The oak tree with the face of a heathen god or demon was a sign that his goal was near. The girl. He could almost feel her warmth. But he also felt the cold hand of fear.

Still staring up at the face etched by the forces of nature in the twisted oak, Nick had wakened in the night wet with sweat. After that, he remembered tossing in his bed, head throbbing rhythmically, for what had seemed like hours before finally falling back into fitful sleep. The dream had faded, only to reemerge now in the light of day.

Nick left the window and moved to light the gas fire at the far end of his room. Pushing a coin into a slot on the wall allowed the fire to hiss to life. He blew out the match and dropped into the armchair near the fire. Nothing really disturbing had occurred in his dream, but it remained vivid in his mind, and he felt again the unnerving sense of dread that he had experienced in the night.

Staring at the flicker of blue flame, Nick felt depressed, hung over, lonely, and more than a little homesick. It was not easy being three thousand miles from home. It would pass, it always did, but for the moment he allowed himself to drift into a dark mood. His head was still aching and the tractor outside still roaring as he closed his eyes and soaked up the warmth of the fire. Sleep soon came to him again. But with sleep came dreams.

The young stranger found himself back in the deep woods. He saw mistletoe growing up the towering sides of an oak tree with a face, but he continued walking, moving steadily forward along a familiar path. He heard the drone of the wind through branches far above his head and heard the gentle hiss of flowing water. He knew that once he crossed the forest stream, he would be near his destination at the edge of the great woods.

It was late evening when he emerged from the trees, and the sky was a uniform gray-blue, broken only by a narrow ribbon of pink along the western horizon. There was still enough light for Nick, standing just under cover of the trees, to make out a strangely familiar landscape. He was on a hilltop, and the land below, crossed in the distance by a small river, was as flat as the fenland around Cambridge. Not far in the distance was an isolated range of low hills, like islands in a calm green sea. He recognized the Gog Magogs and sensed that he had recently come from their relative safety to this hostile, alien place.

The young man skirted the edge of the forest to his right, careful to stay in the shadows of the trees. By the time the village came into view, the sun had set. By the light of a nearly full moon he saw on the slope below him a number of walled enclosures, each containing several circular two-story structures built around open courtyards. Surrounding the entire settlement was a steep embankment and a ditch. Then he waited. Waited for some sign from the woman.

Out of the darkness, a sound came to him from the central compound, carried upward on the wind. It was a steady drone, a chanting by many voices. Though he could not understand the words, Nick was gripped by a sudden fear as the monotonous cadence filled his ears. He knew instinctively that something had gone wrong. Danger! He turned to flee from the sound and those who made it, running aimlessly into the blackness of the great forest. But the chanting stayed with him, its steady drumming undiminished by distance. Still, he ran on, searching for the stream that would take him to the path he knew. Running blindly, he stumbled and fell hard to the ground. Fear paralyzed him, and an icy sweat caressed his spine as he sensed another presence.

On hands and knees, Nick jerked his head upward, though the motion seemed to be occurring through a slow motion lens. Then he felt his mind seize up, his thoughts dissolving into a meaningless buzz as he stared up into the face of a nightmare apparition blocking his path. A huge human figure towered above him, overshadowed only by the night black oaks at its back. Entirely naked, with a thick coil of gleaming gold at its throat, the muscular human form clutched a double-bladed axe in its right hand and a heavy sword in its left. But worse still was the face above that sweat-gleaming body. Or was it a mask? A mask that extended at the temples into two monstrously curving horns flanking an animalistic snout.

Could a mask change expression? Could it twist its features into a snarl of rage? The cruel animal mouth emitted a deadly howl unlike either man or beast. As the axe hand slowly raised, Nick cried out, but there was no sound. He clawed desperately at the earth as he struggled to flee from the savage creature howling at the moon before him.

Nick ran, but his legs were made of lead. Each painful stride left him rooted to the same spot on a forest path that was like a treadmill under his feet. For a moment he was sure that he heard the reedy sound of a flute and the chinking of glass chimes swayed by the wind. Then a hand, hot and pulsing with blood, gripped his shoulder. The drone of heathen chanting filled his skull, and fetid hissing breath was on his cheek. He knew at that terrible moment that this was how it must end.

> Sleep and high places; footprints
> in the dew; and oaks; and brown
> horse-chestnuts, glossy new.
> Rupert Brooke (1887–1915)
> King's College

Nick flung himself upright in bed, eyes staring wide and perspiration standing out on his forehead. He realized immediately that he had been dreaming, but it took time to break free from the effects of his nightmare vision.

The combination of deep sleep and his lingering hangover altered his perception of his surroundings. He stumbled mentally for a while between his dream world and the waking environment, puzzled about which was more real. He could still feel the sensations of his dream buzzing and whirling somewhere in those dark corners of the mind that control sleep. But the dream world was fading; possibly its course was run and its fragile world would disappear, never to come again on another sleepy afternoon. But he could not be sure. Only moments before it had seemed more solid and permanent than this stuffy little room around him now.

The tractor still droned through its rounds outside, and a strong wind blew against the windows of the room. He recognized these noises from his dream—the roar of the wind in the great forest, the drone of savage chanting in an unknown tongue, the flowing of a stream deep in the dream woods now recalled in the hiss of the gas fire.

Soon the numbness left his limbs and the colors and textures of the room gradually softened back to normal before his eyes. The noises around him became unquestionably wind and hissing gas and farm machinery once more. Before long everything was back to comforting normality, and the young man was as sure of this world as he had been of his forest dream a moment before. Finally even the faint buzz at the back of his mind vanished, along with an ancient forest of oaks, strange chanting, and a tree with the face of a man.

A hot shower helped. By the time Nick had brushed his teeth, shaved, and towel-dried his hair, he was once again feeling human. Pulling a robe around himself as he left the drafty bathroom at the end of the hall, Nick saw John Blessed leaning on the door of his flat.

"Well, it's Venus on the half shell."

"You sound pretty chipper," Nick answered. "Sleeping in the Grad Room must agree with you."

"Never felt better."

"Wish I could say the same." Nick squeezed past into his room, and Blessed followed.

"You should try an ancient Celtic hangover cure." The Irishman flopped down in the chair by the fire. "Pint of Guinness as soon as the pub doors open."

"I should have known. But speaking of your Celts, they lived in the forests, didn't they? What do the sagas say about that kind of life?"

Blessed stared at him with mock surprise. "Why, Lombard, I always knew that one day your interests would broaden. But what makes you ask now?"

"Just curious. I seem to have a real fixation with forests lately. Don't know why."

"Hah! Phallic symbols, trees. You've been too long without a woman, Nicko."

"You may be right." Nick held his hands out toward the gas fire. "Didn't they worship in the forests?"

"Right. The Celts had special feelings for the woodlands. Forests, trees—especially oaks and holly—were sacred to the old people. Forests were their temples." He rubbed his bearded chin. "Buggers had a lot more sense than we do today."

The Irishman looked at the clock on the mantel. "Well, Nicky my boy. I'm off." He swung his leg down from the arm of the chair and heaved himself to his feet. "I haven't eaten today. Care to sample the delights of the Curry Center?"

"Tempting," Nick said, "but I still have a small spark of good taste."

"Suit yourself," Blessed shrugged. Then he slouched toward the door, leaving Nick alone with his good taste and an empty stomach.

CHAPTER 6

Sunday afternoon
Trinity Wood

She walks in beauty, like the night
Of cloudless climes and starry skies;
And all that's best of dark and bright
Meet in the aspect of her eyes.

Lord Byron (1788–1824)
Trinity College

At the front door of the old house, Nick stood for a moment facing the deeply sunlit woods. Then he stepped outside. The air was unusually warm for October, carrying a fresh scent from the trees and the recently plowed earth. The tractor had finally retired victorious from the field, and there was no sound now except birdsong and the wind.

Nick wandered around to the side of the rambling building and stood in the shadow of its chimneys, looking at the western sky. The fine blue of the day was rapidly fading to gray, the horizon now streaked with a narrow band of pink like a ribbon between earth and sky. He turned back toward the woods and began walking slowly, distractedly toward the tree line, showing golden now in the dying sunlight. He had intended to go back into the house in search of food, but the strange inclination drawing him toward Trinity Wood was stronger than his hunger.

The soft plowed furrows under his feet slowed his pace and kept him slightly off balance, adding to his growing impression of the strangeness of the moment. There was magic in the evening air. As his unnaturally slow and unsteady steps took him across the earthen boundary of the field, Nick Lombard felt that he was at the same time crossing over another, less obvious boundary line.

At the edge of the trees he saw the girl. She was walking very slowly down the narrow path, coming steadily toward him at a right angle. The setting sun cast an amber glow over the scene, intermittently illuminating and casting into shadow the approaching figure of the girl as she passed through the ranks of the trees. As she drew closer, Nick saw that she was young, probably no more than nineteen. Long blond hair fell across the shoulders of a cornflower blue shawl, and the hem of a white dress swayed gently below the wrap as she walked.

Nearer still, Nick took in every detail of her face, except her eyes, which remained cast down at her feet. He saw high cheekbones and a finely molded nose. Her skin was extremely fair with the coloring of a natural blond. When she was within five feet of him on the path, he caught a glimpse of the gold tracery of sunlight and leaves across her cheek and rose-colored lips. Then she passed him by without looking up.

Nick stopped on the shadowed forest path, his heart pounding and his face flushed with sudden heat. He turned around. The girl had stopped too and had turned as if waiting for his glance. She lifted her eyes, the color of honey, and looked directly at him. He smiled and tried to speak, but no words came.

"No," said a soft voice out of a dream. Then she moved silently to him with a finger pressed gently to her lips. "You don't need words."

Her voice and accent were vaguely Scandinavian, but Nick could not identify the unusual lilt in her speech. He could only look into her deep green gold eyes as he felt her lips draw close to his in a kiss that began gently and quickly turned to passion.

The young American could not stop to consider the strangeness of the encounter. It was as though time had been stopped temporarily so that, as in a dream, events could occur without the cold logic and reason that were the boundaries of the waking world. Fate had led him to walk in Trinity Wood on this dusky evening, and he did not question why, or why this beautiful girl was here too, doing what she did. It was enough to hold her body close and taste the sweetness of her mouth.

As he kissed the warmth and softness of her neck, she spoke again, almost in a whisper. "Not here." Then she took his hand and led him down the forest path to an overgrown turning. Perhaps he should have been suspicious, or at least cautious. A thousand questions whirled in his mind, but dominating them all was a single persistent thought: He wanted this girl who seemed like a beautiful golden goddess in the dying light of the sun, wanted her more than anything.

In a daze of surprise and pleasure, Nick followed the girl deeper into the shadowed woods, crossing fallen timbers and brushing past thick-growing bushes across the narrow path. There was total calm around them. No wind. No birds. The light gradually faded too, but his guide led him steadily forward like some submissive soul entering the half light of the underworld.

Finally they emerged into a forest clearing. In the very heart of the woods, in Trinity Grove, ancient oaks looked down on them in silent majesty around an open circle of honeydew light.

"Now," she whispered, letting go of his hand. "It is meant to be." Her voice had an oddly hypnotic effect. It had to be trusted, must be believed.

The clasp securing her shawl was undone, and soon the whiteness of her dress also slipped from her shoulders and dropped like liquid to the ground. Underneath she was naked, looking up into Nick's face unashamed and proud of her womanhood. He tried to absorb her loveliness, to burn it on his memory. He wanted this picture to still be with him on his dying day.

He saw long, slender legs, the gentle curve of her belly, small, delicate breasts. She stood still and silent for a long moment, letting him savor her body with his eyes, and then she moved toward him. Kneeling, she took his hand and gently pulled him down. Nick shook off the strange inertia that had overtaken him. He stripped urgently as she kissed his neck, his eyes, his chest, and then he felt the soft earth of the clearing under him as they entwined side by side. Her scent was like the forest, fresh, verdant, earthy. She smelled of moss and wildflowers.

The sun had fully set now, and the paleness of moonlight tinged their bodies as they came together under the shadows of the great trees. He entered her as though he had always belonged there, and she closed her eyes and thrust strongly against him as though she too had waited a lifetime for this moment. Nick tried to remember every inch of her body with his hands as her insistent breathing mingled on the night air with the sounds of his own urgency. Her climax came with a cry, and he soon followed with an overwhelming sense of relief that whatever else might happen in his life, he had possessed this strange and beautiful creature and been possessed by her in return.

They lay together in the smoky light on the carpet of leaves in Trinity Grove. There was still no wind to rustle the primeval oaks overhead. No night bird's call interrupted their idyll. Nick pulled her shawl over them as the body heat of their passion melted away. But soon, soft kisses and tender exploratory caresses led to a renewal of desire, and the heat of their body hunger made them kick off the cover to lie together naked once more under the light of the moon.

Their second time together was much slower, more deliberate. They concentrated on prolonging each other's pleasure in every way they knew. Nick floated on a cloud of sensuality, carrying him into a dimension he never knew existed. Feeling her softness yield to his every movement like an extension of his own body and then press upon him with needs of her own, he felt that this was the moment they had both been born for.

Overhead a frigid wind began to stir the ancient oaks of Trinity Grove.

CHAPTER 7

All Hallows' Eve

The plowman homeward plods
...his weary way,
And leaves the world to darkness
...and to me.

Thomas Gray (1716—1771)

The Gog Magog hills lie a few miles southeast of the city of Cambridge, rising incongruously to a height of 250 feet above sea level out of the flat fenland landscape. Taking their name from the biblical nations that made war on the Kingdom of Heaven under Satan's banner, they are better known locally for the remains of a large Roman fort on their commanding heights. A few locals, like Sergeant Colin Church, knew the older history of the hills and the so-called Wandlebury Ring atop them, where the Celtic Queen Boudicca fled with her defeated army after her revolt from Rome had been crushed. Not even Church, however, knew much about the history of the Gog Magogs before the bloodshed of Boudicca's time.

Colin Church was not thinking about history as he rode with Inspector Janeway down the A604 toward the legendary hills. The black Rover handled a sharp corner well, crunching gravel on the verge as the inspector turned off the highway onto a smaller road that would take them close to the commune at Gog Magog Farm.

It was late and both men were tired. The nearly full moon was high in the sky, and Church stared out at its light on the narrow road winding gradually upward from the flatland. He pointed out an easily missed turning onto a single-lane track that would take them to the farm now owned by the Pentacle Commune; at least that was the name on the hand-lettered sign above their stall in the Cambridge market square.

Church had not been near the farm since the commune group had moved in, but he knew it from earlier days. The single lane changed from black macadam to dirt before reaching a gate posted with a sign: "Private Property. No Trespass." A large, rambling farmhouse, a barn, and a number of dark outbuildings crouched in the distance beyond the gate and down a sloping drive. Lights were visible downstairs in the house.

"Shall we pay our respects? It's late, but there are lights." Janeway switched off the engine.

They left the car and climbed the padlocked gate by means of a stile. The rough driveway was dark and difficult to navigate even with their flashlights. Church stumbled once on an uneven spot and cursed under his breath, but an outdoor floodlight aided them in the final approach to the house.

Both men glanced around at the orderly front yard, where a Morris Minor was parked near what Church recognized as a well-maintained threshing machine. There was no peeling paint visible under the lighted roof of the front porch as they climbed the steps. For a moment the inspector reconsidered knocking at the silent house. He looked at Church, who shrugged.

When knocking brought no one, Church stayed by the front door while the inspector walked around to the side of the building, peering into several lighted windows.

Janeway did not see the dog until it was almost too late. The animal had been trained to hug the ground silently until its attack could be made, and only a low growl, a slight flaw in its training, alerted Janeway in time to step back from the bared teeth in the long gray muzzle. The dog, springing toward the intruder, was pulled up short by its tether with a choked-off snarl within inches of the policeman's throat. His cover exposed, the Alsatian strained at its chain, barking wildly. Church came quickly, but the inspector waved his hand in reassurance as he walked unhurriedly back to the front of the house. He had seen nothing unusual in the large, orderly kitchen or in a parlor that appeared to be furnished almost entirely with large cushions scattered around on a hardwood floor.

"What now, sir?"

Janeway removed his hat and smoothed a hand across his brushed-back hair. "Damned odd, no one about at this time of the evening. Even if they were asleep, they would have heard the dog. But we can hardly go on tramping about here in the dark. How large is this farm?"

Sergeant Church pulled on his nose for a moment, as if testing its tensile strength. "Covers most of this hilltop. Fields off to the right, those woods, and another field or two beyond. Probably . . . thirty-five, forty acres."

"And all private property, not to mention it being out of our jurisdiction. Back to the car, I think."

At the end of the rutted drive, Janeway glanced over at his sergeant breathing heavily on the seat beside him. "You suppose they're in there, Inspector?"

"Could be anywhere. Did your friends in the county have an idea how many there are?"

"Well, sir, they told me they think there's as many as fifteen, though they come and go. Supposed to be some children too. God only knows which of the others are their fathers or mothers." He ran a hand back across his broad forehead as if to wipe away the thought of what must go on in a commune after dark.

In the thick woods near the roadside an owl gave a cry in its hunt for small forest creatures. It was a shriek that could equally have been made in the despair of failure or the elation of seizing its prey. Above the trees the constellations were clearly visible on the ultramarine background of the night sky. Janeway lit a Dunhill's without inhaling. Then he held the smoking cylinder quietly as he stared at the heavens.

"There was a sky like this the night before we crossed the Litani during the war. Have I ever told you about that, Church?"

"You never mentioned it, sir." His superior had not often spoken of his past.

"Litani's a river in the Middle East. Syria. We were fighting the French." The inspector laughed. "I know, it seems absurd, us fighting the French instead of the Germans, but that's what kind of war it was. Damned Vichy were trying to hold out, though I don't imagine half the men on either side understood why we were fighting each other."

"You were cavalry, if I'm not mistaken, sir." Church knew that the inspector had served with the Queen's Own Yorkshire Dragoons, but conversation passed the time.

Janeway nodded, gazing now at the glowing tip of his cigarette. "I was a very young lieutenant at the time. Just commissioned in 1940 and sent out to the Middle East the following year. We still had our horses then." He took a drag without fully inhaling, just to keep it burning.

"Did you make it across the river then, sir?"

"What? Oh, yes. We crossed by an undefended bridge, but another group was caught in machine-gun fire from a village. So we formed up ranks, the call was given, and we advanced at the trot." Looking up at an invisible spot on the windshield, Janeway could almost feel his mount breathing under him again.

"Horses against machine guns?" Church's interest was genuinely aroused.

Janeway nodded in affirmation. "You may not believe this, but by the time we got into the charge, damned if the Frogs hadn't run away! Left their bloody machine guns and showed us their tails. One of the last cavalry actions of the war—one of the last ever." He smiled in remembrance. "They had never faced horses in a full charge. It can be a terrifying thing."

The two men silently watched the unchanging face of the farmhouse. No lights went on or off; no vehicles approached or left. The only sound was a sonorous drone of the wind through the trees that gave an impression of distant chanting.

"Sounds like the spirits are out for Samain, Sergeant." Janeway smiled, then he switched on the engine. "Well, pleasant as it is to relax and look at the stars, we can't wait here all night. Find out tomorrow how many vehicles are registered here. We saw the Morris, and I noticed an old truck and a van around at the back." He glanced at the house one more time. "Seems quiet enough tonight, Samain or no Samain."

With just the running lights on, the black Rover coasted past the gate and the dark drive leading to the farmhouse. Lights still burned in the lower windows as the two policemen headed back to Cambridge.

In a darkened room upstairs, a woman sat rocking an infant. Other children were asleep in other rooms. A few had been wakened earlier by loud knocking and a dog's bark, but all had now gone back to sleep. Eleanor Woodbridge was thankful that none of them had cried. Tonight of all nights she did not want uninvited guests.

With sacrifice before the rising morn
Vows have I made by fruitless hope inspired;
And from the infernal Gods, 'mid shades forlorn.
William Wordsworth (1770—1850)
St. John's College

A dozen figures stood on the dark hilltop near Gog Magog
Farm. They circled slowly near a blazing bonfire in a freshly
plowed field surrounded on three sides by dense woods. Age
and sex were concealed by loose-fitting white robes, reflecting yellow in the firelight as the group circled a large natural
rock slab. Many generations of farmers had chosen to drive
their furrows around the obstacle rather than attempting to dig
it out. In earlier times, when the huge stone had been surrounded by uncleared forest, men had seen more profound
reasons for leaving its massive shape where nature had placed
it. Centuries of wind and weather had worn the broad surface
of the stone smooth, and tonight the face of the ancient slab
was covered by a white sheet reflecting the patterns of the
dancing fire.

Standing near the stone was a tall figure in a bloodred
garment. His uncovered head was reddish blond, as was his
pointed beard. As he reached out to grasp the edge of the
white cloth covering the stone, a low, excited humming was
emitted by the group around him, like the sound of some
gigantic insect stirring underground. Earthenware pitchers of
wine and smoking hashish pipes circled continually around
the group, until without a word of command, the circling suddenly stopped and a sonorous chanting was carried out over
the treetops on the wind.

The man in red, hand still grasping the cloth, stared up at
the heavens, reciting a prayer or a curse in an ancient tongue.
A cloud covered the nearly full moon. Then a new sound
came from the gathering, like the rush of air escaping from a
cave, as the white covering on the rock was roughly pulled
away.

A young girl was revealed, lying naked on the cold face of
the stone. Golden blond hair fell across shoulders that were as
white as the cloth that had been torn away. The firelight cast
strange shadows on her flesh as she lay spread-eagle on the
rock, her wrists and ankles tied to stakes driven into the earth

around the massive stone. She stared up at the chanting group surrounding her through dreamy eyes. Her lips moved lazily but found no words.

Raising a pitcher of wine to his mouth, the man in red drank deeply. Then he held the vessel up in the moonlight and slowly poured its scarlet liquid out onto the pale body of the girl bound to the rock before him. The wine ran up her thighs, staining the fair hair on her lower belly; it splashed across her breasts and up to her lips, flowing out over cheeks and chin. The girl squirmed and emitted a low moan as her tongue swept out over her lips, sensuously trying to catch every drop.

The red man cast aside the empty pitcher, and without looking up from the sacrifice spread before him, he extended his right hand, palm upward, toward the circle of figures around him. In an instant, the object he desired was placed in his hand. The blade of the dagger shone silver in the firelight as he raised it high above his head in both hands.

All sound stopped as the fascinated group watched him lower the blade slowly toward the softly heaving breast of the helpless girl. As the tip of the dagger touched the soft, white flesh, a pinprick of crimson blood welled to the surface. Then, with an excited exclamation from the group around him, the man plunged into her body . . . but not with the dagger. It was cast aside as he threw open his robe and lowered himself onto her with a cry of pent-up passion being released.

At this signal the group around the altar stone cried out in reply. White hems of loose garments were pulled roughly upward to reveal even whiter flesh beneath; cloth was torn in the frantic rush for nakedness in the chill night air. Male and female bodies were pulled down, some gently and some with force, into the soft furrows of the freshly plowed field. One young man was smothered by kisses and caresses from two women, one very young and the other middle-aged, while nearby another female reveler led two men of her choice off into the shadows of the trees. Nearer the fire, two women, both with flowing dark hair, entwined sensually, completely lost in their own loveliness. The orange glow of firelight played over the naked dramas being acted out under the moon, and the erotic sounds of pleasure given and received pervaded the night.

This was Samain. A night when all inhibitions could be cast off without guilt. All sexual, social, and moral distinctions could be ignored; long-standing relationships could be put into abeyance for this one night. Commoners could couple with kings. Only pleasure and celebration mattered until dawn, and whatever happened in the darkness would never be mentioned again.

It was Samain. All Saints' Eve. Halloween. The beginning of the ancient Celtic calendar, when demons were abroad and doorways opened between worlds. On this night sacrifices were offered and bonfires lit; animals were mated and so were men and women, to ensure the renewal of life after the long months of winter had finally passed. So long as the old customs were kept, all was allowed during Samain and all would be well in the spring.

At the rock, the bearded man leading the revels withdrew from the sacrificial maiden and called out to his fellow celebrants.

"Now!" he shouted, loud enough to be heard at the edge of the woods. "It is time now. Come!"

Then, leaving their private pleasures, they came. Some came reluctantly, others with eagerness, until a circle once more stood in the firelight. Naked bodies gleamed with the sweat of passion, skin steaming in the cold air. Several figures swayed in an effort to keep balance in a daze of drink and ecstasy. Then the men closed in on the golden girl, still tied to the sacrificial stone. They pressed in close around her as she closed her eyes and quivered in delicious, frightened anticipation. She could feel their heat and catch the scent of their manhood closing in on her. They pressed even nearer now, and each man felt her softness and enjoyed her warmth until every curve of her body was filled by their touch.

The women pushed in behind and between the men, adding their kisses and caresses to the orgy of love being bestowed on the girl. Soon the entire group was as one lost in their desire. Then, one by one, each man's passion spilled over until the sacrifice was truly completed.

Wine and hashish were once again passed around, and the victim, still in a daze of pleasure and drugs, was finally cut free to join the others. The fire was built up, and before long pairings were once again chosen and the night air of Samain was filled with the sounds of abandonment and pleasure in the hills of Gog and Magog.

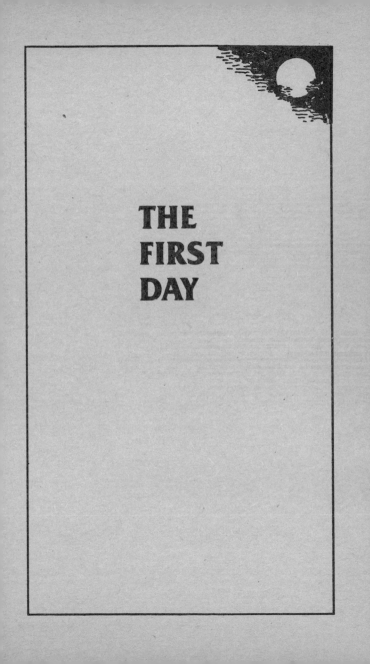

THE
FIRST
DAY

CHAPTER 8

Monday, November 1
Wychfield

This city now doth like a garment wear
The beauty of the morning...All bright
and glittering in the smokeless air.

> William Wordsworth (1770—1850)
> St. John's College

Nick was awake before dawn, having slept only fitfully, thinking of Gwenillan. She had told him her name, though nothing more about who she was or why she had been walking in Trinity Wood. When asked if her name and accent might be Scandinavian, she had simply smiled in what may or may not have been agreement. There was so much about this girl that he wanted to know.

But this morning he had to go to London. Most of his research could only be done among the private papers of various nineteenth century statesmen collected in the British Museum and the London Public Record Office, which he visited at least once a week.

As he stepped out the door, battered briefcase in hand, his feelings were an odd mixture of elation at having met Gwenillan and a certain despondency at knowing so little about her. He could not see her again until the following day at noon. In the suddenness of her departure after their lovemaking, she had not told him why. In fact, their strange meeting now seemed almost to have been a dream, though he could still smell the scent of her body and feel her gentle touch.

The morning air was heavy with humidity. From horizon to horizon the sky was a vast and solid milk white color, without a single crack or rivulet of blue or gray to break its monotony. It was as though the earth had somehow been captured inside a giant dome of opaque white plastic. Somewhere outside the dome, beyond sight, it must have been a beautiful sun-filled day, because the sky, despite its white pall, remained blinding in its brightness.

An hour later, Nick put away the notebook he had been dreaming over and sat idly staring out the train window at the passing landscape. The towns and new housing developments grew thicker as the train left the green belt and approached the sprawling metropolis of London. The city always seemed a magical place, with its fantastic diversity, its color, and the richness of history everywhere under his feet. Even his private melancholy could not prevent a heightening excitement as the train entered the precincts of the great city.

British Rail dived underground into darkness before emerging into the huge enclosure of Liverpool Street Station. As the train pulled headfirst into its appointed platform, a hundred compartment doors swung open along its length to release a new swarm of travelers onto the streets of London. Making his way through the crowd, Nick followed the familiar route of steps, escalators, and bright white tunnels to the Underground that would take him, without ever glimpsing daylight, to Bloomsbury and the British Museum.

He sat in silence in a subway car crowded with sullen-faced workers. Soon he joined them on the long escalators moving slowly toward the light, where he found himself surrounded by bustling crowds of commuters and early morning shoppers. Nick paused for a moment, the crowd that poured forth from underground breaking around him like a rock in a stream as he breathed in the excitement and vitality of the ancient city. People ran for double-decked red buses, and long black taxis made U-turns on pivoting axles in the middle of the busy thoroughfare.

Turning off the main street, Nick strolled into the relative calm of Coptic Street, a short and narrow stretch of lane leading to the British Museum. As always, he glanced into the windows of the small shops lining the street, their mysterious interiors holding wares advertized by signs outside as antiquarian books, objets d'art, occult publications, and exotic imports. He saw an open doorway and, as often was the case, could not resist the temptation to explore.

Inside a tiny storefront bearing the legend "Coptic Books," Nick found himself surrounded by thousands of dusty volumes. The shop's proprietor, equally dusty in appearance and wearing a suit the color of well-worn bindings, was the only other person among the jumbled stacks and piles of books. He saw the elderly man glance up from his scribblings in a ledger, but only for a moment. Nick pulled several used books from the shelves and paged through them without much interest. Wiping dust from his hands, he was about to leave the shop when a worn spine caught his eye. It might have been the faded red binding or the glint of light on time-dulled gold lettering that caused him, almost automatically, to pull it from the shelf.

The title intrigued him: *Lost Gods of the British Forests*. He paid for it with barely a word from the old man behind the cluttered desk, who actually appeared slightly annoyed that a paying customer had interrupted him. Then, with the book in his briefcase, Nick stepped back out into the cold gray light of Coptic Street.

Soon he was climbing the steps of the British Muesum, its Olympian columns soaring overhead. Looking up for a moment, he was reminded of the massive oaks of Trinity Grove, and a heady mixture of thoughts and emotions flooded over him. Once inside, he entered a half-hidden doorway at the back of a gallery, where he showed his reader's pass and was admitted to the Manuscript Reading Room. After filling out a request form with the coded number of two volumes of correspondence for the year 1828, Nick returned to his seat to wait.

He pulled the newly purchased book from his briefcase and glanced again at the faded gold lettering on its cover: *Lost Gods of the British Forests*. Skimming its pages, he quickly gathered that it was a history of ancient religions of the British Isles, before either the Romans or the Christian monks had brought their foreign beliefs to these shores. He paused to study an interesting woodcut illustration of a primitive race of people clustered together in a dark forest clearing with their idols of wood and stone. Then he read a few paragraphs describing the worship of the fertile, life-giving Earth Mother, the female deity venerated in nearly every part of the world until supplanted by the male sky gods of societies dominated by men. According to the author, the roots of the Great Mother's cult had never died away in Britain in rural areas, where constant renewal of the earth through seasonal change remained foremost in men's minds.

Nick read with curious interest how new religions brought by the Roman invaders had been forced upon the conquered

Celtic peoples of Britain. The author contended, and cited numerous proofs, that the old fertility religion was not truly abandoned, though lip service was given to the new Roman pantheon of gods. Names were changed, but the peoples of the forests and fields simply equated the new names with their old deities. The same process occurred when Christianity came to the islands. God the Father, Jesus the martyred son, Mary the mother who gave birth without the intervention of man, even the gallery of saints and angels, all corresponded to long familiar personages and beliefs.

With barely a sound, a thick, leather-bound volume appeared on the desktop near Nick's elbow. Looking up reluctantly from the history of ancient forest gods, he closed one book and opened another. Most of the next six hours was spent concentrating on Foreign Office dispatches. Nick made a genuine effort at concentration. He gave each line of scrawled handwriting and faded ink serious attention, more than most of it deserved. He tried to forget moonlit nights in forest groves and the feel of Gwenillan in his arms. But the moonlight kept slipping in, and the entire afternoon's work was a blank in his mind by evening.

CHAPTER 9

Monday afternoon
Gog Magog Farm

From his brimstone bed, at break of day,
A'walking the Devil is gone,
To look at his little snug farm of the World,
And see how his stock went on.

Robert Southey (1774–1843)

They stood in the farmhouse parlor because there were no chairs. Detective Inspector Janeway remained off to one side of the small group, near the window, having arranged to leave the talking to Sergeant Petrie of the County Constabulary.

Petrie, a stocky man with what might be called a shaggy gray mustache, had made some routine inquiries of the middle-aged woman in the brightly colored caftan who had led them into the sunny parlor. A younger, bearded man had quickly joined them, and Petrie had informed them both of complaints received from neighboring farms concerning late night music and what sounded like chanting and singing from the fields of Gog Magog Farm. The policeman now explained that, because they were newcomers to the area, a routine visit had been overdue even before the complaints. The County Constabulary, he said, liked to maintain a certain visibility with the farmers in the district.

Jan Troop, who had introduced himself as the owner of the farm, nodded in tacit agreement. He had already explained how he, a Dutch citizen, had inherited the property as the only son of the previous owner's sister. "You see," Troop explained with an open smile, "I was suddenly a farmer! But I knew nothing of farming, and I had no money for ... what do you call it?" He looked toward the dark woman standing near him as if she could help him find the right words. "For equipment," he continued, "machinery and all the rest. So I invited Mrs. Woodbridge and several other friends to join me. They invited others ... and we made new friends here in your beautiful country. So," he laughed, sweeping his arms out to his sides, "now there are many of us. We work together. We have a market stall in the town."

"Yes, I've seen it," Petrie commented, twirling his black uniform hat in his hand. "So quite a few of your group are foreign citizens?"

"Some," Troop replied. "We have many friends. Some visit for a time and then move on. I myself plan to apply for status as a resident alien." He smiled brightly, showing even teeth.

"Tell me, do you make the things you sell in the market here at the farm?"

"Yes, we have leather- and metal-working tools and a pottery kiln in the barn." The Dutchman gestured toward the dark woman standing silently near the door. "Eleanor is our chief potterer."

"That's potter, dear boy." Her voice was very British, with indelible traces of country houses and the best schools. Janeway wondered how she came to be here. "What is it exactly that you gentlemen want?" Her dark eyes were cold and impassive.

"Well," Petrie responded without hesitation, "you can begin by telling us how many people live here at present."

"Fourteen adults and four children. Is that all, Sergeant?"

Janeway casually turned from the window. He looked past Eleanor Woodbridge into the large farm kitchen, where two young women, girls really, were kneading dough for bread. One of them was quite striking, with long blond hair. He could not help noticing the soft movement of her body under the loose cotton shift as she pounded the dough. A child of two or three sitting on a little stool watching the baking turned slowly toward the inspector. He smiled, but the child looked away.

"One more question," Petrie was saying. He spoke firmly in response to the woman's hostile attitude. "With regard to the complaints I mentioned, could you tell us what was going on here last night about midnight?"

"Could I ask why you need to know this?" Jan Troop said. Janeway noted for the first time since they had met him, Troop's ready smile was not in evidence.

"It's all right, Jan," Mrs. Woodbridge intervened. "Though we don't have to answer such questions, I will." She folded her arms across her bosom, making her hands disappear inside the loose sleeves of her caftan. "Last night was an important occasion for us. It involves our religious beliefs, which I don't believe I am required to detail for the police. Suffice it to say that we held a small outdoor celebration about midnight. As you are aware, we are on private property here."

"I do know that, madam," Petrie answered, glancing across at Janeway as he lowered his eyes to his wristwatch. "That could perhaps explain the... noises your neighbors complained of?"

"Yes, it could," Jan Troop replied, running his hand across the red fringe of beard. "We have certain ritual songs and music." His smile had returned, unlike the stony face of his companion.

"Other churches do too, if I'm not mistaken," she added, pointedly looking at Janeway rather than Petrie.

"I'm sorry if we were too loud," Troop continued. "We do not want to trouble anyone."

"Do you hold these religious celebrations often, Mr. Troop?" It was the first time Janeway had spoken, and Troop's eyes also turned to him.

"I'm afraid I've missed your name," the dark-haired woman said dryly. He knew she had been quietly studying him since they had entered.

"Janeway," he replied, returning the woman's cool stare.

"Mr. Janeway," Troop began in a matter-of-fact tone, "our festivals coincide with the natural changes of the seasons and the cycles of nature. There was Lammas at the beginning of August, and before that there was the Midsummer festival."

"Midsummer," Janeway repeated.

"Is there anything else? If not, Jan and I have work to do."

Petrie saw Janeway nod slightly. "Yes, I think that will be all. Thank you for your time. If you ever need our assistance, we're as near as your telephone," he added.

Jan Troop's easy smile had returned. "We will try to remember that we have neighbors, even way up here on our hilltop." He laughed his engaging laugh. "England is a small country, like Holland. One always has neighbors."

As the two policemen made their way to the door, Petrie turned back with a final question. "Just out of curiosity, mind, what is your... religion called?"

Troop's grin broadened and his dark companion's mouth

even twisted slightly in shared amusement. "Our religious beliefs are very old, but we have no real church, no name to tell you. Nature is our cathedral," Troop laughed. "Singing outdoors, remember?"

"Names are unimportant," the woman added, as though the statement was a door closing on further discussion.

As Janeway stepped into the hall, he glanced back to see the golden-haired girl in the bright clean kitchen watching him. Her clear green eyes seemed to look beyond his face into his thoughts.

The Morris Minor was still parked near the front of the house. Near it was a large, blond-bearded man. Janeway saw cruel eyes under a protruding brow watching him intently as he followed Petrie up the drive toward their car. The man's height and size in relation to the automobile was startling: he looked as though he could pick it up and carry it away with him if he chose.

Driving back to town, Sergeant Petrie was the first to speak. "What did you make of that lot, Inspector?"

"I'm not sure yet, but I appreciate your help."

"No trouble, sir. Been meaning to look in on them for some time. Glad to have an excuse, and glad I phoned your Sergeant Church about those complaints last night. He'd asked me to keep a finger to the wind. If you need me again, we're as near . . ."

"Yes, as near as the telephone."

The car dropped Janeway at No. 7 Willow Walk rather than at the station. The inspector had a dinner engagement for which he had to change. He pushed open the unlatched front door to the house and walked upstairs to his three-room flat. One wall of the sitting room was lined with books on shelves to the ceiling. Military prints decorated another wall, red coats shining out from dark sepia backgrounds. He glanced up at the soothing pastels of the Impressionist-style painting over his mantelpiece as he walked to the bedroom.

As there were several hours before he was due to meet James Anglesey for dinner, he decided to run a hot tub and relax. Janeway had known the chaplain of Trinity Hall for many years before coming to Cambridge. A shared interest in Anglican Church history had brought the two men together periodically at various conferences and seminars for more than twenty years.

He enjoyed a lengthy, very hot bath, while a cigarette burned untouched in an ashtray nearby. One interest he did not share with his old friend Anglesey, however, was the study of pre-Christian religions. There were a number of questions on that subject he was anxious to put to the chaplain later that evening.

Lewis Janeway leaned back comfortably in the still, hot water as steam clouded the mirror fastened to the bathroom door. He closed his eyes and felt the tensions of the day turn liquid and gradually melt into the water of his bath.

"Midsummer," he repeated softly to himself, "Midsummer."

CHAPTER 10

Monday evening
Trinity Hall

'Tis merry in hall
Where beards wag all.

> Thomas Tusser (1524—1580)
> Trinity Hall

Nick Lombard walked quickly across the deserted market square toward the college, the worn cobbles wet and slick under his feet. The dark shape of Great St. Mary's Church was outlined against the cold glare of streetlights as he crossed King's Parade, shivering against the wind in his thin, wet jacket.

The young American had dined with the Fellowship of the College at High Table once before, and had survived the ordeal rather well, he thought, but this evening was not the best night for a return match. Not only had he spent a long and tiring day in London, and gotten soaked in the process in coming home, he was preoccupied with thoughts of seeing Gwenillan tomorrow and not feeling at all sociable.

Senate House Passage was dark and glistening under the soft glow of its gas lanterns, lighting students and dons on their way to college dining halls, their footsteps on the wet stones fainter echos of Nick's own. Turning into the main gate of Trinity Hall, Nick entered the Porter's Lodge and faced the stout figure of J. Macvicar Swann behind the counter.

The head porter glanced up at the graduate pigeonholes. "Something for you, Mr. Lombard. Looks rather like a bill from the bursar."

Nick groaned as he accepted the disagreeable envelope and thrust it into his pocket unopened. From another pocket he pulled a crumpled black and white necktie with the distinctive crescent of Trinity Hall. Squinting at his reflection in the window, he knotted it under the turned-up collar of his shirt.

Swann ambled into the back room and returned with a towel.

"Thanks, Swann. You're a lifesaver." Nick rubbed his wet hair. "I'm at High Table tonight. Have to look presentable."

The older man hauled a gold watch out of the depths of his waistcoat pocket. "You'd better hurry, sir, if you want to join them for sherry."

The head porter smiled as the young man hurried out into Front Court. Now, where was that blasted Nigel? If he didn't come soon, Swann would miss having his own sherry before dinner; and there were certain ammenities that J. Macvicar Swann did not forgo lightly.

Jan Troop paced the floor of the old barn. It was dark and empty now, its worktables and benches still littered with craft tools and scraps of leather and wood waiting for another workday. In the center of the large open room, a huge cast-iron stove glowed with the heat of burning coals. The Dutchman moved to it and warmed his hands.

Slowly the big barn doors were pulled open from outside, and moonlight cast a spreading fan into the dim interior. Troop turned calmly toward the light and sound intruding on the silence of the barn. The figure of a man, short and dark-bearded, was pushed roughly into view. Behind him appeared the towering bulk of another man, who pulled the doors closed behind them both, cutting off the outside light. The large man then turned and stood threateningly over the other as he hesitated, blinking in the dimness of the shadowed interior.

"Ah, Carpenter," the Dutchman said in a mocking tone of welcome. "Come closer. What are you afraid of?"

When the small, dark man moved only a few halting paces closer, Troop nodded to the other man. "Help him, Harrold." The large, blond man pushed Carpenter forward into the circle of orange light cast by the open door of the iron stove.

"That's better. I've heard some disturbing things about you, David Carpenter. Things I don't like."

Carpenter cringed, looking down at the earth floor, as the leader of the Pentacle Commune stirred the coals with an iron poker and spoke again.

"Several people have told me that you have doubts about some of our activities here. That you think our ceremonies

are . . . how did he put it, Harrold? A lot of rubbish? Is that
it?"

"I never said that," David Carpenter muttered, still staring
down at his feet.

"Well, you're entitled to your opinion." Troop paused sig-
nificantly, strolling over to one of the worktables behind the
other two men. He idly picked up a leatherworking knife and
walked back toward the fire. The blade caught the glow from
the fire as he continued speaking. "Of course, if that is what
you think of our ways, then you don't belong here. What do
you think, Harrold?"

The hulking man at Carpenter's elbow nodded silently and
nudged the other man closer to the fire.

"You see, Harrold agrees with me." Then his smile faded
theatrically into a puzzled frown. "But how could we let you
go? Knowing all that you know, I mean." The curved knife
blade was thrust into the glowing coals for a long, silent moment. When Troop withdrew it and held it up admiringly in
front of his face, the frightened man near him quickly looked
away.

"We've trusted you, David. Trusted you with secrets. Why,
you've even been allowed to see the house in the woods."

Carpenter looked from side to side like a cornered animal,
before his eyes were captured by the glowing orange blade as
the Dutchman took a few paces closer to him.

"Were we wrong to have trusted you, David? I've heard
about the incident in Cambridge last week. You and Horst
Wenger in a pub. Too much to drink. You talking with some
other useless layabouts, telling them things you shouldn't
have. About some of our most private ceremonies." Troop
paused again, a strange, twisted smile on his face as he stared
at the heated blade. "I noticed you didn't think that on Samain
night, rutting with the women like a beast in the dirt. You
certainly seemed a true believer on Samain Eve."

Carpenter cringed away from the smoking blade, now only
inches from his nose. "I didn't mean nothing," he insisted. "I
was drunk! It won't happen again, I swear."

"That's just what you're friend Wenger said. He swore too.
He was glad to swear." Troop continued to hold the slowly
cooling blade in the smaller man's face, its heat caressing his
cheek and making him blink back tears of fear. All trace of a
smile was gone as the Dutchman spoke again.

"I'll accept your oath this time," he said coldly, "because you are swearing on this blade. Harrold and I both know what that means . . . and so do you. If you think of betraying secrets again, just remember this blade and what it could do to a man's face!"

Carpenter tried to back away, but was held fast by the muscular man behind him. Then Troop turned away in disgust, throwing the leatherworking tool onto the nearest table. "Let him go. We all know why Carpenter is here. We know his weakness, and his friend Wenger's. Let him go and get what he needs."

As ordered, Harrold jerked the slightly built man around easily and let him hurry with relief out the door. Then the big man turned back toward the leader of the commune. His voice was deep and his speech slow and deliberate. "The other one is waiting in the van. The boy from the college."

Troop nodded with idle curiosity. "Yes, the boy Eleanor met in the market. Bored with his life, is he? Wants a change? Some excitement?" His crooked smile returned. "Send him to me, Harrold. We can always use an eager young man."

When the big doors eased open again, into the fan-shaped intrusion of light stepped Nigel Pinder, former underporter of Trinity Hall.

> The combination room glowed warm
> when I entered it that evening.
> C. P. Snow (1905–1980)
> Christ's College

It was only a few steps from the Grad Room, where Nick had stopped for a rather soiled academic gown, through a medieval passageway to the Master's Lodge. He adjusted the gown over his damp sport coat as he entered the large hallway lined with oil portraits of college luminaries. The Senior Combination Room, or "SCR," was a long, high-ceilinged room located in the most ancient part of the fourteenth-century college. Its modern renovation contrasted strikingly with the long-case clock and venerable paintings that decorated the Fellows' inner sanctum just as they had for several hundred years before a bright, young architect had surrounded them with blond wood and smoked glass.

The bursar, glass in hand, greeted Nick near the door. "The master has announced dinner, but you should just have time for a drop of sherry."

Nick thanked him and glanced toward the far end of the room, where he saw the chaplain talking to a man with a military-style mustache. A guest, Nick observed. No gown.

Sherry glasses were soon drained and discarded as a casual procession of black-gowned figures formed at the small doorway leading into the dining hall. As guests of the Fellows, both Nick and Inspector Janeway were invited to the head of the procession, to be escorted by the master and the chaplain respectively.

Walking out of the candlelight of the Senior Combination Room onto the raised dais of the head of the long, brightly lit medieval hall was much like making an entrance onstage. Nick glanced down as several hundred students at the long refectory tables stood with much shuffling and scraping of wooden benches.

After a rapid Latin grace, everyone took his seat. John Blessed and a few other late arrivals down in the hall had to step up onto and across the tables—fording past place settings and their fellow diners clutching soup dishes—to slide into vacant seats on benches against the wall. Blessed noted his friend dining in the splendor of High Table and wondered idly if he would ever be invited back after having asked to take the uneaten portion of the senior tutor's filet mignon home last term.

Up on the dais, Nick enjoyed his dinner and a very good claret, talking a little with one of the younger Fellows. The chaplain introduced his guest, an inspector with the city police, and Nick casually listened to them discussing earlier days in their long friendship. He reflected on how many meals and how many conversations, from idle to profound, these walls had witnessed over the centuries. Dinner conversation every night for six hundred odd years, through the Black Death, the Reformation, and two world wars. Above the High Table dais, set high on the wall, was a small Norman window. How many voices could have been overheard through that little window over the years? Despite the gradual evolution into twentieth-century life, Nick realized that anyone looking down from that window this evening would see that almost as much had remained the same in this college hall as had changed over the past six centuries.

Later, back at the long, polished table in the SCR, Nick enjoyed his coffee and a cheroot as he listened to the bursar vent a little of his carefully nursed antagonism toward the senior tutor. "Said the wine cellar expansion was a waste of money!" he explained with disbelief. "And you should hear him on the subject of admitting woman. Hah! You'd think we were limiting enrollment to belly dancers and London prostitutes."

Nick rubbed his thumb over an engraved college crest as he passed a silver snuffbox to his left. The infighting among the dons was not his favorite topic of conversation. "The chaplain's dinner guest," he asked. "Have you met him?"

"Inspector Janeway?" The bursar filled his glass from the port decanter and passed it on to his left. "Yes, I have. In fact, he's the chap who questioned me about what I might have seen or heard on the night of the murder. You remember, the young Spaniard who was killed last summer? Dreadful business."

"Seems an odd sort of combination," Nick observed, "a policeman and a priest."

The bursar shrugged. "Pretty well known as a detective, I gather. With Scotland Yard before he came up here a few years ago. Some sort of stroke, Anglesey said. Needed a slower pace, so where better than Cambridge? And now he's got a murder to deal with."

Nick was only half listening as he watched the chaplain and his guest walking upstairs. Other diners were also standing and talking around the table now as Nick passed a decanter of Madeira and then took his leave of the bursar.

He found Reverend Anglesey and the inspector seated upstairs at a fine old port table, the pride of the SCR. Shaped like a horseshoe to fit against a fireplace, the table was designed with a built-in railway track bisecting its docked-off end. By means of the tiny, ingenious track, a leather bottle holder on wheels allowed a diner to pass a port decanter from one side of the table to the other simply by tipping a hidden slat of wood on the table's underside. The chaplain was demonstrating the device for Janeway with childlike enthusiasm, rolling the bottle carrier across the squared-off end of the table, where a fireplace would otherwise have obstructed the civilized passing of port from right to left around the table.

Nick did not want to interrupt, but as he had hoped, the chaplain soon noticed him and called him over. "Nick, you may be able to add something to our earlier discussion. During dinner, Lewis raised the subject of ancient religions in the British Isles. Your thesis deals with the Celts, doesn't it?"

"Actually," Nick admitted, "that's John Blessed's subject. British foreign policy is all I can offer."

"Of course," the chaplain winced, "I was thinking of your Irish friend. Excuse me."

"What I'm curious about," Janeway said, "is the significance of changing seasons in the old nature religions. What sort of festivals did they celebrate? Take Midsummer, for instance."

Nick noted the authority in the inspector's voice. It was a voice with the easy confidence of a man used to having his questions answered.

"Midsummer," Anglesey mused, "let's see. The Celtic festival of Midsummer was held in honor of the sun, chiefly. There were bonfires and sacrifices. A major part of the festivities, at least in post-Roman times, involved young girls practicing simple magic to find out who their future husbands would be. Very quaint."

"Like a lock of hair under the pillow?" Nick asked.

"Yes, the same sort of thing. They read magical significance into practically everything. Animists, you know. Every stick and stone, every change in the direction of the wind, had a meaning. Of course, that's quite natural if you see all of nature as your god and every stream of water and tree as having a soul."

"Sounds pretty harmless," Janeway observed, "though you did mention sacrifices. What sort of sacrifices?"

James Anglesey took a pinch of snuff from a small silver container on the table. Holding his thumb out stiffly, he placed the pulverized tobacco in the natural hollow formed between his outstretched thumb and the side of his wrist. "Oh, with the Druids it could be almost anything. They sacrificed food, flowers, animals." With an easy motion, he sniffed the soft brown powder up each nostril.

"What about human sacrifice?"

The chaplain looked up at his old friend slowly. "Yes, from what we know, it seems they sometimes sacrificed humans, too. At least in time of war, when they had prisoners. Or perhaps if they felt in special need of help for some reason—say, a drought, or a crop failure, or a run of disease." He paused. "Sometimes, too, punishment for a crime or breaking a tribal taboo could take the form of a sacrifice." His thin lips curled into a wry smile. "Why waste a perfectly good execution?"

Nick watched the inspector's reflection in the highly polished wood. There seemed to be more to his questions than simple curiosity. "What time period are we talking about?" Nick heard himself ask.

"Well," Anglesey began, "Celtic civilization goes back far beyond the Christian era, as you know, but the further back we go, the less material evidence there is about their customs and beliefs. We know a great deal about the later period, though, during the Roman occupation in the first few centuries A.D. Most of what I've mentioned was still true at that time . . . though all these religious rituals and ceremonies originated many centuries earlier."

Janeway lit a cheroot. "What festivals come after Midsummer?"

"Well, there would be Lammas on August first, when the first corn would be ground and the first new loaves baked and dedicated to the gods. It was a jolly sort of festival, lots of dancing and drinking." He smiled at Nick. "Rather like one of the graduates' black-tie dinners."

"There's still a place called Lammas Land in Cambridge, isn't there?" Nick commented.

"Quite right. Just off the Fen Causeway." The chaplain smoothed back his silver hair. "The name, Lammas, goes back to the Saxon *hlef maesse* or 'loaf mass.' The Celts, I believe, called it *Lugnasad*, but it's all the same holy day. The Christian Church picked it up, of course, as they did nearly all the pagan festivals. Easier than trying to make people forget the old ways."

"But, James, isn't there a much less innocent festival about this time of year? My sergeant, a fenman born and bred, called it Samain."

The chaplain's eyes crinkled in a smile. "Ah, Samain. November first—today, in fact! Though in olden times any festivities would have taken place last night, after dark. Like you Americans celebrate Halloween, Nick. The eve was more significant than the day itself. And once again, we Christians still celebrate it, too—All Saints' Day, All Hallows' Eve—part of our rich pagan heritage."

Anglesey took a swallow of port, and after savoring it for a moment on his tongue, he continued. "You're right, Lewis, Samain was one of the more sinister events in the Celtic calendar. They believed that all natural laws were suspended during the night of Samain and that spirits could come back to walk the earth through some sort of . . . chink in the curtain of reality on that particular night. So they prayed and sang and sacrificed to protect themselves. And they enjoyed themselves, too, from what I gather. Suspension of law allowed a certain sexual license, let's say."

He leaned back in his chair, bony elbows resting on its arms, and fingers steepled against his chin. "The demon they were really praying against was winter. By early November they knew the cold was coming, and they could never be sure how many of them would survive the long, dark months to see the spring. It's a very ancient festival, and a very ancient fear."

"Lewis," the chaplain asked after a moment, "does all this have something to do with your investigation? Or shouldn't I ask?"

Janeway smiled at his friend's perception. "I don't want to make too much of it, but do you think there may be people who still celebrate these old festivals?"

"Why, I'm certain there are. You should attend one of my folklore conventions. You'd meet everyone from modern day Druids to self-proclaimed witches. A trifle odd, but entirely harmless; all of them I've met, at any rate." He paused before continuing. "But I can imagine that there are other 'true believers' in the world who are much less harmless. I suppose you have to explore every possibility in a case like this." He turned toward Nick to explain. "The inspector is in charge of our 'Midsummer Murder.' I'm sure you remember it."

"One thing I must mention," Janeway added, "is the need for discretion. I don't want any of this general line of thought to become public knowledge. Can I rely on you?"

"I'm fascinated," Nick admitted, "but I'll keep anything I hear to myself."

"Good. Well, this much you may have read in the papers already. There were traces of several metals found in the wounds of Cordillo's body—copper, iron, and tin. Does that combination suggest anything to you, James?"

"Yes, I recall now that it occurred to me when I first read about it. Bronze—the combination of copper, iron, and tin in specific proportions. I thought it an odd bit of trivia, but now I see how it might fit with a theory of . . . ritual murder, let's say. Though it would take much more than that before I'd take such a theory seriously, as I'm sure you agree, Lewis."

"I don't understand," Nick said.

Anglesey answered. "A bronze instrument has definite connections with pagan times and, therefore, could have a certain ritual significance in someone's warped mind."

"I'm pleased that some of the same thoughts occur to you, James. I only wish that I had a few more theories to explore, however farfetched they may appear."

"Has anything unusual happened on any of the other pagan holy days we talked about?" Nick asked. "Lammas or . . . what was it? Samain?"

"No. Not that we know of." Janeway smoothed his mustache with his thumb. "That's partly where such a theory falls down. Last night was a key date for anyone following a pagan calendar, but it was as quiet as . . . a funeral."

"Bad choice of words," Anglesey chided. "You know, we had our own rather bizarre murder mystery here at Trinity Hall years ago; though the deed actually took place centuries before that."

He glanced up casually to see that he had their full attention before continuing. "A skeleton, the skeleton of a young woman, was unearthed in 1910 during excavations for the Thornton Building near the river. She had evidently been tied to a wooden stake in the river and left to drown as the level of water rose, no doubt during a storm. I don't think it was ever determined just how old the remains were. Methods of dating weren't so precise in those days, and the bones were simply reinterred—in old St. Peter's churchyard at the foot of Castle Hill." He smiled. "I'm not sure which feeling influenced our dons more at the time, religion or superstition, but they were very prompt with the reinterment."

"So no one knows when it happened?" Nick asked.

"It must have happened well before the Middle Ages, when we know the course of the Cam was a few yards east of where it flows today. My guess is that it goes back to pre-

Christian times, judging from . . . circumstantial evidence."
Anglesey threw a wry glance at the police inspector, having
borrowed one of his terms. "Now that I think about it, there
was some piece of jewelry found with the girl's remains that
confirms my guess. It was Celtic in design, dating back to the
early Roman period in Britain. I've seen it in the university
museum—a brooch."

"Must have been a terrible way to die." Janeway involun-
tarily pictured the event taking place so near to where another
body had recently been found.

"Heaven only knows what the poor girl had done to de-
serve such a fate. It would appear to have been one of those
ritual executions I mentioned earlier." Anglesey toyed with
the hidden lever of the port table as each of the three men
imagined the terror in the young girl's eyes waiting helplessly
for the flooding waters to rise and bring a dark, cold release
from her misery.

Nick was anxious to break the mood. "I read that your
investigation is centering around Churchill College now, Inspector. I live nearby, at the Wychfield site."

"Well then, we may get around to asking you some questions soon."

"I haven't run into any Druids or witches lately," Nick
laughed. "Are you looking in our area because the victim's
bike was found at Churchill? That's what I read."

"That and we think he may have had some connection with
a girl from Churchill or somewhere nearby, though we know
very little about her. It's a slim lead. We're simply asking if
anyone saw Cordillo at any time, possibly with a young blond
girl."

"Ah, the life of a policeman," Anglesey said facetiously.
"Do you think this will end up as one of those unsolved
murders we read about in the more lurid morning papers?"

"I'll admit we don't have much to go on, even after several
months, but something will turn up, given time." The inspector looked down at his watch. "Speaking of time, I must go.
Thank you, James, for a delightful evening and for your very
helpful lecture on Celtic ritual."

"You asked for it, Lewis."

Janeway stood and buttoned the center button of his dark
gray suit. "It was a pleasure to have met you, Nick."

"Good luck in solving your case."

The chaplain took his guest off to say good night to the master, and when Nick judged the time was right, he went downstairs to do the same.

Outside, the air was chill after the rain, and the streets were quiet as Nick walked toward Castle Hill and home. Passing the lighted doorway of The Pickeral, he glanced through the frosted glass into the interior of the old pub, where a number of his friends were talking with the landlord. Nick had no intention of joining them tonight.

Soon, however, the wine was having its natural effect and he wished he had used the WC at the pub. Off to one side of the busy Huntingdon Road he saw a familiar wooden gate leading into the dark churchyard of St. Peter's.

The small abandoned church was now minimally maintained by charitable contributions. Nick had been inside once and knew that it was only an empty shell despite its impressive steeple outlined now against the blue-black night sky. He made his way through the tangled weeds amid worn tombstones toward a dark corner that he hoped was sufficiently removed from consecrated ground.

Listening to the sound he made on the leaf-strewn grass, Nick looked up at the old church. He had read once that the site of this almost forgotten building on the little rise of ground at the foot of Castle Hill had been occupied by a Roman temple long before Christianity came to East Anglia. Before the Romans, it had sheltered a pagan place of worship. In fact, for as long as anyone could determine, this had been the site of religious ceremonies, far back into the shadowy centuries before men had kept written records of their worship or their gods. He recalled Anglesey's story about the bones of the girl from the river being reinterred in this very churchyard. Now only the shell of the deserted Christian Church of St. Peter continued to mark the ancient sacredness of the spot.

His relief complete, Nick made his way back through the dark, moss-covered shapes of tombstones and crosses toward the path. A cloud-streaked circle of moon seemed to rest on the very point of the church steeple like some stark modern sculpture. It must have been the wind blowing through the empty husk of the church, but Nick was sure he heard the soft whisper of a voice in the darkness. It was a strangely familiar voice, exciting both anticipation and a certain fear within him. He thought he heard his name, and then something else.

When he stopped walking and stood in the squat, black shadow of the church, the sound became more distinct.

"Forget me . . . forget . . . me . . . forget . . ."

The wind sighed through the bare trees of the churchyard as Nick found the path and quickened his pace.

"Forget me," the wind seemed to whisper, "forgive me."

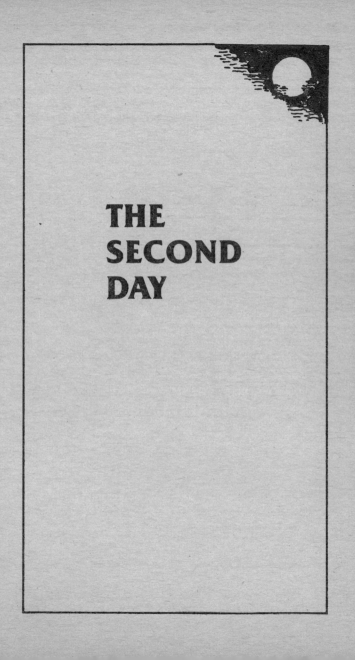

THE
SECOND
DAY

CHAPTER 11

Tuesday, November 2
Cambridge Police
Headquarters

Young men are apt to think themselves wise enough,
As drunken men are apt to think themselves sober
enough.

Lord Chesterfield (1694—1773)
To his son at Trinity Hall

The young reporter was seated in one of the leather armchairs in Janeway's office while the inspector occupied its mirror image across a low coffee table. They made an odd pair, the reporter with his long, sandy hair tied back in a ponytail, dressed in worn jeans, with rolled shirt sleeves and a dark brocade waistcoat, and the older man in his elegantly cut London pinstripe. A knocking interrupted their conversation as the office door was tentatively pushed open.

"Sergeant, this is Mr. Graham of the *Cambridge Evening News*."

The young man nodded. "Terry will be fine." His voice sounded more educated than his appearance had led the sergeant to expect.

"Terry has been telling me about some research of his that may have a bearing on our investigation. He's been digging through the archives of his newspaper, all the way back to the war years." Janeway held out a sheet of paper, a photocopied page from the *Cambridge Evening News* dated 29 June 1943.

Church took the page and sat again on the couch. The worn leather creaked under his weight as he carefully pulled his finger-spotted reading glasses from his breast pocket. He used them to read a lead article concerning the discovery of the mutilated body of a young man near Cambridge. Police gave the cause of death as "multiple stab wounds," but admitted they had no suspects. The deceased had been a prisoner-of-war, a young Italian, put to work on a farm near the village of Madingley.

"Aye, I remember this. Wasn't much more than a lad, but I remember there was a great to-do about the state of the body. Seems to me it was written off in the end as some sort of revenge killing . . . because of the war. Never arrested anyone, if I remember right. So many people dying then, with the war and all, there was no great public outcry to find the culprits."

"Right," Graham agreed. "There were more mentions of it in the paper—'police continue their inquiries'—and one longer article four months later, saying there were still no leads."

"Sounds familiar," Janeway frowned. He crossed his long legs and shifted to face the sergeant more squarely. "Did you note the date?"

"Aye, June 29. Midsummer. Same as our bloke."

"Exactly thirty-three years earlier," the young reporter pointed out. "But I didn't stop there. On an impulse, I went back another thirty-three years to 1910. We were a weekly paper then, but I found this." His eyes showed his excitement as he took another folded sheet of photocopy from his hip pocket and handed it to Janeway.

The inspector saw the date July 2 and banner headlines reporting another gruesome murder. He read aloud:

"Earlier this week, in the early morning hours of 29 June, the decapitated body of a young man was discovered by a man returning from a Public House on King Street."

Janeway paused a moment. "Pubs had later closing times before the 1914 war," Church pointed out. His superior smiled wryly in understanding and continued to read from the article:

"The head and two limbs had been entirely severed from the body, apparently by a heavy, sharpened instrument, not found at the scene. The victim has been identified by his traveling companion as one Adolphe Mazzone, a visitor to our city from Corsica. Police have been able to ascertain no motive for this apparently senseless and brutal crime. Persons residing near Midsummer Common, where the body was discovered, are being questioned. Witnesses' reports that the body had been disemboweled have not been confirmed."

Terry Graham watched the faces of the two policemen as Janeway finished reading. "I'm going back further this afternoon," he explained, holding up a cigarette for approval and then offering the pack. Janeway accepted and offered a match.

"To . . . 1877?"

Terry nodded. "Don't ask me why. The thirty-three-year thing could just be coincidence. I don't know what any of it means." He blew out a cloud of pungent, blue smoke. "When I have a hunch, I follow it."

"There's no substitute for thorough research, though. What do you think, Church?"

The sergeant rubbed his chin and shook his head slowly from side to side. "Like he said, coincidence, most like. I'll admit murder's pretty rare in Cambridge, but the one was a POW—easy to see why someone could have had it in for him. The other one, well—could have been anything. Traveling here from foreign parts, you never know. Article didn't tell us much."

"What does your editor think of all this, Terry?"

The young man reached around and gave his long hair a nervous tug. "My editor is a first-rate newspaperman, but sometimes he lacks a certain . . . imagination."

"So you haven't told him?"

"I will, as soon as I've done some more research."

"Then why bring it to us now?"

Graham looked slightly chargrined. "I wanted to get your reaction. And I thought you should know."

The inspector glanced over at the frowning face of Colin Church. "Well, my reaction—as a man of imagination—is interest. I can't wait to see what else you may turn up." He stabbed out the unsmoked remains of his cigarette. "But as a policeman, I find very little to go on. It's all a little too imaginative for a policeman."

"Wouldn't be a good idea to go writing any kind of article about this," Church added, with a glance at the inspector. "Would cause us no end of problems."

Terry Graham shook his head in what appeared to be agreement. "At first I thought about a sort of general interest story about the coincidence angle. But when I found there was another *coincidence* in 1910— and if I find what I think I might with some more digging—I have too much for a lightweight piece like that. But I don't have enough yet for anything more substantive."

"Well," Janeway emphasized, "even if you do develop something that you think is more substantial, I strongly suggest that you clear it with us before going to print." He uncrossed his legs and looked intently at the young reporter. "A story, even a responsible story, based on the sort of coincidences we've just been discussing would have reporters from every lunatic tabloid in the nation poking their noses into this investigation. I don't think you want that any more than we do."

Terry Graham hid his growing excitement behind a calm face as he made his own point. "I'll talk with you about anything I intend to show my editor, Inspector. But you have to remember that I'm a news reporter, and I have to report what I think is news."

This unresolved exchange was interrupted by the ringing of a telephone on Janeway's desk. Sergeant Church answered and listened for a moment to a voice at the other end.

"Right, we'll be there." He hesitated a moment after replacing the receiver.

"It's all right," the inspector told him.

"They've found bloodstained clothing."

"Where?"

"Half mile west of Churchill College. In the woods off Madingley Road."

"Anything else?"

"Didn't say. Just some clothes: running shorts, shoes, vest. Torn, the constable said, probable bloodstains. One of the dogs turned them up, back a way off the road in the woods."

"Terry, we're going to have to cut this short."

"I want to ride along." The young man looked anxiously from Janeway to Church and then back. "I'm a reporter, and this is news."

"So you said." The inspector was beginning to like Terry Graham. The boy had spirit, even if he was being a pain in the arse. "Get your coat."

Church already had his hand on the door as Janeway glanced back at the clock on his desk. Twelve noon.

CHAPTER 12

Tuesday, noon
Wychfield

And near the sacred gate,
With longing eyes I wait,
Expectant of her.

> William Makepeace Thackeray
> (1811–1863)
> Trinity College

Nick Lombard stared across the field at the dark green facade of Trinity Wood. He had been sitting by his window for more than thirty minutes, waiting for Gwenillan to appear. She was not late, he was anxious. Maybe he would save himself a lot of disappointment and hurt if he just forgot he had ever met her. Maybe in the light of day she was embarrassed by what had happened and wouldn't come. What had passed between them was hard to believe now, almost like a dream.

He watched a small flying insect on the pane of glass. It had somehow found its way into the closed room through a crack or hole in the window frame, and now it could not find the way out. It had been there on the glass for as long as Nick had been watching for Gwenillan, maybe for hours. The tiny creature walked patiently back and forth across the smooth surface, occasionally flying a few inches back from the pane to hurl itself futilely against the unyielding glass. It was a hopeless situation. But the insect continued its fruitless struggle toward the cool and familiar outside world so near through the glass. Nick was idly contemplating raising the sash, intervening like some god of Fate, when he saw her.

It was too far to see clearly, but he knew that the white figure emerging from the forest path was Gwenillan. Snatching his jacket from the back of a chair, he hurried out onto Wychfield's lawn. The trapped insect may have noticed a dark shape pass across the window heading toward Trinity Wood, but it had no effect on its hopeless struggle.

Nick waved and saw an arm move tentatively in reply. Now he could see long, blond hair swinging gently across her shoulders. They met midway along the path that bounded the plowed field, greeting each other shyly, as though for the first time. She looked different than he remembered her in the moonlight. A strand of hair, even more golden in daylight, was pulled back from each temple and pinned in the back. A gray wool skirt and a bulky sweater of undyed wool hid the soft contours of the figure Nick remembered so well.

"I'm sorry I do not speak well." Her look was bold and smiling, and once more Nick found her voice and accent exciting and slightly hypnotic—like a princess from a faraway land.

"My friends say I try to do all the talking anyway," Nick reassured her. "Would you like to walk? Maybe into town? We could look at the gardens along the river?"

She nodded and Nick took her arm to direct her back toward the path through the woods.

"Could we walk that way?" she asked, pointing in the other direction, toward Wychfield. "Is that your home?"

"I have one small room in it." Nick turned his back on Trinity Wood as they began to stroll slowly toward the house and the Huntingdon Road beyond. From behind them, he heard sirens; police or ambulance, he was not sure which. Must have been an accident on Madingley Road.

"I should not be seeing you again," the girl said.

He turned and met her gold-flecked eyes, nearly on a level with his own. "I don't understand."

"I am from far away, and I will not be here long. I should not become . . . connected to anyone." She paused, finding the words for another sentence. "I will have to go back soon. To my family. But when I saw you . . . I knew it was meant to be."

"I know. That evening was very special. Magical. But let's talk about today. I don't know anything about you! You say you won't be here long. Are you a student? A tourist?"

"No," she said simply. "I don't know about you either. Tell me."

Nick laughed at the way she had turned his questions on him. As they walked, he talked quietly to her about himself. Then, leaving the college sports grounds, he questioned her again, speaking over the noise of traffic on the busy road.

"Have you been here long?"

"What?" She hesitated, as if unsure of his meaning.

"How long have you been here? Most visitors come to Cambridge in the summer."

"Yes, I was here in summer." She took his arm and he felt the warmth of her body close to his.

"Do you have the afternoon free?"

"I have until the dark, but . . ."

"But nothing," Nick grinned. "There's no reason we can't spend the afternoon together then. Are you hungry?"

She smiled and shook her head, making her hair sway with the motion. "We can have the afternoon, but we should not get . . . serious."

"Serious! I've never been serious a day in my life." He was rewarded with a smile and the rich sound of her laughter for the first time as they walked on toward Castle Hill and the town. He sensed that Gwenillan was bothered by her difficulty with the language, so he did not press her to talk. It was enough just to walk beside her and breathe in the now familiar scent of moss and wildflowers. He knew it had been foolish to think even for a moment that he could forget her.

Across from the site where William the Conqueror had built a castle to overlook the little river town below, Nick asked again where she was from and was told with a playful look to guess. He guessed Scandinavia and then suggested Sweden as her home.

"Sweden," she repeated coyly, without confirming or denying his guess.

When they turned onto Queens' Road, Nick noticed her fascination with the immaculately trimmed gardens and the graceful old elms that lined their way.

"Beautiful, isn't it? You have a special feeling for the outdoors. I can tell by the way you look up at the trees."

She nodded and smiled as they turned away from the noisy roadway onto a leafy path opening between the trees fringing college gardens along the Backs. "You are from far away," she asked him, "across the ocean?"

"I grew up in a town called Pittsburgh. Lots of smokestacks, not too many trees. So I don't know a lot about nature, but I bet that you do, Gwenillan." He paused. "Can I call you Gwen?"

"Yes, if you like." She let her eyes linger for a moment on

his before looking back at the college gardens. "And you are right. I know them all." Her hand trailed across a few low-hanging leaves still clinging to their branches. "We are all part of the same earth, Nick." It was the first time she had spoken his name.

Nearing King's College, a small pasture stretched out beside them, its black-faced sheep incongruously grazing amidst the formal gardens. A noisy group of undergraduates passed by on their way to the university library across Queens' Road. Nick waited until they had passed before speaking again. "I've only felt that way a few times. The other night in the woods . . . in the grove, with the trees all around overhead and the moss and leaves underneath. And us. I really did feel a part of it all somehow."

He looked at her and found her gently smiling eyes fixed on his. The sensation was so strong, it made him look away. Stopping on King's College Bridge, Gwenillan gazed down over the stone railing at the gently flowing river. The twin spires of King Henry's soaring chapel looked down on them standing side by side on the bridge.

"You can see life in the water. Just below the surface."

Nick leaned on the cool stone balustrade next to her and silently watched the quiet eddies on the dark green surface of the Cam. Their forearms touched.

"My people tell of water spirits who live wherever water flows. They can be gentle, as here, or fierce . . . as in . . ."

"A flood," Nick helped her. "Though I don't know if this old river ever floods."

"It does," she said with calm assurance. Then she turned abruptly away from the river and gazed up at the clouds, which she had seen reflected in the water. "On this bridge, Nick, we are standing between water, land, and air; not a part of any one." Her tone was serious, her face raised toward the sky. "Magic can happen in such a place."

"I'm all for that." Nick smiled as she lowered her eyes from the clouds to face him. When he tried to kiss her, she moved with an easy grace just out of reach. He leaned back against the cool stone, watching another group of students pass by. "We could take out a punt."

"A punt?" she repeated.

It was odd, but the directness of her stare once again made him uncomfortable. "One of those flat boats." He pointed to a long, slim craft on the river with a hardy student wielding a pole at the aft end. "It's late in the year, but the weather is good today."

"Yes, I like being on the water."

"Let's hope we stay on it and not in it," Nick laughed. "But first, let's get a few things for a picnic lunch."

Side by side they left the bridge and the grazing black-faced sheep to walk past the ancient stones of King's College toward the market. The magic of the bridge between earth and sky lay behind them, unused but not forgotten.

The open market square was crowded with lunchtime shoppers. Nick led the way through a jostling crowd of house-wives, looking back several times to see that Gwenillan was following as best she could. They passed a stall with a red-lettered sign that stood out from the others. PENTACLE, it read, and from behind it a dark-haired woman with piercing eyes watched them pass. At a produce stand nearby, he waited his turn to catch the eye of a tattooed man behind the rows of polished fruits and vegetables. Gwenillan browsed nearby, gazing intently at the shining black eggplants on display. In addition to the fruit and some cheese, Nick bought a bottle of Moselle from a wine merchant near the market. Gwen, who had waited outside, smiled as he came out of the shop displaying their treasures.

At the college slipway, Nick righted one of the inverted punts while Gwenillan stood near the edge of the calm water. He helped her climb gracefully into the bow and then he stepped astern and pushed off from shore.

It was a good feeling to move the boat along the smooth surface of the river by his own strength. No motor, no gas fumes, just the fresh air on his face and the cool water running down his arms from the pole each time he pushed it into the muddy river bottom and then yanked it free to be retrieved hand over hand. With every jerk of the pole from the mud of the riverbed, the punt glided smoothly forward. Nick kept it on a straight course by trailing the long pole behind the craft like a rudder. Gwenillan reclined on a cushion, facing him. He watched her gaze dreamily out at college gardens sloping down to the water's edge, one hand trailing lazily over the low side of the boat.

The shallow craft glided silently between the emerald lawns of the Backs and the moss-covered stone of ancient college walls and embankments. Coleridge, Wordsworth, and

Byron had all walked these grassy banks as students. Newton must have studied the flow of the current from the graceful arch of Clare Bridge, which Nick now crouched low to avoid. Erasmus surely reflected on these same ripples and currents, searching for some deeper meaning in the patterns of nature.

For an instant, gliding past the green embankment leading up to the splendid heights of King's College Chapel, a picture flashed into Nick's mind of the terrible corpse found washed up there. But he put all thoughts of sadness and death out of his mind looking down at Gwenillan. Her eyes were closed, and he took the opportunity to study her face. A fresh, outdoor complexion, speaking of sun and rain and windswept open spaces. The coloring was fair, Nordic and healthy, with no trace of makeup on her closed eyelids, no artificial color on cheeks or lips. There was a well-bred but somehow unsophisticated quality about her that puzzled him. Her confident manner and the way she carried herself suggested an upperclass background and a certain maturity beyond her years. But just as strong was an impression of innocence and a kind of simple, rustic charm, a complete change from the smooth and cynical college girls Nick knew. He was still watching her face as her eyes slowly opened and she smiled up at him. There was so much more he wanted to learn about her. He only hoped there would be time.

Downstream, where the river widened, Nick turned toward a shout of his name from the shore. A cluster of figures stood outside The Mill Pub, glasses in hand, enjoying the November sunshine. John Blessed was waving, conspicuous even at a distance with his black beard and the sunlight glinting off a favorite camera hanging on his broad chest.

Nick saw Tom Newell and Ainsley-Hay as the current took the punt nearer to the shore. Gwen heard a shout and raised herself up to look with interest at the group outside the pub.

"When did you become an oarsman, Lombard?"

"I'm trying to avoid boring people in pubs!"

"You don't *always* bore us, old man," Hay called out.

"Hold on! I need a picture of this." John Blessed raised the long lens of his camera and snapped off several shots, zooming in as the punt drifted further downstream.

Looking back, Nick saw Blessed lower his lens and turn to say something to the others. From their laughter, Nick could imagine what they would have to say to him later about the attractive blonde they had just seen with him in the punt. Gwen smiled, too, as though she shared this private thought.

Beyond the town, the river narrowed and became deeper. Willows drooped over the water, causing Nick to duck under low-hanging branches and trail the punt pole behind him. Before long both banks were covered with thick, green vegetation, all signs of buildings, streets, and human habitation left behind. The river wound out into the fenland in a narrow channel, like a green tunnel through the verdant countryside. Several brown female mallards glided along beside the punt, leaving a spreading fan of ripples in their wake; a male companion swam just ahead, the sun highlighting brilliant green as he turned his head back toward his harem. Gwen watched the ducks with amusement, trailing one hand in the water to create a wake of her own alongside the boat.

When Nick found a place where the bank was low and the trees gave way to flat fenland fields, he steered the craft toward shore.

"You are tired," Gwenillan innocently observed.

"Tired? No way." Nick maneuvered the long side of the punt parallel to the shoreline as Gwenillan reached out and grasped a handful of long grass to aid in the docking.

They found a flat, grassy spot near the water and enjoyed their wine and cheese and Israeli oranges. Then Nick lay back on the grass while Gwenillan strolled along the riverside. He watched her stop and gaze down at some drama below the bottle-green surface of the water.

When he joined her by the river, putting an arm gently around her shoulders, she smiled and stood quietly with him, watching the flow of the water. Later, sitting side by side on the grass, they watched clouds blown in from the North Sea join, pull apart, and rejoin like a constantly changing jigsaw puzzle. Nick felt a spreading warmth of contentment both in body and mind. He felt alive. There was blood and electrical charge in him, and the earth beneath his back was as solid and full of life as his own body. He wanted Gwenillan to share the feeling that she was largely the cause of.

"Gwen, I'm not sure you'll understand all of this, but have you ever felt that there are moments in your life that are nearly perfect? When everything comes together just right?

It's really those few moments in an entire lifetime that make all the rest worthwhile."

He rolled over onto one side and looked at the girl lying near him. She was watching his face with the same unnerving intensity he had noticed earlier.

"A person can live for seventy or eighty years, and what he'll remember most at the end of it all are maybe five or six minutes when everything seemed to gel. Those moments are so special because they're so rare. Usually something will go wrong—the phone will ring, or you'll stumble making your grand entrance." He looked up at Gwenillan and laughed. "Or the girl you're punting with will overturn the boat. But perfect moments do come, and that possibility is what makes life so . . . great."

Nick leaned back to stare up at the sky, already losing some of its color and brilliance. "Anyway, Gwen, what I'm trying to say is that, for me, *this* is one of those special moments—one of the perfect ones worth waiting for. Does any of this make sense to you?"

"Yes," she said after a moment of silence. "I understand. There are special moments from my life. They come back to me . . . over and over." She rolled onto her side, away from Nick, but he had noticed the tears. He moved to her and brushed back the hair from her wet cheeks.

"What is it? Did I say something . . . ?"

"No. There are sad moments too." She touched his cheek and then kissed him lightly. He returned a stronger kiss, but she gently pulled away. "Nick, it is too late."

Reluctantly he looked up to see the sun drawing closer to the western horizon. "November afternoons are short."

Gwenillan did not repeat her warning or tell him that she had not meant the time of day. "The dark months come," she said, "after Samain."

"What?"

"November," she said, brushing her skirt as she stood. "Then the dark."

The girl leaned forward and kissed him once more very long and very softly, like a flower brushed against his lips as he bent to capture its scent. "It is late," she said again. "Too late."

There is an hour wherein a man
Might be happy all his life,
Could he find it.
                    George Herbert (1593—1633)
                    Trinity College

Punting back to Cambridge was like a dream, the fading light giving an eerie effect to overhanging creepers and leaves on the deserted riverbanks. Without the sun's illumination, the water course seemed narrower, even more like a tunnel, its verdant green sides pulsing with life all around the small boat and its two passengers. Alone in their wooden craft, cut from a living forest, they were neither on land, in the air, or water. Surrounded by all three realms of nature, they were once again not a part of any one.

Later, after docking and pulling the punt ashore at Trinity Hall's slipway, Nick was still feeling the magic of the river: the magic of the day and being with Gwenillan. Their walk through the streets of Cambridge in the early evening darkness was quiet and contented. Nick wondered about their relationship, where it would go from here.

He looked in at the lights of The Pickeral. "We could stop for a drink?"

She declined, saying that it was already after dark.

"Can I walk you home then?"

She smiled, but once again her response was negative. "Walk with me, Nick, back to where we met. I will leave you there, close to your home."

Why didn't she want him to know where she lived? Could there be a husband, a jealous boyfriend? More likely she was thinking ahead to a time when she would have to leave, and trying to make it easier for them both.

As they walked up Castle Hill, past the dark shape of St. Peter's Church, Nick suggested that it would be shorter if they went by way of Madingley Road. "Then I'll cut through Trinity Wood and you won't have to walk through the woods alone."

She kept her eyes downcast on the uneven pavement. "If we take the longer way, we can be together a little more."

Thick clouds had begun to gather overhead, scudding darkly across the nearly full moon. There was a scent of rain in the air. Students on bicycles passed by on their way from outlying student housing to evening meals in ancient college halls. One rang a bell and waved. Nick turned to see Kebby Mlanga breezing down the hill, black gown flapping around him in the wind. He smiled and told Gwenillan that she had just seen a future cabinet minister of Kenya.

When the rain came, only a few blocks from Wychfield, they ran, laughing, with Nick a few steps ahead leading the way. Large, cold drops hit their faces and stung their skin as they ran through the open gateway, charging through water already running in streams.

"In here!" Nick shouted, taking the girl's hand and pulling her toward the gabled porch of a rambling Victorian structure converted by the college into a modern sports hall. "We can get some towels in here and wait until it lets up."

She clung to him, shivering and breathing hard. Nick put his arms around her, feeling as though he were comforting some cold and frightened forest animal: a beautiful young doe looking up at him with liquid eyes.

"You're freezing. Let's go inside."

The sports hall was deserted, its two racquetball courts empty, and no sounds coming from the changing rooms. Nick knew that everyone would be at dinner as he gathered up two large, white towels. Gwen used one to dry her hair, changed to dull bronze by the wetness. He wrapped her once more in his arms and felt her shiver.

"You still have a chill." He rubbed her shoulders through her soaking sweater and breathed in the musky animal scent of the damp wool. "There's a sauna here. It will warm you up while we wait for the rain to stop. You can change in there."

Gwenillan smiled and squeezed his hand as she turned toward the door he had indicated. "Yes, I will get naked." She disappeared through the changing room door, leaving Nick to take in a deep breath and let it out noisily in anticipation.

Nick stripped in the other changing room and wrapped a towel around his waist before returning to the sauna. A dry blast of heat slapped his face, making him remember standing with his father as a boy in front of the open grate of their coal furnace.

But the sight that greeted him inside the sauna was more warming than any furnace blast. Gwenillan was stretched out on the wooden bench with her eyes closed, a white towel spread out beneath her beautifully naked form, already glistening with small beads of perspiration. Her hair was still damp, and she pushed back a strand as she opened her eyes and greeted Nick with an innocent, open smile.

In the forest shadows of Trinity Grove her nakedness had glowed dimly in the moonlight, but now Nick was startled by the full effect of her beauty. He sat on the bench opposite her, back to the wall, feeling as though he had only made love to this woman in a dream. Not sure what to say or do, he tried not to be too obvious in his appreciative glances along her long, firm calves and thighs. They were brushed with fine hair, the color of summer cornsilk. Gwenillan shifted slightly as she saw his response to her. With a delicate sensuality she moved her hand across the firm rose tip of one breast. He glimpsed the cornsilk hair under her uplifted arm as she spoke to him softly.

"Love me again, Nick."

He poured water on the brazier, causing clouds of steam to rise up and coat the glass panel in the door with a damp gray film. Though he knew everyone should be at dinner, the possibility of being seen added to his growing excitement as he moved toward the beautiful girl.

They made love on the hard redwood floor. Nick breathed in the rich aroma of the wood and felt its rough grain against his bare back as Gwenillan knelt across his hips, hands on his shoulders and face turned up toward the low ceiling. He cupped the softness of her breasts and then ran his hands down the length of her back and across the delicious female roundness of her hips, engraving every curve of her body on his memory with his touch. Once more he smelled the fragrance of her body and felt the soft down on her limbs.

They moved together with a fluid and natural rhythm amid the clouds of hot steam. It was like making love in the clouds, or in the heat of a primeval rain forest where two human beings had never before joined in the act of love. They changed position, Nick rolling on top, and their skin slid together wetly with the slickness of perspiration as their passion increased toward its climax.

CHAPTER 13

Tuesday evening
Trinity Wood

The night is chill; the forest bare;
Is it the wind that moaneth bleak?

Samuel Taylor Coleridge
(1772–1834)
Jesus College

It was darker than Terry Graham had imagined inside the wood. He wished now that he had replaced the batteries in the flashlight he had taken from the glove box of his car. It cast a weak, yellow glow across thick tree trunks and the web of branches that obscured the path he was attempting to follow.

He knew that the police had cordoned off the area of the woods along the Madingley Road where the bloodstained clothing had been found earlier in the day. He had visited the scene with Inspector Janeway, and he felt strongly that there was significance in the clothing being found here, in this woods. He did not believe that the evidence had been dumped here randomly. Evidently the inspector had similar suspicions, because a constable had been posted at the site even after teams had completed a further search of the woods.

Back in his office that afternoon, the young reporter had studied an ordnance survey map of Cambridge and found that the woods could also be entered from the Trinity Hall sports ground at Wychfield. Then he had spent several hours in the newspaper archives, where what he found had increased his determination to go back to the woods under cover of darkness.

Terry was not sure what he expected to find. His reporter's instinct told him that the police had missed something. He sensed a big story—maybe something much more than a story. His afternoon's research had given him cause enough to be curious about the little woods off the Madingley Road, and being on the scene was the only way he could work when his excitement was running this high.

Nevertheless, it was dark and cold, too dark to see much of anything under the trees. The branches above his head twined together in a dark canopy that blocked out even the light of the moon. Limbs brushed against his cheek and caught in his long hair.

Terry pulled his worn leather jacket closed against a sudden cold as he pushed deeper into the woods. It had rained earlier, and his feet were already soaked by the thick underbrush. When he was nearly ready to turn back, he noticed the silence. There were none of the natural noises of the woodland after dark; no wind in the trees, no rustlings of small creatures in the fallen leaves, no owl's hoot to break the stillness of the night. Terry made a quick determination to return to his car.

After a few minutes of backtracking, he stopped and looked around. The path that he was following had disappeared. All he saw as he cast his light around was a tangled tapestry of black and swaying branches. With a growing sense of apprehension he realized that this was not the way he had come. He swung his flashlight in a slow arc. It was already flickering, the worn batteries nearly gone. Then he noticed the clearing off to his right. The moonlight through the gap in the forest canopy acted as a beacon, drawing his eye to the low-hanging ground fog in the open circle of Trinity Grove.

Terry felt the wind pick up. Saving his failing batteries for the darker parts of the woods, he inched his way toward the light of the forest clearing, holding one hand in front of his face against the prickly, clawing branches that seemed to be suddenly thicker all around him. As the trees overhead sang in the quickening wind, Terry thought he could almost make out words, but the language was unknown to him.

In the clearing he found himself surrounded by towering columns of oak rising up out of the mist like the legs of giants. He felt disoriented and slightly heady, a sensation heightened by a sudden smell of ozone in the air promising another evening storm. Looking and listening intently for a sound or a light to give him back his sense of direction, Terry could hear only the rising wind. And all he could see were spidery black shapes of moving branches in the gaps between even blacker trunks of oak and elm. He leaned against a slender willow growing up in the shadow of the most massive of the ancient oaks surrounding the moonlit clearing. Closing his eyes just for a moment and rubbing a damp palm across the throbbing in his temples did nothing to ease the dizziness that was threatening to overtake him. He wanted only to get out of this woods; back to his car at Wychfield or to the Madingley Road, it no longer mattered which. If he could just regain some sense of bearing and balance . . .

The howl of the wind died out to a single persistent note as the young reporter looked up directly into the face from which the sound came. The living tissue of the gnarled tree looming above him had been contorted by the forces of nature into a grotesque approximation of a human face. The distended lips of a knothole below a noselike protuberance issued the whine of the wind from deep within the ancient hollows of the trunk. Then another sound reached his ears, like the wind but more distinct. Music. It was music, haunting and discordant, blending with the natural cadence of the wind and dark forest rustlings; a flute or some simple wind instrument growing louder and closer.

Terry Graham whirled around toward the sound—the sound that was to ring in his mind over and over again, blocking out all else for the rest of his life.

> Who loves not wine, women, and song,
> He is a fool his whole life long.
> > William Makepeace Thackeray
> > (1811–1863)
> > Trinity College

After they had showered together and rubbed each other dry with rough cotton towels, Nick stood close to his secretive lover on the porch of the old sports hall. The rain had stopped and the moon hung low over Trinity Wood, lying silent across the length of a playing field from where they stood.

"Can't I walk you home now?"

"Nick, don't do this." Her tone made it clear that argument would be useless. "Enjoy our time together. It was only meant to be once, but . . ." Her voice trailed off in the silence with a certain sadness. Then she added more softly that she needed time alone to think about what had happened. "About what is happening . . . between us."

Nick leaned on the scaling paint of a pillar, his other arm around Gwen's slender waist, as he looked up at the evening sky. "Can't you tell me anything about yourself? What about your family, your father'?"

"My father is dead."

"I'm sorry." Nick squeezed her shoulders and cast his eyes, with hers, down at the porch.

"It happened a long time ago."

"My mother is dead," he offered, not sure why except that it lent credence to his sympathy. "It happened a long time ago, like you say, but a lot of times I feel like she's still here with me."

"She is. Just as those I have loved are with me." She pulled away from him and walked to the end of the gabled porch. "Some live now, some then, others are yet to be born. The only difference is time." She spoke slowly, searching for the right words, while Nick waited patiently, knowing that she wanted to continue.

"Death is only a change. . . . Time goes on. Life cannot end in such a simple way . . . when a person is already part of a much greater life all around us."

It was quite a speech for her in English, and the concentration showed on her face when she looked back into his eyes. "That is what I believe. What I know. Can you understand, Nick?"

"I understand a lot of things that I didn't before today. I have a different feeling about things that have been around me my whole life. Just from being with you."

His words caused them both to look out into the darkness toward Trinity Wood, picturing their first coming together under the gnarled oaks of the grove hidden deep within. Gwenillan watched his face. There was a dreamy, withdrawn look there she had seen before in the face of another young man far from his own country.

"I'd really like to believe what you say, Gwen, about us all being part of something larger and more lasting. It must be a very comforting view of life . . . and death, too. Like a religion."

"Nick," she said quietly, barely causing a ripple on the evening air. "I must not see you again."

"What'? Gwen, but why?"

"Wait! Don't always question what has to be." She turned

her face away from him. "I was wrong. I should not have chosen you."

"Chosen me! No, I don't believe it. I don't believe that you don't want to see me again." He reached out, turning her head to face him, and saw tears making wet stripes across her cheeks. "There's something else. What is it?"

Pulling her face forcefully from his hands, she stepped away. "Yes, yes!" she said angrily. "You are right. I love you."

He moved close to hold her once again, and the softness in his voice returned. "You can't leave me now. Can't you see how much I want you, Gwen?"

The girl allowed herself to be enfolded in his arms. "Yes, it is already too late," she murmured softly. "I want you, too."

Nick heard voices and laughter in the darkness. A group of students passed under a streetlight near one of the undergraduate houses. Then he felt the warmth of lips brushing his cheek.

"Tomorrow evening. Eight o'clock. But not here. On the bridge, Magdalene Bridge."

Then she was gone, running out into the darkness of the playing field toward the path through the woods. She was a black, then a gray shadow dissolving rapidly into the steam rising from the rain-drenched field. For a moment her airy figure seemed frozen in motion, then she was gone; still close by but hidden behind the blank, gray curtain of the fog. Soon all Nick could see was the unintelligible face of Trinity Wood rising black and intimidating above the mist.

CHAPTER 14

Tuesday evening
Trinity College

Of college labours, of the Lecturer's room...
With loyal students, faithful to their books,
Half-and-half idlers, hardy recusants,
And honest dunces.

William Wordsworth (1770—1850)
St. John's College

"In fact, the rate of illegitimate births in Biggleswade in 1865 was eighty-three per one thousand births. In Luton it was even higher, ninety-three!" the young don added with a gravity more than adequate to the weight of this revelation.

Nick struggled to keep his eyes open. While the chill in the room helped, the glass of sherry in his hand worked against him. Being with Gwenillan had made him forget entirely about his evening seminar.

"County parish records give a clear picture of the birthrate in Buckinghamshire over the entire quarter-century span we have in view. How this relates . . ."

Nick wondered where the professor had found this one; sounded like a visiting Australian, but Nick had missed the introduction. "Child Labour and Straw Plaiting in the Mid-Victorian Home Counties" was a subject that would have been trying enough even without the nasal accent.

Professor G. K. C. Boys-Menzies was an elderly bachelor and the permanent sitting-tenant of the grandest set of rooms in Trinity College. His fortnightly evening seminar with a dozen or so research students was a tradition, and Nick appreciated the honor of being a member of the group known as *Boy's Boys*. Over the past thirty years, the group had included many of the leading historians of the age. It was to learn from men like Boys-Menzies that Nick had made the three-thousand-mile journey across the Atlantic. But tonight he could not generate any enthusiasm for the tribulations of the freely fornicating straw-plaiters of Victorian Buckinghamshire. All he could think about was Gwen.

When the floor was finally open for questions, Nick did not take part. He left it to the others to ferret out weak spots, undocumented references, and unprofessional generalizations, putting forward the most perverse and onerous questions their years of Cambridge training could bring to bear on the unfortunate presenter. They knew that only by showing real initiative would they be invited to stay for that warm time later in the evening when the whiskey would be liberated from its cherrywood cabinet and chairs moved in closer to the fire for conversation until the professor's 11:15 bedtime.

After a time, Boys-Menzies carefully raised his considerable bulk out of the deep armchair—his cheeks even rosier than usual from the closeness of the fire and several glasses of dry fino—to officially end the seminar. He glanced approvingly over his departing scholars, discreetly inviting two or three to stay behind. "Get more rest, Lombard," he suggested, though Nick could have sworn that he'd not looked in his direction all evening.

The moist evening air on his face as he left the spiral stairs from the tower room brought to mind the rain earlier and what it had led to. Walking past the elegant range of Christopher Wren's library, he was surrounded by the subdued sounds of college life at the end of the day. In the arched shadows of the cloisters he heard a student's voice call out a name from an embrasured window above him. Nearby a chapel bell tolled slowly and solemnly, its sound drifting with the wind downriver and across chimney pots and clunch-stone walls.

Nick paused on Trinity Bridge, looking downstream at the other spans across the Cam ranked in order before him: the familiar modern arch leading to Trinity Hall, and beyond it the graceful sweep of Clare Bridge. Farther downriver, past Clare in the darkness, lay King's College Bridge, where a few hours earlier he and Gwen had stood looking out at the recent scene of bloodshed on the banks of the Cam.

Tonight the river was peaceful, flowing dark and silent below him. He turned to face upriver where it stretched out northward under St. John's famous Bridge of Sighs to lap around the mossy stone foundations of Magdalene Bridge beyond, where Nick was to meet Gwenillan on the following evening. He watched the effortless motion of a swan gliding under the bridge toward its nest hidden somewhere in the shadows. The moonlight on the graceful curve of the creature's body made it shine with an inward phosphorescent glow.

There was a cold wind on Castle Hill, where he paused to catch his breath and look back at the lights of the town. Under a moon nearly three-quarters full, he could see the dark rise of the Gog Magog Hills. There was something about the scene that evoked a discomforting feeling of déjà vu, something lingering with him as if from a dream.

The dark silhouette of the distant hills was strangely compelling. It was odd to think of Roman legionaries tramping across this terrain so far from the sunny, poplar-lined roads of Italy. Evidently the Romans had thought the same; Nick remembered reading that they had called Britain "a country of the setting sun, remote from our world." From their hilltop fortress the Romans must have fanned out across the fens, dominating the bridge across the Cam and its mud and wattle native settlement. They would have brought their own gods and icons to the pagan shrine at the foot of Castle Hill, where the shell of St. Peter's now stood. Roman sandals would surely have trod this strategic hilltop and beyond it to Wychfield and the ancient woods nearby. Nick breathed it all in. He knew he would never lose his sense of wonder at the multiple layers of history all around him here in this "country of the setting sun, remote from his own world."

There was still a rain-washed freshness in the air as Nick retraced the steps he and Gwenillan had taken earlier. The sudden downpour that had sent them seeking shelter in the sports hall had washed the pavements clean and left puddles of dark water wherever the natural nourishment of the rain had not found a place to soak into the earth.

Nick saw the flashing blue lights before he reached Wychfield's gate. A uniformed constable blocked the entrance, and among the figures gathered outside, Nick recognized Ainsley-Hay and Samantha. He joined them just as the constable was moving the group back to allow an ambulance to exit, lights whirling and siren warning motorists out of its way as it headed toward the town. A black Rover with a blue light flashing on its dash followed the ambulance racing down the A604. Then, as the constable stepped back to allow the group through, Nick joined Samantha and St. John. He could see other policemen, some with dogs, fanning out across the playing fields, the probing beams of their lights scanning the tree-rimmed face of Trinity Wood.

"What the hell is going on?"

"Don't know, old man. We've just come back from The Pickeral."

"He takes me to all the best places," Samantha commented drolly. "Look, there's Guy. Let's ask him."

Guy Chamberlain approached from the direction of the sports hall, dressed for racquetball. He told them quickly and with some importance that he had seen the entire thing.

"Some chap gone completely bonkers," he said bluntly in his odd Anglo-French accent. "I was coming back from the sports hall when I nearly ran into him."

"Who?"

"Don't know. He staggered up to two undergrads, shouting something totally incoherent. Then, by God, he had one of them by the collar, screaming into the poor fellow's face." He walked with the others toward the house as he continued. "What a commotion! Enough to wake the dead."

"Was he drunk?" Samantha asked, affecting a casual disinterest in the answer.

"That's what I thought at first, but when he was right in my bloody face, there was no smell of alcohol."

"Yes, *you* would notice that."

"But you should have seen his eyes! Staring at me like a madman." Guy was getting into the spirit of his narrative now, sounding more and more like vintage Ronald Coleman. "Poor devil. His clothes were all torn, and his hair—it was long and tangled—hanging down past his shoulders and full of burrs and leaves as though he'd been running headlong through the woods. That's what I told the police. His face was scratched and bleeding, but his eyes were the worst."

"Was he a student?" Nick asked.

"I don't think so."

"*C'est terrible!*" Samantha was scandalized. "We should have porters here to keep out the townies."

"Who called the police?" It seemed to Nick that quite a lot of constables and patrol cars had been called out for what seemed like a minor disturbance.

"Don't know, but there have been police roaming around here off and on all afternoon."

"Where have you been?" Ainsley-Hay broke in. "You know the murder last summer? Well, today they found the poor sod's clothes over at the edge of the woods, along the Madingley Road. Tom Newell told me that when he tried to take the shortcut through the woods around dinnertime, they stopped him. Had a whole section of the woods cordoned off, where they found the clothing, I suppose."

"How do you think this lunatic got into the woods then?"

Nick, recalling Gwenillan walking alone toward the woods from the sports hall after dark, did not hear the question. He was picturing a young man with tangled hair and a bloody face running blindly through Trinity Woods—the way he tried to run on another night, the way the red-cloaked man in his dream ran. He tried to picture what had made them run.

"Guy, do you know what he was trying to say?"

The Frenchman stopped walking and the others stopped too, turning back to look at him. "That was the strangest part. Most of what he said was incoherent, but I could make out one thing. He was babbling something about . . . about a *mask*."

Guy paused. He wanted to be sure that he got the phrasing right. "What the devil he meant, I don't know, but he kept saying over and over again that it was not a mask. Yes, that's it—not a mask."

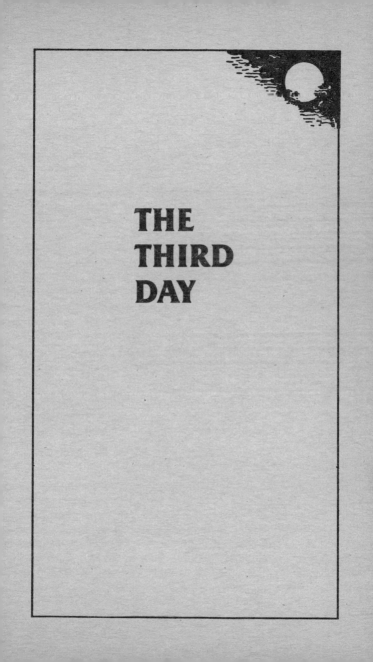

THE
THIRD
DAY

CHAPTER 15

Wednesday, 1 A.M.
Lensfield Road

Except wind stands as never it stood,
It is an ill wind that turns none to good.
> Thomas Tusser (1524—1580)
> Trinity Hall

The radio call came in soon after Janeway and Church had left the hospital. They had spent a few minutes with Terry Graham and several anxious hours outside his room while the young reporter was examined by a number of physicians. In those few moments that Terry had been conscious, they had heard a great deal of incoherent babbling and had endured the vacant, terrified stares with which the young man had looked through them. Janeway hated seeing Terry in that state, thinking back to the self-confident young reporter who had come into his office less than twenty-four hours before. It had been an entirely different person lying before him in the hospital bed looking out with reddened eyes on another world beyond his understanding.

To stop his raving, the physician attending had sedated him, and it was only when this medication had begun to take effect that Terry had finally said something that Janeway could understand. In a drowsy, mumbling state just before sleep he had suddenly opened his eyes wide and stared directly into the inspector's face. Then, as if in a momentary flash of recognition, Terry Graham had lifted himself upright in the bed with surprising strength and grasped Janeway's jacket, speaking softly so that only he could hear. The words were not clear on first hearing, but when Terry repeated them, Janeway heard: "Five days ... the fifth day."

The inspector was still puzzling over what the boy could have meant when the call came over the radio in the Rover. Sergeant Church looked over at him as the dispatcher reported a break-in in progress on a side street in the Burleigh district.

The car was already headed in that direction with Church at the wheel. They would probably be the first car there, but Church did not switch on the siren or light.

Instead, he nosed the car to the curb and killed the engine as soon as they arrived near the scene. Then both men stepped out onto a rather seedy frontage of small shops and dingy cafés, all closed for the night. Across the empty street was a high-rise council estate, and just ahead, Crispin Lane. It was little more than an alley really, where a caller had reported two men trying locks on doors.

Approaching the corner, they were joined by a young constable on foot patrol; Janeway recognized him as a fast bowler on the police cricket team named Mathers. Together the three men cautiously approached the dark entrance to the narrow lane. Church peered around the corner first, and as his eyes adjusted to the darkness, he made out two youngish men, one kneeling in front of the lock on a large warehouse door while his companion held a pencil light over his shoulder. The sergeant turned back to Janeway and nodded, holding up two fingers. Then they stepped back into a doorway while Mathers kept watch at the corner.

"What do we have?"

"A warehouse on the right, about twenty yards down the alley. Two men, young. No weapons in sight."

Janeway explained his plan, and then left to take the car and block the other exit from Crispin Lane. He was nearly in position when Church confronted the suspects.

"Police! Stand where you are!"

Constable Mathers shined his torch into the dimness, illuminating the surprised faces of the two men, one black-bearded like his own and the other pale and fringed with dull blond hair. For a moment the two stood frozen, looking toward the lights, uncertain of what to do. Church and Mathers watched cautiously, knowing that if weapons were to appear, it would be now.

Suddenly both figures turned to run. Expecting this, Janeway waited. The constable's light danced across the backs of the running men as the two policemen dashed into the alley in pursuit. Mathers had his nightstick out, and after a few athletic strides, he was in a position to throw. The weighted stick caught the smaller man at the back of the knee, bringing him heavily to the ground.

"Go on after the other one!" Church shouted, already breathing heavily as he stopped to handcuff the stunned man. Mathers sprinted on, his whistle now clenched in his teeth blasting an alarm.

As the footfalls on the bricks came nearer, Janeway pulled forward with a squeal of tires into a blocking position across the alley. His timing was right, but the fleeing man was more agile than expected. The tall man hesitated only a moment in his stride before leaping up onto and over the bonnet of the Rover to continue running toward a vacant, weed-choked lot ahead. Janeway considered pursuit, but saw that young Mathers was already past him and narrowing the lead of the fleeing man.

Throwing the car into reverse, the inspector roared back down the narrow lane the way he had come and then wheeled around in the direction the suspect had fled. Ahead of him he saw a panda car approaching from the opposite direction, siren and lights flaring in the night. It screeched to a halt to avoid a running, swerving figure illuminated for a moment in its headlights like a picture from a slide show. Janeway pulled up at an angle to the patrol car.

In the deserted car park, lighted now by his headlamps, he watched the young constable land the running man with a rugby tackle. The lanky, blond man resisted, throwing a wild punch toward the policeman's bearded jaw. Mathers easily fended off the blow and landed a beefy fist under the other man's chin to settle the matter very effectively.

"Firearms," Janeway said softly to himself as he walked over to where several uniformed constables were pulling the winded suspect to his feet. "Pray God, we can get on without them for a good long time."

Another panda car arrived with Church sitting beside the dark-bearded man in handcuffs in the back. When the second man had also been loaded into the car and Constable Mathers congratulated on a job well done, Janeway and Church climbed into the black Rover and headed toward the station.

"All we needed was a little more excitement today."

"Or to begin a new day, more like," Church answered wearily, looking at his watch.

"Ever seen either of those two before?" Both suspects had refused to give their names, and neither had been carrying identification. They seemed unusually frightened and uncooperative considering that they had only been taken for loitering with intent.

"Yes."

"What's that?"

"Yes," the sergeant repeated, "I've seen one of them before. The blond-haired bloke with the long legs."

"Well?" Janeway steered the car into the parking lot behind the modern station house.

"In the market, in the stall run by that commune."

"You mean they're from the farm?"

"Aye," the sergeant said. "From Gog Magog Farm."

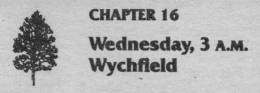

CHAPTER 16

Wednesday, 3 A.M.
Wychfield

I cannot see the features right
When on the gloom I try to paint
The face I know; the hues are faint
And mix with hollow masks of night.

Alfred Lord Tennyson (1809–1892)
Trinity College

In his dream, Nick was once again in the familiar forest land-scape. The dream was a puzzle of things he had heard and seen and thought in the past several days, but its diverse pieces seemed to fit together with a natural symmetry now.

He saw the same woodland path as in earlier dreams, crossed the same forest stream, and he emerged from the woods to look out over the same strangely familiar moonlit valley toward the distant hills. Only, this time he was detached from the action, floating easily above the scene at treetop level.

It was night, but a bright moon, three-quarters full, illu-minated the drama below him. The cloaked and hooded figure he saw on the forest path was a young man; dark-haired, though the features were hidden. The cloak was red, bloodred above sandaled feet.

Nick watched a slender form cloaked and hooded in white step out from behind a cluster of willows halfway down the hillside. She held up her hands in warning, causing the young man to come to a halt and look around. Drawing closer to the scene, Nick saw the girl's lips move in speech. Most of her face remained shadowed by her hood, but there was a certain familiarity in the easy grace with which she moved. The man was being warned to stay away. "Forget me," she pleaded, "forgive me!"

Protesting, the young man took a few steps closer. But she was now in tears, shaking her head and then pointing back over her shoulder toward the woodsmoke coming from around the curve of the hill.

"Cendl," she whispered, and Nick watched the man instinctively reach for a short sword concealed under his red military cloak.

They were very close now, almost close enough to touch, but she avoided his outstretched hand. Instead she threw back her hood, and blond hair flew in the night wind. The man moved closer as she backed away, almost hysterical now in her effort to make him save himself.

"Cendl!" she repeated more urgently. While Nick stared into sobbing, gold-flecked eyes, a hideous shriek cut the air like a scythe. It was promptly answered by a howl from the direction of the woods, like a human imitation of an animal cry for blood.

The girl turned away from the young stranger who had come for her in the night; she would never see his land far from the setting sun. With a sobbing cry she began to run blindly down the black hillside, following the drifting woodsmoke back to its source.

The man hesitated, looking after her until another baying cry caused him to whirl around. Nick saw torches flaming not far off in the shadow of the trees. A line of fire ran along the black curtain of the forest like a spreading flame put to a trail of wax. The red cloak raced back toward the nearest trees, crashing into the underbrush in a frenzy to find the path. Nick felt himself tied to the fleeing man, like a kite to its grounded pilot. He saw the figure below him stumble in the darkness, and he felt cold water hit the man's face as he landed, arm outstretched, in a rushing stream.

The hunted man pulled himself to his feet and ran on, splashing through the shallow water in the hope that the stream would lead him back to the path he sought. There were more wild cries to both his left and right as he ran through the darkness of the forest, losing his footing more than once on the slick stones of the stream bed. Then suddenly silence descended on the woods just as the running figure at last found the path, stretching out before him through the blackness like a welcoming tunnel to salvation.

Nick could almost feel the frightened man's heart pumping as he bounded up the familiar pathway with the wind whipping at his cloak and rustling the dry winter oaks. Suddenly he stopped. Through his eyes, Nick saw the flicker of torches blocking the way ahead.

The dreadful whoops of his pursuers now began to sound on the path behind him and in the darkness on both sides. The sounds were slower now, more deliberate, like an animal closing in on its cornered prey. Amid these chilling sounds the man in red ran toward the light of a small clearing. There, blocked on all fronts, he turned his gaze upward to the towering oaks all around him; he seemed to be looking directly at Nick, still hovering above him on a level with the tops of the great trees, but the shadows concealed his expression.

The trapped man backed up against the largest and oldest of the trees, its gnarled features oddly resembling a human face looking down stoically on his plight. He opened his cloak and drew forth a short sword from the gilded leather scabbard at his belt. Very slowly the howling circle closed in on the young stranger in the sacred grove, but his eyes were fixed now on another danger.

Two bright eyes burned in the forest like diamonds on velvet. He watched, breathing hard, as they approached him slowly and steadily, side by side, never wavering as they pierced the darkness. Underbrush crashed with sickening force as they moved relentlessly forward. The man in red turned away in the moonlight, hopelessly looking up at the ancient trees for succor, and Nick Lombard stared into his own face drenched in a cold sweat of terror and despair.

> A sight to dream of,
> Not to tell!
>
> Samuel Taylor Coleridge
> (1772–1834)
> Jesus College

Sara Larsen awoke with a dull throbbing in her temple. The room was dark; 3:40 on the bedside clock. She pulled herself to a sitting position on the edge of the bed, palms pressed to her damp forehead. The sticky web of the dream still clung to her, drawing her back to the dark woods and what she had seen there under the three-quarter moon. Slowly she lifted herself to her feet, and then, allowing her eyes to adjust to the familiarity of the room, she broke free.

The cotton nightgown clung damply to her as she made her way quietly toward the closed bedroom door. She was careful not to wake the woman and small girl with whom she shared a room in the commune. Then she hurried down the chilly hallway to the small bathroom, where she drank a glass of cold water from the tap. Even in the glaring white light of the tiled bathroom she could not entirely clear her mind of the dream. Despair was the strongest emotion that remained, hopeless despair.

Sara switched off the fluorescent glare of the bathroom fixture and stood shivering slightly in the dim light. Through the sheer curtain at the window she could see the lighted farmyard and, beyond the peak of the barn roof, the black rise of the Gog Magogs. Samain, that's when the dreams had started. She remembered almost nothing of the Samain Eve revels; it was almost as though that had been the first dream. She had been proud to be chosen as Samain Maiden, having been with the group for only a few months. But afterwards she realized that she had been tricked and used, though she remembered very little except music and stars in the clear night sky. It was the not remembering that bothered her most.

Maybe she had been wrong to run off to Europe. Her parents were so against the marriage plans, and she saw now that it never would have worked. She had told Emillio to forget her before she left California. She had to leave, she told herself, to save them both. She knew what must be at the root of her dreams of hopeless lovers, but that did not ease the pain.

She lifted one bare foot, then the other, off the cold tiles, hugging herself with her arms. The warmth of the bed was waiting, but sleep meant dreams, more dreams. Sara thought again about leaving the commune. She had decided that joining the Pentacle Commune was a mistake. In London, cold, wet, and tired, with no money and nowhere to stay, the offer of a ride to Cambridge and a warm farmhouse where she could work for her keep had seemed like a godsend. Jan Troop had been so nice, like the older brother she had left at home. Now she saw the way he looked at her . . . and the way the others feared him.

An owl hooted outside, and Sara looked at her watch. Not long until dawn; she had to get back to bed. Turning, she saw her face in the silver rectangle of the mirror over the sink. She was pretty, she knew it. Mrs. Woodbridge was always telling her that she was "like a goddess" in that funny way of hers. Eleanor was so good to her, like a mother, helping her and giving her loving hugs and compliments on the pottery she made. And bringing her the special tea she brewed three times a day.

Sara squinted her eyes against the cold light in the hallway. Of course, she didn't believe in the religious nonsense Mrs. Woodbridge was always preaching. But it was the least she could do to listen and pretend to be interested. God knows, she had met enough religious kooks in California, and she had learned early that it was easiest just to listen and nod your head. Eleanor got so much pleasure out of telling her stories, what was the harm in humoring her even though she would never be what the older woman called a "true believer"?

Some of it even made sense, about the beauty of nature and the environment, things Sara had always believed in. And some of the singing and little ceremonies had been fun at first. There was no real harm in any of it, but Sara knew that she couldn't go on pretending forever. She had to tell them she was leaving, but talking and drinking tea with Eleanor always made her so relaxed. Decisions seemed to take so much energy, and lately she just didn't seem to have energy for anything. It was so much easier just to drift.

She tiptoed to her bed and sank gratefully into its warmth without disturbing the others in the room. Time passed, and eventually her rolling and turning slowed as she fell deeper into a dream state.

She was near a small river, like the River Cam, but different. There were no stone college buildings and no gardens on the riverbank, just a few rough structures made of wood and thatch. Not far downstream she saw a crude wooden bridge crossing the water, made of logs roughly tied together with heavy ropes of twine.

It was raining hard and a stiff wind blew the downpour in sheets, whipping up waves on the surface of the water. Sara did not feel the wetness or the cold. She walked along the muddy shore in her nightgown, passing through a huddled crowd near the bank like a shadow. No one looked at her, but soon she began to wonder why a crowd had gathered in the rain at this unlikely spot. Then she saw the rough wooden stake driven into the mud of the river bottom about ten feet from the bank. It leaned slightly askew, with the wind-driven river current crashing against it in a flood tide. Drifting easily through the milling crowd, Sara emerged close to the river. All around her she saw talking, laughing faces, but she heard nothing except the cold rush of mud brown water.

Then she saw that the post driven into the flooding river did not stand alone. A weak figure, head hung low, clung—no, was tied—to the wooden stake with thick, knotted ropes. The figure moved slightly, blond hair reflecting the weak, cloud-filtered light, looking like dulled bronze. The hair was close-cropped, having been crudely hacked into a ragged fringe, but the form was female. She raised her head once painfully to glance up at the jeering crowd, but quickly turned away. Either from shock or defiance, she did not cry out or beg for mercy, nor did she struggle against her bonds. But the churning water was already high on her chest. Waves splashed up into her face, driven by the wind as they broke across her heaving breast.

Lost in the crowd, Sara watched a tall, bearded man, a warrior's helmet on his brow, turn and stoically walk away; a weeping woman of middle years clung to his powerful arm. The gray, rain-soaked sky seemed to hang low, only yards above the ugly crowd that remained. Sara looked around at their faces; a few more somber, but most were laughing or sneering, their mouths moving in shouts or jests as they relished the final moments of the drowning girl. Rough, unshaven faces looked out on the scene with cruel delight from under greasy leather caps. Pockmarked women jeered as they clutched steaming cloths over their heads against the downpour.

The girl seemed to swoon once and her head dropped low, but the cold water roused her, filling her nose and mouth until she pulled herself up choking. The driving rain was raising the level of the river by the minute. It almost reached her chin now, and flashes of lightning over the fens promised that the storm would only worsen. Sara leaned desperately into the face of a fat man near her in the crowd, his lips curled over broken teeth in a cruel grin. She reached out to shake the man by the shoulder, but the ruffian turned casually to a drunken companion to share a joke and a drink from an earthenware jug, simply scratching at the shoulder where Sara had laid her hand.

The girl in the river was fully awake now. Sara watched her face as she looked up directly into her eyes; she seemed to see the fair-haired stranger who could have been her sister, though no one else did. It was painful for Sara to meet her look and see the despair in the green-gold eyes below the cut and ragged hairline. Her face was terrible in its familiarity, a face last seen in the silver rectangle of a shadowed mirror.

Sara sensed the other's terror as the waves rose higher and the wind blew stinging spray into her nose and eyes, but there was nothing she could do. It was only a matter of time until the jeering crowd no longer had a focus for their cruel attentions. Gradually drifting off to seek shelter from the rain and fires to dry themselves, they would remember this day's grisly work for the rest of their short, brutal lives. They might even repeat to their children how the chieftain of the hill tribe had come to the town by the river to sacrifice his daughter. The story might even be passed on to grandchildren by the people of the river crossing, but soon the world would forget the girl staked out in the flooding river to die. Why such a hideous death at the hands of her own family? What cruel gods had to be satisfied? Vaguely, in the subconscious dream state, Sara Larsen knew the answer.

Then she was drifting up into the slate gray sky like a hot-air balloon, above the smoking town by the river, over hilltops and trees. She drifted upward above clouds bursting with rain to a region where the sun shone brightly and the sky faded from brilliant blue to white above her.

Drifting upward above clouds bursting with rain to a region where the sky faded from brilliant blue to white, Nick Lombard opened his eyes onto the ceiling above his bed, reflecting the warmth of the morning sun.

He realized immediately the connection between his dream and Reverend Anglesey's story. It was only natural, too, that he should dream of Gwenillan and give her face to the girl in the river. Still, the vividness of the dreams and his disturbing feeling of personal involvement were still with him as he wandered toward the town on a beautiful autumn morning.

Attracted by the gardens on Castle Hill, he strolled distractedly among the welcoming greenery of the empty park overlooking the peaceful symmetry of the university town by the river. He saw church towers and steeples, smoking chimneys, modern architecture, silhouetted against ancient college buildings, all set in twisting streets laid out in the Middle Ages. It was a city Nick had come to love. He thought of having to leave someday. Then he thought of Gwenillan. She would leave too, but when? With him or without him? He refused to think further than today, further than meeting her tonight.

His mind drifted back to the previous evening; beads of sweat on honey-colored skin, the feel of Gwen pressed against him, the smell of redwood in the steam-filled sauna. No, he could not let her go. He pictured her in the punt on the quiet evening river, and then running beside him through the rain to the shelter of the sports hall. He could not imagine anything she could tell him that would make him give her up.

He sensed a presence near him just before a voice spoke softly in the silence of the empty garden. "You were thinking of me." It was a statement, not a question.

Nick turned to see the girl near him, her hands tucked behind her and one foot lifted to rest against the gray trunk of a willow tree.

"How long have you been here?"

"Oh, a long time."

"I didn't expect to see you until this evening." Nick held out his hand and she allowed him to kiss her lips. "I was just thinking how much I missed you."

They stood together quietly and watched the traffic flow down into the narrow streets of the town. A bell tolled from a college chapel below them. Then Gwenillan drew his attention to the range of hills just visible in the distance beyond the spires of the town.

"Do you see those hills, Nick?"

"The Gog Magogs?"

"There was once a Roman camp there. A great fort with many soldiers."

"The Wandlebury Ring. I've thought about having a look at it, but . . . no car. It's a long way to walk."

"A man can walk that far in half a day," she said. Then she changed the subject abruptly. "Nick, do you truly want to be with me?"

"You must know that I do," he assured her. "You seem to know everything I'm thinking, you must know that."

"Even though you know so little about me?"

"I know enough," he said, "and I want to know more when you decide you're ready to tell me."

She looked into his eyes, and again he felt the power of her concentration as she spoke. "What if I told you it is dangerous to love me?"

Nick laughed. "Don't you know, men are always attracted to a dangerous woman."

"I'm serious. There are many things you do not know."

"I'm serious too." He looked deep into the green-gold of her steady gaze. "I don't intend to let you go now that I've found you. I'll learn all your secrets in time, and I'll accept the bad with the good if it has to be that way. I can't imagine anything that would change the way I feel."

Gwenillan turned her face away. "There are many things you can't imagine," she said softly.

Nick touched her face, returning her eyes to his. "Come on, it can't be so terrible. I love you, Gwen."

"You loved me even before we met."

Nick smiled at her self-confidence. "When you're ready, you can tell me everything. Right now there's just one thing I want to know. Do *you* want to be with *me?*"

When she spoke her voice was even, but he sensed the emotion behind her steady words. "I love you, Nick. I should not, but I do." There were tears at the corners of her eyes as she turned away.

"What's this? Why shouldn't you fall in love? Love is a good thing; don't cry."

She took a few paces away from him toward the willow tree. "You don't understand. It's the first time. You are the first one." With her back to him, Nick saw her hands go to her face. "The first since . . . No! Love is not always good! Not always."

There was a moment of silence, as her desperate words were blown on the wind toward the distant hills, before he went to her and placed his hands on her shoulders. "I don't know what may have happened in the past, but it doesn't matter. You don't have to tell me now."

"We are from different worlds, Nick. You do not know my world, and I cannot be part of yours."

"Sure, we're different. There's a lot for both of us to learn and accept. I'm a city boy from across the ocean and you're a country girl from a whole other world. That's true, but it doesn't mean we can't learn from our differences . . . and maybe create a world of our own, together." He watched for some sign of acceptance and found it in her smile. "I'm changing already. Look where you found me this morning. In a park, not in some dusty library. Whose influence do you think that is? Just give me time."

The quiet smile remained on her lovely lips. "Time. Yes, we will have time." She looked past him at the grass and trees. Two gardeners were entering the park, rakes across their shoulders like weapons.

"Will I see you this evening? On Magdalene Bridge?"

"Yes, but now I must go."

"Where are you going? I'll walk with you."

She came close and kissed his cheek quickly before turning away. "I must go," she repeated, and then she was running with long, graceful strides toward the gate. "Stay here," she called back. "Look around you and think of me."

Before Nick could answer, she was out of sight behind a hedgerow, dashing past the two gardeners ambling along the gravel path. She vanished like a young deer and Nick was left alone, looking at the trees of the park and the distant hills. Oblivious to the nasal mutterings of the approaching workmen, he thought only of the girl he was now sure that he loved.

CHAPTER 17

Wednesday morning
Cambridge Police
Headquarters

The trumpet's loud clangour excites us to arms,
With shrill notes of anger, and mortal alarms.
John Dryden (1631–1700)
Trinity College

"Better enjoy your tea." Inspector Janeway was speaking from behind the heavy oak desk in his office. "We have another hard day ahead."

Colin Church groaned inwardly. He'd had almost no sleep, and a day spent anywhere other than in his own bed would be considered a hard day.

Janeway had nearly completed plotting the troop dispositions at Austerlitz on the sheet of yellow paper in front of him. He added a Russian Guards battalion and thought about the state of his investigation. Things were finally moving. Vincente Cordillo's clothing had been found in Trinity Wood and identified by hair and bloodstains matched to police samples. Then there was the bizarre incident involving Terry Graham to consider, occurring in those same woods. The police search of the area, interrupted by darkness yesterday, would continue today. There was momentum at last, and Janeway felt it in a region of his nervous system that only seemed to come alive at times like these.

He placed Napoleon's mounted grenediers and the chasseurs of the Guard on the left flank and added a few batteries of Australian artillery to the opposing side near the Russian Noble Guard. The French cuirassiers and the rest of the heavy cavalry went behind the center of the line, and Davout's corps was concealed for the great trap Napoleon laid for the Russians on his right.

Janeway had not slept at all. He badly wanted a strong cup of coffee, a cigarette, a whiskey—preferably in that order—but he resisted all his forsaken vices and continued to arrange the *Grand Armée* on paper. It was a device he had learned years ago to help him relax in times of stress. He was sure that Church sometimes wondered about his sanity, but Janeway had confidence in the effectiveness of his own rather eccentric therapy. As he had ordered his thoughts, along with the emperor's divisons, in the past several hours, a number of things had begun to come clear. He placed the French Imperial Guard in reserve for a crushing breakthrough later and then leaned back in his chair.

"How is young Graham this morning? Any change?"

Church looked up from the dregs of his tea. He had been trying to read his future in them, but all he could visualize was a soft, warm mattress. "Aye, for the worse. He's gone into a coma."

The inspector swore aloud and stood abruptly from behind the desk as Church continued his report.

"Doctors have moved him into a special unit and hooked him up to their machines. Told me it looks bad for the lad. He won't be telling us any more today, any rate. They'll phone if there's any change."

"A coma! Damn it all!" He paced before the blue rectangle of his window, and gradually his expression and his tone softened. "Bloody shame what happened to the boy . . . whatever the devil it was."

"He seemed a good sort," Church conceded, "for a reporter."

"We know that someone or something frightened him badly out there, but more than that must have happened. He was a level-headed sort to have gone over the brink like this."

"Doctors said there was no physical harm done. No head injury, no concussion."

Janeway's face showed his consternation. "My first suspicion was drugs. Any sign of that in his tests?"

Church shook his head, suppressing a yawn with great difficulty. "Nothing. Shock, the doctors said. Damned strange if you ask me. Could be some drug that doesn't show up in the blood maybe . . . but I'm no doctor."

Finally Janeway stopped pacing and sat down facing the other man. "I've been sitting here for the past four hours thinking about the papers we found in young Graham's pockets last night. He withdrew several folded sheets of paper from his inside jacket pocket and opened them on the desktop.

"It's a working list of notes for the article he told us about. He evidently went back to the newspaper archives yesterday afternoon. He's made notes here about an unsolved murder in Cambridge in 1943 and an unexplained disappearance in 1910."

"But we know about those," Church said, "the POW and the Wop tourist."

"No, not those. Two *other* incidents in those same years, but later in the year. First week of November in both cases."

"Like now, first week of November." Samain, Church thought, but he did not say it.

The inspector followed Terry's notes with his index finger. "A Portuguese soldier here for training was found stabbed to death in forty-three and in 1910 a Canadian student went off on a nature walk with a university group and was never heard from again. Last seen in the vicinity of Trinity Wood."

He paused and leaned back in his chair. "I want to keep this tightly under wraps, but have one of our young constables check these references in the files of the *Evening News*."

"I still don't see—"

"Wait, there's more. Terry went back in the records to 1877, thirty-three years earlier than the incidents in 1910."

"Same thing?"

"Two murders. One late in June, the other early in November. The first body found, quote 'in a disfigured state' on Butt Green."

"That's at the edge of Midsummer Common."

"Yes, like the first incident in 1910. Newspaper headline even called it the Midsummer Murder." The inspector handed Terry Graham's notes to Church.

The sergeant fished his reading glasses from his breast pocket, adding another set of fingerprints to the layers already there. "Says here that the bloke in November might have been done in with a sword. S'truth!" Church removed his spectacles and rubbed tired and swollen eyes. "All a bit hard to fathom. You've been thinking it over, Inspector; what do you make of all this?"

"Maybe nothing at all," Janeway admitted tiredly. "But I'm planning to put a few ideas to a friend of mine at the university later this afternoon. He's something of an expert on local history . . . and other things."

The inspector stood and straightened the creases in his suit.

"Now, if you can rouse yourself to the task, Sergeant, I'd like to put a few questions to our guests downstairs."

"You mean the two from the commune?"

"Right first time." Janeway picked up his swagger stick from the desk and strode briskly across the room, through the door, and out into the hallway.

Sergeant Church dragged himself wearily to his feet. His thoughts turned idly to retirement: only working from dawn to dusk instead of dawn to dawn, with a pair of heavy horses and a few Guernseys for company instead of the thieves and layabouts in the city jail. Dreamily visualizing the layout of his future pigsty, he followed the inspector through the door that had been left standing open for him.

Downstairs a constable led the way to the cell where the first prisoner was being held. "They'll be out soon," Church pointed out. "Solicitor's negotiating bail now. My guess is that Dutch bloke, Troop, is putting up the brass." The electric door to the cellblock slid open with the smooth sound of a sword withdrawn from a scabbard.

"What have you found on these two, Church?"

"One is a foreigner, West German. That's the blond-haired lad—our sprinter. Horst Wenger." He gave the name a distinctly anglicized pronunciation. "Immigration says he's been here about four months this trip, but he's been in and out of the country a lot in the past few years. Gives his residence as a German town called Koln."

"Cologne, eh? What about the other one?" They continued walking down the modern corridor of closed cells, their footsteps in uneven cadence on the tiles.

"Bearded chap is English. David Carpenter, from Bristol. Merchant seaman before he lost his card. One conviction—possession of drugs. Found a kilo of hashish in his footlocker when his boat docked in Southampton two years ago. Served seven months." They had reached a heavy metal door with a small glassed and barred window at eye level, a special holding cell for troublesome prisoners.

"Wenger was giving the lads some trouble last night, dragging his feet and swearing at them in German. We put him in here to cool off."

The door opened on the sound of low moaning, like a person might make in the midst of a bad dream. Then suddenly a scream ripped the air and went reverberating down the long corridor of the cellblock. Horst Wenger flung himself off the bunk and crouched down in the corner of the small room farthest from the open door, long legs tucked up under his chin, and arms shielding his face from some unseen terror. He screamed again and then went back to moaning and gibbering unintelligibly. Before the constable could reach him, he had fallen over onto his side and begun to twitch uncontrollably.

"Get a doctor," Janeway ordered, and the constable went running back down the corridor as Church took his place kneeling by the prisoner's side. Together Janeway and Church got him stretched out flat on his back and tried to calm his shaking. The inspector pulled a blanket from the cot and wrapped it around the young man on the floor, who continued to shiver and pull his legs up into the fetal position, alternately whimpering and crying out in pain.

"Look at his arm."

Janeway saw the needle marks in the crook of the young German's arm where his sleeve had been pushed up in the scuffle. "An addict! Why wasn't this noticed when he was processed last night?"

Church swore at himself, to himself. "Like I said, sir, he was fighting us every step of the way in here. Couldn't put him through regular processing."

The constable returned with a paramedic. "A doctor is on the way, sir."

"Good. Tell him this man is an addict suffering from withdrawal. He may have to be transferred to hospital, but keep him under guard. Understood?" Janeway turned away from the kicking, screaming figure now fighting against the attentions of the paramedic. "Church, you come with me. Constable, give us your keys."

They went back out into the corridor, now echoing with the cries of the suffering man inside. "Leave the door open," the inspector said. "I want someone else to hear this. Where is the other one, Sergeant?"

Colin Church led the way to David Carpenter's cell, where they found him standing by the door, his face pressed up against the wire-reinforced glass panel, listening intently to the screams and moaning from the direction they had come. He backed off as Church unlocked the door and the full volume of the noise reached his ears. Janeway immediately marched in and gripped the young, black-bearded man by the wrist. Tucking his stick under one arm, he pushed back the man's sleeve with his other hand. There were no marks.

"Sit!" he commanded.

"'Ere, what is this . . . ?"

"Sit!"

With Church's aid, the young man was perfunctorily seated on the side of his cot. "Trousers," Janeway ordered. The sergeant in charge of the cellblock assisted Church in pulling off the loudly protesting prisoner's trousers, leaving him sitting on the bed in his shorts. Then, taking hold of one ankle, Church twisted him roughly over onto his stomach. The tracks of the needle were there behind both knees.

"Take it easy," Carpenter protested. "You got no right!"

"Easy?" Church cut him off. "We'll take it ever so easy, Your Highness. You just be glad I've been up the whole bloody night and I'm feelin' a little fagged out, or you'd see what *easy* is, my lad."

Janeway stared hard at the frightened man. "I want answers. Quick. No nonsense. We know your weakness. You may not be as far gone on the stuff as your friend down the hall, but my guess is that before long you'll be as badly off as he is—screaming for someone to put you out of your misery. Do you hear him screaming, your mate Wenger?"

"Piss off!" Carpenter shouted in a brave show, causing Church to step in closer. "You can't do this. You have to get me a doctor."

"We *can* get you a doctor," Janeway said calmly. "We can see that you don't end up like Wenger, groveling about on the floor with demons picking at your vitals." The inspector moved in close, eloquently slapping his swagger stick into the palm of his hand as he constructed his next sentence.

"What were you after in that warehouse last night? We know that one floor is rented to a chemists' supply house. Was it drugs?"

Carpenter mumbled something about not having to answer, looking down at his bare legs.

"Was it drugs?" Church repeated less kindly.

"So what if it was? We didn't even get in. You got nothing on us."

"No? Your friends will get you out on bail, won't they? Your friends at Gog Magog Farm."

David Carpenter reacted as Janeway had expected. "How

do you know about that?" he demanded angrily.

"Why don't you tell us about your friends. About Jan Troop and the others. What do they have to do with this?"

"Nothing! They had nothing to do with it. And you got nothing on me either," he added with diminishing confidence.

Sergeant Church leaned close into his face. "I wouldn't bet the next few years of my life on that, matey. Breaking and entering, resisting arrest . . . assaulting an officer."

"Wait! I didn't bash nobody! That was Horst, he—"

"So you say," Church told him. "But I was alone with you in the alley. Remember? And I got this loose tooth back here. See?"

Janeway intervened. "We know all about your previous conviction. Drugs, wasn't it? Things could go very hard for you this time, Carpenter."

"You could go down for a long time protecting someone else," Church added. "Lot like being on a long sea voyage, being in prison. Cramped quarters, no pubs . . . no women. But then, you know all that."

"On the other hand," Janeway continued, "if you can tell us something of interest, things could go more easily for you. No promises, but we'll be asked about your cooperativeness."

"Or your bloody-mindedness," Church put in, with another meaningful tug on his tooth.

"All right," Carpenter said quietly, looking up at Janeway but avoiding the sergeant's eye. "I do know a few things . . . and I don't owe that lot at the farm anything, that's for damn sure. But I want to see a doctor first." Wenger's moaning had died away a few minutes earlier with the arrival of a physician and a sedative.

"Later," Janeway told him. "If I were you, I'd tell all I know rather quickly. You're beginning to twitch ever so slightly."

"All right, all right, but at least give me a fag."

Church obliged him with a cigarette and then lit it for him as the inspector watched his dark-bearded face. Janeway could picture David Carpenter a few years younger in a Borstal school and a few years older in Dartmoor Prison. It was a face he had seen a hundred times before, but it was not one of the strong hardcase faces. David Carpenter would talk.

The young man drew deeply on the cigarette to ease his fear. "Troop is a dealer. Horst and one or two others bring the stuff in from the continent; a lot of them are foreigners, like Wenger, from all over Europe. They come and go all the time. But I don't have any part in that," he insisted, "not since I left the ships. Lost my card after I was nicked."

Janeway concealed his enthusiasm behind a quiet manner. "What kind of drugs?"

"Pills and angel dust mostly."

"What else?" Church prodded. "Come on, come on! You're an addict, goddamn it. You and Wenger, where do you get your supply? From the Dutchman, right?"

"Bloody hell! All right, you may as well have it all. I'm finished with that crew anyway. Troop gets hard stuff from a dealer he knows in Amsterdam—but I swear I don't know any more about that side of things." He looked up into the inspector's skeptical eyes. "Hell, you don't think they got their money from that rubbish they sell in the market?"

"Hard stuff, you say? What exactly?"

Seeing the young man's nervous hesitation, Church repeated the inspector's question with more force.

"All right, but I want a doctor bloody quick." Carpenter stared down at his bare legs across the edge of the cot. "Heroin," he mumbled.

Janeway and Church exchanged a glance. "And was this little break-in Troop's idea, too?"

"No way," Carpenter said wearily. "That bloody stupid idea was Wenger's. Him and me decided we could make a little easy money for ourselves without telling Troop. Maybe we could get enough together to split on our own, he said. Don't know how I let him talk me into it." He smoked his fag nervously. "No, bloody Jan Troop wouldn't be stupid enough to try a stunt like this."

"Tell me about Troop." Janeway's voice was easy now, encouraging.

"Smooth businessman, he is, bloody clever. That's why I hitched on with him in the first place. But . . ." he hesitated.

"But what?"

"Well, he's got these crazy ideas. And most of the others are just as far gone as he is—always out gazin' at the moon and chantin' or some bloody nonsense. That's the part I couldn't take. All the bloody useless rubbish I had to listen to. But I had to pretend to go along with all of it. That woman of his watched us all like a hawk."

"Eleanor Woodbridge?"

Carpenter looked up with surprise. "Yeah. But I'm well out of all that now anyway." He stubbed out the butt of his cigarette. "I don't like to think what would happen to me if they knew what I'm tellin' you. You got to protect me now. I don't want no bail."

"I want to talk with you more later, a lot more," Janeway told him. "Sergeant, get Mr. Carpenter a statement form so that he can put all this in writing. While he's doing that, fetch him a doctor. Oh, and Sergeant, give him back his trousers."

Colin Church tossed the trousers at Carpenter's face and then handed over another smoke before moving toward the cell door.

Janeway moved in closer. "You know, David, I'll follow up what you've given me so far. It may just help us both. But I think there may be something else you can tell me. You say the heroin supply comes from across the Channel. Where does Troop get his PCP? You did say 'angel dust,' right?"

"Right." Carpenter rubbed his beard nervously. "Where's that bloody doctor? Oh, hell. He buys some, I'm not sure of the source. But they make a lot of it themselves."

Janeway glanced back at Church near the door. "Where is the lab? At the farm?"

"Not bloody likely," Carpenter sneered. "No, there's another place. More isolated. A lot of beakers and such set up in an old house. I seen it once—just went up there to unload some furniture," he added quickly. "Troop's very touchy about who sees that place. My guess is the bastard has some of the profits stashed up there somewhere."

"Up where?" Janeway asked as calmly as he could. He heard footsteps approaching down the long hallway and he wanted an answer before the doctor arrived to break his uneasy rapport with the prisoner.

The young man heard the footsteps too. He drew deeply on the second cigarette and watched the door, his free hand clutching and unclutching spasmodically at his side.

"Where?" the inspector demanded, causing him to flinch with the unexpected force of the command.

Carpenter blew out a stream of smoke toward the floor. "Jan bought a little piece of land up the Huntingdon Road a mile or so from the city center. It's out of the way, well back from the road. There's an old wreck of a cottage there, back in the woods."

"In the woods?" Janeway said half to himself as he pictured the by now familiar site of Trinity Wood in his mind.

"That's right," David Carpenter answered testily, "a bleedin' woods. So what? Now, where's that bloody doctor?"

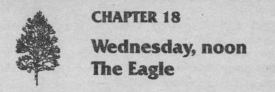

CHAPTER 18

Wednesday, noon
The Eagle

The presence of a body of well-instructed men,
who have not to labour for their daily bread,
is important to a degree which cannot be overestimated.

Charles Darwin (1809–1882)
Christ's College

St. John Ainsley-Hay was leaning languidly against the bar when Nick entered the pub. The Eagle was crowded at lunchtime with a good mixture of young and old, male and female, students and locals from the shops and colleges nearby. A makeshift food service line was set up across one corner of the crowded room offering cold meats and salad, shepherd's pie, an excessively yellow curry, and other luncheon fare.

Nick greeted his friend, who made enough room at the bar for him to have some hope of attracting the busy barmaid's attention; she was a pretty girl in a low-cut black sweater, which explained why Ainsley-Hay had stayed by the bar. By the time Nick had been served with a pint of Greene King and some sausages, the press of the crowd had begun to outweigh the pleasantness of watching the barmaid bend over the tap.

Outside, the air was chilly in the cobbled courtyard of the old coaching inn, but it provided some relief from the noise, smoke, and elbows inside.

"Well, Lombard," St. John said, cradling his gin and tonic in both hands, "why aren't you in London today bashing away at the scribbling of some poor, long dead statesman who never did you any harm?"

"I could just as well ask why you're not in the law library."

"I'm checking out the proverbial local talent—of which, you may have noticed, there is a considerable dearth."

"Oh?" Nick said, picking up one of his sausages impaled

on a toothpick. "I saw the smile you got from the girl behind the bar."

"Mandy?" Hay replied with an innocent incredulity. "Smiles are cheap." He brushed an invisible speck of lint off his blazer sleeve. "No, Lombard, that's precisely the problem with this place. The only time a fellow has a prayer is in summer, when the tourists descend."

Nick took a long, appreciative swallow of his beer. "Oh, I don't know about that."

"What's this? Has Lombard discovered a hidden blossom in this wasteland? Do tell, old man; who is this secret flower?"

"Her name is Gwen. Met her on Sunday." Without changing his expression, he added nonchalantly: "She's Swedish."

St. John set down his drink and looked at his friend with amazement. "Swedish! You're sure you haven't just dreamt this?" He raised his hands in supplication to the gods who had passed him by. "While thousands starve, Lombard of Pittsborough . . ."

"Pittsburgh," Nick corrected.

". . . Lombard enjoys a feast known only in men's fantasies. Tell me, does this goddess have a sister or a friend? A mother, perhaps?"

"You'll be the first to know if she turns out to be twins."

"Tell me more," Hay insisted.

Nick frowned into his beer, thinking how little he actually knew about Gwen despite his boasting. "Not much to tell, except that she's beautiful . . . and wonderful, and smart, and—"

"Enough, enough! Where did you find her?"

"In Trinity Wood of all places," Nick confided.

"Well, this calls for another drink. I'll even buy. But I want an introduction." Then he sauntered off to the bar while Nick finished the last of his sausage and mustard. It made him feel good to be able to one-up St. John Ainsley-Hay. He glanced around at the old pub and thought about bringing Gwen here on a cold winter evening. They would sit in the snug stone seats built into the huge fireplace. That was, if he ever saw her again after this evening.

Hay returned, glass in hand, standing aside at the doorway to allow a noisy group of shopgirls to exit ahead of him. "Did you see that, Lombard? Not a word of thanks, not a second glance. A wasteland, I tell you, except for your mysterious Swede."

He handed over Nick's beer, the dark amber liquid giving form to the winter sunlight through the thick windowpane mug. "Cheers! Sorry I can't stay here boozing with you all afternoon. Duty calls in the savorless form of the law library. But stop by The Pickeral this evening—Guy's birthday, you know."

"Okay. Blessed warned me that you were planning something suitable to the occasion. I may see you there."

"Ah, the life of an American at Cambridge." Hay adjusted a black ascot with the white stripe of Trinity Hall and then added dreamy recitation: "With prudes for proctors, dowagers for deans, and sweet girl graduates with golden hair."

"Keats?" Nick guessed. "And how did you know she's blond?"

"Tennyson. And aren't dream girls always blondes?" Hay made a great show of sighing enviously. Then Nick watched his friend's long gray flannel legs stride confidently across the cobbles. He turned once and grinned back at Nick. "A real mystery woman! Some chaps have all the luck." Then, shaking his head theatrically, St. John turned with an elegant economy of movement and disappeared through the arched gateway into the street.

Watching him go, Nick was glad that he had finally told someone about his luck. He hoped that it would last.

Eleanor Woodbridge stood in the doorway of the workroom watching the girl working at the potter's wheel. The light caught the rich blond hair in a way that turned it to bronze and then back to gold as she inclined her head in her work. In the short time Sara Larsen had been with them, Mrs. Woodbridge's interest in her had grown, though she had been careful to keep secret the small favors and personal attentions she allowed the American girl when they were alone.

Her shoulders, working with the clay on the wheel, moved with a gentle female strength under the thin cotton blouse. Mrs. Woodbridge watched as the younger woman raised a bare forearm to wipe moisture from her brow, her clay-covered hand hanging still in the air for a moment like a terracotta sculpture. How delicate her hands were, but what youth and strength there were in that slim, young body, in those firm, gold-flecked limbs. The dark woman remembered a summer afternoon watching Sara and the other young women of the commune bathing nude in the farm pond; she shifted her stance to hide the voluptuous shudder that coursed up her thighs. Such youth, such an innocent sensuality. It was clear that, although the girl certainly knew that she was attractive, she had no idea of her potential sexual power. The power of the Great Mother in her . . . or how to use it.

Eleanor Woodbridge knew such things. At Sara's age she had already discovered the power of female sexuality, and she had used it at the right times, with the right men and women, perfecting her skills, putting a fine edge on her art. She still possessed those female skills and could use them when needed. The fragile beauty of youth was gone—a useful tool for quick seduction, but nothing more. Now she had maturity, a look that spoke of exquisite sensual experience, a look that could still attract. And once attracted, once alone in the dark, she could work magic. Jan Troop knew that. But there were things even the young Dutchman had still to learn.

She watched the silent girl at her wheel among the others, a fluted vase taking shape between her glistening wet palms like a straining red-brown phallus. Sara would come to her soon in the dark of night, she would come of her own free will. It was merely a question of time. Patience was part of the art. Special care must be taken because the girl had the potential to be a true believer, to carry on what Eleanor Woodbridge had begun here.

Jan had told her of the innocent perfection of Sara's role on the night of Samain. The older woman relished the picture of the naked girl on the cold stone slab in the field, surrounded by the wildly lusting men and women of the commune at the height of the ceremony of fertility. She wished that she had been there, if only to have touched that soft skin for a moment, to have caressed the delicate, pink-tipped breast almost visible now through the sheer white blouse. To have felt the cold night air on her own bare flesh and tasted salt on the young girl's damp thigh.

There would be time later for all that and more. It would have been beneath her dignity to have stripped off and cavorted with the others in the ceremony. A temptation she had to resist. Besides, if she had been rutting with the rest on Samain Eve instead of at home with the children, she would not have seen the two policemen prowling around the farmhouse. She smiled as she thought of the dog going for the smug inspector's throat; a few more inches.

Seeing them had given her an advantage, preparing her for their next visit. And later, after their ridiculous interview in the farmhouse parlor, she had made discreet inquiries of her own about Detective Inspector Lewis Janeway. Why had he come to the farm twice even though it was out of his jursidiction? That still troubled her, that and the arrest of Carpenter and Wenger. In his arrogance, Jan insisted that it was nothing to concern them; they had no legal responsibility for other commune members, and the two fools were too afraid to talk.

Mrs. Woodbridge's gaze wandered around the small workroom in the barn, touching on the three women and two young men making planters, vases, and mugs for sale in the market stall. Dull, unimaginative people, she thought with disdain. Weak people, meant to be used. They didn't really believe in the old ways; they wanted to be loved, accepted, so they affected belief. Or worse, they believed without understanding.

Still, they served a purpose, and soon they would no longer be needed. Neither would Jan Troop, Harrold, and the others like Carpenter and Horst Wenger. Weak men whose motives were so far from pure. Soon, with their help, there would be enough money, and money would set her free.

She glanced again at the golden girl. Where had she come from? Some California town with a Spanish name. So far from home, so sad when they had found her, and so young. But she would blossom with tenderness and guidance. She would be a true believer. Not like the others. Skills could be taught, but belief had to come from within.

"Here, let me show you, Sara," the older woman said. "You need to mold the clay just so." Her fine hands covered the girl's on the rim of the pot, taking up the wet terra-cotta stain like litmus paper touching acid.

> That blessed mood,
> In which the burthen of the mystery
> is lightened.
> William Wordsworth (1770–1850)
> St. John's College

"Well, that's what we have, James." Detective Inspector Janeway paused as the crowd shouted encouragement to their teams. The chaplain glanced downfield at the match and then looked back at his friend as he resumed speaking. "It may have some bearing on the case and it may not. The point is, I can't put any of my men to digging further through the records and history of Cambridge. I have superiors to answer to—and there are certain people in my department who might consider this line of investigation highly irregular."

The royal blue jerseys of the Peterhouse ruggers were being pursued downfield by Trinity Hall's black and white. Janeway could have thought of better places to discuss his ideas with his old friend, but things were happening quickly now after a long lull and he did not want to wait.

Finding Anglesey at the university rugby grounds, huddled inside an oversize topcoat on the sidelines, the inspector had explained the course of events involving Terry Graham and the notes the young reporter had made. Meanwhile a fairly sluggish intercollege rugby match had periodically erupted and subsided around them. They stood in one place as most of the other spectators moved up and down the sidelines with the players, leaving them to converse as freely as the flow of the match permitted.

"Besides," Janeway continued, "I simply don't have anyone qualified to do research outside police records and newspaper files, and those don't go back much further than poor Terry Graham has gone already."

"So you'd like my assistance," James Anglesey filled in while attending to an itch under the clerical collar hidden beneath a sweater and overcoat. "Well, I'll be glad to help, Lewis, in any way I can."

"It's just that having you here and knowing your expertise in the history of the area . . ."

"Beware flattery, Lewis."

Janeway smiled. "Really, if the police can't find expert assistance in Cambridge, I don't know where they can."

"Oxford?" the chaplain suggested with a wry smile.

"Go Hall! Go Hall!" came a sustained cheer from a cluster of undergraduates a little way downfield.

The chaplain watched Janeway light a second cigarette though he had held the first smoldering but unsmoked until it had burnt to its filter in his hand. He had never seen this nervousness in his friend before, but then, he had never before observed him in the environment of his police work.

"Another reason I've come to you, James, is that there may be some connection here with . . . the occult, for want of a better term. You may remember me hinting rather broadly at that the other evening in some of my questions about ritual sacrifice and so forth." He tapped the ash off the end of his cigarette, but did not put it to his mouth. "There is certainly more than the beginning of a pattern here."

"I remember very well." Anglesey lowered his voice as a student stopped near his shoulder. "In fact, your questions caused me to give the matter some thought. You know, Lewis, one particularly favored method of ritual murder practiced by the Celts and many other ancient peoples was disembowelment."

The chaplain paused and watched Janeway's face as the spectators moving past them sighed their disappointment at a failed try. "They did it," he continued, "preferably to a living victim, then they read the poor devil's entrails. Beastly business, but it fit their view of the world and the forces that governed their lives."

Janeway grimaced. "Oh, I should mention, too, that there are some people we have under surveillance—they call themselves a 'communc.' They're almost certainly mixed up in drugs and possibly some sort of black magic trumpery as well. They may be using it as a cover for their criminal activities, I don't know yet. Or their leader may just be using this hocus-pocus nonsense to frighten the rest into doing what he wants."

"One thing before we go on, Lewis." Anglesey glanced toward the scrum and then back at his friend. "The occult, as you have termed it, is not necessarily 'nonsense.' Often it is in practice, but not by definition. If I'm going to help you, then you must accept my word for that much. We're talking about murder, possibly a series of murders—murders committed in an extremely brutal, ritualistic manner. Nothing associated with this kind of crime can be dismissed as nonsense."

"Point taken and accepted," Janeway said with unaccustomed humility. "James, if you agree to look into this angle of the investigation, I will be extremely grateful. And I promise to defer to your judgment in all matters . . . extraterrestrial." The inspector shifted his stance and scratched at his mustache with an apologetic look. "Sorry. I mean it, James. I wouldn't have come to you if I didn't take this aspect of things seriously."

"Once again, Lewis, I'll be most happy to help. Just leave me those copies of poor Mr. Graham's notes and I'll begin from there this afternoon."

"Good," Janeway said. "There is a certain urgency to all this—if there is anything in this theory of Graham's about a pattern. This week following Samain appears to be a crucial time, and we're already well into it."

The blue shirts and mud-spattered black and white were joined in another scrum, reminding Janeway of a single multicolored beast moving in a slow and awkward mating dance.

"By the way," Anglesey said over the noise of the crowd once again moving their way, "did young Graham speak to anyone at his newspaper about what he had found?"

"I don't believe so. I called on his editor, of course, to ask what Terry had been doing in Trinity Wood. He didn't know. I gathered he hadn't heard a word about this line of inquiry—and believe me, he'd have been asking me questions if he'd had any inkling of Terry's theory. Said he assumed the finding of Cordillo's clothing had led the boy up there."

Several students in college scarves pushed noisily by, and Janeway lowered his voice. "In any case, I requested that the paper play down what happened to Terry for the moment."

"And the boy is still in a coma?" Anglesey asked, thinking of a number of students near Terry Graham's age who had come to him for help and advice over the years.

"Doctors aren't holding out much hope of him coming out of it soon—maybe never. A specialist's coming up from London later in the week, but I don't think we can count on hearing any more from Terry Graham, unfortunately."

Booing erupted at what Hall supporters saw as a bad call from the black-shirted referee.

"So," Anglesey sighed, "I'm beginning with all you have?"

"Sadly, everything we have. I'll brief you further on this commune group as that aspect of things develops. At the moment, though, there's no solid connection there with the murder investigation. I only mentioned it because of the occult activities of the group."

The chaplain put a hand to his back where it was beginning

to stiffen from standing for too long in the cold. The college sports teams would soon have to do without his conscientious support at every match.

"I'll do my best for you, Lewis, but I can't promise that anything useful will result." Then he looked across at his friend with a smile. "It is rather exciting, though—for a tired old academic like myself, I mean."

"Tired old academic! James, you amaze me. Why, you've done at least as much detective work as I have. Sifting through museums, archaeological digs, God knows what else."

"Probably more than you have," the chaplain agreed smugly. "Evidently you haven't read my latest article on the antiquities of Roman Norwich?"

Janeway laughed aloud at his friend's facetious egotism, but Anglesey maintained a stoical facade. "You're quite right," the inspector conceded, "probably more."

Black-and-white-striped jerseys spread out across the field in a staggered line, like a wave breaking. A quick series of lateral passes, reinforced by several bone-shaking blocks and tackles, led to a strong run around the end of the Peterhouse blue shirts, culminating in a successful try for Trinity Hall. The scoring player, marked out by a bloodied nose, was embraced by his teammates and cheered from the sidelines for one of the few goals of the afternoon.

"Well," the chaplain said, after adding his applause to the general noise around them, "I had better be getting on with all the extra work you've given me if I want to keep my Sherlockian reputation."

Janeway was used to and fond of his old friend's insouciant attitude: calmness and humor in the face of all things. He thought, not for the first time, that James Anglesey would have made a first-rate soldier if he had not chosen the cloth. Then he thought of the several generations of students who had brought their problems, personal and academic, to the cool, imperturbable gentleman standing next to him. Anglesey was looking thinner and a little grayer these days, and his back was more perceptibly bent each year, but his old college was very fortunate to have him.

"I'll give you a lift," he offered, straightening his hat as he turned away from the field, where a Hall player was now writhing in pain and holding his knee.

"Thank you, Lewis. I can't say I was looking forward to the walk."

Offering his arm to the chaplain in crossing a rough patch of ground, Janeway smiled at the incongruous look of the long college scarf thrown rakishly across one bony shoulder. "Just one more thing, James. You might give some thought to the only halfway lucid thing young Graham said to me in hospital. Something about 'five days.' He seemed to recognize me for a moment, then he said to me very clearly, 'five days, the fifth day.' No idea what he might have meant."

Janeway shook his head, thinking of the state in which the young man had been found. "I really want to find out what happened to him that night. I've seen men break down before —in wartime—but it's always hard to accept that there's such a fragile wall between sanity and . . . well, I'm going on a bit. I'll let you solve all the riddles for me."

From behind them a raucous cheer went up from the Peterhouse side of the ground as Anglesey spoke. "Lewis, it's terrible what happened to the boy, but it's not your fault. He didn't tell you he was going up there poking about after dark. If he had, you'd surely have stopped him. Whatever it was that happened, there's nothing you could have done."

Janeway nodded grimly. "Nothing except catch the bastards responsible," he said very evenly, but with obvious feeling.

As the two tall figures walked side by side toward the black Rover waiting on Grange Road, thirty tired and muddied young men trudged off the field toward the nearest pub to exaggerate their afternoon exploits and compare bruises over many pints of beer.

CHAPTER 19

Wednesday evening
Castle Hill

For though thy being be but show,
'Tis chiefly night which men to thee allow;
And choose t'enjoy thee, when thou least art thou.

Abraham Cowley (1618—1667)
Trinity College

A sleeping pill borrowed from John Blessed had allowed Nick a short afternoon nap. But the pill had not prevented dreams, which were still clear in his mind as he walked through the crisp autumn air to meet Gwenillan in the town. He pulled his old tweed jacket closer around him against a cold wind blowing up the hill from the river.

In his imagination, he was back in the dream woods looking down from a great height, level with the tops of the massive trees. It was night, and below him were a man and woman, naked together in the moonlight. There was a familiar clearing surrounded by oaks, and in the distance, the rushing sound of a stream. Their limbs were entwined and the woman's long golden hair obscured their faces as they kissed, lying on a bloodred cloak spread out on the shimmering floor of the moon-washed clearing. Their movements together were unnaturally slow as Nick watched their lovemaking from above. He felt serene in watching; not like a voyeur, but as though he and every other part of the scene—trees, earth, sky—were all involved equally in the moment. All were part of the same tableau, which would have been incomplete and meaningless without any one. He saw colors. White bodies glowing against a crimson background and surrounded by the dark greens and browns of the forest; the yellow of the girl's spreading hair and the light of the three-quarter moon.

* * *

That pleasing vision had stayed with him for a long time, soothing his troubled mind and spirit. So much so that he had been totally unprepared when the Horned Man had once again intruded, crashing into the dream and causing the beautiful scene in the clearing to vanish and the threatening blackness of the forest to close in. Nick saw again the snarling animal face, the thick golden necklace on a glistening naked torso, and then the double-bladed axe. Something was entwined around the long, curving horns as the creature pushed its way through the forest undergrowth. Holly. The shape of the leaf was clear and Nick had recognized it for what it was.

He had watched the man-beast stride into the suddenly empty clearing by the Grove and stop, nostrils twitching grotesquely at the air. The thing had stood for a moment breathing hard, plumes of steam forming where its warm animal breath met the cold night air. Slowly it had turned and craned its bull neck upward toward the trees. For a moment Nick had felt the anger in those hot, red eyes and sensed the torpid animal intelligence behind them, as the beast had stared up at the point where his mind's eye hovered near the tops of the trees. Still gazing upward, the creature had bayed at the moon—a hideous, unearthly sound, neither animal nor human—before striding off in the direction it had come.

Even now, walking down Castle Hill surrounded by the mundane noises of traffic and the town, Nick could still hear that monstrous sound. He dreaded sleeping again, dreaming more. Earlier that morning he had mentioned his trouble sleeping to Swann, and the porter had suggested that he talk to Reverend Anglesey if something was troubling him. Maybe Swann was right . . . or maybe he shouldn't have mentioned it at all.

Soon after passing by the abandoned shell of St. Peter's Church, Nick arrived at a busy intersection and stood waiting to cross. He could see Magdalene Bridge in the distance, but it was too far to tell if Gwen was there. He hoped that tonight they could sort things out. Surely the dreams were only reflecting his fears of losing her.

Then he saw a slender figure standing at the center of the arched rise of Magdalene Bridge, almost like a ghostly gray statue gazing out at the river. She did not appear to hear him as he approached and casually leaned up on the railing close by her side. The lights of passing cars swept across her face as she turned toward his voice.

"Excuse me, miss, but I reserved this spot."

She smiled and leaned onto his shoulder. "I've been watching the river. Isn't the water beautiful and calm?"

"Hope you haven't been waiting long. I fell asleep. Have you eaten? We could—"

"Can we just walk?" she interrupted. "Somewhere quiet, where we can talk?"

Nick suggested Magdalene College gardens just across the road. As they turned together and began to walk, he reviewed the speech he had been preparing since the previous evening. He planned to bring everything out into the open, even the dreams. Gwenillan took his arm in crossing the street, leaving the sounds of talking and laughter from a group of students on the bridge behind them. The pressure of her body made him feel good as they walked shoulder to shoulder, her height almost equal to his.

"I know there are gardens in here somewhere," he assured her as they passed through the large, arched entryway into the old college. He noticed obvious glances from a don and one of his students as they passed on by on their way out. It was a nice feeling to have an attractive young woman on your arm.

Nick led the way through the empty main court past stones that had been laid in the last years of Henry VIII's reign. Passing by the open door of the dining hall, he pointed out the soft glow of candles from the only college hall in Cambridge never to have installed electricity.

"The founder of this college was lord chancellor during the trial of Thomas More," he commented, but Gwen's face showed no reaction. "Anne Boleyn, too." Gwen nodded, but Nick noted that she did not show any interest or appear even to recognize the names he had mentioned. He wondered again about her background. Had he crossed the ocean to the greatest university in the world only to fall in love with a sweet, uneducated country girl? It was ironic, but he didn't care.

Entering another court, they strolled past the impressive Renaissance library built to house Samuel Pepys' diaries, but Nick made no mention of it.

"Oh, look," Gwen said as they rounded the corner of the building. "There they are." She pointed toward the trees and neatly planted hedges and the dormant flower beds of the college gardens. Excitedly she led him by the hand across the gently sloping lawn, the smell of recently raked grass and leaves rising up to meet them in welcome.

Now it was her turn to talk of something that interested her, and Nick's turn to listen quietly like a novice. He ambled along beside her, hands in his pockets, looking from side to side as she pointed out each species of plant and shrub and each variety of tree that they passed. The garden was deserted except for another strolling couple, who nodded in greeting as they passed by toward the library. Gwenillan went on with her absorbed narrative as though she did not see them. She seemed to have been longing for the fresh open air and greenery.

"That tree there, Nick. Look." She held his arm to stop him as she pointed to a thick gray trunk a few feet away. "Do you see the small green leaves growing up its side?"

Nick had to strain his eyes in the dusky light to see. "Some kind of ivy, isn't it?"

"No!" Her laugh was pleasant and throaty, and Nick enjoyed her surprise at his lack of knowledge. "It's mistletoe." She reached up and picked a small cluster of the round, green leaves with their translucent white berries reflecting the moonlight. When she handed them to Nick, he felt the waxiness of the leaf and the coolness of her hand. He looked down at the milky white berries and thought of snow and roast turkey and a pine tree hung with colored lights.

"This may surprise you, Gwen, but I don't think I've ever seen real mistletoe before. Where I come from, we buy *plastic* mistletoe and hang it in doorways at Christmas. Sounds terrible, doesn't it?"

She smiled with him. "We use it in our celebrations, too. It is a very special plant. Do you know why?"

"Wait, don't tell me." Nick stood close to her under the gnarled limbs of the old tree and pretended to be deep in thought as he stroked her hair.

"The mistletoe grows between heaven and earth," she explained. "It is not rooted in either one, and that makes it magical. It grows with a tree. And when it grows on one like this—an oak—it is even more special."

Gwenillan was involved in her narrative now, speaking slowly, searching for the right words in an unfamiliar language. "Because oak is the king of all trees. He lives for hundreds of years . . . and from him spring many new trees in his lifetime, so that he never really dies."

Nick looked up at the wizened old trunk with new admiration. He had always had a certain reverence for old trees, just as he had for old buildings, paintings, or books, but Gwenillan's enthusiasm was infectious. He had never thought of his natural surroundings this way before. There was a whole realm of existence he had virtually ignored, simply taking it for granted all his life. Nick was reminded of his dream of the Horned Man. "What about holly?"

"Holly?" She ran her hand gently over the scarred skin of the old tree. "Yes, holly is special too. We use it on our holy days, in our ceremonies."

"Really?" Nick moved closer to her and held out the sprig of mistletoe. "Well, we have one ceremony I like very much. I hold the mistletoe over your head and . . ." He slid his arm around her narrow waist and pulled her close. Then, with the soft pressure of her body against him, they kissed. It was not a kiss of passion, but a long, soft intermingling of lips and tongues, a gentle, lingering exploration that neither of them wanted to end. As they kissed, a night breeze blew through the deserted garden, carrying with it the verdant scents of grass and late-blooming flowers and rustling the dry branches of the winter oak above them.

Laying her head contentedly on his shoulder, Gwenillan spoke softly in his ear. "Nick, I will not leave you."

The words he had so badly wanted to hear flowed past him for a moment. With one simple statement she had made all his rehearsed speeches, all his arguments, unnecessary.

"I don't want to lose you," he began, feeling he should say something, but unsure how much.

Her voice was oddly sad as she spoke again. "It is too late. Too late for either of us." She touched his cheek and he felt lost for a long moment in the golden depths of her eyes. "We will come to know each other better, and you will understand more than you do now. There are so many things . . . but we will have time."

Then her head was back on his shoulder and he felt the warm wetness of tears against his neck. He tried to comfort her, hoping these were tears of happiness, but she backed away slightly and dried her own cheek.

"I must go soon," she told him softly.

Nick protested, but she looked away from him as she spoke. "I would like to stay with you here . . . to stay with you all night, but I am not always free to do as I want."

"Why not?" Nick demanded. "Why aren't you free to stay all night if you want to? Who says you have to go? You haven't told me anything about—"

"Don't!" she warned, and then her voice softened. "I'll explain everything in time. Be patient. Be glad we have this hour now." She looked up at the moon and then back at him, smiling this time. "But I have a little more time."

"It's just there's so much I want to know about you—your home, your family, what you like and don't like. I don't even know your last name."

She seemed unsure of what he meant until he explained. "Your other name, besides Gwenillan. Your family name."

"Family name," she repeated hesitantly. "My people are the Celangi. My family is Cendl."

Nick smiled. "Kendel, Gwenillan Kendel."

"In my village, I was also called Rhia. But I like your name for me better. Gwen."

"You know," he said thoughtfully, "I don't even know my real family name. When my great-grandfather came to America from Italy, his name was too difficult for the immigration people to spell, so they just gave him the name of the part of Italy he came from—Lombardy. The old man was so proud of his new 'American' name that he even dropped the final y to make it sound less foreign. So I'm Nick Lombard. Well, what's in a name?"

The wind had turned cold and a slight drizzle was beginning to fall on the garden. Nick suggested going across the street to The Pickeral, where they could be warm and dry. Then he remembered Guy's birthday celebration in the pub. Gwen agreed that they should avoid the party, saying again that she should leave.

Before they could decide anything, there was a crack of thunder and the clouds opened. Nick had to shout above the noise of rain hitting the dry leaves above their heads. "Come on!" He held her hand tightly and pulled her behind him through the fragrant half light of the college gardens toward the street. "We'll find a quiet corner," he promised. "I don't want to share you with anyone tonight."

The old pub by the bridge was crowded as they pushed into

the light and warmth of its interior, leaving the rain-wet gardens behind like another world. Through the smoke clustering around each low-hanging lamp like a halo, Nick saw his friends packed into a small back room. They did not notice him, brushing water from his jacket and hair as he led the way to a small table in a relatively deserted corner. Gwen took a seat facing out into the room with her back to the wall while Nick went to the bar. He was surprised when she told him she was not hungry and did not want a drink.

Moving down the bar, trying to attract the barman's attention, he attracted Tom Newell's instead. Tom called out a greeting, asking when Nick was joining the party. Just then, there was a bright flash from the back room. "New camera," Tom explained. "Birthday present for Guy. It's one of those American instant-picture aberrations." Then he gathered up two hands full of drinks and weaved his way back to the raucous group in the back.

Turning from the bar with his beer and a sandwich, Nick was surprised to see someone sitting at the table with Gwenillan. A skinny young man with lank blond hair sat with his back to the bar, facing Gwen across the table as he fondled a glass of beer. He wasn't talking to the girl, just staring across the table at her face.

"Hey, that's my seat."

The other man—younger and several inches shorter than Nick as he stood—mumbled something that could have been a grudging apology before slouching off to the bar. Nick recognized him as he walked away: an underporter at Trinity Hall. Nigel something.

"Do you know him?" Nick whispered as he reclaimed his seat with his back to the bar.

"No. He just sat down."

"Lot of nerve, but I can see why. You look beautiful."

Gwenillan smiled. "You eat, Nick, and I will talk." Then she began, telling of being born and growing up in farming country. She had lived in a small village where she had known every person, every animal, every stick and stone for miles around. The little farm area and forest were her whole world for all the years she was growing up. That was where she had learned so much about plants and trees and the natural mysteries of the forests and rivers. Nick was right, she'd had very little formal education, being taught at home by her mother and by an old woman in her isolated village. She said she admired Nick for having read so many books, studied so many interesting things, and traveled so far from his home.

"I want to learn so much from you in our time together," she told him as he sat silently eating and listening.

Then, from behind him, Nick heard his name. He turned to see Guy Chamberlain at the corner of the bar, swaying slightly and holding his new camera unsteadily to one eye.

"Say 'Stilton,' old chap!"

Nick grinned into the lens. There was a short, blinding flash, and when he turned back to Gwenillan, she was smiling at Guy's efforts to collect his drinks and stagger back to his party. Nick shrugged apologetically for his drunken friend, inviting her to continue her story. As she did, he glanced back at the bar, where Nigel was eyeing him curiously. The young underporter turned away quickly rather than meet his glance, but Nick noted that he was sitting at the bar with a striking blond girl. Her long hair was pinned up on her head in a braid . . . but the eyes, the long, tapered legs inside faded jeans . . . she could have been Gwen's sister. Maybe that explained Nigel's confusion.

As Nick turned away from the pair at the bar, Gwen was talking about her family. Her father had been an important man in the village, which she explained was why she was called "Rhia" by the people of the district. Nick didn't quite understand, but he listened as she gaily talked about a big family with seven brothers and a baby sister that she had been a second mother to in her teenage years.

There was a long pause before she spoke again. "They are all dead now," she said, her voice growing soft and her eyes suddenly very far-away. She did not explain fully the tragedy she said had befallen her village, and Nick, seeing how painful it was for her, did not press her for details. He was picturing a disastrous fire or flood or perhaps an avalanche and searching for words of sympathy when she abruptly changed the subject.

She had been in love once, she said, when she was still living with her family in the village. The boy had been a foreigner, a stranger in her part of the world whom she had met one day while walking by a forest stream. Like Nick, he had spoken another language and had a different background and customs, but they had fallen in love despite these differences. Her parents had been violently opposed to the match.

Nick thought of their own situation as she told him they had not had much time together, meeting in secret and always having to part before they were ready. "We made a plan to run away together to his country."

She stared down at the scarred wood of the tabletop for a long time before continuing, but Nick did not interrupt her private thoughts. Before they could carry out their plan, she said finally, in a voice that was almost a whisper, the boy had been killed. Looking up at Nick and speaking very quickly, she added that it was then that the tragedy had befallen her village. The sudden loss of everyone she had ever loved had been too much for her to overcome. "That is why I am here," she whispered. "Why it means so much to me to find you."

Nick wanted to say something comforting, but before he could speak, she blinked away the tears welling up in her eyes. "So if I sometimes seem like . . . like I am somewhere else in my thoughts, or if what I do seems strange, please understand."

Nick reached across the small table and silently placed his hand on hers. A lot was clear to him now. Gwen had gone through a terrible shock. He understood why she was sometimes distant and secretive, wary of forming new commitments, and he had a new sense of admiration for her strength.

"Nick, I want to be with you, but I am sorry. I did not want to make my tragedy yours."

Nick wanted to reply, to reassure her and tell her that he understood and loved her, but he found that all he could do was look into her eyes. It was as though he were staring into a deep green gold tunnel that carried him across time and space. It was a strange feeling, almost like dreaming while being awake; a loss of control, but a comforting sensation despite that. He let himself drift toward whatever fate awaited him, whatever was meant to be, as if carried along by a swift current or by his own subconscious in sleep.

From somewhere very far away, Nick heard a voice. It was Gwenillan speaking, her voice breaking her own strange spell. She said that she had been crying and must dry her face. He watched her walk away toward the rest rooms, her body graceful and confident under the simple white wool of her dress.

She was barely out of sight when Nick felt a comradely

hand clasp his shoulder. "What's this skulking over here in the corner, Lombard?" This came from St. John Ainsley-Hay in his usual affected tone of disinterest. "Never mind. All I care about right now is finding the pisser." Then he wandered off with a quip about John Blessed missing the party, too, and how there was that much more for the rest of them to drink.

Nick smiled, wondering what could have kept Blessed John away from a party. He turned around to look at the crowd in the pub, intermittent flashes of light indicating that Guy had not yet exhausted his supply of flash cubes. Leaving the table, he walked to the bar with his empty mug aloft to catch the attention of the landlord.

Waiting for his second pint of bitter, he again noticed the pretty blonde in blue jeans. She had noticed him too, he was sure of it, but she coyly glanced back at the scruffy young man still by her side as Nick looked away. She was pretty, almost as striking as Gwen if only she'd been dressed a little less like a farmhand. He tried to picture her long hair down, or pinned back at the sides as Gwen wore it. What in hell was she doing with someone like Nigel?

Ainsley-Hay on his way back from the WC tapped him on the shoulder in passing. "If you wait much longer, the guest of honor may well have passed out entirely."

"Nothing new in that." Turning away from the bar, Nick saw Gwenillan waiting for him in their quiet corner. As he took his seat, she told him that now she really must go.

"Damn it! Already?" he protested. Noticing the couple at the nearest table turning toward him, he moved his chair so that his back was more toward them.

"I'm sorry, Nick. Believe me, I don't want to go, but there is nothing more to say now."

He knew what a strain it must have been for her to tell him about the loss of her family. "I understand," he said softly. Then he drank off as much of his pint as he could in a single swallow as Gwenillan stood and draped her shawl across her shoulders.

"I will follow you," she said, once again allowing Nick to lead the way.

The rain had stopped and the cold night air was refreshing after the press of people and the smoke of the pub. As they strolled back up the hump of Magdalene Bridge, Nick could feel the threat of rain still in the air. Gwenillan stopped near the center of the old bridge, built where a natural deposit of gravel had provided a dry approach to the Cam for as long as it had flowed along the edge of the East Anglian fenland.

"I'll leave you here, Nick."

"Still won't tell me where you live or let me walk with you, I suppose?"

"Nick, I should not have seen you at all tonight."

"Should not? Could not? Gwen, why do you have to keep secrets from me?" He was ready to protest more, to demand some explanation, when she spoke again.

"Tomorrow," she said. "Tomorrow you will know everything." Before he could ask what she meant, she drew his eye to the river. "Look, a swan. See how she shines in the moonlight?" Together they watched the beautiful creature glide silently down the dark river, glowing white with reflected moonlight.

"She is a creature of the Great Trinity of water, land, and air." Her voice had the odd sort of reverence Nick had heard before. Somehow it meant more to him now.

"More magic?"

"A good sign. For us."

Still watching the swan disappear into the darkness along the misty banks of the Cam, Gwen spoke again softly. "Nick, I want you to have this." She reached to the shoulder of her shawl and removed a gold clasp. Nick had noticed its curious design their first night together in Trinity Grove. Gwenillan squeezed it for a moment near her breast and then pressed it into Nick's hand. "Keep it near you tonight, and I will be with you."

Nick held up the brooch in his palm and saw its pattern of intertwining figures, like serpents woven into an intricate geometric design, as it reflected gold in the moonlight. He began to speak but was stopped by the soft pressure of her finger on his lips.

"When we met, Nick, I told you it was meant to be. Do you remember? From the first it was not in our hands." She removed her finger from his lips and replaced it with a kiss. "Tomorrow," she said, "tomorrow you will understand."

"Tomorrow," Nick repeated, trying to stop her from going. "But when will I meet you? Where?"

She looked back at him from a few paces away. "You will

know." Then her face turned reluctantly away from his like a ship leaving shore on the tide.

Nick watched her slim, graceful figure disappear over the crest of the bridge and thought of the swan on the moonlight of the Cam. He stood for a long time in the magical spot at the center of the bridge, poised between earth and sky, before returning to the noise and heat of the pub.

> The oak that in summer was sweet to hear
> And rustled its leaves in the fall of the year,
> And whistled and roared in the winter alone...
>> Samuel Taylor Coleridge (1772–1834)
>> Jesus College

John Blessed was totally relaxed; so relaxed, he had only now remembered Guy's party and had no idea of the time. It was dark outside his window, but that didn't tell him much. Since he had no watch and did not allow a clock of any kind in his room, he realized that he would have to go further afield.

He decided that one more joint was in order if he was going on an expedition. Having already found excuses for several others, he saw no harm in one more. Just getting ready mentally, he rationalized, for Guy's birthday celebration. He took a prerolled reefer from the shoe box on his dresser and lit it as he ambled through his door and out into the hallway. Blessed's room was in the attic portion of the old farmhouse under the bare beams of its ancient rafters. It was smaller than most of the rooms, but more private, and he liked it that way. He banged on the locked door of the other attic room, but Tom Newell was evidently already gone.

Cursing happily, Blessed John shambled down the steep attic stairs. Lombard would know the time, Americans always knew the time. He stumbled on the bottom step but eventually arrived intact at the ground floor, where he proceeded to Nick's room, singing a Gaelic folk tune punctuated by his hand slamming against closed doors as he went. From behind one, a voice called out for quiet.

"Got the time?" Blessed shouted in return.

"Piss off!"

Lombard's door was closed but not locked. Blessed swung in from the hall, calling out his friend's name. He found an alarm clock by the bed in the empty room. Late, but Blessed liked late arrivals, having started life a month later than his mother's doctor had predicted. Not too late for a small drink, he told himself, if Lombard still had that bottle of Kentucky bourbon his father had sent. He searched the dresser top and then the bookcase, where he found the empty Jack Daniel's bottle acting as a bookend.

Turning away in disgust, his eye was caught by a book lying askew on the shelf. Automatically he bent to straighten it, and the title aroused his interest: *Lost Gods of the British Forests*. Looked old. Taking another deep drag on his joint, he glanced at a few of the woodcut illustrations and decided that the book was worthy of borrowing; he might even get a quote for his ever-developing dissertation.

Musing to himself on the rewards of a scholarly life, he wandered back upstairs trying to continue his earlier singing while holding a lungful of smoke. Back in the attic room, he flopped onto his bed, one arm hanging over the side with the dangling butt of his marijuana cigarette and the other balancing the book on his stomach. He decided to read a little before setting off for Guy's party.

Skimming for a time, he discovered a chapter of some interest. It concerned events in the area of Cambridgeshire during the Roman occupation. He read about the Roman encampment at the Wandlebury Ring in the God Magogs and how they had ruled the surrounding area from their stronghold. It mentioned Cantabrigia, the Roman name for the native settlement at the Cam River crossing. Seems that a hill tribe in a village nearby had given the Romans some trouble....

John Blessed looked up as a hard rain began to hit the window he had opened earlier to vent the smoke in his room. Getting up to close it, he noted that there was quite a storm outside. He watched it for a moment, looking out into the darkness toward Trinity Wood. A strong wind was blowing the rain against the house with surprising force, and it seemed to be increasing even as he watched. Looked like he could expect to get soaked getting to the party unless it blew itself out.

After closing the window, he went back to wait out the storm. The author's narrative, as he continued reading, explained how the Romans had taken revenge on the village of the hill tribe, a people called the Celangi, but he had missed the reason they wanted revenge against the poor sods. He began paging backward, casually looking for the origin of the dispute. His mind was functioning at half speed after three joints, but to him it seemed that he had never been more lucid. Suddenly it seemed very important to prove this by finding the reason for the massacre of this forgotten people of the Cambridgeshire forests two thousand years ago. "Truth!" Blessed mused to himself. "The mission of the historian."

A tree branch slammed hard against the roof outside, causing him to look up with a start. He went back to his reading, but it happened again, this time closer to his window. Placing the open book facedown on the rumpled bed, he dragged himself to his feet once more and walked to the black pane of glass, reflecting the jumble of his room back at him. He switched off the overhead light so that he could better look outside, where he saw the huge oak nearest the house swinging its uppermost branches against the peaked roof. "The hanging tree," Blessed mumbled for his own amusement, recalling stories about the medieval lord of Wychfield hanging poachers from the tree outside. "No poachers here," he laughed. "Go knock on some other window!"

In his bemused state the whole thing seemed hilarious. He was still laughing when, in turning away from the window, his eye was drawn to Trinity Wood. Its blank gray face stared back at him like a wall of stone. But just for a moment, just as he had begun to turn away, he swore that it had moved. He watched the wood intently now, waiting for anything out of the ordinary. Smaller trees nearest to him swayed with the force of the wind, but certainly the forest hadn't moved! How ridiculous to think that it had, even in his state. He held one finger aloft and spoke out in a stentorian voice: "'Till Birnam Wood shall come to Dunsinane . . .'"

His recitation was cut off by a resounding crash as though a gigantic fist had been slammed down on the roof above his head. Blessed stared up at the ceiling beams in amazement and then looked back out the window. Trinity Wood had moved! Moved closer to the house by yards! He leaned closer to the liquid black of the glass and rubbed his smoke-reddened eyes. Everything was normal. Trinity Wood hung like a motionless black curtain across the field.

Blessed John turned back to the bed. Too much, he told

himself; he should learn when to quit. He shook his head to clear his senses, thinking he might skip the party and stay home to read himself to sleep. Reaching out for the book, he was frozen in motion by the resounding crash of a heavy limb slamming against the outside wall, followed closely by the rifle-crack sound of splintering glass. He whirled around, covering his face with his arm, to be assailed by a frigid, rain-filled wind and flying slivers of glass. After a startled moment he struggled against the wind and rain toward the shattered window, grabbing up a blanket from the foot of the bed in the faint hope of somehow blocking the opening gaping before him like a jagged, hungry mouth.

With a stunning suddenness, the scarred and spiny branch of the ancient oak struck him like some gigantic arm reaching in through the smashed window. Then it heaved itself into the attic room, pushing the fragile human in its path to the floor as it clawed forward on elbows of gnarled oak. Wood of windowsill and floor grated against living wood of the tree as the monstrous limb pushed inward and then recoiled with the unnatural wind that drove it forward and then back. Wind and rain screamed into the tiny room, swirling between floor and ceiling like a spectral being.

John Blessed cowered in terror before the clutching branches reaching out for him in a vision more terrifying than any he had seen after his worst binges. The book he had been reading a moment before was blown from the bed, its pages fluttering frantically like the wings of a trapped bird as it flew to the floor and then was pushed by the wind under a heavy dresser against the wall. Blessed did not see it. Nor did he see Trinity Wood move closer. Close enough to look into the little attic room through the shattered eye of its broken window.

CHAPTER 20

Wednesday evening
The Pickeral

Her face was veiled, yet to my fancied sight,
Love, sweetness, goodness in her person shined.

John Milton (1608—1674)
Christ's College

The atmosphere inside the pub was thick with tobacco and beer and the sounds of conversation. Nick made his way apathetically toward the crowded bar, where he found Kebby Mlanga and Ainsley-Hay ordering drinks for what must have been a small army on bivouac nearby.

"So, Lombard, finally joining the party?"

"Cheers, Nick," Kebby said brightly, handing him a beer.

Nick shook off his melancholy and decided that he should celebrate. Tomorrow he would see Gwen again and she would explain everything that was puzzling him now. "Cheers!" He drank off half the pint of bitter in a single long swallow.

Guy Chamberlain's birthday celebration was still going strong. Grouped around three tables pushed together in the small back room of the pub were most of Nick's friends. Tom Newell was there, along with Mo Roper and his wife, Thelma. Kevin and Julie Rees looked up and smiled as Nick approached. Samantha kissed his cheek as she went to help St. John and Kebby with the drinks. Everyone was there, Nick noted, except John Blessed.

"Nicky, have you come to rescue me from these Philistines?" Samantha asked in an exaggerated tone of desperation as she lifted Guy's limp hand from her thigh and deposited it gently on the table.

"Happy birthday, Guy," Nick said, but there was no response. "His eyes are open. Is he awake?"

"This will rouse him," St. John suggested, leaning close to his drunken friend's ear. "Time, gentlemen! Last call!"

"Merde!" Guy shouted, reverting for a moment to the

country of his birth. "What? Last what?" He struggled toward the waking world. "Where's my bloody glass?"

"It's all right, we have another one here for you," Julie Rees told him, steadying his hand on the glass.

Guy smiled dreamily, his hand clasping hers. "Lombard, old chap, where the blazes have you been? Don't you know it's my bloody whatdoyoucallit . . . birthday?"

Hay answered for him. "Why, Dr. Lombard has been conducting research, I wouldn't doubt, on the mating habits of northern European birds." He winked at Nick and then checked to be sure he had the attention of the others. "Don't you know? Nick prayed to the gods and has been sent—wait for it—a Scandinavian maiden who thinks fate brought her here just to meet him. In fact, why aren't you with her now!"

Hay turned to Nick amid the friendly sounds of surprise and envy from around the tables. "Hope you weren't planning to keep it a secret," he half whispered.

"So you saw her, did you?"

St. John smiled and shook his head. "Should I have? No, but I'm looking forward to the pleasure."

"Why, Nicky," Samantha cooed, "have you been keeping secrets?"

Mo Roper reached a long, check-shirted arm across the table and clasped Nick's shoulder. "Why didn't you bring the little lady with you?" he drawled.

"We did stop by a while ago, but she couldn't stay."

"Well, next time bring her along, Nicko." John Blessed spoke from the corner of the bar. "You'll be wanting our expert appraisal before you go and do anything rash."

"Where the hell have you been?" the guest of honor demanded.

"Fell asleep," the Irishman explained innocently to a chorus of jeers, "reading." He did not mention the other events that already seemed like a drunken blur in his mind.

"So tell us, Nick," Tom Newell continued when Blessed had gone back to the bar with Kevin for more drinks, "is she blond and beautiful, like the Swedish girl in my dreams?"

Nick took a swallow of beer and grinned self-consciously. "Very blond and very beautiful. You saw her, Tom. It was at a distance, but you saw her with me yesterday afternoon. You were there too, St. John, and so was Blessed."

Ainsley-Hay and Tom Newell looked at each other quizzically as Nick continued. "You remember, we were in a punt and you were all out in front of The Mill? Swilling beer, as usual," he laughed.

"I certainly remember you punting, old man," St. John admitted. "Who could forget a sight like that? But I don't recall anyone with you . . . unless you had her lying down in the bottom of the boat." There was general laughter at this.

Tom shook his head in agreement. "Actually, we thought it a bit odd, you out punting all on your own like that."

"Well, she was leaning back on the cushions . . . but you should have seen her."

Blessed and Kevin returned from the bar with another round. "Here, Blessed John, do you remember a girl with Lombard on the river yesterday?"

"Girl? You're dreamin' if you saw a girl. Nicko was poling along all alone . . . looked like Charon on the Styx. I'd have noticed a girl, believe me!"

"Don't listen to them, Nick," Samantha broke in. "They were probably too drunk to notice your girl."

"I'm never that drunk, my darlin'," Blessed retorted, dropping his hand to her knee to prove his point.

"Now, wait a minute," Nick said more firmly, leaning forward on the table now and setting down his drink. "This is absurd! Kebby, you saw us together yesterday, too. You were cycling down Castle Hill at dinnertime. You waved, remember?"

Kebby Mianga toyed with the glass in front of him. "Yes, I remember, Nick. But I can't say for sure there was anyone with you. . . . I was going pretty fast downhill and watching traffic, you know."

"Maybe she—" Mo Roper began.

"Oh, I see," Nick cut in, "this is some kind of joke. Well, okay, enough is enough. You've all had a laugh. I know you saw her, you must have. Guy," he said, shaking the shoulder of the drowsy Frenchman across the table. "You saw her here with me this evening!"

"Don't recall, old chap."

"You took a picture of us, goddamn it! With that new camera of yours."

"Steady on." St. John put his hand on Nick's arm.

"Picture?" Guy said laconically, his consciousness beginning to surface. "I do remember snapping your picture.

Bloody marvelous little camera—American, you know." He laughed a staccato, drunken laugh. "Develops pictures right on the spot. Bloody clever. Never seen anything like—"

Nick reached across the table, picked up the camera, then slammed it down hard on the tabletop. There was sudden silence. "Where is the damned picture now?"

"Picture?" Guy stammered. "It's here somewhere." He groped in one pocket and then another before finally bringing out a handful of squares of Polaroid paper and fumbling them onto the wet surface of the table.

"Go easy, Nick," Blessed advised, turning to Guy. "Give me some of those, Chamberlain old sod, and I'll lend a hand." He gathered up the stack of photographs and began sorting through them.

"Here's one of you, Nicko. You're smiling like a banshee, but you're all alone." He handed the photo to Nick, who saw himself seated at a table in The Pickeral facing the camera and smiling broadly. The chair against the wall behind him was empty.

"She must have been in the ladies."

"Maybe you're the one playing the joke," Tom Newell suggested. "When I saw you at the bar, you were only ordering for one. Remember?"

"She didn't want a drink!" Nick said hotly. "Does everyone around here have to be a damned alcoholic?"

"When I saw you later on my way to the WC you were by yourself, too, old man," Ainsley-Hay added quietly.

"She was in the loo! I told you, she had to be." There was a long moment of uncomfortable silence as Nick desperately clutched at Gwen's brooch in his pocket.

Thelma Roper whispered something softly to her husband. "Well, we're gonna have to be pushin' off," the big Texan said. "Happy birthday, Guy. Enjoy yourself, you hear?"

"We'll see y'all later," Thelma added with an embarrassed little laugh.

Kevin and Julie Rees pushed back their chairs and stood. "We have to be going, too. Many happy returns, Guy. Someone see that he gets home all right," Julie ordered.

It was nearly closing time and the crowd was thinning out, providing an excuse to leave what had become an uncomfortable situation for everyone at the party.

"We'd better get the birthday boy on his feet," Tom said.

Samantha finished her wine and stood. "Well, I must get my beauty sleep." She touched Nick's arm as she turned toward the door. "Nicky, don't worry about . . . well, just don't worry. I'm sure there's some logical explanation." Then she breezed out of the pub, trailing a short mink jacket over one shoulder like a hussar.

Nick and John Blessed were soon left alone at the table. People were leaving the pub, taking clouds of smoke and light with them each time the door swung open into the cold night air. John Blessed waited, wondering what had happened to Nick. It must be something more than this girl he claimed to have met. The Irishman thought of the unsettling experience he had just come from in his attic room; he had not yet come to grips with what really could have happened.

"Nick, I—"

"You know, Johnny boy," Nick interrupted in an ostensibly cheerful tone helped along by too much drink, "I think I must be dreaming all this. I've been dreaming a lot lately . . . dreaming but not really sleeping. Hardly had any rest for three days. Dreaming about forests—like I told you—forests and floods, and oak trees with faces . . . and men that aren't really men, men with horns . . . and girls I meet in the woods and go on the river with, and—"

"Come on, Nick," Blessed broke in, putting a hand on his friend's shoulder. "Don't you think you'd better go home now and get some sleep?"

"Sleep?" Nick laughed. "You know, I've heard about people who live in a dreamworld all the time—crazy people." He laughed again and pulled Guy's photograph from his pocket. He stared at it hard and then very slowly, very deliberately tore it into small pieces.

Blessed thought of steering the conversation in another direction, maybe confiding to Nick what had happened earlier while he'd been reading Nick's book . . . Nick's book? Before he could pull his thoughts together, Nick began ranting again in a maudlin, drunken voice.

"What's so crazy about seeing a girl who's not there? Going on a picnic with her, making love—" Suddenly he stopped speaking, his features struggling for composure as a sober thought came to him through a haze of alcohol and doubt.

"You know, I was beginning to believe all of you. You really had me going!"

"I can only follow half of what you're saying, Nicko."

"Well, I'll tell you, Blessed John, what I'm saying is that you may not have noticed Gwen in the punt with me yesterday, but she was there! And I can prove it!"

"Nick, I swear to you, I didn't see anyone—"

"You may not have noticed her," Nick repeated with growing confidence, "but you did take a picture of her. You must remember snapping pictures with that long lens of yours. I saw you! And photos don't lie."

Nick saw his friend glance down at the torn Polaroid at his feet. "I know, I know. But Guy evidently took his bloody picture while Gwen was in the ladies. God, he was drunker than I am now. The pub was crowded, noisy. I don't remember every move we made all evening. But your picture, Johnny boy, your picture will have to show her there in the boat with me. Where is it?"

"I haven't developed the film yet. It's still in my locker at the Camera Club. So what?"

"So, we're going to go develop that film."

"What, now? It's after eleven! The darkroom is locked."

"You have a key, and we have all night."

"You gentlemen planning to sleep here tonight?" The landlord's voice came out in a vent of smoke from the cigarette permanently glued to his lower lip. There would be late results of the evening's soccer on television and he was anxious to get home to watch them in comfort.

John Blessed sighed and stood. "Cheers, Arthur, we're just going to develop some pictures." Halfway to the door, he turned back with a gladiator's salute. "*Morituri te salutamus! We who are about to die salute you!*" Laughing, he followed Nick out the door. What the hell, maybe humoring his friend was better than going back to his cold attic room.

Arthur watched the pair exit his pub. Students, he reflected idly. Strange lot. You never knew what to expect. Still, he had to admit they were good for business, so long as you didn't expect anything they said to you to make any sense.

CHAPTER 21

Wednesday, 11 P.M.
University Library

There was a door to which I found no key;
There was a veil through which I might not see.

> *Rubaiyat of Omar Khayyám,*
> translated by
> Edward FitzGerald (1809—1883)
> Trinity College

Passing under the arch of King's Memorial Court, James Anglesey was unable to avoid looking up at the flat, graceless facade of the university library. An immense, phallic tower jutted up from its midsection like some lost grain silo from the western Canadian plains. The chaplain had often said to his colleagues that it was a monstrous building, totally out of tune with the architecture of the university and the town. But even Anglesey had to admit that it was one of the world's great repositories of knowledge. He knew that the information he sought was somewhere within that vast and unendearing exterior, among the rows and stacks and shelves of well-thumbed volumes without which this university could not have functioned for the past seven hundred years.

Anglesey's request to use the library after hours had been unusual, but he had some standing in the university and was a personal friend of the curator of books. It was already eleven o'clock when he arrived at the massive doors and rang the night bell. Students and dons had been gone for an hour, but fortunately a few staff members were still on duty, closing the facility for the day. Anglesey showed his pass to the rather surprised young clerk who answered the bell and was asked to wait in the monumental lobby. When the clerk's echoing footsteps returned, the chaplain was given back his pass with an added signature from the assistant librarian on duty.

"We'll all be leaving in a few minutes, Dr. Anglesey," the young man said. "Sure you'll be all right, sir?"

"I'll be fine, thank you." Impatient to get on with his work, Anglesey began to climb the marble steps to the main level of the library. The young clerk called after him.

"Oh, the elevators are down for the night. Sorry. Hope you don't need to walk up too many floors."

Only five, Anglesey groaned to himself, only five. On the stairs he passed a cleaning woman—a black-haired female of middle age with piercing eyes that stared at him with unconcealed surliness for invading her domain after closing. The chaplain was not in any mood for surly charwomen, being faced with three more flights of steps. He gave the woman what he thought of as his *withering glance*. She did not, however, seem the least bit withered as she continued down the stairs with her bucket and mop, stopping to look back at him with undiminished malice when she reached the landing.

She was right in a way, he thought more kindly, stopping to catch his breath on the fourth floor. In the long hours before dawn, this grotesque building and all it contained belonged more clearly to her than to any of the students or dons of the university that employed her. He was the intruder here tonight.

Nevertheless there were certain volumes here that he must consult without delay. After what he had read earlier in the day, he could not wait until morning. He had begun that afternoon looking through his own small, specialized collection of books on local history. Then he had visited the university archives at the Old Schools instead of going to dinner. Immediately afterward he had phoned the curator for permission to use the university library after closing.

A clock chimed the half hour as he walked down a resounding hallway on the fifth floor. He wondered if he was entirely alone in the building now; surely cleaning people would be about for a time, and possibly there was a security guard on site overnight, though he was not sure of it. He pushed open a door and entered the British history stacks, where he had so often browsed through the volumes on the history of Cambridge and the county that bore its name. He was surrounded by silence as he walked down a long aisle running alongside twenty-five ranks of floor-to-ceiling bookshelves. The overhead lights were off and he found his way by the dim light from the high windows until he reached a reading desk near the bookcase he sought. Then he switched on a small reading lamp over the desk and put down his note-pad and pencils.

He stood and looked back down the long row of identical chairs and desks running the entire length of the wall, all dark now except his own. A light glowed dimly through a small window in the closed door to the outer corridor. He twisted a dial which immediately lit a single aisle of books, its auto-matic timing mechanism ticking off the seconds until it would again go dark. Anglesey walked back into the stacks, scan-ning the shelves for a few moments before recognizing the worn spine of the volume he needed. It required a stretch to reach the book even for a man of Anglesey's height, and his spine protested at the effort. He glanced through the hard-won volume and then found two more, located in more civilized positions on the shelves, before returning to his desk. Behind him the light in the stacks clicked off abruptly.

During his researches earlier in the day the chaplain had discovered a number of things. In addition to the incidents Terry Graham had documented, he had so far found references to twelve similar unsolved murders or disappearances of young men in Cambridge or its environs over a period ranging back to the thirteenth century. Of course, there had been many more such incidents mentioned in the sources he had paged through—and he admitted that he had skimmed them very quickly—but he had easily found twelve that fit the pattern. Most were brutal, mutilation murders, though only two men-tioned anything that could be construed as disembowelment. The victims in each case had been foreigners, and the motives and methods of all the killings were unresolved.

He knew that there must be any number of similar crimes for which some poor wretch had paid with his life for being in the wrong place at the wrong time. Other incidents he had passed over for being too easily explained in their historical context. It had to be assumed, too, that there were many other killings or disappearances that had never been recorded in any chronicle or history. But the startling thing was that in a single day of research he had found twelve incidents that matched such a specific set of criteria.

Perhaps even more troubling, Anglesey had found that ten of the murders—spaced out over a period of nearly six cen-turies—fit into a perfect thirty-three-year sequence of dates when he counted back. And these were in addition to those identified by poor Terry Graham. The chaplain scratched at his unshaven chin as he considered again the implications of what he had found so far.

Every reference that mentioned a specific date or time of year in relation to one of the killings had the crime taking place either in midsummer or late autumn; three actually mentioned Midsummer Day, and two sources—one in the late Middle Ages, and the other two hundred years later—referred to the mutilated body of a murder victim being found near the Feast of All Souls.

One of the ten in particular had captured the chaplain's interest. An eighteenth-century source, referring back to an earlier history of Cambridgeshire, spoke of a disemboweled body discovered at a site called Wychfield in 1646. The savaged body had been found lying in a farmer's field adjoining a woods, and near it was the head of a young man impaled on a stake in the manner of the ancient Celts who had once inhabited the area. The people of the time had suspected witchcraft, and the murder had been cited as evidence in a trial for necromancy, which was the only reason a record had been preserved of the incident for Anglesey to read 330 years later. He wondered again how many other grisly murders had never been recorded over the centuries.

Using the books before him on the desk, the tired, elderly scholar searched for other references to Wychfield. He knew the present site, of course, and was familiar with its history as a Trinity Hall property, but he wanted to learn more. According to one author, the very place-name had originated because of a long association of the place and the forested area nearby with unexplained occurrences and violent death. Another eighteenth-century source described Wychfield as "lying near the King's Highway to Huntingdon, half a league from the Church of St. Peter the Lesser at Castle Hill." On a reproduction of a map dated 1680, he had found Wychfield clearly marked, lying between the Huntingdon Road and a smaller track leading toward the village of Madingley. Bounding it was a wooded area labeled "Trinitie Grove."

Anglesey removed his wire-rimmed reading glasses and rubbed his strained eyes. His angular features stared back at him, blurred without his spectacles, from the black pool of the window glass at eye level above his desk. He was too tired to go on, but a growing sense of urgency made him persevere. It was becoming increasingly clear to him that someone's life might well depend on what he could learn from these dusty old volumes.

Replacing his glasses, he drew a deep breath. He was tired, and there was little point in continuing to search for more examples of unsolved murders. The point was made and a pattern validated as much as it could be in such limited time. Closing the books in front of him, the chaplain stood wearily to his feet. Something told him that to find the origins of the mystery, he would have to go back much further, at least to the shadowy centuries before the Dark Ages when Rome had ruled the world and Britain had been the home of wild tribes and ancient customs. It was the period he knew best, and what he had learned so far drew him toward it now.

Turning the timer dial again before entering the stacks, he searched through the familiar shelves of reference works on ancient Britain. He gathered up several books, including Dudley and Webster's *The Rebellion of Boudicca* and *Bagendon, A Belgic Oppidum,* by E. M. Clifford, and was starting back to his seat when a gold-edged binding caught his eye. As familiar as he was with this aisle of books after thirty years of study, he could not recall this slender volume low down on a bottom shelf. He stooped to retrieve it just as the timer clicked and the lights went out. Cursing his luck and his aching back, Anglesey shambled to the light switch and then deposited the other books on the desk before returning for the unfamiliar volume. It took a moment to find it again, but soon it was in his hands. Under the reactivated lights he read on its worn spine a title he surprisingly had not encountered before: *Lost Gods of the British Forests.* Thumbing through it curiously, he trudged back to the circle of lamplight at his desk.

Time passed, and the chaplain was cross-referencing the volumes spread out in front of him when he heard the noise. It came from the stairwell and sounded like a door being slammed back hard against the wall.

"Who's there?" he called out once. Then he listened, heard nothing, and returned to his work.

It was several minutes before he heard another sound, a kind of distant howling followed by a low moaning that made him suspect the wind rushing in through an open window. Anglesey stood and was considering going into the hallway to find the source of the disturbing noise when it suddenly grew several fold in intensity. It was definitely coming from the stairwell at the end of the hall and building rapidly in volume as it came closer, rushing and swirling up five flights of stairs, one landing at a time. The chaplain stood rigid, holding on to the back of his chair as he listened to the crescendo of sound flowing toward him like a tidal wave roaring to a crest.

An instant later the heavy door thirty feet down the aisle from where Anglesey stood blew open with a force that shook the wall. A flood of noise and wind flowed over the elderly man, knocking him to the floor and holding him there with its force. The wind carried with it a heavy animal scent, a pungent smell of woodland and farmyard mingled with a stench of the slaughterhouse. Anglesey's eyelids were pressed open by the blast as the reeking squall filled his nose and mouth, choking off his feeble breath.

His books, notes, and reading glasses were blown against the wall as if thrown there by an unseen hand. At the same time, the light in the outer hall slowly died and the desk lamp also flickered in a dying SOS, throwing the room into total darkness. Still pinned to the floor, the chaplain painfully forced his right hand to his chest against the strength of the blast. He clutched the small silver cross he wore under his shirt and collar. Then, wide-eyed, he watched a strange phosphorescent glow materialize in the open doorway leading to the corridor and the howling stairwell beyond. For an instant Anglesey was sure that he saw a dark outline silhouetted in the doorframe against the sickly green glow. It was human but inhuman, animal but man, with steaming nostrils and grotesquely curving horns. He clutched at his crucifix and prayed aloud against the demon being looming over him, struggling for breath in the stinking maelstrom that swirled around him.

Then, as suddenly as they had come, the wind and the nightmare shape in the doorway were gone. Only a lingering stench of animal musk remained, but it was rapidly fading. The desk lamp fluttered back to life as the row of overhead lights blinked on in the corridor, and if Anglesey had not been lying on the floor with his notes scattered around him, it might have seemed that nothing had happened at all.

He looked around carefully before attempting to stand. The door to the hall abruptly swung shut as though it had never burst open, and then there was silence. The thousands of volumes in the stacks behind him were untouched; the platoon of reading desks stood sentry in their undisturbed ranks. The full force of the blast had been directed at him, Anglesey realized . . . or at his work.

Slowly he eased himself to his feet, holding on to the desk with one hand and supporting his back with the other, hoping there were no vertebrae dislocated by the fall. Then he righted the overturned chair and searched until he found his spectacles, bent but unbroken, like himself. He gathered up his scattered notes and the books he had been reading, carefully stooping to his knees for each one. He half expected a security guard, or even the surly cleaning woman, to come through the door at any moment to investigate the commotion that had just passed. But no one came. The only sound was a clock slowly sounding midnight. He could not stop now to look for help. Though badly shaken, the chaplain knew now what he must do.

He tried desperately to concentrate. The threatening disturbance had ironically given a direction and an added urgency to his search. There had been two books open in front of him—Clifford's *Oppidum* and . . . and the book he had just discovered, *Lost Gods of the British Forests*. The key must lie there, he was sure. He recalled that he had put Clifford's book to one side and had actually been reading in the other volume.

His hands trembled as he turned the pages again, seeking the exact page where he had been stopped from his reading by the strange intrusion of wind and noise. He recalled the author's description of the rebellion against Roman rule by the Celtic Queen Boudicca. In the first century after Christ her Iceni people had fought against the Roman legions in the area around Cambridge. He reread every paragraph now more carefully, through the author's description of the major suppression of the Iceni rebellion in A.D. 60 and the occupation by the Romans of the Celtic hill fort of Wandlebury in the Gog Magog Hills. He read on, studying each sentence for any possible significance, until he recognized several lines where his reading had been abruptly broken off.

Various minor military operations and local disturbances had continued in the years A.D. 61 and 62. Anglesey turned the page. His eye was immediately drawn to a reference to Cantabrigia near the middle of the page. He went back and read the full paragraph preceding it, which told of a raid by a detachment of the Roman XIV Legion on a native settlement

near the river crossing of the Cam. The tribe, an obscure Can-
tuvellauni people known as the Celangi, were totally annihi-
lated by the Roman attack. According to the author, the
Celangi were never again mentioned in the reports of Roman
governors of Britain.

Anglesey read further. The author of *Lost Gods* wrote of
the massacre of the Celangi in their sacred grove on a day of
worship for the Celts across all of Europe. The tribal chief and
his seven sons had all been slain defending the sacred oak
grove, as had the entire war band, the *Teulu,* and the extended
family of the chief, the *Cendl.* While the men were fighting
and dying with their gods in the forest grove, their village had
been put to the torch and their wives and children slain in a
brutal slaughter of annihilation.

Anglesey adjusted his glasses and reread the final sentence
on the page several times. The author referred to a Roman
consul's report, which gave the reason for the savage extinc-
tion of the tribe. "The Celangi ceased to exist because of their
brutal murder of a young Roman officer, the son of a Senator,
who had violated their Sacred Grove honoring the supreme
Trinity: Earth, Sun, and Sky."

The specific violation of the Grove of the Trinity was not
known, but the author used the example of the young
Roman's ritual murder—and the vengeful massacre that en-
sued—to illustrate the strong survival of tribal beliefs despite
the subjugation of the Celts by Rome. The massacre was reported to have taken place during the pagan festival of Samain
in the year A.D. 62.

The chaplain laid his spectacles aside and wiped his sweating brow. He gazed out into the silent darkness of the stacks to
rest his eyes and calm his racing mind. Then he carefully
adjusted the beam of his reading lamp more directly onto the
book and papers in front of him. Samain, he recited to himself
like a mantra, the festival of Samain. His fingers trembled as
he took up his pencil. The span of time from the present back
to the year A.D. 62 was 1,914 years . . . a figure exactly divisi-
ble by 33.

CHAPTER 22

Wednesday, late evening Cambridge

She was a Phantom of delight
When first she gleamed upon my sight...
William Wordsworth (1770–1850)
St. John's College

Outside The Pickeral, the dimming of the lights through the frosted glass lightened the shadows of the two young men on the now quiet street. It was cold and late, and John Blessed was tired.

"Kebby left his bike, and mine's here. Let's at least cycle down to the darkroom to save time."

They wheeled their bicycles out to the curb and then set off through the silent streets of the university town, their tires whirring smoothly on the wet pavement. The wind was cold on their faces, and John Blessed's beard collected a fine, chilly drizzle. Nick tried not to think about the questions pulling at his mind. He tried not to think about Magdalene gardens or the bridge they had just crossed, but it was useless.

The moon emerged from clouds as they coasted past a tall steel derrick towering over the center of town like some colossal gibbet waiting for a victim from Brobdignag. In the morning light it would begin another day's work of erecting a modern shopping center for modern Cambridge. A few minutes later their cycle lamps cast roving beams across the stone front of Emmanuel College.

"You're sure you want me to go through with this?" Blessed asked wearily. "All right, all right. I have to develop the bloody film sometime." He searched through his pockets for a key ring.

"I'll wait here." Nick watched the thickset form of his friend disappear, grumbling into his beard, past the Porter's Lodge toward the darkroom used by the University Camera Club. Then he sat on a low stone wall in front of the college that had already been old when John Harvard had enrolled there. Only a few cars passed by, and the shops across the way were dark. He watched the noisy progress of a group of students returning from a pub crawl.

Sitting in the sterile glare of yellow streetlights, the young American felt as though things were coming apart in his life. Whatever Blessed's photographs showed, Nick had begun to question much of what Gwenillan had led him to believe. He should have asked her more, and pressed her for real answers. He had wanted so much to believe her—still wanted to believe her—but the seeds of doubt were the quick-growing variety.

Thunder sounded in the distance over the fens, and the mist in the air became a steady rain. Nick moved back under the arched gateway and tried to empty his mind by counting the seconds between the few passing cars. A clock in an inner courtyard sounded the same doleful note twelve times. Watching his breath cloud the moist night air, he finally heard footsteps on the wet cobbles of the interior court. Eventually they brought John Blessed into view.

"Damned foul night you've dragged me out on." When Nick did not reply, Blessed continued. "Well, there's this one. A little blurred—my hand wasn't too steady, I'll admit—and it was taken at a distance."

He presented a print, which Nick held up to the light of a large lantern in the entryway. "You can't much tell if there's one person in the boat or three!" John's forced laugh echoed alone off the stones of the passage.

"Let me see the others."

Blessed handed over two more photos. As Nick held them in the light, his friend took a few steps away, rubbing his hand across his beard. These two pictures, taken with the zoom lens, had a much clearer image of the punt. The photographer's hand had been steady and the focus was accurate. In both photos Nick saw himself clearly alone, a stupid, self-satisfied grin on his face.

"Nicko . . ."

"John, why don't you start on back."

"Do you want to talk?"

Nick shook his head.

John Blessed rested a hand on his friend's shoulder for a moment. Then he took his cycle and pushed off into the night.

The dark stranger watched him go, listening to the whir of his tires on the wet surface of the street and allowing his mind to wander anywhere other than to what he had just learned.

> I saw her on nearer view,
> A Spirit, yet a Woman too!
> > William Wordsworth (1770—1850)
> > St. John's College

After a time, he did not know how long, Nick stepped out into the chill drizzle. Kebby's bicycle remained behind, forgotten. Walking back toward Castle Hill, the young man felt numbed. There were thoughts, devastating thoughts, trying to break through to his consciousness, but he blocked them out. He did not feel the rain hitting his face or hear the ominous thunder drawing closer.

A small knot of sallow-faced teenagers lounged in a store-front. Fueled by greasy burgers and beer, they were feeling nasty and a bit sluggish, almost ready to slouch off home at the end of another vacuous day. Nick did not notice their wide, shortened trousers and heavy boots. He did not hear the ripple of nasal mutterings as he passed them by.

Beams of headlights searched across his blank face as he followed the curve of the street past Christ's College and Marks and Spencer. His mind remained a blank gray canvas as he continued past the darkened facades of the shopping district and the crouching shape of the Norman Round Church. It was only in crossing Magdalene Bridge that the demons inside him threatened to break through.

Rain began falling harder and the crash of lightning struck somewhere nearby as Nick marched steadily, unhurriedly, past the unlighted windows of The Pickeral. By the time he reached the empty intersection at the foot of Castle Hill, the rain had changed to hail and the hammering of frozen ice pellets finally brought him to his senses. He ran. The hail-stones grew larger, stinging his face painfully as the storm intensified and lightning flashed overhead.

Once again Nick sought relief in the abandoned Church of St. Peter. He fumbled with the latched gate before dashing blindly up a twisting path, the hailstorm making a curtain of ice to block his way across the sacred ground that had been a place of refuge and worship for countless generations before him. Clawlike branches of black and twisted trees bent under the wind, snatching at his running form, until finally he grasped the cold iron ring on the church door and twisted. It groaned open to admit him to sanctuary.

Leaning back against the heavy wooden door and panting for breath, Nick could feel the hail pounding for admittance at his back. He looked around the dark interior of the cramped building and was struck by its bareness each time lightning illuminated the stone crucible surrounding him. A barren altar stone crouched at the far end of a short nave under the arch of the steepled roof. Except for an ancient baptismal font, the tiny abandoned church was entirely empty. Outside, the wind swooped and howled, insuring that he should not forget its presence or the fact that only a few thin panes of colored glass separated his cold sanctum from the heart of the maelstrom.

Nick moved away from the door to a corner in the stone wall farthest from the large stained-glass window, backlighted now by intermittent flashes of electricity cracking the night sky. As the storm increased in force, the wind took on a wild baying quality, bringing with it disquieting half-remembered dreams of a chase, a blood hunt.

The hail drove harder against the ancient leaded glass, hard enough, Nick saw, to cause the large central panel across from him to bow inward with its force. He felt sweat under his clothes and knew that it was caused by more than running. His sanctuary had become a cold stone trap, surrounded and beset by the forces of nature. The trap, he knew, could become a tomb.

Lightning flashes abated for a moment as a dark cloud covered the moon, throwing the interior of the building into almost total darkness. Nick pressed his shaking body deeper into the natural recess formed by the conflux of two ancient stone walls. The wind died momentarily and then raced toward a new crescendo, sending gales of rock-hard hailstones against the worn clunch walls of the medieval church. In a suddenly renewed lightning flash, Nick watched in terror as the weakened panes of leaded glass above him curved inward as if in slow motion and then shattered into a cascade of colored fragments. They rained down, splintering and echoing on the flagstones below. Nick's hand flew to his face, but a jagged shard of bloodred glass struck him on the forehead, sending him staggering along the wall and clutching at its smooth, worn stones for support.

The wind gusting in through the jagged fringe of torn leading was a visible entity as it coursed and swirled around the shadowed interior of the building. Its effect on Nick was hypnotic. As it eddied and funneled and danced before him, he saw strange pictures forming on its thick, spinning surface.

The barren room began to take on a new form as Nick watched dazed and in awe. He saw carved wooden pews take shape on what had been a cold and empty floor. There were flowers on a cloth-covered altar; candles flickered through the swirling mist, and the whine of the wind became a hymn. A choir slowly materialized before his eyes, while pews appeared and then filled with dark frock-coated men, and women in bonnets and long-skirted gowns.

Gradually the music changed, the sweet, high female voices being overshadowed by the drone of a male chorus intoning a doleful Latin chant. The worshipers in the pews changed, too, in a slow metamorphosis to doublet and hose beneath fur-lined coats with wide, embroidered sleeves. Near the silver-decked altar were dark, tonsured figures, their hands raised in prayer.

Then Nick stared in silent fascination through the gusting whirlwind as the very fabric of the building seemed to change around him. Pillars of marble rose upward as medieval stone walls melted away, and the floor beneath his feet took on a mosaic pattern of entwined foliage and serpents and horsemen in pursuit of game. Nude statues emerged from the mists to line the wall of columns, and figures in tunics no less white than the marble marched in silent procession to the altar stone.

There before the altar was a milk white lamb held fast by a young boy, staring upward at a towering female figure poised above him with a knife upraised to the sky. The Latin chant remained, but it, too, had changed, grown more discordant, more of a rhythmic recitation than a song. It ceased abruptly as the knife blade curved downward in a single sweep, spilling the lamb's crimson blood out onto white marble and into a silver cup, poised to capture its flow. Then there was silence.

Nick continued to watch as the mists before him thickened and then parted again on a moonlit landscape. What had been marble columns a moment before now sprouted upward to incredible heights, taking on the gray and wrinkled skin of

full-grown oaks. The floral mosaic became a green forest carpet beneath Nick's feet as he stared out at a solemn gathering
in an ancient sacred place.

The wind carried sounds of a reed flute and the gentle
chink of bronze and glass hung from tree limbs swayed by the
breeze. A sonorous hum came from shadowy figures gathered
in the gloom beneath the great trees; most were dressed darkly
in leather and rough woolen tunics, but some wore long white
robes, luminescent in the filtered predawn light of the grove.
All around the perimeter of the majestic forest cathedral were
carved wooden figures, stylized male and female symbols and
other creatures out of dreams, all driven on sharpened stakes
into the ground.

A shape in the shadows moved slightly and a dark crouching form came into view: a black-haired youth on his knees,
head bent forward and held in check by a gold-bearded warrior chieftain. Above him a broad-shouldered figure in white
stood in the shadow of the largest oak, arms outstretched,
holding aloft the golden instrument of sacrifice, a double-
bladed axe. With stoic disdain, the chieftain roughly pulled a
torn and dirty bloodred cloak from the bent shoulders of the
kneeling youth. The war band murmured approval.

Prayers for strength and prayers for vengeance were
shouted out to the Dark Mother who gave life to all things,
and to her servant, the horned god of death and revenge. Then
in a glittering arc the axe blade fell like a monstrous pendulum
on its backswing. Nick's mind went numb as the blade
thunked home. He pressed himself to the wall, trying desperately to meld into its cold and senseless stones to escape the
terrible drama being played out before him.

After a moment Nick slowly opened his eyes to find the
church returned to its natural form, but filled now with light
and noise and a musky animal scent carried on the still-howl-
ing wind. There was a movement at the far end of the nave,
then the rasping sound of stone grating on stone. Nick stared
in horror as the heavy granite altar moved, heaving itself off
its foundations and then slowly, steadily levitating upward. As
the altar hung motionless midway between the vaulted ceiling
and its torn foundation, a shape took form on it: a human
shape, its pale, naked flesh distinguishable as female even in
the gloom. Through the swirling mists Nick watched a
masked figure in white raise a fistful of shining yellow hair

and cruelly hack it off with the slash of a golden blade.

Suddenly his eyes were torn from this spectacle by a bone-shaking shudder and rumbling beneath his feet, like thunder underground. With a terrible ripping sound rising above the mad howl of the wind, the stones in the center of the floor were pushed upward from below and then heaved broken to either side. A fiery orange glow illuminated the small room from underground as a figure of huge dimensions, powerful as a whirlwind but intangible as the wind, rose up from the smoking fissure in the floor. Thick and black like the smoke of an oil fire, it took shape, filling the cramped structure to its rafters and then hanging before the levitating altar stone, humming potently with kinetic energy.

For a moment, the ancient church was filled with electrical charge. Nick felt the hair on his neck bristle and tasted the metallic tang of ozone on the dry surface of his tongue. Lightning flashed and crackled outside the shattered window above him like the death throes of the world. Pulsing with life, the night black figure, its horns now taking shape, bent forward between Nick and the helpless female form on the altar.

In cold desperation, too shocked to think why, Nick dug into his pocket and grasped the gold talisman Gwenillan had given him, his only real link with her now. With a strangled cry he threw it wildly at the beast reaching out for him.

The crash of the altar stone was terrible dropping back onto its shattered foundations as the nightmare figure collapsed inward on itself like so much oily smoke. Nick collapsed with it to the cold stone floor and the blessed relief of oblivion.

THE
FOURTH
DAY

CHAPTER 23

Thursday, 1 A.M.
Gog Magog Farm

... a lamentation and an ancient tale of wrong,
Like a tale of little meaning though the words are
   strong;
Chanted for an ill-used race of men that cleave the
   soil...
Till they perish and they suffer, some 'tis whispered
   down in hell.

Alfred Lord Tennyson (1809—1892)
Trinity College

The soldiers came out of the trees on horseback. Several hundred strong, the sound of their beasts' hooves pounding the earth was like thunder underground.

Dawn was a narrow ribbon of pink along the horizon, its arrival a silent signal for the charge. The rosy first light touched on metal at shoulders and chests of horsemen and glinted off bronze cheek guards on crested helmets. At their vanguard rode the officers, marked out by flowing red horsehair crests and billowing capes. These red-cloaked leaders brandished swords, while the others carried iron-tipped spears or blazing torches, leaving traces of flame on the air as they bounded down the hillside. The thunderclap and shout of their charge brought forth the frightened faces of women and children from the darkened doorways of the village below them. The soldiers knew where the men of the tribe were on this dawn of a heathen holy day, and they knew what horror awaited them there in their sacred grove.

The mounted men swept down on the undefended village like reapers into a standing field of corn. Many leaped the surrounding ditch and urged their mounts up and over the earthen bank and down among the huddled dwellings, while others funneled in through the unprotected gateway in the earthworks. Torches arched through the air onto dry roofs of thatch. Fleeing women, some clutching infants to their breasts, were struck down with sword and spear. A mounted trumpeter reined in his rearing mount and blew a brassy note on the horn curved around his chest, announcing the admittance to another world of three generations of mothers, daughters, and wives.

The terrified wailing of children mingled with shrieks of the dying. A girl child of five or six, kneeling in shock by the side of her slain grandmother, was hoisted and carried a dozen yards on the point of a lance without making a sound; her frantic mother running after her was trampled under iron-shod hooves. The horse soldiers circled and eddied among the burning huts. Mounted archers cut down any who fled toward the open country or the shelter of the trees. The long hall at the center of the mud-brick and wattle settlement was ablaze, its timber skeleton glowing orange behind a curtain of fire. Black smoke rose in a pall to blot out the rising sun.

At the center of the circling horsemen a woman of middle age and noble bearing stood her ground, an infant girl clutching at the hem of her torn gown. She had dragged a chieftain's broadsword from her burning home and now held it in both hands poised for striking. A crippled horse and dying rider already lay at her bare, bloodied feet. Hatred was in her green gold eyes and a pagan curse on her lips. From the midst of the melee a horse bore down on her, and a figure in a swirling bloodred cloak knocked the unwieldy weapon from her hands with the clang of metal striking metal. Then the rider wheeled his horse around. The tall woman raised her arm in a futile reflex motion as his short sword began its sure and deadly backswing. . . .

Sara's arm struck hard against the oak headboard of her bed. She pulled a painful knuckle to her lips and tasted blood. Then she remembered the dream. What could it all mean, and why were the dreams so unrelenting, coming to her every night all week?

She slid her legs over the side of the bed and groped for a cotton dressing gown. Then she walked quietly past the sleeping woman and child across the room. Her watch told her that it was after midnight. Regretfully she remembered that this was one of the nights when the entire commune would be awakened soon for one of their prayer ceremonies. In silence she swore a good old American curse with Angle-Saxon roots that even Eleanor Woodbridge would have approved. She had to leave here soon. If only she had a little more money. If only she had somewhere to go . . . or someone to go to.

She wandered out into the hall feeling very lost and alone. Her intention was to go downstairs for a cup of hot milk to help her sleep at least until the prayer meeting. Passing by the bedroom shared by Mrs. Woodbridge and Jan Troop, however, she was startled by a loud voice.

"Jan, you fool!" Then Eleanor Woodbridge's voice dropped in volume, but not in tone. "How can you even think of going through with it now?"

Sara listened, but she did not intend to eavesdrop further until she heard her name.

"Keep it down, Eleanor; do you want to wake the whole house? Your precious Sara is right down the hall—and I'm sure she'd love to hear your plans."

Sara moved nearer the door, glancing back over her shoulder to be sure no one else was about. The bedroom door had been left slightly ajar so that Mrs. Woodbridge's cat could slink in and out during the night. Her voice, speaking more softly now, carried through the crack.

"Leave my plans out of this. We're talking about *your* insane plans. Doesn't it mean anything to you that the police have been here twice in the past week?"

"County police," the Dutchman sneered. "Country bumpkins."

"What about this Inspector Janeway? He's no fool. I tell you we have to be careful."

Sara heard the sound of creaking bedsprings as Jan Troop rolled over onto his side. "Janeway has no jurisdiction here, I told you."

"But he has jurisdiction over David Carpenter and that ass Wenger. I'm worried, Jan. Why have they refused bail?"

Having no answer, Troop tried to obviate the question. "Carpenter and Wenger are cowards. They'll never talk to the police, they're too scared. They know what would happen to them. Anyway, it's all the more reason to move quickly."

The woman's anger was growing, but she kept it under rein. The man with her was a fool, she knew that, but he was not going to drag her down with him. Sara listened as Mrs. Woodbridge threw back the covers and left the bed. The girl hugged the wall, preparing to make a hasty escape, but she heard footsteps moving across the room, away from the door.

"Jan, I'm only going to say this once. If you go through with what you have planned for tomorrow night, then I'm leaving. It's far too dangerous now."

"Go then! Now let me get some sleep before this bloody ceremony you have scheduled for the fucking middle of the night. It will be the last one of those, believe me!"

"I know that you've never believed, Jan," the woman said calmly. "I've used you all along."

"You used me! Eleanor, *no one* believes in all this non-sense the way you do. None of us! Sure, some of them are frightened or stupid...or drugged up enough to think they believe, but they don't, not like you." His laugh was cruel as he rolled away from her response.

Sara strained to hear what Mrs. Woodbridge was saying, but her words were muffled by the man's laughter and by his sneering comments spit back at her even as she spoke. She could make out only the end of the woman's speech.

"Tonight is the end! Tomorrow I'm leaving...and I'm taking Sara with me."

CHAPTER 24

Thursday, 3 A.M.
Gog Magog Farm

Still echoes the dread Name that o'er the earth
Let slip the storm and woke the brood of Hell.
Samuel Taylor Coleridge (1772–1834)
Jesus College

Somewhere not far from the roadside there was the sound of an owl's mournful screech. Not like the cry of a night-hunter, a bird of prey, it was lachrymose, more like the plaintive sound of a harried victim than a carnivore on a blood hunt. Colin Church listened with disinterest. He had been sitting in the unmarked Ford Escort for several hours, waiting and watching, in a small lay-by overlooking Gog Magog Farm.

The storm had been heavy for some time, with high winds and hail, but it had passed now, though dark clouds pushed along by a stiff wind continued to move in steady progression across the moon. Church, who had his window cracked half-way for his cigarette, could see his breath mixed with each exhalation of smoke. Pulling his overcoat closer around his chest, he was tempted to switch on the engine for the heater.

Very little of note had happened during his vigil. Soon after his arrival, a car had pulled into the rutted lane to the farm-house; it was one of the vehicles registered at the farm, driven by the heavyset man called Harrold. All four of the vehicles registered at the farm were now parked in the lighted farm-yard.

Church could just see the front of the house; for a closer look, he would have to leave the car. A light that had been burning in the downstairs parlor window went out. Then, as he watched, the other lights that had been visible also went dark. So they had finally turned in, the sergeant thought, and about time. A county constable would relieve him at 5 A.M., but that was still several hours away. Church leaned back into the seat, trying to make his back conform to the molded vinyl of the Ford's upholstery. Then he noticed that the light in the front parlor had been replaced by a softer glow with the flicker of candlelight.

Pulling himself upright, Church opened his door and then closed it quietly as he climbed out. Flashlight in hand and military-issue binoculars around his neck, he stepped into the fringe of trees. The night air was cold, but full of a crisp, clean scent from the earlier rain. The same rain had made the ground slippery under his feet as he moved forward slowly through fallen leaves and mud until he had a clear view of the house.

Adjusting the notched metal focusing wheel, he watched the blur of the parlor window clear into a glowing tableau backlit by candlelight. A strangely hooded figure stood, back to the window, arms gesturing dramatically as though addressing a group. Oddly, though the window revealed this figure at waist level, no one else was visible in the room. The window was open slightly and Church could see tendrils of blue smoke escaping into the night air, but the speaker's words did not carry.

The sergeant had begun to move closer when the figure at the window raised its arms and a high-pitched humming sound emanated from the apparently empty farmhouse parlor. The strange sound carried on the still country air like the voice of a single being. Church stopped and raised his glasses in time to see the speaker turn slowly toward the window. He saw the intense eyes and dark features of Eleanor Woodbridge under the red hood as the woman spread her arms, reaching for the drapes hanging on either side of the window frame. Behind her, the disembodied voices took shape as a dozen or more men, women, and children rose from their sitting positions on the floor. All were draped in loose white robes. For an instant, Church caught sight of Harrold leading a girl with golden hair toward the front of the group. He was struck by the empty, glazed look in the girl's eyes just before the heavy drapes were yanked together, blotting out the scene entirely.

At that instant the humming also ceased and the glow of candles behind the curtains was snuffed out. Church was left wondering if he had seen anything at all. Once again he was surrounded only by wet grass and trees and the somnolent sounds of night in the country.

Back in the car, Church switched on the engine. As the heat took the chill from his bones, he lit a fag. Somewhere nearby the owl again sounded its ambiguous cry. Janeway would make his move soon, he told himself, maybe before this day was out. When he did, Mr. Jan Troop and company would be humming a very different tune. Sergeant Church drew deeply on his smoke and leaned back in the seat, smiling with satisfaction at his choice of words.

> Grey twilight poured on dewy pastures, dewy trees
> Softer than sleep—all things in order stored,
> A haunt of ancient peace.
> > Alfred Lord Tennyson (1809–1892)
> > Trinity College

It was dark under the shadow of the ancient trees in the grove. A multitude of men and boys were gathered in silence, some armed and all dressed in their finest clothing, armor, and furs. Nick saw it all through the window of sleep from the cold floor of St. Peter's.

There was the glint of gold and copper and bronze among the crowd facing the white-robed holy men. A heavy gold torque shone at the throat of the high priest, the Magus, standing at the center of the congregation and flanked by two Druids on either side. The steely gray of his beard showed his age, while his position beside the war chief gave evidence of his high status.

The tribal chieftain, with his golden mustaches and conical helmet of polished bronze, was no taller, no more bull-shouldered, than the high priest by his side. Around the chief stood his seven sons, the oldest not yet twenty-one and the youngest barely ten. All were dressed in tunics dyed with the brightest colors and armed with broadswords hand-crafted to their varying sizes and strengths.

Ranged behind the priests, the chief, and his sons were the oldest and most noble of warriors, the personal bodyguard, each man marked with the scars of his years of service. Among them stood the relatives of the chieftain, his blood kin, the Cendl. Farther back under the trees around the clearing, behind the warriors, were the other men of the tribe—farmers, herdsmen, and artisans. By their sides were their

*sons who had not yet reached manhood and also the old men
of the tribe, some leaning on swords or spears that had tasted
blood in their youth and now served them better as canes.*

*All the men of the Celangi waited in silence in the clearing
for the dawn. Ornaments of glass and metal hanging down
from ghostly tree branches overhead made discordant music
on the early morning breeze, while a reed flute wove a me-
lodic harmony with their irregular counterpoint. Stylized
images of carved wood protruded from the ground fog eddy-
ing around the bases of the great oaks that formed their temple. Nearby a natural spring added its gentle sound as it
boiled over from an opening in the earth to form a stream
through the forest. It was a scene familiar to countless generations of men—from the shadowed Isles of Erin to the vast
steppes beyond the Black Sea—for millennial ages before the
triumph of the Christian God.*

*The wind seemed to die as the Magus turned his back to
the assembled warriors and tribesmen, dramatically raising
his arms above his head. His eyes remained closed until his
back was to them. Stretching out before the high priest was
the pathway from the Sacred Grove to the edge of the forest,
running straight and true to the east and sloping slightly like a
dark, green tunnel toward the horizon line on the flatlands
below. Slowly the Magus lowered one hand, his inverted palm
outstretched so that from where the men of the tribe stood, it
seemed to rest on the very horizon at the end of their line of
sight. Small boys peered out at the spectacle from behind their
fathers' knees. Then, with painful slowness, the hand inched
upward, and with it came first a hazy pink luminescence and
then the glowing red orb of the sun, as though attached and
pulled upward by the downturned palm of the Magus.*

*There was an audible intake of breath from the assembled
crowd and murmurs of approval and prayer. Surely this
would mean an easy winter and good planting in the spring;
there were taxes to be paid to the Roman governor, and years
of warfare had taken the lives of many young men who would
be missed at times of planting and harvest and in the hunt. All
those gathered under the sacred oaks prayed that the Sky God
would change the fortunes of the Celangi. All hoped that the
powers of the Magus would make it happen. But there were
many men in the forest clearing who still put their trust in the
older gods, in the Great Mother. They whispered prayers to*

her as the god of the Druids showed his fiery face above the horizon. These men cursed the peace that had been forced on them by the Romans, and some relished the vengeance that had recently been inflicted on a son of Rome for his violation of their Grove and the defilement of the daughter of their chief.

Then, suddenly, a new shape filled the light at the end of the forest path to the horizon. A dark and moving shape, blotting out the rim of the sun. A steady drumbeat was carried to their ears along with the rhythmic tramp of military sandals. The Magus dropped his arms and spun around toward the alarmed crowd. Warriors looked to their weapons, and children stared around with frightened eyes. In the distance there was a trumpet call and the ominous sound of hoofbeats like thunder underground. A common thought ran through the brains of all the Celangi like an iron-tipped arrow. The village! The women! Wives, mothers, daughters!

As the dark outline of shapes moved closer, the warriors saw men pressed close together, marching three abreast up the path. Shields and spears took shape, and polished steel helmets reflected coral in the rising sun. The men in the clearing looked for escape from the trap, but in every direction they heard the tramp of feet through the dry autumn underbrush of the forest. More horns sounded above the steady thunder of military drums. Smoke darkened the sky visible at the backs of the marching troops, and the screams of loved ones in the burning village were in every man's ears.

The chieftain tried not to think of his wife and infant daughter. Instead the face of his older daughter formed unbidden in his mind: he saw again the look of sadness in her eyes at their last parting. It was because he loved her so, loved her more than any father loved a daughter, that he had promised her to the gods as a priestess. That she die under the swirling river waters had been demanded by the gods. It was the girl who had brought this tragedy upon her people; she and the dark outland boy who had tried to take her away from her people, away from the Sacred Grove where she was sworn to serve for all her days. The shame of what they had done could not be washed away even with his death and her ritual drowning.

The war chief turned away from his own thoughts and urged his panicking men to stand fast. They quickly formed up *with him in a circle around the clearing, the priests, the old men, and boys in the center. Those who did not have better weapons with them picked up fallen branches and drew eating knives from their belts. Two of the white-robed Druids with enough youth and strength to fight were given swords by old veterans no longer able to wield them. Then the chieftain gathered his sons around him and touched each of the seven on the shoulder tenderly, stroking the white-blond head of his youngest one last time before turning to face the foe.*

The steady beat of drums and marching feet drew nearer as the enemy came into view. Through the mist rising from the forest floor a wall of shields took shape, crashing through the underbrush on all sides of the Grove and its now-crowded clearing. Behind the sturdy rectangular shields were the brown campaign tunics and steel armor of Roman legionaries, but only their hobnail sandals and the metal curve of cheek plates and helmets showed to their enemies.

Only when the trap had fully closed around the outnumbered men in the forest clearing was the order given to halt. Then there was silence for a long moment. The gentle chink of wind chimes and the dry rustle of oak leaves could again be heard, incongruous with the suppressed violence in the air.

On a shouted command, the deadly Roman throwing spears were released and the men in the clearing fell like wheat under a storm of hail. Though many of the Romans could not throw well in the cramped conditions, few of the defenders had brought shields and they had no defense against the withering pilum *that fell on them. The youngest son of the chief was one of the first to fall, pierced through the throat by a short, steel-tipped spear. The war chief's face twisted in a grimace of anger and pain as he looked down on the boy who had been his favorite in all things. He raised his sword to heaven and bellowed a curse that could be heard even above the screams of the wounded and dying around him.*

There was a smooth metallic whisper, like a scythe cutting through the air, as the Romans drew their swords. Commands were shouted, trumpets blared, and the wall of shields began to close on the stunned warriors in the clearing. The advancing ranks parted and re-formed as troops pushed their way through the forest, circumventing the larger trees and trampling saplings underfoot. The undergrowth was too thick to

*allow a charge, but the battle-hardened legionaries advanced
slowly and steadily, like a machine of metal and oiled leather
controlled by some unseen clockwork mechanism. It was unnerving to the Celts, used to the shrieking and running of their
own wild charges into battle. They waited now for the onslaught, shaken and depleted by the rain of javelins. Wounded
men leaned on their comrades for support, and young boys
cried as they clung to their fathers' legs.*

*There were tears of rage on the chieftain's face as he
shouted out a command to the warriors of the Cendl. They
answered his call with shouts of defiance and then followed
him forward, screaming for blood and vengeance as they
hurled themselves on the advancing ranks of the foreign in-
vader. They were warriors and they would die in the attack,
not standing and waiting for their enemy to fall upon them.*

*For a short time, the ancient grove was filled with the
sounds of struggle and exhortation. Sharpened steel struck
sparks from iron and cut through bronze and bone as cries of
exhilaration and pain mingled with the clash of arms. Adrena-
line was furiously pumped into men's blood only to be released by a sword thrust or the savage hack of a battle axe
slicing through sinew and veins to spill the crimson life force
onto the dark forest floor. The Celangi fought madly, out of
desperation and despair, and the roots of the great oaks drank
up the blood of hundreds before the sun was high on the eastern horizon.*

*The chieftain saw the old comrades of his war band fall
one by one to the short, stabbing swords of the Romans,
though many of the dark outlanders fell beside them. Six of his
seven sons lay dead, their youthful weapons lying shattered
and trampled under Roman sandals. Following the warriors
into the fray, the lightly armed farmers and artisans had been
no match for the trained legionaries, and soon only the war
chief, his eldest son, and the high priest remained on their
feet, exhausted and drenched in blood. But the Romans
paused for a moment before their final, irresistible charge.
Wild-eyed legionaries and half-savage mercenary troops from
the German forests and Netherlands marshes caught up in the
blood lust of battle were reined in with difficulty by their officers.*

*A young general on horseback, his face weather-beaten
and looking older than his thirty-six years, stared down with*

stony eyes as the three embattled Celts staggered back toward their sacred shrine. They rooted themselves in the shadows of the tallest oak for a final stand, surrounded by their icons and images of their gods and demons. Here they would die. Their enemy was barely a sword-thrust away, but the Romans were held in check by their commander. The Celtic chieftain, his helmet gone and a deep gash in one shoulder, stared deeply into the eyes of his only surviving son. He tilted the boy's trembling chin upward in proud defiance.

Wind chimes and the cries of the wounded blended with the sounds of creaking leather and the chink of metal. In the shadowed branches of the sacred tree, a face of oak seemed to look down with equal dispassion on the terror of the dying and the dark resolve of those still standing.

Throwing down the broken blade of a broadsword that had served him well, the high priest turned toward the base of the oak tree with a face. His back to his enemies in contempt, he ripped the bloodied white robes of priesthood from his muscular body. Then the Magus leaned down toward what he knew lay hidden in the morning fog at the gnarled roots of the holy tree. When he stood and turned once more toward them, the Romans saw the powerful, sweat-glistening torso of a man . . . crowned by the horned head of a snarling beast. Sacred mistletoe twined around the curving horns of the mask, and the ceremonial double-headed axe he raised in his strong right hand was cast in the same precious metal as the gleaming torque at his throat.

There were murmurs from the Roman ranks. Prayers were whispered to Mars, the soldiers' god. Other legionaries, initiates of the mystery cult of Mithras, called on their deity, personified like the god of the Celts in the rising sun at their backs. The general on horseback raised his baton to quiet his troops in preparation for signaling the attack. His arm hanging motionless in the air, he spoke aloud in the conquering Latin tongue that both the chieftain and the high priest grudgingly understood.

"People of the Celangi, you have brought this punishment upon yourselves. You must have known that the great emperor and the gods of Rome would demand exacting vengeance for the slaying of the young officer. Sacrificing a girl, even your own daughter, is not enough to atone . . ."

At the mention of his daughter, the chieftain's piercing cry sounded through the blood-drenched forest. Then the voice of the Magus behind his sacred mask chanted a blood curse in the old tongue, calling down the wrath of the gods of earth and sky, the vengeance of the Dark Mother and the God of Thunder on the dark foreigners who had slaughtered his people in the Sacred Grove of the Trinity.

"Death to you and to your sons in every generation!" he cursed them. "Every generation will taste death twice for this black day!"

The Roman waited to hear no more. He lowered his baton and his troops rolled forward to the sound of drum and horn, swallowing up the final desperate resistance of the Celts in a sea of armor, leather, and slashing steel. Almost before his curse had died on the air, the Magus had fallen beside his dead chieftain and the chieftain's son. But no man dared reach for the golden prize at the High Priest's throat, or even for the cast-gold axe lying in the dead Druid's blood. Not yet. For, although the bodies of slain warriors lay scattered and broken in the forest clearing, sprawled in the awkwardness of death, they were only empty husks. Even as the victors watched, they later swore they had seen the shades of the fallen Celangi rise upward and merge into the living trunks of the trees that formed their temple—from one life to another.

The Roman ranks parted and drew back as their red-cloaked general pushed forward, urging his mount over the bodies of the dead toward the Sacred Grove. There, among the carved wooden images thrusting up from the mist-shrouded roots of ancient trees, he saw what he had come to avenge. One twisted face impaled on a wooden stake was not a pagan deity or totem of fertility carved from wood like the others and hung with glass and gold and holly. Black matted hair crowned this head staked out in the Grove of the Sacred Trinity, and empty, staring eyes the color of the summer sky blankly surveyed the blood-soaked woods.

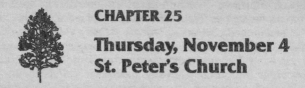

CHAPTER 25

Thursday, November 4
St. Peter's Church

A fire was once within my brain;
And in my head a dull, dull pain;
And fiendish faces, one, two, three,
Hung at my breast, and pulled at me.

William Wordsworth (1770—1850)
St. John's College

Nick felt the hardness of the stone against his spine, then the cold. Slowly he opened his eyes on the empty room. Dream images still spluttered in his mind like the afterburn of a Roman candle on a dark evening sky. He remembered the sounds of a horn and drum, and a noise like thunder underground. There were dim recollections of warriors, and of trees, their forms merging wraithlike one into the other. A shouted curse. And there was blood.

Weak gray sunlight filtered in to lighten patches on the flagstone floor of the old church. Nick's joints ached from sleeping on those cold stones, but he gradually shook off the mooring lines of sleep and remembered why he was here. Then, reluctantly, he remembered more.

Standing now, he looked around at the silent emptiness of the Church of St. Peter. No shards of colored glass littered the flagstones; the lead-bound window was intact. There was no gaping fissure where the floor could have been heaved up monstrously from below. Nick was sure the visions that came to him now were more than dreams. They were too clear, and the feelings they evoked too strong. Yet the squat stone altar stood unmoved on its foundations, just as it had when he had entered seeking sanctuary from the storm. Near it on the floor, his eye was attracted by a glint of metal. He walked toward it and stood over the yellow gold of Gwenillan's brooch, staring down at it for a long time as he recalled an unbelievable sequence of events. The coldness of the metal sent a chill up his spine as he bent and retrieved Gwenillan's parting gift. "Keep it near you tonight, and I will be with you," she had said. Suddenly his urge to leave the church was overwhelming.

He pushed open the heavy iron-bound door onto a dismal November morning. The sky had been painted with thick slabs of charcoal gray, hanging motionless, untouched by sun or wind. The storm the night before had freshened the air, but it was cold through Nick's damp tweed jacket. He sneezed as he walked down the narrow path through the moss-covered tombstones, his throat dry and sore from sleeping in wet clothing on a bare stone floor. But he stopped himself from going further in recounting the roots of his present misery. Once he began to concentrate, he did not know where it might lead.

The strong, even features of Gwenillan's face took shape in his mind, but he rejected the image. He felt as worn and beaten in body and spirit as the weathered tombstones around him, leaning drunkenly askew and announcing the passing of men and women already dead for centuries. Nick did not think about their bones under his feet or the dust of even more ancient people buried below them in this long-sacred ground.

A hot shower, dry clothes, and aspirin, he repeated to himself. Hot shower, dry clothes, aspirin. It drove all other thoughts out of his feverish mind. He paused for a moment with his hand on the damp metal of the gate latch to look back at the church's thick and graceless spire looming above him. Surrounded as it now was by more modern buildings and the busy traffic of the Huntingdon Road, it seemed to have been artificially placed here on consecrated ground from some other world and time. Consecrated ground, Nick thought. Remembering what he had seen and heard there in the dark of night, he knew that such things had never been consecrated— not by any hand in heaven above.

His head ached and he thought again of the shower and aspirin that awaited him at Wychfield. After that . . . he did not know. Despite the chill of the morning, he felt a sticky sweat on his face. As his hand went to his forehead to wipe it away, he felt the roughness of a small gash, sealed over now with dried blood: the kind of cut that would be made by a jagged splinter of flying glass.

> The soft complaining flute
> In dying notes discovers
> The woes of hopeless lovers.
> > John Dryden (1631–1700)
> > Trinity College

There was something about a spot of polish on the gloss black toe of a shoe that appealed to J. Macvicar Swann. Like shining brasswork or cleaning his pipe, it gave him a deep feeling of satisfaction. He undertook each of these small tasks with elaborate and unvarying ritual. His cloth was linen, one of a number of torn or soiled dinner napkins provided by the college butler. It took the Saddler's polish well, allowing Swann to smooth the paste wax into the leather in slow concentric circles until the entire surface of the shoe appeared in a haze, as though seen through frosted glass.

Old Ted was on duty at the front desk, sorting the morning post and handing out parcels. Ted was Swann's senior by more than a decade, but his senior only in age. With the front desk under control, the head porter could relax with a certain contentment in the back room of the Lodge, the warmth of the gas fire on his knees and the agreeable smells of polish and leather in his nostrils. After a last admiring glance, he placed his handiwork to bake in the heat of the gas stove and leaned back in his chair to do the same.

When the spindly form of Old Ted presented itself in the doorway, clearing its throat for attention, the head porter reluctantly opened his eyes and acknowledged the interruption with a noblesse oblige befitting his position.

"Young gentleman to see you, Mr. Swann," Ted announced in a voice that could just as well have been on forty-year-old celluloid. "Mr. Lombard."

So much for a nap. "I'll be right out."

"Don't get up." Nick Lombard's head appeared over Ted's bony shoulder. "I just wondered if you could spare a minute."

The head porter looked around uneasily. "No trouble at all, sir." He made room by the fire, noting the anxiety in the young American's voice.

Nick sat on a straight-backed chair. "Sorry to barge in like this. I was on my way to see the chaplain, like you suggested, and I thought . . . Swann, you've been here a good many years, you must have seen some strange things."

Swann directed a glance at Old Ted, who turned to amble back to his duties. "Strange things? I suppose so." He looked down at his shoes, quite dry now by the fire. "Do you mind if . . . ?"

"No, go ahead." Nick looked down at his own shoes as he tried to think how to begin. "You must have seen students break down, Swann. Mentally, I mean, so they'd have trouble telling what's going on in their minds from what's really happening."

Swann rubbed rhythmically on the toe of a shoe, bringing out a liquid gloss from the back depths of the leather. "Do you know someone who's having that kind of trouble?"

"I think maybe I am. . . . So do most of my friends. Somehow, I don't know, my dreams seem to be . . . well, taking over."

"You mentioned dreams the last time we talked."

Nick nodded as he watched the porter spit onto his polishing cloth, hardly missing a stroke in his smooth buffing motion. "There are things that I'm sure are real, but if I think about it logically, I know they can't actually have happened —except in a dream. Do you remember the other day, Swann, when I mentioned meeting a girl? Well, when I've been with her, everything has made sense, but when . . . when she's not with me, I wonder if any of it is actually true."

"Young women have lied to young men before, and I daresay young men have done the same." Swann set down one gleaming oxford and slipped his beefy hand into the shank of its mate. Then he paused, extracting his hand and setting the shoe aside, still cloudy with dried polish. "I don't mean to make light of it, Nick, but it sounds a fairly common situation. I think there's something more serious bothering you. Am I right?"

"You're right. It's not so much that she's lied to me—she's hardly told me anything, as a matter of fact. It's just that, right now, I'm half-convinced that I must have dreamed the whole damned thing. Meeting her . . . everything. I can't be sure that anything that's happened to me in the past week is real."

Swann frowned. "I'm a little out of my depth, but if I could suggest . . . Why don't you just sit down with this girl and talk things over?"

"You don't understand. I'm not talking metaphorically. I really don't know anymore if she exists! I don't know where she is . . . who she is! God, I don't know anything . . . after last night." As his voice trailed off, Nick pictured his fist slamming hard into the wall with a gratifying crunch, the plaster forming a crackling mosaic around his hand.

"What happened last night?"

"Too much to explain. Too much I *can't* explain. But that's one reason I'm here. I'm looking for that new porter; Nigel, I think his name is."

"Well, I can save you some time there." Swann's bushy brow furrowed as he thought of Nigel Pinder. "Nigel's not likely to be seen around here. Quit, he did, just yesterday. Running off to join some group of other layabouts on a farm, I gather."

Nick knew that Nigel and the girl he had been with at the bar must have seen Gwenillan, if anyone had, but he despaired of finding either of them now. "Thanks for lending an ear, Swann. I'm going to dump all my problems on Reverend Anglesey." Nick's laugh was feeble as he moved toward the door.

"If you want to talk again, any time at all, Nick . . ."

The young man nodded his thanks and then walked out through the Porter's Lodge past the watery gaze of Old Ted. Swann watched him go before bending with some effort to retrieve the shoe he had set aside by the grate. He picked up his polishing cloth and held it poised over the wax-clouded toe. He was sure there was something more Nick was not telling him. He didn't like the way the boy seemed to be looking out at the world from some other place. Perhaps, the head porter thought, he should also have a word with Reverend Anglesey.

CHAPTER 26

Thursday afternoon
Trinity Hall

I am afraid that, under cover of a revival
of ancient literature, paganism may attempt
to rear its head—as there are some among
Christians that acknowledge Christ in name,
but breathe inwardly a heathen spirit.

> Erasmus of Rotterdam (1466—1536)
> Queens College

"Lewis, I believe I know what Terry Graham meant by the 'fifth day.'" As he spoke, James Anglesey was standing, hands clasped behind his back, near a window in his rooms overlooking the front court of Trinity Hall. They had just finished a light lunch, and Inspector Janeway, to whom he was speaking, pushed aside a plate of Bath biscuits and Double Gloucester cheese.

"I've come across a curious fact—well, quite a number of them actually, as I've just been telling you—but one thing in particular seems to make some sense of this fifth day business." He gazed intently at the gray November sky filling his window as the inspector watched his tired features in profile.

"In every instance where I found a specific date mentioned in relation to one of these curious unsolved murders, it was within five days of either Midsummer's Day or the Eve of All Souls. Usually the body was found on the fifth day after one of those two calendar dates."

Janeway looked thoughtfully down at the glass of pale yellow wine resting on the arm of his chair. "Yes, I've noticed the same coincidence of dates in Terry's notes, but I have trouble seeing what the significance could be. If we are, in fact, searching for some tie-in with a cult religion or ritual murder, then I agree the date of the crime would be significant. Midsummer I can understand. All Souls, yes. But what

is significant about the fifth day *after* those dates? That's
where the theory seems to fall down."

"I've given that a great deal of thought." Anglesey had not
told his old friend about the strange occurrences in the university library or what he had read of the massacre of the Celangi
during the feast of Samain. And he did not intend to.

"You know," he said instead, "we talk about specific dates
and events, days and years, as if these concepts have always
been the same. Actually, time is relative, and our modern
perceptions of it are of very recent origin. We think of All
Hallows' Eve as the last day in October, and Midsummer as
June twenty-fourth, but those are simply dates we have in-
vented for our own use. The events to which they relate are
much more ancient, corresponding to the changing seasons
and movements of the stars. Things men have watched for in
the heavens since long before there was any set calendar.
Who's to say that the dates on our modern calendar correspond to anything fundamental anymore? We think of our calendar in terms of business appointments and vacations, not as
a mystic means of measuring the conjunction of nature with
the cosmos."

Janeway methodically lit a pipe as he listened, his attentive
silence encouraging Anglesey to continue.

"For that matter, the calendar itself is a terribly artificial
thing. The Chinese and the Maya had their own, similar to
ours but not the same. So did the Romans. The European
world used that one for about thirteen hundred years—despite
an error of one day every one hundred and twenty-five years
or so. Finally Pope Gregory got the idea that everything
should be put straight with a new calendar in 1582. Of course,
being English, we didn't reform our calendar here until the
middle of the eighteenth century! That caused no end of confusion for several hundred years.

"But my point is that we have had a rather haphazard progress toward our present system of reckoning the days and
months of the year. Other people at other times have had entirely different systems, equally valid for them. Going back
even before the Romans, men living here where we sit today
had their own methods of counting off the seasons and marking their feast days."

Anglesey poured another glass from the chilled bottle of
Chablis in front of him and offered to do the same for his

guest. The inspector declined and put down his pipe as he spoke. "Yes, I can see how four or five days could easily be lost in the shuffle over the centuries. But I'm still not sure that I see your point."

"Let me try to explain. If, as I believe, this strange series of coincidences has its origin in events that began long before our own time, then there's no reason to suppose that specific modern calendar dates should correspond exactly to what has happened in the past—or what may be about to happen now."

The chaplain stood and paced once more to his window. "Nevertheless, what Terry Graham discovered, and what my brief researches seem to confirm, is that there is a significance to the fifth day after certain calendar dates as we now reckon them—five days after Midsummer and the same number of days after the Eve of All Souls. It's as though there is another, much more ancient, calendar operating in parallel to our own. Perhaps a calendar that has never undergone either a Roman or a Gregorian reformation. A primeval calendar based entirely on the seasons and the circuits of the stars."

Janeway's pipe bowl glowed orange as he inhaled and then expelled a stream of powder blue smoke toward the ceiling. "James, I'm not sure I understand the implications of all you're saying, but if you are suggesting the possibility of some secret society—some sort of religious cult, perpetrating ritual murder over a period of many centuries . . ."

"I know you're uncomfortable with this line of thought, Lewis, but please bear with me. There have been certain events over the past several days that I haven't yet mentioned to you—some that I can't mention even now—but I'm convinced that we are dealing here with something deeper than surface appearances."

Janeway tapped the bowl of the pipe on the ceramic edge of an ashtray. A last few shreds of blackened tobacco needed prying loose with a finger, which then had to be wiped clean on his handkerchief; the nuisance of the contraption had nearly convinced him to risk his doctor's anger by going back to cigarettes. "So you believe that because tomorrow is the fifth day—that is, the fifth day after All Souls' Eve—there's likely to be another murder?"

"I do. There is a pattern here we may not understand fully, but we cannot afford to ignore it. Poor Terry Graham saw it, or the beginning of it."

"What about the thirty-three-year interval?" Janeway asked. "Why thirty-three years between each pair of murders and the next?"

Anglesey shifted some irrelevant papers on his desk. "I don't have all the answers, Lewis. I can only guess, but I do know that 'three' has been a mystical number for as long as men have kept records of their beliefs. Why? Well, there's earth, fire, and water; land, sea, and air; man, woman, child. The triumvirate is basic to our understanding of the world around us. Think of our own religion—Father, Son, and Holy Spirit, three Persons in one God. This very college is named after the Trinity. So are the woods where you found Terry Graham."

The chaplain leaned back on his chair, running his palms over the carved beaks of goshawks on its arms. "The Greeks had their triumviral gods, too—the three brothers, Zeus, Poseidon, and Hades, ruling over the three realms of nature. So did the Romans, of course, and many other ancient peoples. Even the Japanese had their gods of heaven, earth, and hell. Here in Britain, the number 'three' was an important mystical number for the Celts, whose beliefs seem to figure in this in more ways than one."

Janeway did not attempt to relight his pipe, content simply to clutch its lingering warmth in his palm. "Yes, but why *thirty*-three, if you can continue your educated guesswork?"

Anglesey shrugged. "Three taken ten times? The sacred number written twice? I don't know. But traditionally thirty-three has been taken to represent one generation of human life. For example, we're told that Christ lived on earth for thirty-three years. Now, no one knows for certain how many years Jesus actually lived as a man, but the writers of the Gospels knew the significance in the ancient world of a thirty-three-year time span. One generation."

He sipped at the pale wine without really tasting its crispness. "Whatever the reason, the pattern we've discovered has one, sometimes two, murders taking place in similar circumstances in intervals of thirty-three years. Killings in every generation for almost two thousand years."

"Of course, there are gaps in your research," the inspector observed, scratching his mustache. "I know you've had very little time, and I agree there seems to be a pattern. I just don't understand why."

"Don't you see? *Why* doesn't really matter! What is important is that someone's life may be in danger as we sit here talking!"

Anglesey calmed himself before continuing. "One more thing, Lewis. I've said that the murders were *reported* five days after those dates. Many of the bodies were discovered in the early morning—like young Cordillo—which would indicate that the killings actually took place during the hours of darkness between the fourth and fifth days."

"And today is the fourth day after the Eve of All Saints," Janeway continued. "So we are right now at the time of greatest danger—if we are serious about following the natural extension of the pattern you've outlined."

"I'm very serious, Lewis. I believe that tonight there will be another killing. I would almost go so far as to say that after tonight or tomorrow morning, the danger may be past—at least for this generation."

"Which leaves us very little time."

"Very little time," the chaplain agreed.

"But what in hell should we be on guard against?"

" 'What in hell' may be more apt than you think, Lewis. But please, let's give it our attention. I believe there is a young man somewhere in Cambridge who is in grave danger at this very moment."

"But who? There are thousands of students, thousands more young men in the town, not to mention visitors, tourists—"

"Yes," Anglesey cut in, "a foreign visitor would be most likely. Many of the victims in the past have been from Mediterranean countries—'the dark men from the sea' our ancestors called them, because they always came in ships."

"Among the thousands of foreigners in Cambridge, where do we look? Why, in the university alone there are—"

"I know, Lewis, I know. The odds against us are tremendous."

The inspector was alarmed by the way his friend's face seemed to have aged years in just the past few days. "One more thing about this evening," he said. "As I mentioned to you, we've been watching a commune group that has taken up residence in the Gog Magogs. Two of them are in custody and they have become very cooperative since their solicitor explained what they might gain by testifying against their former colleagues. According to them, tonight is an important night, as well, for the Pentacle Commune."

"Pentacle? A cabalistic sign. Interesting. Go on."

The inspector looked at his watch and thought of all he had to do before that evening. "I'm telling you this in strictest confidence, but there is a drug raid planned for tonight, and I've called out every available man. We're watching a cottage near the Huntingdon Road where the transaction is supposed to take place, and there will also be a search at the group's farm in the Gog Magog area. So you see, I simply won't have the manpower to devote to anything else tonight." He watched frustration twist the silent features of his old friend's face.

Stretching his legs out in front of him, Janeway tugged at his trouser legs just above the knee and then stood. He walked to the book-lined windowsill. "James, whatever we may know about patterns and times, we still have no idea where the threat may be coming from. Even if I had every constable on the force available tonight, I wouldn't know what instructions to give them. Follow every young foreign man in the city? Put out an alert for warlocks?"

Anglesey also stood and turned away in irritation.

"I'm sorry, James, but surely you see what I mean. Certainly what you have been saying has made an impression on me. I take your advice very seriously, but as a policeman, I'm left with very little to act on!" The inspector sighed as he looked at his friend's rigid back. "All I can promise is to do what I can with what I have."

There was a knock at the door, and Janeway watched the chaplain's long, stooping back cross the room and disappear into a small foyer. The inspector had to admit that he was confused. He had learned long ago to respect Anglesey's intelligence and insight on a great variety of matters, but he was beginning to doubt that it had been wise to bring the chaplain into a matter as grave as this; he had already gone much further than Janeway had anticipated when asking for assistance. Now he could not reconcile what he heard from the chaplain with his own rational investigations. His theories and Anglesey's were like oil and water; both had substance, but they were of differing natures and would not mix. What bothered him, perhaps more than anything, was that after more than four months on this case, Anglesey's rather extraordinary theories seemed more substantive to him than any of his own.

But what could he do about it, with time apparently so short?

He heard voices and the closing of a door before the chaplain returned to the room, smiling apologetically for the interruption. "Just one of the students," he explained.

"I'm just about to leave, if you have an appointment."

"No, no," the chaplain assured him. "It was only Nick Lombard, the young American you met at dinner. He just stopped by to chat. Probably nothing serious. I asked him to stop back later."

Janeway watched his friend ease his arthritic joints back into a sitting position behind his bird-of-prey desk. "You're right," the chaplain continued. "I confess, I don't know what to do either. But I have a terrible feeling that time is running out."

The inspector was worried that Anglesey was right, but he had no idea what could be done about it. He glanced at his watch as he rose. "I must go, James. I've got quite a lot to do before this evening." He stopped and smiled for the first time during their talk. "Mind you, if everything does go as planned, it will be the biggest coup for the department in quite some time."

Anglesey did not return his smile. "I understand that you won't have men to spare, but if you can just—"

Janeway took the older man's arm as they walked toward the door. "Every constable on the force will be at his peak tonight, primed for action. This sort of operation doesn't come our way often. What's more, I promise you that every one of them will be under direct orders from me to be on the alert for anything out of the ordinary. Absolutely anything, whether it appears to have any connection with our drug arrests or not."

The two men moved across the worn Chinese carpet arm in arm. In the cramped foyer Janeway paused, one hand on the doorknob. "James, this group, this commune, they're involved in drugs and in some sort of cult religion that appears to have a very powerful hold over most of them. In moving against them, I believe we may also be taking a step toward solving the larger question we're both concerned about. In any case, it's the only positive action I can conceive of right now. Once we have these people in custody, I intend to make them talk about anything that could have the slightest bearing on last summer's murder . . . and what happened to Terry Graham. The woods where he was found, and where we found Cordillo's clothing, is very close to the cottage they're so secretive about."

"Yes, Trinity Wood," the chaplain said thoughtfully. "You may be right, Lewis. I sincerely hope you are."

James Anglesey closed the door slowly behind the inspector and then listened to his fading footsteps on the stone stairs winding down from his rooms. He remained standing in the dim light of the narrow entryway and reflected on the events of the past several days and what might lay ahead tonight. He knew that Janeway would do his job well; his men would be out in force and as alert for action as if they were preparing to cross the Litani with the young lieutenant at dawn. But the chaplain was also aware that the police would be operating on a different level, in a different dimension than the one in which he was now convinced the danger lay. He realized that he also had a task ahead of him on the threshold of the fifth day after All Hallows' Eve. Suddenly he felt very weak and unprepared, but he knew there was a role for him that he could not expect the police to comprehend.

CHAPTER 27

Thursday afternoon
Trinity Hall

Alone!—that worn-out word,
So idly spoken, and so coldly heard.
> Edward Bulwer Lytton (1803—1873)
> Trinity Hall

Even as Nick Lombard climbed down the narrow stone steps of "F" Staircase, he was not sure why he had gone to see the chaplain. How could he have put his fears into words when he was not even sure what they were? Stop by later, Anglesey had offered, but Nick was not certain he would. It was difficult to remember being certain about anything.

His headache was persistent now, throbbing painfully as he followed the walk bisecting the brilliant green of the quadrangle. He didn't imagine that a drink would take the pounding away, but it might help him to forget what had caused it. There was a soreness in his joints and a feverish ache from lying on the cold stone floor of St. Peter's. He buttoned his red flannel jacket with clumsy fingers. All his movements, physical and mental, were in low gear as he pulled himself up the stone stairway toward the college bar. It was more than lack of sleep that made him feel as he did. It was a lack of something else—of perspective. A lack of logic.

His sense of balance and proportion in daily activities, a formerly unquestioned belief in action and reaction in a constant flux of readjustment, had been shaken by the events of the past few days. Logic and reason, the reliable guides he had always lived by and clung to in times of stress, had been challenged and called into doubt. There was more at stake now than just an aching desire to see Gwenillan. He felt that his own sanity was in question. More and more he felt rooted in the dreams that came to him every time he closed his eyes; so much so that he dreaded sleep at the same time that another part of him longed to sleep and even to dream, if dreams were the only way he would find her again. He knew that there was something hidden in those dark forest dreams, something to be feared, though he could never entirely grasp its meaning.

The most troubling question, the question he could not put out of his mind, was how he could have spent most of three evenings and one full afternoon with someone who had only been there in his imagination. Could there really have been no one by his side walking down Castle Hill, standing on Magdalene Bridge or talking in the gardens, punting on the Cam? As soon as his hopes began to rise that surely his friends must have been mistaken, the hard fact of John Blessed's photographs dragged him back to an unwilling acceptance of what surely must be reality.

If he had been alone, he wondered why no one had noticed. But would there have been anything to notice? What if the undergraduate walking toward him now imagined that the Queen Mother was ambling along beside him, holding his arm and telling him secrets of the royal family?

During nearly all his conversations with Gwenillan, they had been alone: in Trinity Grove, at the sports hall, on their picnic, in Magdalene gardens. He suddenly recalled the curious glances of a don and his companion in Magdalene College. And what about the puzzled look from Nigel in The Pickeral when Nick had accused the young porter of taking his seat? For most of the thirty minutes or so that they—no, he forced himself to accept it, *he*—had been in the crowded, noisy pub, Nigel or anyone else looking in his direction would simply have seen a young man seated with his back to the bar eating sandwiches and drinking a beer. They would not have known that he was listening to Gwenillan tell him about her life and the tragic deaths of her family.

John Blessed's hearty laughter met him at the doorway even before he could see the Irishman standing at the bar with Ainsley-Hay and Guy Chamberlain. He nearly turned to leave, but Blessed spotted his red jacket and called out. Nick reconsidered. Maybe a drink and a talk with friends would do him more good than an hour of soul-searching with Reverend Anglesey.

Blessed tried to make it easy for him, continuing to talk about a planned trip to Dublin and allowing Nick to listen quietly. Guy affected disinterest, asking Nick what he was drinking.

"Whiskey," Nick said, thinking of bourbon. The barman reached for Scotch, but was stopped by a shout from John Blessed, who pointed to Jamison's Irish. "He said, 'whiskey'! Now, where was I?"

"Halfway to Dublin," St. John reminded him.

"Ah, the things I could show you in Dublin."

Nick listened, sipping at his drink. The easy conversation of his friends made him feel better, but he could not join in.

"The only travel I have planned for Michaelmas Term is St. Moritz," Ainsley-Hay said in a tone that made it sound like an obligation any sane man would dread.

"Speaking of 'Alps,' are you taking Christina with you?" Guy laughed at his own quip and then turned to Nick. "What about your girl, Nick? Seems to me I heard last night that you'd found one?" It was obvious that Guy had no recollection of how things had ended the previous evening in The Pickeral, but the embarrassed looks of his two companions made it clear that they did.

"You know," St. John said quickly, "if we don't get down to hall soon, we'll get no lunch." Guy protested that he hadn't finished his drink, but Blessed told him to take it with him, pushing him toward the door with Hay's assistance.

"Tell me more about this goddess later!" Guy shouted.

John Blessed took a last swallow of Guinness and wiped the foam from his beard. "Had lunch yet, Nicko?"

"Not really hungry. Think I'll stay here awhile."

"No, walk down with me anyway," Blessed insisted. "You look awful. Fresh air will do you more good than whiskey."

"That's news, coming from you."

The two friends left the bar by way of a modern outdoor terrace. Walking down the broad, cascading steps encircled by the medieval brick and stone, neither of them noticed the incongruity of their surroundings.

"Feeling any better this morning?"

"Flu coming on, I think." Nick looked down at his feet where the crunch of the gravel walk began. "But it's more than that."

"Sorry about Guy just now."

"Well, I'm glad someone's forgotten the fool I made of myself."

"Look here, mate, there must be a way to reason this out. This girl . . . what was her name?"

Nick noted that he used the past tense. "Gwenillan," he said. The sound of her name spoken aloud brought Gwen's face to him again. He blinked away the painful image.

"What else did she tell you about herself?"

They had stopped on the gravel path near the corner of the old library. "Said she came from a small country village. I gathered her father was some sort of local bigwig. But he's dead. In fact, her whole family was killed, parents, baby sister, and I think she said seven brothers. She didn't say how it happened, and I didn't ask, but it must have been a hell of a shock for her."

"Whew, I can imagine. What else?"

"Can't we just forget it? I don't need this needling."

"No," Blessed insisted. "I want to help. What else? What's she like?"

Present tense, Nick noted. He looked up at the black and white crescent of Trinity Hall on the peaked roof of the library as he considered the question. "It's strange, but she has almost a sixth sense about nature. I've never met anyone so in touch with their surroundings. From growing up in the country, I suppose, but she's shown me a whole new way of looking at the world."

For a moment, Nick forgot his melancholy and smiled. "She looks at a duck on the river, and where you or I would see a duck, she sees some sort of magical creature that's equally at home on water, land, or in the air. The simplest things have magic for her." He explained what she had told him about mistletoe and oak, how everything held some special meaning for her. "And when she told me all this, it was impossible to be cynical or make a joke of it, she was so natural and matter-of-fact about it all."

Nick was lost in his thoughts now, back in Magdalene garden. "It's as though every plant and tree is alive for her—I mean, really alive, as though they each have a soul. She has a way of making life take on a new dimension. That's what's really magical."

John Blessed ran his fingers through the black tangle of his beard. He watched Nick's face as he talked and saw the memories forming there. He also saw that what was being remembered must be more than a dream. He did not speak until Nick had finished, not wanting to bring his friend back down to earth with too hard a fall.

"Why don't you just phone her up and sort things out?"

"No phone number. Don't know where she lives." Nick looked down at the pattern made by his shoe in the fine gravel. "I first met her coming through Trinity Wood from Madingley Road." He laughed despondently. "So this morning I walked halfway to Madingley looking at goddamn mailboxes."

"You've got it bad, mate. Your word that you met this girl is good enough for me, but it looks like she's been leading you on, maybe about a lot of things. You'll do well to forget about her." He waited until several students had passed. "Nick, you're on a downhill road. Not like yourself at all, and people are noticing it. Drinking more than usual, moping around, quick to lose your temper. Not working, I suppose?"

Nick shook his head in agreement. Then he reached for a handkerchief to catch a series of violent sneezes.

"I think you know what I mean, Nicko. Look at yourself! How did you do that to your head?"

Nick ran a finger across the cut on his forehead, sealed over now by a fresh scab. "An accident."

"Walked into a door, I suppose? And what about this trouble sleeping? Still having dreams?"

"Every time I manage to fall asleep. And they're getting worse, more real. Gotten so I don't want to sleep, however tired I am."

"Is it always the same dream?"

"No, always different . . . but the same in a lot of ways, like they're all linked together somehow. Gwen is in some of them, and a lot of what happens is connected with things we've done together. That's natural, I guess, but other things are . . . well, strange."

"How strange?" John pressed. "Tell me."

Nick watched a group of undergrads cross the court, laughing, joking, the way he would have been not long ago. Then he pictured the dream woods in his mind. "Usually it's like seeing a story being played out, like watching a movie almost. Except there's no order to the scenes. I seem to get different parts of a story in each dream, and I can't figure out how they all fit together."

He concentrated on what he could remember in the light of day. "There are always trees, a forest . . . and one tree seems to have a face. I see people, but they're not like us. They're out of another time, and they talk, but I can't understand most of the words. And there's a strong sense of danger . . . danger and death."

His friend watched Nick's face darken in remembering. "Do you ever remember what's being said?"

"Usually I don't even hear the words. Once, though, I did hear a word very clearly . . . if I can remember it now." Nick tried to recapture his dream of the man in the red cloak. "There was a hunt. Men with spears and swords, and they had torches because it was at night. But they weren't hunting animals. It was a man they were after, and he was running through a forest. I remember someone warned him. A girl warned him that there was danger, that they were after him. One word she said came through to me—she said it with such strong feeling—and he understood the danger."

"Well, what was it?"

Nick laughed weakly. "It doesn't make any sense. It sounded like 'candle,' but that can't be it. Just one of those stupid things in a dream—" Then, quite suddenly, his mind made a connection. "Wait a minute. When I asked Gwen her family name, she told me . . . 'my family is Kendel,' she said, but . . . but that was *after* I'd had the dream. She told me that just last night."

"Look," Blessed said, "I've got to get moving or I'll miss old Cramer's seminar. Meet me at dinner. Okay?"

"Sure. Thanks for listening. But hold on a minute, there's something I want to show you." Nick dug into his pocket and came out with his hand closed over the brooch Gwenillan had given him. He held it out to Blessed, palm upward so that it caught the weak sunlight. "Just so you don't think I'm completely crazy. I didn't dream all this, John. I did meet her, and she gave me this."

John Blessed held the intricately cast golden circle in his hand, looking closely at the pattern of intertwining serpents. The style was very familiar, but it couldn't be the real thing. . . . Still, the workmanship was so good. He turned it over in his palm.

"I'd say it was real gold. Not marked, though. Certainly seems old enough to be interesting, but it couldn't be what it looks like. My guess is that it's a copy of something much older . . . a damn good copy. Did she tell you anything about this? Where she got it?"

"Not a word. She just slipped it into my hand the last time I saw her. Last night."

Blessed puzzled over the ornament. "You said you thought she was Scandinavian? Could be Norse, but it looks more Celtic to me."

Nick agreed. "Maybe you could show it to Professor Cramer after your seminar? See what he thinks."

"Good idea. And I'd better get my arse moving if I'm going to make it there." Blessed turned to leave, but then hesitated. "Oh, there's something I have to give you, too." He dug in his briefcase and came out with the book he had found under his dresser that morning: *Lost Gods of the British Forests*. "Sorry about the torn pages. There was . . . an accident. I'll tell you about it at dinner."

"Right," Nick promised, "I'll see you at first hall."

Before he had gone far, Blessed turned back to his friend, now walking toward the river embankment. "Hey," he called out, "if she's in Cambridge, we'll find her! I'll ask around. . . . Kendel, right? Gwen Kendel?"

"Right. And she told me another name . . . sort of nickname. Said that back home they called her 'Rhia.'"

"This wench has her fair share of names!" Then the Irishman gave an abrupt wave before hurrying to his seminar.

Nick sneezed again as he slipped the small book into the pocket of his red flannel jacket. His throat was dry and sore. All the same, as he crossed the arched span of a bridge across the Cam, suspended for a moment between water and sky, he found that he was feeling a little better for having confided in someone. He hoped it would last.

> For sure they did not seem
> To be begot of any earthly seed.
> Edmund Spenser (1552?–1599)
> Pembroke Hall

It was unusual for him to be invited into Inspector Janeway's home, but for Colin Church this was an unusual day. Driving back from the inspector's lunch at Trinity Hall, the sergeant had sensed a change in his superior's attitude. He seemed distracted, preoccupied with something more than the police action planned for that evening. Church was preoccupied too;

preoccupied with his lack of sleep and a meager lunch from the college buttery while Janeway had been with his friend Anglesey. Having been excluded from that chin-wag, he now wondered what the old chaplain had said to bring on this change.

After looking in on Terry Graham's unchanged condition at the hospital, they had driven to Janeway's flat at No. 7 Willow Walk so that he could shower and change before a long evening, perhaps all night, on duty. Expecting to return to the station to do the same, Church had been surprised when asked to stay.

Sergeant Church did not sit as he waited in the sitting room for the other man. He paced slowly around the room, studying the surroundings as a reflection of a man he did not fully understand. It was not a large room, rather dark, and furnished with the same solid wood and leather found in the inspector's office: a sofa, bookshelves filling one wall, a few scattered tables and chairs, and a cherrywood camp desk in one corner near a bay window. The rugs, like the one in the office, had most likely been bought during Janeway's years in the East.

One wall, painted the color of green baize, held an arrangement of military prints, the sepia tones of backgrounds and horseflesh setting off the scarlet of military coats. Silver-framed black and white photographs on the desk were windows into the world of British Palestine half a lifetime ago. Church studied the face of the young cavalry officer, peaked cap tilted slightly to one side, standing with the reins of his mount in hand, or, in another picture, smiling with a group of fellow officers in the bazaar. The mustache was darker, the face less lined, but the eyes were the same.

The manic screech of the kettle led Church to a small, seldom-used kitchen, where he added hot water to a simple china pot for tea. The fragrant odors of Darjeeling rose up to him as the boiling water began its magical transformation, bringing India to this stuffy little room halfway around the world.

Inspector Janeway emerged from his bedroom as Church was arranging cups and saucers on a tray. He had changed into a comfortable-looking suit of gray green moleskin and sturdy oxblood walking shoes bought years ago at Bally on Bond Street. "Thank you, Church. There's a pitcher for some milk in the drying rack, and you might bring some of those biscuits on the counter there."

Carrying the tea things into the sitting room, Church found the inspector standing, looking very intently at the large oil painting hanging over his dark oak mantel. It was a peaceful pastel landscape done in the Impressionist manner. Even Church, who freely admitted to an ignorance of art, could see that it seemed out of place in these somber, masculine surroundings.

"Where should I put these, sir?"

Janeway reluctantly pulled his attention from the restful colors of the French countryside. His thoughts lingered for a moment on a spring afternoon in Beaune long ago with the woman who had later painted this picture for him. He helped the sergeant arrange their tea on a low table near the sofa, watching Church's large, gnarled knuckles grasp the handle of the china pot like a man with a child's toy as he poured.

He took a cup and saucer from the tray and reached for the milk. "I think we'll need this before the end of the day." Then he sat on the sofa across from the armchair in which Church had ensconced himself to pour the tea.

"I wanted a little peace and quiet to go over our final plans for this evening. Arrangements have been made, as you know, for all the extra manpower possible, and for a number of them to be armed."

For the next thirty minutes, Church methodically picked out the bourbon creams from the plate of assorted biscuits as his superior outlined the plan for putting an end to the Pentacle Commune.

"So that's basically it," Janeway said finally. "But I also want you and every constable on the force to be on the alert for anything that might seem the least bit out of the ordinary tonight. Anything at all." He paused for effect. "Remember that our murder investigation is still of primary importance, and I believe that this evening may be crucial in that regard, too."

"You mean you're convinced now that Troop and his lot are mixed up somehow in the murder?" Church sought confirmation of his own strong suspicions.

"I didn't say that. We'll find out more when we have them in custody and when we can search the farm properly. I mean only what I said. Tonight I don't want anything suspicious to be overlooked—particularly in the vicinity of that damned woods. Instruct everyone to be alert, whether things seem to have anything to do with our drug raid or not. Now, are you clear about your role?"

"Yes, sir. I've got it down pat, except on thing. When I'm in position around this cottage in the woods, where will you be?"

Janeway set down his empty cup. "I'll be in contact. I plan to do a bit of roving, keeping tabs on your action at the cottage and Petrie's at the farm, as well as pursuing some ideas of my own."

He leaned back on the sofa, one elbow up on its back, his hands clasped across his chest. "Tell me, Church; you've interrogated our informants. Do you think we're going to have a show tonight?"

Church finished chewing the last of the chocolate cream biscuits and swallowed. "I think Carpenter is scared enough to be straight with us, sir. The other one, I'm not so sure about. Wenger changed his tune too fast. He's been cooperating, takin' part in his methadone program and all, but I still remember when we brought him in. They're both damn scared, that much I know."

Janeway was skeptical. "This talk about black magic and threats may just be an excuse to put all the blame on Jan Troop."

Church took a final swallow of tea and toweled his lip on the back of his hand. "They both tell the same story. Seems Troop and the Woodbridge woman make everyone take part in these weird ceremonies—lots of naked dancin' in the moonlight, chantin' incantations and such. Most of them are pretty keen on it, too, according to Carpenter. Course, he says he wasn't. Says Troop makes everyone cut their wrists and swear a blood oath of secrecy. Told them he could call up the demons of hell if they cross him."

Janeway puffed energetically on his pipe and watched it, nonetheless, go out. "I can see how the group of misfits and drug addicts Troop has gathered around him might just believe that. His so-called religion not only gives him a supply of brainwashed helpers, it provides a plausible cover when questions are asked about strange noises and movements in the night. What was it Mrs. Woodbridge told us? A religious celebration?"

"Aye, she's another one, sir. Carpenter says she's the one he's most afraid of, and Wenger fairly turns white when he talks about her. Says he fears for his soul!"

"And well he should, though I don't think Eleanor Wood-bridge will have anything to do with it."

A Victorian mantel clock chimed four times, just as it had at teatime every afternoon for the past hundred years. "So," Janeway announced as a prelude to standing, "we'll get back to the station in time for you to shower up if you want and have a bite to eat. If what David Carpenter has told us is accurate, we'll be moving in about midnight, but I want everyone in place by eight."

The inspector moved toward the door to retrieve his coat and hat and his stick. He shut off the gas fire, and then, holding open the door from the sitting room to the hall for Church, he glanced back at the tranquil pinks and greens of the painting above his mantel. Thinking about the upcoming raid as well as his conversation with James Anglesey, Janeway heartily wished that he could take a bit of that peaceful Impressionistic landscape with him through the hours ahead. He switched off the light.

CHAPTER 28

Trinity Hall, 7 P.M.

Twilight and evening bell
And after that the dark.

Alfred Lord Tennyson (1802–1892)
Trinity College

The air was filled with the sound of bells as John Blessed left the college dining hall. Clare, Trinity, Caius, all were ringing in the evening at seven o'clock. No one he spoke to at dinner had seen Nick since lunch, and he glanced now into the Porter's Lodge to see mail still in the pigeonhole marked "Lombard."

There was a cold wind and the scent of rain in Senate House Passage where Blessed recognized a familiar shape striding toward him in the lamplight. It was rounded all over, with no angles or edges, from the glinting toes of polished black oxfords, past a formidable girth, to the level-set crown of a porter's bowler.

"Swann, have you seen Nick Lombard today?"

The head porter stopped in the cobbled lane under a tall gas lamp. "Matter of fact, I did, sir. Came by to see me this morning, late, nearly lunchtime."

"You haven't seen him since then?"

"No. Anything wrong?"

Blessed rubbed a hand across his beard. "Just he was supposed to meet me at first hall. Nick's been a bit down lately, and I wanted to talk to him, that's all."

"Actually," Swann said, "that's what he stopped by to see me about. Trouble sleeping and such . . . dreams?"

"And a girl he's met?"

"That's right." The head porter lowered his voice though the passageway was empty except for them. "I'm not one to betray confidences, but I'm fond of young Mr. Lombard, and

I know the two of you are close. I suggested he go by to see Reverend Anglesey."

"I think I'd better find out if he did."

The two walked together back toward the college, John Blessed's plimsolls silently slapping along the cobbles beside the clicking heels of the older man. "Frankly, I've been a bit concerned about him, too," Swann confided. "Friend of his father's, you know."

Their arrival in the Lodge was acknowledged by Old Ted, who, when asked if he had seen the chaplain, announced that Anglesey was likely to be found in the old library.

"Asked me to bring the key to let him in, Mr. Swann. 'Bout an hour ago. Don't know who had more trouble with them steps, him or me." Ted laughed a laugh like crackling glass.

Swann accompanied John Blessed across the main quad toward the small library that had stood at the center of Trinity Hall since the time of Elizabeth Tudor. They walked silently past the Georgian stone facings of North Court and then climbed the outside staircase to the library entrance on the upper floor.

The door was open. Stepping down a few steps into the narrow Elizabethan room, they saw the thin form of Trinity Hall's chaplain outlined against a window of leaded glass and backlit dimly by the moon. A single reading lamp burned in the nave of the old building. Anglesey, standing at an upright medieval reading desk, looked up from the volume open before him as they entered.

The head porter noticed an unfamiliar nervousness in the chaplain's movements as he removed his reading glasses. "What is it, Swann?"

"Sorry to disturb you, Dr. Anglesey, but . . . well, we were wondering, sir, if you'd seen Mr. Lombard anytime today. At my suggestion, he was going 'round to call on you."

Anglesey, obviously tired, leaned on the chest-level desk. "Yes, he did come by, but I had another visitor. I asked him to stop back. I was in my rooms until . . . let's see, nearly six, but he didn't come by again."

When neither of the others said anything immediately, the chaplain rubbed his spectacles nervously between his thumb and forefinger, badly smearing one lens. "Is it anything important? I'm really quite busy."

John Blessed and the porter exchanged a glance. "It could be important," John ventured. "At least, we think it could."

Anglesey reasserted his customary patience. "Nick didn't say what he wanted. I gather you two know something about it?"

"Well, it's a bit difficult to explain," Swann began, scratching at a shaggy cheek. Then he summarized his last several conversations with Nick, as the chaplain listened with increasing interest.

"Dreams?" he interrupted. "And a girl, you say? He met a girl? Blond?"

"So he said," Blessed answered. "But there's more. It's odd."

"What is? What's odd?" Anglesey demanded, his impatience resurfacing now for another reason.

"Well, it sounds silly, really. Nick insists that he brought her into The Pickeral last night, but there were a dozen of us there and no one saw a girl with him. The same thing happened the other day on the river. All of us saw Nick, but no girl, though he swears she was there."

"So you see why we're worried about the lad," Swann added. "He was to meet Mr. Blessed here at dinner, but no one has seen him since . . ."

"Not since you," Blessed told him.

Anglesey toyed with the iron chain that secured the heavy volume on the desktop to the padlocked iron rail below. "What else did he tell you about these dreams?"

Swann shook his head, but John Blessed described what he had been told about Nick's dreams of forests and people who appeared to be from another time. When Anglesey insisted on more detail, he recounted everything he could remember, including Nick's description of men with spears and torches hunting a fleeing man in a bloodred cloak through a forest.

"A red cloak," Anglesey repeated. "Is there anything else you remember? Anything at all? I can't explain now, but any detail could be very important."

John was puzzled, but he struggled to remember his conversation with Nick. "He told me there was a warning in the dream. A girl warned the man. Just one word, Nick said, and he didn't know what it meant. Sounded like 'candle,' he said, but that doesn't make any sense."

"Candle?" Anglesey searched his memory, replacing his smudged spectacles as if that would help. "A blood hunt... forests and men with spears... There's a Celtic word, John; you might know it. *Cendl*. It was the kindred group of a king or chief, related to him by blood. When a wrong was done to anyone in the family group of the chief, the Cendl acted as one in seeking a bloody revenge against the transgressor. The vengeance of the Cendl could be a fearsome thing."

"But how would Nick know a word like that?" John protested. Then it struck him. "Wait a minute! The girl... Nick told me her name. Gwen... Gwenillan—"

"Yes, yes, an old name," Anglesey cut in excitedly, "but—"

"Wait!" John Blessed insisted. "It's her last name I mean. She told him her family name was 'Kendel'.... Could that be 'Cendl'?"

As the two scholars considered this in silence, the head porter cleared his throat. "Couldn't it be," he offered, "that she told him her name *first*, and that's why the word came up in his dream?"

"No matter," the chaplain said urgently. "What else do you know about this girl... this girl that no one else has seen?" He would have to tell Lewis Janeway about this as soon as possible.

Blessed related what Nick had told him of Gwenillan, about her unusual fascination with nature—the stories of the swan and mistletoe. Anglesey saw the significance immediately, his mind fighting for clear thought as new facts and implications rushed in on him too fast to be digested adequately.

"I'm a damned fool! I sent him away. Pray to God for my soul."

As Blessed and the porter stared at each other in confused silence, the chaplain braced himself with both hands on the old desk. "Both of you listen to me carefully," he ordered in a tone neither of them had heard from this gentle man before. "I believe that Nick is in serious danger. There is too much for me even to try to explain. Simply take my word that our friend needs our help now... tonight!"

The young Irishman's face behind the black of his beard had gone white, while the head porter's cheeks were flushed. "Can't you tell us," Blessed began, "what sort of danger...?"

"No! I don't know myself. But if you want to help Nick, do exactly as I ask. I'm deadly serious about this. If we don't find Nick in the next several hours, it may be too late for anyone to help him."

The chaplain's tone told Swann even more than his words. "We'll do exactly as you say."

"Good. Swann, go back to the Porter's Lodge and stay there. Send anyone available out to make rounds of the college with instructions to watch for Nick. Then phone Inspector Lewis Janeway of the City Police. You'll probably have to leave a message, as I imagine he'll be away from the station. Say that I believe it is vital that we locate Nick Lombard. Suggest anywhere you think he could have gone, and give the police Nick's description and the Wychfield address. Tell Janeway I'll be there later. And tell him about this girl— Gwenillan Kendel. John, did Nick give you any idea how we might find her?"

"He didn't even know that himself."

"I expected as much." Anglesey was standing up straight now, no longer leaning on the desk for support. "If Nick comes into college, Swann, keep him with you until Inspector Janeway or I can get to you. Don't let him out of your sight! I'll be in contact, and you have the Wychfield phone number. Blessed will be there. Have you got all that?"

Swann lifted his bowler from his head and rubbed a palm across the damp expanse of his forehead as he let his orders sink in. Even this moment of hesitation was too much for Anglesey.

"Well, go on, man! A young man's life may be at stake here."

"Yes, sir!" Swann responded, lifting his chin and thrusting out his already expansive chest as he turned, with a glance at John Blessed, toward the door.

As his broad back disappeared through a medieval doorway designed for much lesser men, the head porter was reciting to himself, "Call Inspector Janeway, message, Wychfield, search college, ours not to reason why..." At last he had been called upon for action, service suitable to the gravity of his station. And who did he have to rely upon as his subordinate on this crucial night? Old Ted! It took all his resolution to keep his chin high as he rumbled down the stairs into North Court.

"What about me?" Blessed asked impatiently.

Anglesey's answer was prompt and unvarnished, more like a general issuing orders than a churchman of scholarly bent. "First, go to the Grad Room and the college bar. Gather up as many of your friends as you can find and tell them that it is extremely important that I find Nick. Don't bother about why, just send them out around the town—pubs, the cinema, cafés, the university library—anywhere they can think of. Get them all out looking, then you go to Nick's room at Wychfield and wait there for me. Check in periodically with Swann by phone."

"Right. But I have to ask one thing. What conclusions are you drawing from these dreams? I think I see part of it, but—"

"You know Celtic mythology, John," the chaplain explained quickly as he walked with the younger man to the door. "You know the significance of mistletoe and oak groves . . . and the *Cendl*. And the animistic world view this young woman has expressed to Nick."

"Yes, I know all that. I should have seen it myself. But why is Nick in danger?"

Practically pushing the young man out the door by his elbow, Anglesey gave a partial answer. "There is a connection between the girl, the dreams, and the danger. Don't ask me any more." Privately he was thinking of another young man, this one dressed in a bloodred cloak, a Roman officer's cloak, and of Nick Lombard telling him with pride about his Italian ancestry. A terrible, but by now familiar, pattern was taking shape.

John Blessed stood his ground for a moment longer in the dark doorway. From his pocket he drew forth the gold brooch and held it out. He didn't have to say a word as he watched the chaplain's eyes go immediately to it and stare with a sort of reverence, or fear.

"The girl," Anglesey whispered, "the girl gave him this?"

"That's what he told me. I showed it to Professor Cramer this afternoon and he said he can't accept that it's a copy . . . but he can't believe it's real."

"Romano-British," the older man said softly, "first century."

Again Blessed nodded. "Cramer said he's seen another almost exactly like it. He wanted to keep it to study, but I told him it wasn't mine to lend. Still, it gives me a strange feeling just carrying it around. Would you keep it until we find Nick?"

James Anglesey held the golden circle in his hands, its intertwining serpents staring up at him with a half dozen eyes. He knew what it must be, but a part of his intelligence continued to reject all that he had learned in the past quarter hour.

"I'll keep it," he said, his voice sounding as though it came from somewhere far away. "I know what I must do." The clergyman placed the brooch slowly and carefully in the inside pocket of his black suit jacket.

Seeing a look of intense concentration cover the chaplain's face like a tragic mask, John Blessed hurried away without saying more. Halfway down the steps he heard the sound of his name.

"John, if Nick should come to Wychfield, don't let him out of your sight, whatever he might do or say."

The young man shook his head solemnly. "What about you? Is there anything I can do to help?"

"No. Go now, quickly. I'll come to Wychfield as soon as I can, but there are things I have to do first. Things you can't help me with." Then, listening to John Blessed's footfalls clattering down the stone steps outside the old library, he continued softly to himself. "No one can help me."

The chaplain adjusted his spectacles and bent over the ancient desk. He closed the chained book he had been studying and lifted it down onto the waist-level shelf built into the standing desk. Then, scanning the shelf carefully, he found the volume he needed and pulled it from its place. The weight of the dusty, leather-bound manuscript put a strain on his back as he slid its rattling chain along the iron rail running the length of the row of desks and then lifted it up onto the slanted reading surface before him. In all the hours he had spent in the unique chained library of Trinity Hall, he had only had occasion to consult this book a few times, and never under circumstances that he took so seriously.

Anglesey spent the next twenty minutes hurriedly copying unfamiliar words and phrases—some in Latin, others in archaic Greek—from the chained volume in the narrowly focused circle of lamplight. In the gloom around him, the upright medieval reading desks in rank and file down the nave of the library seemed to be watching the elderly scholar in their midst, straining to see over his bent shoulders what ancient knowledge was being stolen.

The chaplain had never before read the full rite of exorcism dating from the time when Christ still walked the earth as a man. It was a slow and painstaking process. At another time he would have stopped to rest his eyes after copying only a few phrases, perhaps going back to his rooms for tea and a comfortable fire. But now he forced himself to persevere for a much more urgent purpose than mere scholarship. Anglesey knew, like his friend Lewis Janeway, that a soldier going into battle is only as good as his weapons.

CHAPTER 29

Huntingdon Road, evening

Lo! in the middle of the wood...
Sun-steeped at noon, and in the moon
Nightly dew-fed.

> Alfred Lord Tennyson (1809–1982)
> Trinity College

It was dark under the trees that shielded the old house from the road. Only a few traffic noises carried from the invisible highway to compete with the night sounds of the woods. To one side of the house lay a flat stretch of fallow field, dark and empty now under a cloudy night sky. On the other three sides were the trees of Trinity Wood, and under them Sergeant Colin Church, enduring what was proving to be a long, cold wait.

His men were in position in the shadows around the small house: ten constables, half of them specially armed with twelve-gauge shotguns, and another three marksmen issued with .45-caliber revolvers. Shortly after eight o'clock two young men had arrived, both recognized as commune members. Church stared through the trees at their green Morris Minor parked near the battered front porch of the cottage. Lights showed in two of the six curtained windows under the overhanging eaves of the single-story structure, but there was no sign of movement inside the house, and no noise. Now they must wait for the others. For Church, waiting was the cruelest part of a policeman's lot.

He looked up at the dark clouds alternately covering and uncovering the moon like a lunar shell game. Nearby, the hunting cry of an owl momentarily burst forth only to be obscured by the muffled roar of a heavy lorry speeding down the old Roman road toward Huntingdon and the industrial midlands beyond. Church signaled to the nearest constable, pointing toward the road where his unmarked car was parked on the nearest side street. Then, staying well back from the un-paved drive curving through the trees, he walked along in the shadows toward the road. Confident that the situation was under control, he wanted to check in on the car radio with the station and with Inspector Janeway at Gog Magog Farm. He could have radioed from the stakeout, but he felt the need to move about, and he had to admit that he was looking forward to a few moments of comparative comfort in the car.

So here he was again, tramping about in a woods after dark. There must be a better way, he thought, for a man his age to earn a living. Church knew that the stand of trees around the cottage ran into the woods where the young re-porter had been found. The thought had occurred to him ear-lier as he had driven here, passing by the entrance to Trinity Hall's Wychfield site less than a kilometer down the Hunting-don Road from the almost hidden turning to Jan Troop's cot-tage in the trees.

Knowing that he was in those same woods made the ser-geant uncomfortable as he also recalled the bloodstained clothing found at the other end of Trinity Wood. He knew it was an irrational feeling, but he moved more quickly through the darkness along the edge of the trees, not wanting to use any light in making his way back to the road. Somewhere off to his right a creature stirred in the blackness. Church turned toward the sound. He wondered for the first time if he had done the right thing in disdainfully turning down the firearm he had been offered, but he resolutely shook off the feeling of uneasiness as the lights of the road came into view.

> Sable-vested night,
> eldest of things.
> > John Milton (1608–1674)
> > Christ's College

From where he sat in the lay-by overlooking Gog Magog Farm, Inspector Janeway could see a black van and a battered farm truck parked in the farmyard of the Pentacle Commune. The only other vehicle registered at the farm, a blue Hillman, had been followed that morning taking Mrs. Woodbridge to the commune's stall in the Cambridge market. With her had been the blond girl identified as Sara Larsen, an American. At last report, the car was still parked near the now-deserted market square. The whereabouts of the two women was unknown, and that bothered Lewis Janeway very much.

Sergeant Petrie and several of his men were stationed at observation points nearby, watching lights steadily burning in the farmhouse windows. Additional men were waiting in their vehicles at various positions for Petrie's instructions to move in. In the past ninety minutes of watching, lights had gone on several times in upstairs bedrooms, and in one uncurtained room a woman had been seen putting several small children to bed. It appeared to be a quiet evening at home for the Pentacle Commune.

Janeway recognized the possibility that all their preparation might be for nothing. David Carpenter and Horst Wenger could have had any number of reasons for fabricating a story about drug dealing. If so, it would be an embarrassment, but Janeway felt that was a necessary risk.

The inspector scanned the blackness of the landscape and the farm. Only an outdoor light above the peaked roof of the old barn cast any significant artificial illumination into the scene. Not a single car had passed the Rover sitting in darkness on the unlit country lane for more than an hour. The Gog Magog hilltops might have been another world or time except for the few lights of the house and barn. Janeway's gaze scanned the blue-black arch of the night sky, its aubergine depth obscured by streaks of silver cloud passing across the moon.

There were too many thoughts demanding his attention. He recalled the look of anxiety in Anglesey's eyes when he had spoken of things that had "happened to him" in the past few days, without further elaboration. Then the uncharacteristic look of fear on the face of his old friend faded in Janeway's mind, slowly merging into the look of stark terror in Terry Graham's eyes after he had withdrawn inside himself from something his mind could not accept.

Janeway reminded himself that Anglesey was right; what had happened to Terry Graham was not his fault. He would have stopped the boy, if he could have . . . if he had known where he was going. That woods, he thought, there was something about that damned woods. And now another young man might be in danger. Anglesey seemed so sure of it, sure that tonight was crucial. But who? Where?

He struck a match, holding it low below the car windows as he warmed a slim cigar and then lit it. He had decided that cheroots, smoked without inhaling and without the bloody nuisance of a pipe, might be the solution to his smoking dilemma. The pungent smoke as he drew on the cigar made the anxious waiting more bearable.

Suddenly the radio sparked to life with his code name for the evening's operation. "Shadow One. Come in, Shadow One."

"Shadow One here," Janeway responded. "Go on."

"Personal message for you, sir, from a . . . James Anglesey. A porter from his college phoned in for him earlier in the evening," the young constable explained. "Sorry, sir, but with all the activity, it sort of got . . . mislaid. Hope it's not important."

"Get on with it, constable," Janeway snapped.

"Well, sir, I'm to tell you that the young man Dr. Anglesey spoke to you about may be . . . Nick Lombard. Says you met him recently at a college dinner?"

"Yes, I remember. What else?"

"I'll read it, sir." The constable proceeded to relay Swann's description of Nick and the message that Reverend Anglesey would be waiting at Wychfield later in the evening. "Oh, and he said to tell you, sir, that this Lombard had recently started seeing a girl, a blond girl. He didn't say any more than that, sir."

Janeway quickly issued instructions to give Nick's description to all constables on patrol. If the young man could be found, he was to be escorted home and kept under police protection, and the inspector was to be notified immediately. "And don't let this message get 'mislaid' . . . Hedges, isn't it?"

He had barely acknowledged young Hedges' apologetic reply when a change in the configuration of lights at the farmhouse caught his eye. It was difficult to see clearly through the fringe of trees, but the front door had opened. As he watched, he saw several figures in silhouette before the door closed, snuffing out the light from the foyer. A moment later there was movement near the vehicles in the farmyard and the sound of car doors and an engine starting. A county constable, who had been standing in the shadow of the trees with binoculars, came up to the window of the Rover.

"Three men, sir, in the van. One of them is tall with a red beard. You said to watch for him."

Janeway crushed out his cigar in the ashtray under the dash. "Tell Sergeant Petrie that I'll follow the van."

As the constable hurried away, Janeway watched twin headlamps moving up the rutted land from the farmhouse. About thirty yards away from where he watched, they stopped. There was the hollow sound of a door opening and closing as one man climbed out to unlatch the gate. He would have to follow at some distance on such a deserted stretch of road, but he felt certain he knew where they were going. The door clanged again and then headlight beams lanced out from the driveway and the van lurched forward, kicking up dirt and gravel from the unpaved surface.

When the red glow of taillights had disappeared around the first curve, Janeway started his engine and drove slowly past the entrance to the farm. As he rounded the first curve, the other vehicle was somewhere out of sight ahead on the curving downhill lane. A few minutes later he reached the paved road to the village of Fulbourne and turned in the opposite direction toward the A604 and Cambridge. There was more traffic here, and he hoped he could close the gap. He could see taillights ahead in the blackness. Two vehicles. He used his radio.

"Shadow One to Shadow Five and Six."

When the two unmarked cars waiting near the city limits had responded, Janeway continued. "I'm following a black Volkswagen van, tag number HVE 18F, coming from the direction of Shadowland One. It should reach position Five in less than ten minutes. Shadow Five will follow the vehicle without notice until Shadow Six takes over surveillance. Do not, I repeat, do not follow the target vehicle if it leaves the main roadway at Shadowland Two."

A car passed by in the opposite direction. Janeway could see other lights behind him now as traffic picked up approaching the main highway. He increased speed to narrow the distance before the two vehicles ahead reached the intersection of the Cambridge road. He approached them at the traffic circle, where they waited for a cluster of cars on the A604 to pass. A moment later, when both vehicles turned toward Cambridge, the inspector saw that neither of them was the black van.

He looked around despairingly at the cars waiting impatiently behind him at the intersection and at the empty black stretch of road beyond them. Then he pulled onto the shoulder, swearing under his breath. The van must have turned toward Fulbourne at the first intersection. But why? Had he been seen? If so, would Troop call off his plans? Before radioing the two waiting tail cars and putting out a general alert for the van, he called Colin Church.

When he heard the familiar voice of the sergeant, he did not say anything immediately. He stared dispassionately ahead as a huge articulated lorry with West German tags screamed past, headlamps flaring through the darkness on the A604 toward Cambridge.

"Church," he said when the scream had died, "I've lost them."

> I pass like night from land to land;
> I have strange power of speech.
>> Samuel Taylor Coleridge
>> (1772–1834)
>> Jesus College

There is a legend in Cambridge that some evenings after dark, the crouching stone lions guarding the Fitzwilliam Museum case themselves down from their cold granite pedestals and slouch forward to drink from the deep stone gutters in front of the old building. James Anglesey thought of that story briefly as he approached the steps leading up toward the massive columns of the university museum. The lions watched his approach and his glance at the metal-lined gutters, black-shadowed under the amber glare of streetlights.

The iron gates were open, and as the chaplain slowly climbed the steps, the museum doors also swung open. A high-pitched female voice—slightly wavering and much too loud—spoke his name.

"James! Such a delight to see you, but I really would have preferred a more conventional time and place!"

"Thank you, Winifred, for coming down to unlock on such short notice. I'm very grateful," Anglesey said wearily as the tiny figure of Winifred Adams popped from the lighted doorway beneath the huge museum doors. "It's very important, or I shouldn't have troubled you like this."

He had nearly reached the top of the long climb when Winifred scurried down the last few steps to take his arm. Completing the climb with him, she insisted that he pause for breath when they reached the portico. Anglesey knew that the little woman hanging on to his arm and chattering away was at least his age, but he wished that tonight he had half her energy.

"I won't even ask what's so urgent," she bubbled. "I'm just glad of an excuse to see you again . . . Jamie. It's been an age since we last got together! When was it? Oh, yes," she went on without a pause as they stood on the landing, "that recital at Girton. Months ago! We must really get together more often. Perhaps next Sunday, for tea . . . or something? It's been so lonely for me at weekends since sweet William died."

"Yes," Anglesey responded, not entirely sure to what he was agreeing on Sunday.

"What?" came the reply.

Winifred's failing hearing explained her own rather piercing manner of speech. "Can we go inside now, Winifred?" he said more loudly. "I really must be in a bit of a rush!"

"I've asked you a hundred times to call me 'Winnie,'" she returned with a girlish smile, and, indeed, she had.

"Now, Jamie, I imagine you'll need my help in finding whatever it is you're looking for," she continued, still clinging to his arm as she led the way inside. "I'll be glad to come with you. I'll admit I'm a bit frightened being in this big place all alone after closing, but with you it could be great fun. Like a parlor game!" Then a faraway look came over her sparkling blue eyes. "William so loved playing games in the dark."

"Uhumm." The chaplain smiled feebly as he tried to free his arm. "Thank you, Winif . . . Winnie, but I know just what it is I want to see, and I'm sure I can find it on my own. Should just take a moment, really."

"Well," she said with a reluctant pout, "if you're certain I can't help, I'll wait in the office. But don't rush because of me. I'll be waiting for you. And I have a car, so don't even think of walking back to college."

Winnie Adams stood in the grand entry hall of the Fitzwilliam, surrounded by its baroque smorgasbord of every type and hue of marble, watching the tall, angular form of the chaplain slowly climb the multicolored stairs. He had always been such an attractive man, she thought, even when William was alive. "Just switch on the lights as you go, Jamie! And remember, Winnie will be here for you whenever you're ready." Her descant invitation reverberated in the lofty spaces of the grand foyer, meaning precisely what it promised.

At the top of the stairs, he turned into a darkened exhibition room. He found a light switch on the wall and continued walking, illuminating one gallery after another as he passed through the deserted museum, and leaving a trail of white light behind him as he went. The quiet was almost a tangible thing. Only the hollow sounds of his own footsteps echoed off the high plaster ceilings.

His passage through the galleries brought to light all around him the treasures of past ages in glass cases, on walls, and display stands. Porcelain, precious metals, glass, and stone. Faces and scenes out of the past looked down on him from painted canvas, as the silence and emptiness of the enormous building took the chaplain's mind racing back to the fifth floor of the university library. His imagination struggled for free rein to conjure up the sounds of an unnatural wind gusting through the galleries and the slam of doors being blown back on their hinges, but Anglesey kept control as he paced steadily forward toward his goal.

Exhibits that had seemed mundane to him many times in daylight now took on a sinister quality in the darkened rooms in that moment before the light switch brought them out of the shadows. Burnished steel suits of armor stared out at him through empty helmet slits, and headless female forms in Victorian lace cried out for attention as he passed them by. Beasts long dead and stuffed snarled hatefully at the intruder in their midst. More than once, Anglesey resisted an urgent desire to whirl around and catch some motion, some small change in position behind his back.

Finally he reached a corner that turned into the darkened gallery that he sought. His fingers found the light switch, but it brought no light to the blackness of the room. Repeated clicking of the switch had no effect.

The chaplain stared into the square, high-ceilinged room. A range of windows on the far wall framed a moon still nearly full, and a beam of its pale honey light fell on a glass case in the center of the gallery. Anglesey could almost see his goal in the watered-gold shaft of moonlight. Murmuring a phrase stolen earlier from the chained book in Trinity Hall's library, he entered the darkened chamber. A Roman cuirass and the remnants of a crested helmet took shape in the gloom of one corner as his eyes adjusted to the dimness. A painting below it showed an artist's conception of a red-cloaked officer in full uniform, its fleshless face seeming to watch his every movement. Early British and Celtic pottery filled glass-fronted cases around the walls of the lofty room, and high up on one wall the Romano-British Gallery was dominated by the remains of an iron-rimmed chariot wheel, carved from wood that was cut while Christ walked in Galilee. Anglesey had seen the room many times before. He knew it and all its contents well, but now, cloaked in shadows and moonlight, it all seemed changed.

A thick, low-slung cloud, charcoal-colored and filled with rain, had been riding the wind westward since dusk from the choppy crests and risers of the Channel inland across the fens. Now, as the clergyman walked toward the flat glass case at the center of the museum gallery, it covered the moon like a blanket thrown over a lantern to douse its light.

Anglesey stopped where he stood, the relics of past civilizations around him suddenly passing into darkness. The force of the wind that had pushed the cloud forward on its course now rushed against the ceiling-high windows as the chaplain fumbled in his pockets for a match. Finally striking a light, he watched the flame gradually cast a tiny circle of illumination in the void, helping him to make his way forward. He had to see what was in that case, and he would not be driven back by noises and the dark.

The glass of the flat-topped display case gave Anglesey's reflection back to him as he leaned over it with his match. His eye caught the glint of gold before he had to snuff out the burning stub of matchstick in his fingers. Then he stood in total darkness again for a moment, listening to the threatening whine of the wind and struggling to light another match. It suddenly flared orange, and as its flame subsided to a steady glow, the chaplain again bent over the display of Romano-British jewelry. The brooch was there in a prominent spot. Its serpentine forms intertwined with an elaborate grace, a primitive theme cast in sophisticated abstraction. Deep-set crystalline eyes, half-hidden in its gilded coils, glared up at the old man with his intrusive flame.

A museum card explained the discovery of the exhibit during the excavation of Trinity Hall's garden court: a brooch found near the skeletal remains of a young female and a water-logged wooden stake.

"Celtic brooch," the card read. "Early Romano-British." The date given was circa 60 A.D. Yet it was the same! Every curve and swirl the same. Anglesey stared in fascination at the nearly two-thousand-year-old ornament he knew he had seen in his own hand that very evening. Then the faint glow of his match sputtered and died.

As the moon emerged from the charcoal cloud, passing on now toward the heartland of England and beyond to the Atlantic breakers by dawn, he slowly reached inside his jacket pocket. The room was once again dimly lighted by moonlight, illuminating the chaplain's face as it registered surprise and then growing alarm. He frantically searched every pocket, though he knew precisely where he had placed Gwenillan's brooch for safekeeping. There could be no mistake. It simply was no longer there. The tensed muscles in his face relaxed as he realized that he really should not have expected it to be.

Forcing himself to remain calm, he looked again at the glint of ancient gold in the dimly lighted case. The sinuous curve of the pagan emblem seemed to glance back at him with a mocking smile. Then another cloud covered the moon, casting darkness into the gallery once more like a huge shadow looming over his shoulder.

Anglesey turned toward the doorway, the glow of electric light from the next gallery beckoning to him like another world where sanity and logic still prevailed. Turning the corner and entering the brightly lit room was like returning from a bad dream. But Anglesey knew it was no dream that had led him there and was leading him forward now, perhaps to another encounter with a mystery two thousand years in the making.

He made his way as quickly as his aching joints would allow toward the next chamber. In his excited imagination, he watched the lights of the galleries stretched out ahead of him and pictured them dying out one by one as he approached, leaving him in terrifying blackness. He recalled the slaughterhouse odor, and for an instant he expected to glimpse the towering shadow of the horned man on the wall above him. But nothing happened. Everything was deceptively normal as the weary clergyman made his way back to the main staircase, switching off lights as he went and leaving darkness behind him like a wake.

Winifred Adams was waiting for him at the foot of the great marble staircase with a glass of amontillado in each dimpled hand. Her smile was wide and winsome, pressing the corners of her sapphire eyes into a river delta of wrinkles. She did not appear to notice that the chaplain did not return her cheery greeting.

"You will have time for a small glass of sherry with an old friend, won't you, Jamie?" she called out as he navigated his way carefully down the wide, polished stairs. "I say an old 'friend,' but I could just as well say an old 'admirer,' I think ... not that either of us is so old, really. I was just thinking of when we first met," she continued dreamily. "Between the wars. ... Oh, Jamie, it was a wonderful time to be a young girl. I was ever so fond of you, even then, but William ..." Her voice trailed off as Anglesey reached the bottom of the stairs.

"Here you are, you dear man," she began again, thrusting the sherry into his hand and precluding any decision on his part. "You really look as though you could do with a little. Those stairs! So tiring. Why don't we go into my office, where we can be comfortable?" Winnie reattached herself to the chaplain's arm, without allowing even a momentary pause in her soliloquy. "The fire is on and it's really quite cozy." She looked up at him and then lowered her eyes demurely. "There is even a divan there, if you would like to lie down for a bit. These long days are so tiring ... I might even be tempted to join you," she giggled, "but, of course, there is only one divan."

Winifred Adams was nonplussed, to the remarkable extent of being momentarily speechless, when the chaplain lifted the sherry she had just given him and downed the entire glassful in one hasty swallow.

"Why, Jamie," she began with some hesitation, "I never—"

"Winifred," the chaplain interjected forcefully, "no arguments, please. Go switch off the gas fire and collect your things, and I'll be very glad to accept your kind offer of a ride. I have an urgent appointment at our graduate hostel at Wychfield, if you can drive me that far."

She stared up at the tall, determined man standing beside her. "Of course I can. I've never seen you so . . . so masterful! Whatever you say . . . James."

He silently handed her his empty glass, which she held uncertainly for a moment before scurrying off to do as she had been told.

Outside, under the shadows of the triumphal columns, the stone lions were waiting, biding their time and nursing a thirst, until the elderly couple inside switched off the lights and walked down the steps past them to the car parked by the metal-clad gutter on the street.

CHAPTER 30

Grantchester, evening

And from the infernal Gods,
Mid shades forlorn of night,
My slaughtered Lord have I required.

William Wordsworth (1770—1850)
St. Johns College

Nick walked with slow and disconsolate steps down the dark country road toward Cambridge, thinking about the events of the past several hours. His afternoon wanderings after leaving Anglesey's rooms had led him three miles from Cambridge to the quiet serenity of Grantchester. The village had welcomed him, an unchanging oasis of thatch-roofed solitude surrounded by woods and river and fallow fields. Even cars passing by him earlier in the sinking sunlight of the November afternoon had not disturbed Nick's impression that he was somehow walking back in time.

Near the village by the river he had rested, sitting under a knotty, thick-trunked oak, its brown autumn leaves rattling in the wind overhead. Sitting and staring vacantly at the flowing water of the Cam, he had finally allowed his mind to grapple with his confusion. All his thoughts, his doubts and fears, had flooded out and joined the flow of the river current.

If he accepted that he had actually met Gwenillan, touched her, loved her, as he knew he had, then who was she? Where had she come from, and why? Why had she told him their meeting was meant to be? And where was she now?

Later, leaning back against the trunk of the old oak, Nick had glanced through the book John Blessed had returned to him, *Lost Gods of the British Forests*. It was strange. First the old volume had seemed to demand that he buy it, and now, on the most unnerving day of his life, it had found its way into his hands again and almost called out to him to be read.

Maybe there was a reason. Maybe it would help him forget for a while.

He had paged through the book, watching chapter headings fly by until one drew his attention: "The Bleeding God." He read of the arrival in ancient Britain of the Mediterranean cult of the Great Earth Mother, the primeval life-giver. First coming to northern Europe about the time of Christ, she was called Nerthus, though the Mother had many names. The author told how the ancient Britons who worshiped in the dark forest glades and sacred groves had combined the worship of the Mother goddess with their own pantheon of male gods—particularly with Balder, called the Bleeding God.

Balder was a god of the Celts killed in a bloody murder by other warrior gods. He was invulnerable to all their weapons until struck by a shaft of sacred mistletoe, the Celts' "tree of glory." Then the old chronicles said that Balder died "laced with blood" in a sacred forest grove. The ancient people of Britain combined this legend with their new worship of the female deity Nerthus, who they said took Balder as her lover before his murder. The lovers were blissfully happy until autumn and the onset of winter. Then, after Samain, the young god had to die his terrible, bloody death to ensure the recovery of the earth in the spring.

In the fading afternoon sunlight, Nick had read about the importance to all ancient peoples of seasonal death to win the promise of nature's renewal. Most myths combined it with the "Great Rite," meaning ritual copulation in a sacred place. This was the essential role human men and women could play in the grand mystery. The goddess and her young lover, they believed, joined with the human lovers under the sacred branches of oak and holly and Balder's fatal mistletoe, growing halfway between earth and the gods.

Nick's eyes did not leave the yellowed pages until he had read the entire chapter. When Christianity later came to the British Isles, the native peoples had simply further adapted their ancient beliefs to fit another new mythology that found its way to them from the Near East via Rome. Nerthus, the Earth Mother, became the Virgin Mary; and Balder, the oldest of all the old gods, whose very name means lord, became the Lord God of the Christians. The Bleeding God, dying so that life could be renewed, became Christ on the cross—the "tree of glory"—saving mankind by rising from a bloody death.

It all fit so well. The continuity of sacred myth and belief was an appealing concept, but it was more than curiosity that had kept Nick Lombard reading until well after dark. When he had finally closed the book and sat resting tired eyes, the confusion in his mind had begun to clear. He had almost glimpsed the deeper meaning in his dreams . . . in everything he had experienced since his first night with Gwenillan under the great oaks. It was then that he knew he must go back there, back to Trinity Grove. Tonight.

But even now, walking toward Cambridge through the cold, dark dreamscape of the lonely countryside, he was not sure why.

> Oft in glimmering bowers and glades he met her,
> And in secret shades of woody Ida's inmost grove . . .
> Alfred Lord Tennyson (1802–1892)
> Trinity College

The roar and smoke of a heavy lorry made Nick look up from the patchy brown grass of the verge as traffic picked up near the center of Cambridge. The lights of passing cars made twin streams of red and white in the darkness along Queens' Road near the College Backs. He waited for a chance to ford the river of lights and noise. A horn blared and an angry driver shouted at the student sprinting through the headlights, but Nick did not look back. He ran on up the tree-lined path leading toward King's Bridge and the soaring spires of King's College Chapel beyond. Then suddenly he stopped. It was a figure standing alone on the bridge that attracted his attention. A slender figure dressed in a pale-colored coat reflecting the moonlight. A girl.

Nick stood in the shadows of the trees for a moment, watching. The long golden hair, the arms resting on the stone balustrade, were just as he remembered them. The girl turned her head, and he glimpsed her profile etched against the night sky by the lights of the college.

"Gwen!" he called out, fighting the excitement that rose from his chest to lodge in his throat. "Gwen, it's me!"

The girl whirled toward the sound of his choked-off shout. She paused for a moment in a rigid posture, muscles tense and instincts wary, and then she turned to run. In disbelief, Nick watched her flee with long strides across the open grass that led up from the river toward the looming spires of King's Chapel. He called out her name once more and then began to sprint after her.

The girl was breathing heavily by the time she dashed into the dark stone alcove outside the huge oak doors of the chapel. She had looked back twice to see the figure of a man in a red jacket pursuing her, and she had heard him shout something. Her hand was damp grasping the heavy iron ring on the door and pulling at it frantically. Locked, the chapel doors were locked for the evening! She swung around to see the outline of the man in red straddling the entrance to the chapel alcove, and she knew there was nowhere else to run. It was over, she was caught.

Nick's eyes adjusted slowly to the blackness of the enclosed entryway. The girl's light-colored clothing and hair came into focus first, and then he searched for her face. A moment later he knew that it was not Gwen.

Sara Larsen was still breathing hard. "Who the hell are you?" she demanded bravely. "What do you want?"

"I'm sorry," Nick stammered. "I . . . I thought you were someone else." He relaxed his stance and backed away from the doorway.

Sara lost no time in edging her way cautiously out into the open, away from the darkened doorway. In the light, Nick could see her clearly. So much like Gwenillan, but not her.

"You're not from the farm?" the girl asked hesitantly. Her relief was growing, but she was still suspicious. Surely they would come after her. If not this one, then someone else. She had to get away from Cambridge.

"Farm?" Nick repeated. "No. I just . . . You look so much like someone else."

Sara shrugged. All she wanted was to go, somewhere quiet, somewhere safe, until morning. She turned quickly and began to walk away.

"Listen, I'm sorry. Really!" Nick followed behind her, keeping his distance. He knew now where he had seen her before. "You may not remember, but I saw you last night in a pub. You were with Nigel, right? Isn't that his name? Please wait."

Sara did not slow her pace. He knew Nigel. Maybe she was not safe yet. "Go away. Let me alone."

Nick dashed ahead of her and began to walk backward as they crossed the broad quadrangle of King's. "Please," he persisted. "Do you remember seeing me there? It's very important."

Grudgingly she glanced up at his face. American. A nice face, nice dark hair, sort of Italian. "I guess I saw you," she admitted. "So what?"

Nick breathed a sigh of relief and smiled broadly. "Please, can we stop walking for just a minute? I only want to ask you one question and then I'll go away. Promise."

He had a nice smile . . . and the quad was well lit. "All right," she told him, taking a cautious stance a few feet away.

Nick put his hands in the pockets of his jacket to put her more at ease. "When you saw me last night," he began, speaking slowly to show the seriousness of his question, "was I with anyone? At the table, I mean. You were sitting at the bar. Think carefully, did you see anyone with me at the table?"

The girl gave a small laugh, and Nick was reminded of Gwen's smile. "Just Nigel," she answered. "I thought you were going to hit him, the way you snarled that it was your table."

Nick's hopes had been crushed so often that he was almost numb to it now. "So when I booted Nigel out, there was no one else sitting at the table? Just Nigel and me?"

Sara frowned quizzically. "No, there was no one else. Who were you expecting, the Queen?"

Nick's dejection came out in his voice. "Thanks," he said. "I'm sorry if I scared you back there." Then, hands still jammed in the pockets of his red jacket, he turned back toward the river and began to walk away.

She watched him for a moment, thinking, considering the possibilities. There was a chance he could help. "Wait," she called after him. "I'm sorry, too. It looks like you were being straight with me."

Nick paused and looked back as she took a few steps toward him and then spoke again. "Listen, I answered your question, now maybe you can help me."

"Sure, if I can."

"I'm in a jam," she began, wondering how much she should reveal about running away from Mrs. Woodbridge and the Pentacle Commune. "I'm getting a bus to London in the morning . . . but . . . well, I only have enough money for the ticket, and nowhere to stay tonight. You're a student, aren't you? I was thinking maybe you'd know somewhere I could crash . . . just for tonight. Maybe a dorm, or somewhere in your college?"

"All-male college," Nick told her. "There are porters—and they're not all like Nigel." They shared a laugh as Nick considered her request. Any other time, a pretty girl asking to spend the night would be a godsend, but he had so much on his mind tonight that it was just one more problem.

"I'm just talking about a place to sleep," Sara emphasized, "nothing else."

"I guess you could come up to Wychfield. There's a graduate hostel there, where I live. Let me tell you how to find it, in case you don't find anything better." He gave her directions to the Wychfield site and his room number, wondering even as he did if it was a good idea.

Sara treated him to another smile, even more beautiful now that she trusted him. "I'm not going home yet, or you could just come with me," he said, explaining that he was supposed to meet a friend.

"That's okay," she said quickly, "I can find it by myself later if I need to." Sara had her own reasons for wanting to stay alone and out of sight this evening. "But thanks . . . What's your name?"

Nick told her and was told hers in return. He thought again how attractive she was. Could he put Gwen out of his mind . . . forget about going to Trinity Grove and get on with his life?

"Thanks, Nick. Maybe I'll see you later then."

Nick smiled ruefully as he watched her go. "Maybe," he said to himself, *"maybe* I'll see her again. Story of my life."

The effects of his cold, lack of sleep, and hunger were taking their toll. Nick felt light-headed and feverish after the excitement and confusion of his encounter with Sara Larsen. He decided not to look for John Blessed, but to continue directly to Trinity Wood and then home. Focusing his thoughts on that, as well as he was able, he paced steadily forward along the Madingley Road.

The pathway when he found it was dark, roofed over by a latticed arch of leafless branches. The police guard had been removed, and Nick was totally alone entering the dark tunnel through the woods. There were noises around him, wind in the upper branches and the stirrings of small night creatures close to the ground, but the damp carpet of decaying leaves was soft and soundless under his feet. It was like walking on air, with no sound or substance to his footfalls in the darkness. His shirt was damp with sweat and he felt slightly delirious, his head throbbing and his thoughts wandering, but he continued to plod wearily forward. Was there really a woods around him, or was it being projected there against the walls of some massive white room? Nothing made sense. Why was he here? Why not home safe in his bed?

The sound of the reed flute was suddenly quite distinct. Then it faded into the discordant music of the wind in the trees. Nick listened as he walked, but when it came again, it was not as clear. Only the wind, he told himself. He had reached the overgrown turning that would take him into the secret depths of the woods, to Trinity Grove. Part of him yearned to escape the fascination that was drawing him to the dark heart of the forest. Ahead, he could see the light at the end of the pathway opening onto the field of Wychfield Farm. In a matter of minutes he could be home.

When the wind stopped abruptly, Nick stood still, looking up at the suddenly stilled branches above his head. Then the soft, reedy music came to him again, but not from outside. The haunting strains of the flute in a primitive melisma of tones seemed to reach him from somewhere deep within himself. Lowering his eyes from the silent treetops, he saw her, standing dressed in white before him.

> I waked, she fled,
> And day brought back my sight.
> > John Milton (1608–1674)
> > Christ's College

Sara Larsen stayed in the shadows of Kings College gazing across at the lighted shopfronts of King's Parade. Beyond them was the market square where she had slipped away from Eleanor Woodbridge that afternoon. She wondered if they would still be searching for her. Perhaps the Woodbridge woman had given up by now . . . but she recalled the conversation overheard in the dark hallway of Gog Magog Farm. It was obvious from her argument with Jan Troop that Eleanor had plans for Sara that she would not give up easily. But what were they?

Curiosity made Sara edge her way up the darker side of the street to where she could get a better view of the closed stalls of the market. She wondered if Eleanor's car was still parked where she had last seen it. The dark shape of Great St. Mary's church loomed across the road, closer to the market. The American girl made a dash for its sheltering walls, moving quickly past the few pedestrians still on the street and merging into the shadows of the recessed church door. She peered around the corner of the building toward the deserted market square. There in the artificial glare of the streetlights was Eleanor's car.

She felt the pressure of a strong hand on her shoulder just as she heard the familiar voice.

"Hello, Sara. I've been watching you, wondering when you would come back to me."

Sara tried to pull away, but Eleanor's grasp was too firm. When she tried to speak, to protest, a scarf was pulled across her face and bound tight against her mouth as a gag. The huge church door groaned open like the mouth of a gigantic beast, and the girl was no match for the larger woman dragging her into the darkened interior.

"I'm sorry, my dear," Eleanor told her in a voice filled with a perverted affection. "But I want you to be quiet and listen while I do the talking. I have so much to tell you . . . about the grand new life we will have together. You and I!"

Sara struggled and shouted against the gag as she was dragged up the central aisle toward the altar. The two women entwined in the embrace of their struggle looked like a creature from medieval myth as they passed through the shafts of misty colored light coming through stained glass set high in the ancient walls. "You are the chosen one, Sara. Not just for Samain, but for the rest of your lifetime. And it will be a wonderful life . . . so much to accomplish!" Eleanor's speech came out in gasps as she dragged the younger woman forward. "You are a true believer . . . I know it . . . and you will too . . . soon . . . sooner than you think."

At the high altar, Mrs. Woodbridge loosened her grip for a moment to open the altar gate. Seeing her chance, Sara wedged her foot behind the ankle of the larger woman and pushed. When Eleanor fell with a startled cry to the marble floor, Sara, her eyes wide with fear, turned to run. She had barely gone a single stride when a fist with the strength of iron circled her ankle, bringing her down to the floor with her captor.

With Sara crying out against the stifling gag, Eleanor Woodbridge got to her feet and pulled the girl up with her. She was panting with exertion and a trickle of blood dribbled from a cut on her forehead down into her dark eyebrows. "You mustn't fight against it, Sara. It's meant to be." Holding the girl with one hand, she pulled the belt from her raincoat with the other. Then, grasping both Sara's wrists in front of her, she began to tie the belt around them.

"You'll see ... when we're away from this place ... away from Jan Troop and the others ... you'll see." Eleanor tried to concentrate on tying Sara's arms, but the girl was so close. The scent of fear rose from her fresh young skin, so soft to the touch. The older woman's hands brushed against the girl's jeans and sweater as she tied the knots. "You'll see, my darling girl." Her motions slowed as she gazed into Sara's face. Her hands brushed more deliberately against the softness beneath the worn jeans. "You'll see, my love."

Eleanor's right hand closed over the girl's breast, and her eyes eased shut in a moment of shuddering emotion as a sigh of desire escaped her lips. Sara pulled her bound hands together in front of her chest and pushed the distracted woman away. Then she ran blindly through the darkened church. Tears streaming from her eyes, she searched for a way to escape. A small door in a corner of the nave caught her eye just as she turned to see Eleanor Woodbridge striding toward her, arms outstretched and blood streaming down her face.

The door was unlocked, but it did not lead outside. Instead, a long, curving flight of stone steps led upward, but it was too late to turn back. Sara raised her tied hands and pulled the scarf from her mouth to release a pent-up scream. Still bound, the terrified girl fled up the stairs of the bell tower. Behind her she heard Eleanor Woodbridge's slow and deliberate tread on the steps, her jumbled words floating up ahead of her to Sara's ears. "It's no use running. There's nowhere you can go. You are meant to be with me ... to serve the Mother. It's been promised."

Suddenly Sara was at the top of the stairs, breathless and

panting. All around her was stone and open air looking out onto the rooftops and streets of Cambridge far below. Above her were the cast-bronze bells of Great St. Mary's. She looked around frantically, but there was nowhere to go. Mrs. Woodbridge's ranting voice was coming nearer, closing on the final curve of the stairs before reaching the top.

Very slowly, in no hurry now, Eleanor Woodbridge rounded the final corner and gazed upward at the frightened girl, a look of triumphant lust in her dark eyes. Once again her arms stretched outward, strong white palms upturned in supplication or in confident demand, and a twisted smile on her heavy lips. Blood was on her cheek. She reached to her own chest and grasped the front of her blouse beneath the raincoat. The thin white cloth tore under her passioned grip as she pulled the blouse apart, allowing her full, flushed breasts to fall free. "Come to me, Sara. Come to the Great Mother of us all."

All Sara's fear and anger lashed out in a single gesture. With an anguished cry she struck the crazed woman before her with both bound fists. Certainty of victory draining from her face, Eleanor Woodbridge felt her footing lose its balance on the worn steps. She tumbled backward in the narrow passage and disappeared with a defeated screech out of Sara's sight around the corner of the curving stairway. A moment later she lay twisted across the stairs, her last thought as her neck had snapped . . . an ancient, almost vanished religion that she would never see reborn.

> Of forests and enchantments drear,
> Where more is meant than meets the ear.
> John Milton (1608–1674)
> Christ's College

"Attention inside! This is the Cambridge City Police. The house is completely surrounded." Church's voice through the bullhorn was slightly rasping, but it carried authority, as did the powerful beams of police spotlights suddenly illuminating the run-down cottage in the woods.

"Throw out any weapons, well clear of the house. Then come out by the front door, single file, hands above your heads. You have two minutes . . . from now!"

Church looked at the inspector near him under the trees. The armed constables leveled their weapons at the ramshackle house. A curtain moved slightly. There was silence.

The black Volkswagen van was parked beside the Morris in front of the house. It had arrived soon after Janeway had joined his men at the cottage. Having had time to think, the inspector guessed that Jan Troop had taken the indirect route by way of Fulbourne in order to collect a cache of drugs to be sold in the transaction that they had just interrupted. On their arrival at the cottage, Troop and Harrold had carried in two large suitcases that they had not had with them at Gog Magog Farm.

It disturbed Janeway that a young man he had seen leaving the farm with them, a pale and scrawny boy identified as Nigel Pinder, was not with them now. Perhaps he had been left behind in Fulbourne or wherever the goods were stored. The inspector wanted very much to know where that was, but there would be time for that and many other questions soon.

Parked next to the van, between it and where Janeway stood, was a battered blue Ford. It had arrived soon after Jan Troop, with the two apparent buyers. One man was young and the other middle-aged, both wearing dark raincoats. Janeway had given them only a few minutes inside together before handing Church the bullhorn.

"One minute!" the sergeant announced tersely now.

Thirty seconds passed before the front door of the cottage eased open slightly. Marksmen in the darkness under the trees tensed, their safety catches off and fingers resting lightly against trigger guards. Twin beams of spotlights focused on the slowly opening door. Then there were two soft thumps as one handgun and then another were tossed out onto the dirt of the yard.

"All right! We're coming out!"

The voice was immediately familiar to Janeway and Church. "Don't shoot!" the speaker added nervously in Jan Troop's accented English.

A thin man dressed in jeans and a light jacket was the first to come out, hands above his head, followed by the other young man from the commune who had arrived with him in the green Morris earlier.

"Keep three paces between you," Church ordered through the bullhorn, "and continue to walk toward the sound of my voice until I tell you to stop. Hands high over your heads. Palms open!"

The two men continued walking down the steps and into the yard, followed by the large, bearded man known to the police as Charles Harrold. As the big man reached the edge of the porch, Jan Troop appeared in the doorway, glancing around and squinting into the blinding glare of spotlights. Church looked at the inspector and saw him nod in silent understanding. "Only two more," Church said quietly, feeling sweat on his palms. "Our two buyers."

Jan Troop's foot was on the bottom porch step when the door behind him was suddenly kicked shut from within. Simultaneously there was the icy sound of breaking glass, and rapid-fire shooting from an automatic pistol flashed out from a side window of the cottage. Janeway and Church crouched low behind the trees as more shots flared from a window at the front.

Jan Troop and the three other men strung out across the yard threw themselves flat on the ground at the sound of the gunfire. One figure rolled toward the cover of the parked vehicles.

"Watch that one!" Janeway shouted to an armed marksman.

"Throw out your weapons!" Sergeant Church called out. "There won't be another warning!"

A renewed blast of gunfire from the parlor window was immediately answered by a shouted order from Janeway and the thump of six shotgun loads fired from the woods, closely followed by the crash of heavy slugs from police revolvers slamming into the sides of the house. A second shotgun salvo shattered the glass of every window. The disarmed men in the yard crouched low, covering their heads as the barrage of police gunfire peppered the house.

Janeway barely heard the engine of the van turn over amidst the firing. With a jerk, the van jumped backward, reversing out of its position between the other two parked vehicles. Janeway drew the Smith & Wesson semiautomatic he had nearly left at home and snapped a shell into the chamber. He had time for two shots and the marksman near him for two more as the van paused, momentarily facing them, to shift from reverse to first gear. The dark-tinted windshield shattered, but the unseen driver managed to de-clutch and depress the accelerator before collapsing. The driverless van lurched forward, careening wildly into the trees at the edge of the narrow drive before crashing into the trunk of a large elm.

"Hold your fire!" Church shouted through the bullhorn. There was sudden silence followed in a moment by the sound of a handgun being dropped weakly onto the wooden floorboards of the porch.

"We're coming out!" came a voice from the side window. "Don't shoot!" The Irish accent was clear. Then the police spotlights showed a second weapon being tossed from a shattered windowsill.

A moment later the two men in raincoats emerged through the front door, the older man supporting his younger companion, who was bleeding from a cut on his head. A swarm of constables moved from their cover around the house as Church gave the "all clear."

As the suspects in the yard were being pulled to their feet, frisked, and handcuffed, a constable ran toward the crashed van. Janeway was close behind. He knew who had rolled toward the parked van during the firefight. As he neared the steaming wreckage, the inspector wondered if Jan Troop was still alive. If not, there were questions that might never be answered.

Ambulance sirens screamed up the Huntingdon Road as Janeway approached the constable holding open the driver's door of the battered van. A bleeding figure was sprawled across the seat, moaning in a low, pained voice. He lifted his head as the inspector leaned over him, and a trickle of blood ran down from beneath his greasy blond hair.

"What the bloody hell happened?"

Nigel Pinder, brought along only for the dirty job of digging up the buried suitcases, had waited as ordered in the back of the van until the shooting started. Jan Troop was nowhere in sight.

CHAPTER 31

Wychfield, 11:45 P.M.

My dwelling is the shadow of the night,
Why doth thy magic torture me with light?
                    Lord Byron (1788–1824)
                    Trinity College

John Blessed sat in the orange glow of the gas fire in Nick's room. A shaded lamp burned near the window, but James Anglesey chose to sit in the shadows at a small table across the room. Between the two men, Inspector Janeway paced back and forth across the narrow confines of the room, his shadow cast large and wavering on the back wall by the light of the fire.

"So the boy is still out there somewhere?" The policeman's voice was weary, but the tone of concern was genuine.

The chaplain sat quietly staring down at the tabletop in front of him as though it were covered with some intricate and fascinating puzzle. John Blessed spoke when Anglesey did not respond.

"Everyone I know has been out looking. Now that the pubs are closed, I don't know what to think."

Anglesey looked up slowly from the table. "What about this raid of yours, Lewis? Can we learn anything from these people?"

Janeway sighed and stopped his pacing, staring out into the darkness of the fields of Wychfield Farm. "They're being booked now, but the ones I most want to question are missing."

"The leader? This Dutchman you mentioned?"

"Yes, I'm afraid so. There was some shooting. Unavoidable, but no one was injured apart from a few cuts and bruises. In any case, under cover of the gunfire, the Dutchman slipped away from us somehow." In his mind, he pictured Jan Troop crawling out of the van after it had crashed to a stop at the edge of the woods . . . or slipping away earlier as all attention was focused on Nigel Pinder attempting to escape alone in the van.

"However he did it, he can't have gotten far. My men are searching the woods now. Less than a kilometer from here, actually. I really should be there with them, but I came here as you asked, James, as soon as I possibly could."

"And I appreciate that, but what about the others in this . . . commune?" Anglesey rubbed his palm across the surface of the table as though erasing a picture he had drawn there with his mind. "Can they tell us anything?"

"The County Constabulary are conducting a warrant search at the farm now. Everyone will be taken in for questioning, but at least two members of the group haven't been accounted for." Janeway pictured the dark, saturnine face of Mrs. Woodbridge as it had appeared in the doorway of Gog Magog Farm on his second visit there. "One woman in particular I want to question, but she and another young woman gave us the slip earlier in the day, in the market."

He glanced impatiently at his watch. "I must get back to the station soon and start questioning the others. But damn it all, James, I just don't know what to ask in connection with this theory of yours. I don't know where to begin to get at what you told me this afternoon. I've been a soldier and a policeman, but I'm no scholar. Your explanation about ancient calendars and Celtic legends . . . and murders that happened in the Middle Ages made some sense to me at the time. You can be very convincing. But now it's almost midnight and my mind is set on drug deals, and missing suspects, and last summer's murder."

"Lewis," the chaplain began, "I really can't tell you how important this is. . . ."

"I know," Janeway said wearily. "I said I would help, and I will, as far as I am able. Just tell me where to begin!"

John Blessed slumped in the armchair by the fire, his bearded profile half in shadow and half glowing red as he watched the two older men behind him. He wished that he could understand why they were so concerned about Nick, why tonight was so important.

The chaplain looked up slowly at the tall figure standing above him. "Lewis, I know you want to help. But please, sit down. I'm at least as agitated as you, and your pacing only makes it worse."

Janeway smiled weakly, pulling out a straight-backed chair from the table as the other continued to speak, leaning forward with his bony elbows resting on the table and his palms steepled against his chin. "This cottage where you made your arrests, you say it's close by, set back in the woods? That would be part of the same . . . part of our woods here? Trinity Wood?"

"Right," John Blessed confirmed. "Trinity Wood isn't as small as you might think. I took a wrong turning in it once and it took me the better part of an hour to find my way out."

"It stretches at least a mile to the north," Janeway added, "and over to the Madingley Road on the south."

"Where the bloodstained clothing was found," Blessed put in, looking up to catch the inspector's reaction.

Now it was Anglesey who stood and paced to the window. The drapes were pulled back, and the black liquid surface of the glass reflected Janeway's eyes as he turned to watch his friend walking away. The chaplain stood very close to the glass in order to look out across the field at the dark silhouette of Trinity Wood. Then he turned back to the inspector.

"You asked where to begin, Lewis. The woods, that's the key. Begin with those damned woods. Nick will be there."

"What?" Janeway was genuinely perplexed. "How can you know that? Really, James, this thing—"

"I don't know it!" The chaplain's outburst reflected the tension that had been building in him all day. "I *feel* it!" Then he walked back to the table and stood across from the inspector, leaning unsteadily on the tabletop with both hands for support. "Do this one thing for me, Lewis," he said more calmly. "Go to the woods. Go now!" He thought of Nick's dreams, and of the murders he had read about through the centuries, so many of them connected with Trinity Wood. "It's already terribly late."

Janeway looked up at his old friend, his mind filling with questions, excuses to dissuade Anglesey from this strange request. A battered clock on Nick's mantelpiece began sounding twelve slow, mournful chimes, its mechanism running down for want of winding.

"Please, Lewis. I simply don't have the strength to go myself. Take John with you. You'll go, won't you, Blessed?"

"Anything," John Blessed offered. "If you're sure . . ."

"I'm not sure of anything. Not anymore. But this may be our last hope of preventing a deadly tragedy." The old man stared down at the tabletop, all the force now drained from his voice. "I don't have the strength. I just . . . I don't . . ."

Janeway stood and placed an arm around the chaplain's shoulders, helping him to sit. "I'll go, James. But I'll go alone. There's still a dangerous man loose somewhere in those woods."

Anglesey wished silently that Jan Troop was his only worry.

"Inspector," John Blessed said, pulling himself up from the armchair, "I have great respect for the law, and I'm no hero, but let me put it this way: Nick is my friend, and if Reverend Anglesey thinks he's in trouble in those woods, then I can either come with you . . . or you can look over your shoulder and see me a dozen paces behind you."

Lewis Janeway smiled in spite of himself. "All right, we'll have a look together. But let's not waste any time. I have some torches in the car, and I have to radio in." He retrieved his hat and coat from the bed as he spoke. "Meet me in front of the house."

At the door Janeway tucked his stick under his arm as he took hold of the knob, looking back at Anglesey. "James, why don't I get someone to drive you back to your rooms?"

The chaplain waved away the suggestion. "Lewis, John, be careful."

With a final nod, Janeway closed the door on his friend's warning, and Anglesey turned to the young Irishman. "Don't worry," Blessed told him, "we'll be as careful as a fox stealing eggs. And if Nick is in those woods, we'll find him."

The young man's back was to the chaplain and he did not hear him reply softly, "That's what frightens me." But then Anglesey spoke more loudly, stopping John as he opened the door. "This girl, you told me her name, do you remember? Didn't it mean anything to you when you heard it?"

John Blessed paused and thought for a moment. "Gwenillan?" he said. "No . . . just a foreign-sounding name."

Anglesey leaned on the table, feeling drained in body and spirit, aware of his true age for the first time. "No," he said steadily, though the effort showed in his face, "the familiar name she mentioned."

"What, Rhia?" Blessed queried.

"Rhia," the chaplain answered, "Celtic for lady or for queen. And Rhia Annon——"

"My God!" Blessed cut in, aware of what the chaplain was preparing to say next. "But I don't understand. Nick doesn't know a thing about Celtic language. Why would he make up the name of . . . ?"

"Just go, John. Go quickly, and take this." Anglesey pressed a sterling silver cross into the young man's hand. It had never before left his person since his ordination. He clearly recalled clutching it in fear on the fifth floor of the university library as a wind from hell had pressed him to the floor, choking off his life's breath.

John Blessed took the cross, his usual smile and good humor entirely gone from his face. Thinking again of what had happened so recently in his room just above them, he looked into the elderly churchman's eyes. What he saw there returned a still familiar chill to the base of his spine.

A few moments later James Anglesey stood alone by the window staring out into the darkness. He could just make out the figure of Lewis Janeway and the shorter, stocky form of John Blessed beside him as they passed among the large black columns of trees near the house. By the time they reached the edge of the plowed field separating Wychfield from the woods, all that was visible were the yellow beams of their lights stirring the ground fog that covered the furrows like shallow blue water.

The soft orange glow of the gas fire flickered across the page as Anglesey stood by the window reading from a sheet of notepaper held close to his face. The nervous trembling of his hands as he had written the words earlier made his task more difficult now as he tried to read them. The phrases were still strange to him, but after tonight he felt sure that they would become familiar. They would never be far from his side in whatever time might be left to him in this life. And tonight would never be far from his thoughts.

Much of the Latin was a very archaic form, dating from the earliest days of the Church when Christians had been forced to hide in the darkness of caves and catacombs scratched with the ambiguous signs of the fish and the lamb and the crossed bars of a Roman instrument of torture that had become their emblem. But there was power in the ancient phrases. He could feel it now as he read aloud the incantations to protect mortal souls from the demons of darkness and the pit. He recited them for Janeway and Blessed, and for "the dark man from the sea," Nick Lombard.

Nevertheless, when he looked up from the page to catch a glimpse of flashlights still probing across the blackness of the field, it was not a Latin phrase that leaped into the chaplain's mind. As a strong wind began to beat against the fragile pane of glass between him and the night, the words James Anglesey recited to himself were much older than Latin, older than the religion of Christ the Redeemer. They reached back to the time of another "Bleeding God."

"Rhia," he said softly, his breath clouding the cold glass of the window, "Lady. Rhia Annon, the name that is not spoken. The Lady of Darkness and Death, mistress of the world below."

There were footsteps in the hall and then a sudden knocking at the door. Anglesey turned slowly and moved toward the sound, staring at the thin wooden door and wondering what lay on the other side. Another sharp rapping, but too light to be one of Janeway's constables. It demanded that he hurry.

The chaplain's palm was wet as he grasped the knob and turned, pulling the door toward the rapidly beating heart within his chest. A female figure stood silently in the unlighted hallway, her features suddenly flooded by the light from the room. A girl. Young . . . blond . . . with blood on her face.

And when the sun begins to fling his flaring beams,
Me, goddess, bring to arched walks of twilight groves...
                    Alfred Lord Tennyson (1809—1892)
                    Trinity College

The fragrance of moss was fresh, but musty at the same time. It smelled of both life and death, giving off multifarious scents of woodland and cool places that Nick had never noticed before. Now, with his face pressed so close to the moss-covered trunk of a forest willow, close enough to see every crease and swirl of its bark, he studied a patch of lime green moss in glorious detail. It was an entire, perfectly formed forest in a microcosm, a brilliant green world with a depth and life of its own.

He felt Gwenillan's body stir and he pressed her more tightly to him, her back resting against the tree trunk and her arms around his neck. They had been standing like this for what seemed to Nick like hours, but he was content to let the world go on and time pass as they kept their silent embrace. Even when he had heard what sounded like the rapid-fire crackle of fireworks in the distance earlier, he had said nothing. He just wanted to hold her, letting his doubts and fears melt away. So long as he felt the warmth of her body against his, he knew this was no dream.

Nick's chin rested on Gwen's shoulder, his lips near the warmth of her neck and the rich smell of moss and trees. He could not see her face, but he sensed that she was smiling. There were so many things he wanted to ask, so many questions to be answered, but when they had met on the dark forest path, all he could do was hold her. She had embraced him just as urgently, but also in silence, as though in speaking they would lose the moment or break the spell. They had kissed, and now as she leaned back against the curve of the tree, Nick caressed her body again, convincing himself that finally he had her. The firmness of her flesh under his touch was not his imagination. Gwenillan had come back to him, and he would not let her go again.

She moved against his chest, and Nick felt her lips on his neck. Then her embrace loosened and he pulled away slowly so that he could look into her face. She smiled slightly and looked up at him, her eyes like the forest, green-gold and cool with random shafts of light adding sparkle and life.

"Gwen," he began softly, interrupting the magic, "you don't know what I've been through since last night. I have to ask . . ."

She looked down, denying him the lovely mystery of her eyes. It was clear she did not want to hear his questions, but he had to continue.

"Gwenillan, where have you come from? Why were you waiting here at this time of night?"

Her enigmatic smile returned as she held him gently at arm's length. Then she stepped away from the cool trunk of the willow, warmed now along one side by the heat of their bodies. "That is not important," she said very quietly, but with a trace of haughtiness he had not heard in her voice before.

She seemed to be taunting him, making light of what she had put him through. "All right then," he heard himself say, "let me ask something that is important." He walked a few paces in the opposite direction and then turned to face her where she stood toying with the branch of a holly bush. "Who are you, Gwen? Why are you really here . . . and what do you want from me?"

The girl continued to look down at the leafy branch twirling in her hands. The smile no longer played across her lips.

"Gwenillan. Answer me. What is there to hide? I'll understand whatever it is you're afraid to tell me." When her silence persisted, Nick felt his face growing hot.

"Why have you lied to me? Tell me the truth now." He grasped her by the shoulders and felt her hair like silk against his hand. Her eyes gazed back at him nearly level with his own.

"Nick, you really do love me, don't you?"

"Yes! Yes, I love you. That's why I have to know the truth!"

Her beautiful face remained impassive as she spoke again, resisting his attempt to pull her closer. "Do not answer lightly, Nick. Do you want to be with me? Do you want that more than anything?"

Nick was held by her eyes like a mariner with his gaze fastened on a far horizon. His reason and emotions and physical longing all struggled to arrive at the answer she demanded. When he spoke, it was with conviction, his voice firm and steady in the forest darkness. "Gwenillan, being with you means more to me than anything I can imagine . . . now or ever."

"That is your free decision, truthfully spoken?" she questioned him, still holding back from his embrace, almost as though she hoped to dissuade him from offering himself to her in love.

"Do you love me?" he responded simply.

The girl did not smile as she replied. "I should not, but I do love you, Nick Lombard. You are the only one I have loved."

Nick looked into her eyes with relief. "Then why this mystery? Why can't you tell me everything?"

Gwenillan took a step backward, away from his tender hold on her shoulders. She did not answer, clasping her hands instead across her breasts as though locked in some internal struggle she could not speak of even with the man to whom she had just pledged her love. Thunder sounded in the distance over the desolate fens.

"Gwen, you know about the dreams, don't you? The forest, the man in red . . . the girl at the river. You know what it all means."

When she simply stood staring into his face, making no effort to respond, he turned away and threw up his hands in exasperation. "What the hell do you want from me?" he shouted, his voice resounding in the stillness of the forest.

"Nothing, I want nothing. Go away, Nick. Just go now and leave me alone. I won't see you again."

Nick turned back to her in surprise, reaching out for her arm, but she pulled away with unexpected strength.

"I lied," she said coldly. "I don't love you. Go home! Your friends are there. Leave me alone!" Then, turning her back to him, she raised her clenched fists in the air and screamed once very loud, a wail of despair stronger than any emotion Nick had ever seen displayed. "Go, now! Before it's too late!" she cried out to him, her voice cracking as she turned in tears toward the trees. Then she ran, plunging headlong into the thickest part of the woods like a swimmer diving into the ocean. She did not look back.

"Gwenillan!" Nick hesitated only a moment before sprinting after her. Branches caught at his face and clothing and he could barely see her running form ahead of him, but he followed in her wake through the dark underbrush and trees.

He called out after her a few more times, but soon he needed all his breath for running. She passed through the darkness and trees like a young deer as Nick followed, the chase having an almost hypnotic effect on him. Soon he had no idea how long he had been running deeper and deeper into the woods, and no idea where he might be. His only concern was keeping Gwenillan's dark running figure in sight. She was well ahead, her slender form appearing and disappearing from view as she passed among the dark shapes of the ever-thickening trees.

Nick shielded his face from branches, but before long he hardly felt it when a root stubbed his toe or a branch whipped across his body. The running became automatic, so that he began to notice other things . . . the three-quarter moon resting atop the dark branches above his head, a strong wind stirring the treetops, the sounds of night birds and running creatures that he disturbed in crashing through the brush.

Almost without noticing the transition, Nick found himself running down a clear pathway. He thought he could still see Gwenillan ahead, but he was no longer sure. The trees around him were much larger than any he had seen in Trinity Wood before, towering over his head like the dark and massive columns of some gigantic temple. He realized suddenly that the haunting music of the reed flute was in his ears once again, but he could not be sure if the sound was real or if he was creating it in his fevered imagination. The pumping of his lungs and the agitated pounding of his heart as he ran added percussion to the primitive rhythms of the unseen instrument.

Suddenly the level surface of the path was gone and Nick fell, sprawling forward headlong until icy water hit him like the crack of a whip where a shallow stream crossed the path. He thought he knew the woods well, but he had never before found a stream. Pulling himself to his feet, bruised and wet, he heard the terrible baying sound in the distance. Was it animal or man? He could not be sure, but it seemed to be on three sides of him now, like the sound made by hunters driving game into a trap.

With faltering steps, Nick began to run down the packed earth of the path stretching out before him into the shadows of the great trees. The light of the moon was entirely obscured by the gigantic shapes all around him, but he knew Gwenillan must be somewhere in the darkness ahead.

When he reached the clearing of Trinity Grove, the opening in the forest canopy above had transformed it into a golden lake of moonlight in the center of the forest blackness. It was as it had been on the night of their first meeting, but larger somehow, surrounded by more massive oaks than he remembered. Nick stopped at the edge of the clearing, panting for breath. Gwenillan was there in the center of the circle of honeyed light, the three-quarter moon above her head making a golden halo of her shining hair. She was running easily across the open space toward the trees. Nick called out to her, but she did not look back.

He ran out into the open light of the clearing and stopped near the center. Gwenillan had just reached the trees when she paused and turned back toward the young man pursuing her, his red flannel coat deceiving her for a moment in the moonlight. Tears welled up in her eyes before she turned away for the last time, the image of a man in red once again burned onto her memory forever. She was close enough for Nick to glimpse her tear-streaked face, and then she was gone, fading into the shadow of a gray-green willow.

Nick stood dumbly looking at the dark facade of the Grove, like a living Stonehenge around the clearing. Surely it hadn't looked like this, not this huge, this ancient, less than a week before? The baying sounds had stopped. So had the music. He was surrounded by total silence, no wind, no forest stirrings or night sounds. He listened for the slightest noise, an owl's cry, a rustling of leaves . . . a girl running through the brush beyond the willow . . . but there was nothing.

Slowly, gradually, he began to feel the earth tremble under his feet. With it came a faint rumbling like thunder underground. As he felt the tremor spread up his body along his spine, he swore he could hear the muted echo of shouts, of screaming and cries of pain somewhere in the distance.

Then there was silence before the music began again, closer this time as the flute wove a melody around the hollow thumping of a crude drum. Nick was drawn toward the nearest trees, where a gentle tinkle and clash of metal and glass was carried by the wind now sweeping across the forest clearing. He moved steadily toward the gap in the trees through which Gwenillan had disappeared. As he approached it, he gazed up at the largest oak in the Grove, lying directly ahead of him, next to the willow. Searching for the source of a strange whistling noise, like the sound of wind escaping from the depths of the earth, his eye traveled up the scarred trunk of the ancient tree until it reached a knotted configuration of bark in the shape of a human face. Nick knew every line in that horrible face from his dreams. He recognized the knotty brow, the swollen cheeks, the twisted knothole mouth that issued forth a wind from the hollows of the enormous trunk.

Staring up in horror at the oak tree with the face of a man, Nick felt his legs weaken under him as all his nightmares came rushing back upon him. Still sweating from the running, he nonetheless felt suddenly chilled all over. Slowly he forced his eyes to leave the nightmare face on the tree. It was then that he saw the light in the darkness near him. Peering into the blackness beyond the edge of the forest clearing, he could see the flicker of a small flame.

Nick moved toward the light, calling out as he went. "Hey, what are you doing there?" He saw a dark figure crouched low to the ground near the jewel of flame. "You can't start a fire here. The whole woods could go up!"

The red-bearded man, interrupted in the act of covering his escape, whirled around on the intruder. He glanced down at the small pile of brush that he had just set alight and then stood near the wood he had gathered. "Stay out of this, boy!" he ordered venomously. "I'm warning you."

Nick noted the heavy accent, similar to Gwen's. Then he allowed his anger and frustration to focus on this intruder in Gwenillan's woods. "Warn me all you want, mister," he challenged, continuing to walk cautiously toward the taller man. "I can't let you burn down the Grove."

Stepping between the dark-haired boy and the fire, Jan Troop took up a threatening stance. Nick barely saw the glint of the knife blade reflecting the flames in time to jump back as it slashed toward him.

"I warned you," the Dutchman hissed. "Now run away while you still can."

Nick stood defiantly a few feet out of reach, crouched in a defensive posture. "I can't let you burn down the Grove," he repeated coldly, not sure why he was being so brave, but thinking of Gwen at risk somewhere in the darkness of the trees.

Before Nick's words had died on the night air, Troop lunged again. This time Nick not only ducked, he reached out, grasping the hand that held the knife. The two men struggled, Nick twisting the knife hand and then swinging his assailant's arm so that it struck hard on the rough and unyielding trunk of an oak. Troop cried out in pain as he dropped his weapon into the shadows at the trunk of the great tree. With two hands free now, the larger man tried to throttle the breath from the young American. Why was he here? Where had he come from? Not police . . . but he knew they would catch up soon, unless . . .

Nick was close to blacking out, his breathing choked off, when the Dutchman tripped over a massive tree root, causing him to stumble backward and loosen his deadly grip. The two men fell together into the small fire struggling to life. As they rolled for position, the burning embers were scattered into the dry underbrush. Furious now, Troop used his superior strength to gain an upper position. His right hand flailed about and came up with a new weapon. The dead branch came down with a sickening thud on the head of the young man. The Dutchman was about to strike the unconscious boy again when he heard the noise. It came from behind him in the forest darkness. Troop rose up quickly and stood defensively, the bloodstained branch in his hand, to face this new threat.

He did not cry out when he saw the horned man looming up in the shadows of the trees. It stood squarely before him, nostrils flaring and eyes burning with the vacant brutality of a beast. Troop stood frozen to the spot in fear as the creature parted its hideous black lips in an animal snarl, bathing him in the foul odors of the charnel house. Then he stumbled backward, searching for a way out. As the howling wind rose with sudden and unnatural force above the trees, the creature behind him reared back its bullish neck and ripped the air with a bestial roar that challenged the wind for mastery of the night.

Jan Troop staggered out into the clearing. When he forced himself to look back, the horned man was gone. Its animal stench lingered, but the man-beast was gone. Gone, too, was the body of the American boy. The red jacket was nowhere in sight. But more important, the scattered embers had ignited the brush in a half dozen spots, and flames were rapidly spreading to connect them into a fire that was growing larger by the minute.

The frightened fugitive wandered in a daze across the clearing until he was confronted by a massive oak tree with the face of a man blocking his way. All he wanted now was a path to escape, away from the fire he had started and from his police pursuers, away from this nightmare woods.

The chink of glass chimes sounded on the steadily rising wind. As the Dutchman stared in disbelief, a faint blue mist began to form around the slate gray trunk of the ancient tree. It took shape slowly, like a shadow, forming the limbs and torso of a man. Then there were weapons, a battle axe and shield, and finally a head, its features obscured by the conical shape of a metal helmet.

Troop looked around frantically, but the spreading fire blocked any retreat. All around him, at every tree in the Grove, the shades of fallen warriors were taking shape, emerging from the resting places where they had sought unattainable solace for two millennia. Like faceless shadows the Cendl emerged once again to seek a bloody vengeance. Unearthly figures moved forward with a spiderlike gait. For the Celangi. In the name of the Dark Mother! Death to the outlander in every generation!

Jan Troop screamed now, but it was too late. A pall of oil-black smoke from the burning woods blew along the ground to mingle with the rising mist. The clash of metal and terrible sounds of massacre were in the air, and an unnatural wind rushed to a crescendo over the blood-nourished oaks of Trinity Grove.

> I am the rider of the wind,
> The stirrer of the storm.
> Lord Byron (1788—1824)
> Trinity College

John Blessed lost his footing more than once crossing the field. Blasted furrows, he couldn't see them in the darkness, and this damned blue mist everywhere wasn't any help. The black curtain of Trinity Wood lay ahead of them, silently guarding its secrets from the two men approaching from the east.

Lewis Janeway was tired, very tired. He had let the van give him the slip . . . Mrs. Woodbridge and the American girl had disappeared. The raid had ended in a blasted shooting match—with the main culprit getting away! Now he had a gaol full of suspects, two warrant searches in progress, a pair of suspected Irish terrorists in custody, and a potentially dangerous fugitive at large. All that, and here he was tramping across a farmer's field in the dark looking for a lost college boy. All because his old friend had a wild theory that the boy was in danger and that for some unknown reason he would be in this woods after midnight.

It was all too much for one day. Janeway didn't think it was just his age; it would have been difficult for a man half his years. And it was far from over.

The inspector wished silently that the young man stumbling along beside him had had sense enough not to insist on coming along, or that he had been sensible enough to prevent it. Jan Troop could be anywhere in these woods, in addition to whatever it was Anglesey suspected of lurking there in the darkness. As he continued to pick his way across the field, one unsteady step at a time, Janeway was aware of the weight of the Smith & Wesson bumping against his hip in his jacket pocket.

He stopped for a moment and lifted his light from the misty furrows, sweeping its beam across the blank face of the woods. Somehow the forest reminded him for an instant of a gigantic sleeping animal, quiet now but watchful, breathing softly with potential violence. John Blessed stopped beside him, taking the opportunity to pull his coat closer around him. As he did, he felt the sharp corner of the chaplain's silver crucifix.

"Do you know what we're doing out here, Inspector? I mean, do you really know what this is all about?"

Janeway continued to scan the woods. Seeing nothing, he pulled the beam of light back to rest in the gently swirling mist at his feet. "What I know is James Anglesey," he said. "I've known him for nearly twenty years, and I've never seen him upset by anything before. If he asked me to trek across three fields this size, I'd do it." He settled the Irish tweed more securely on his head. "No, John, I have no more idea than you what we can expect to find in those woods."

Even as he spoke, the inspector felt the wind pick up. It was coming at them from the west, from the direction of the woods, not as was usual from the northeast off the Baltic and the North Sea. But it was as cold as any Baltic wind, sending a chill through both men with its first touch.

Blessed glanced at the older man, and they both looked toward the woods. John lifted his flashlight beam. "Look there!"

A black column of smoke rose on the wind from the depths of the forest, writhing back upon itself as it emerged above the treetops like some obscenely huge black snake. "Let's go," the inspector ordered, and they both began to move as quickly as they could toward the woods. They had only gone a few steps, however, when the tempest increased tenfold in its force. It swirled across the treetops, whipping the smoke into a rearing and snapping serpentine shape amid a resounding clatter of dry winter branches. Then the wind swept down on the open field with a roar like thunder. Janeway covered his face with his arm. Blessed turned his back and bent over under the force of the blast.

They were making little headway even before the hail came. Hard icy pellets beat down on the field like bullets, forcing both men to crouch low under the onslaught. The shelter of the house was too far away.

"Run for the trees!" Janeway shouted over the roar of the wind, still increasing at a pitch louder than any natural sound he had ever heard.

They tried to run, but the force of the storm was too great. John Blessed fell first. He stumbled in a furrow and could not rise as the storm of hail beat down on his back with stones half as large as a man's fist. He screamed out something, but it was immediately swept away on the wind.

Janeway did not see him fall. He struggled on until he too was knocked to the ground by unrelenting wind and hail. As his flashlight fell from his hand, it was picked up by the wind and thrown across the field like a flaring rocket gone wildly out of control.

Above them both, above it all, the wind swooped and howled, whipping across the face of Trinity Wood in its fury. But hidden deep within the wood, in Trinity Grove, all was now quiet.

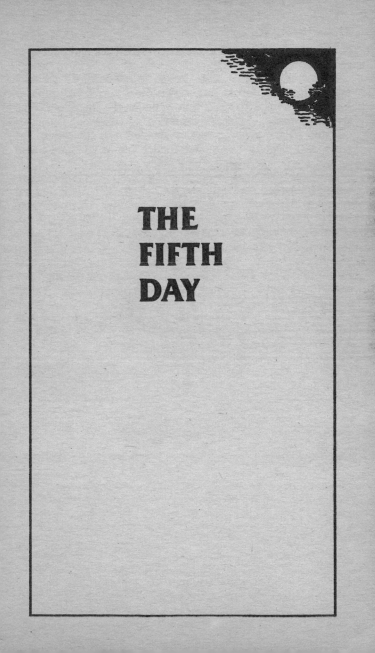

THE
FIFTH
DAY

EPILOGUE

Soon fades the spell, soon comes the night;
Say will it not be then the same,
Whether we played the black or white,
Whether we lost or won the game?

Lord Macaulay (1800–1859)
Trinity College

Jan Troop could see the cluster of figures near the center of the clearing, surrounded on all sides by the charred and smoking ruins of the great oaks. They had been there for some time, talking among themselves and roping off a section of the clearing. They had not seen him.

From where he was, he could not see the body. In any case, the mutilated corpse had been covered with a plastic sheet, the police photographers having finished their grisly work in the weak early morning light. It was just after dawn now, and what little remained of the once great Grove was water-soaked from the sudden storm of hail and rain that had doused the fire before it could spread to the entire wood. The sun cast a rosy glow into the open bowl of the clearing. It would be a lovely day.

The tall man with the battered tweed hat, the inspector from the City Police, was standing off to one side alone. He looked tired, tired and troubled. About what, Jan Troop did not know or care. Even had he known that the inspector was thinking about Eleanor Woodbridge—the American girl had told him the whole story—it would not have concerned the Dutchman now.

A tall, thin, slightly stooping figure stood near the roped-off area. Reverend Anglesey had been up all night, too. Now his head was bowed and he seemed to be reciting some sort of prayer. Nearby stood John Blessed, with a bandage around his head. Guy and St. John and Tom Newell were standing nearby, silent for once all three of them.

Sara Larsen had given the chaplain quite a fright, arriving unannounced at the door of Wychfield. She stood now by Anglesey's side, looking around at the blackened, smoking trees. Turning slightly, Sara smiled at Nick Lombard.

Nick's head was bandaged, like Blessed's, having been treated by the police medics after he had been found. He knew who had saved him. Not that he remembered very clearly being lifted and carried through the forest, still half-unconscious. All he could recall was the crash of the brush underfoot and a raw scent of animal musk as strong arms had carried him away from the burning Grove and placed him carefully in a safe place. *She* had not carried him, but she had saved him. He touched his cheek now as he remembered her last kiss, a brief brushing of silken hair and tender lips before he was left alone at the edge of the dark woods.

He looked up and found Sara offering her smile. Smiling back, he thought of Gwen. There were so many things she had to tell him, but he was beginning to understand. He leaned gently against the seared grey green trunk of a willow. There was so much to learn. And she would always be here to guide him.

Off to one side, a stocky police sergeant in a brown trilby hat was giving orders to a group of constables, their uniforms and checkered hatbands marking them out from the others gathered in the clearing. On the sergeant's orders, the policemen began to fan out into the fringes of the now dead forest grove, looking carefully down at their feet as they walked.

For a moment, Jan Troop was fearful as they came his way, toward the charred remnants of the ancient oak. They might see him. If they looked up.

Troop knew that he had changed. His cheeks were swollen, his brow knotted and enlarged. In truth, his entire face was horribly distorted, and blackened now by the fire, his mouth twisted to one side and open where the wind sometimes whistled through like breath from the center of the earth.

The morning sun was up now above the trees, shining down on the small group around the plastic-covered lump of dead flesh in the clearing. The cursed outlander saw it all. If the others looked up, one of them might even notice a flash of blue in the deep-set eye sockets of the burnt-black oak tree with the face of a man.

A gentle breeze stirred what remained of his dead upper branches, making them rattle like bones as he stared out forever across the ruined treetops of Trinity Grove.

Avon Books presents
your worst nightmares—

...haunted houses

ADDISON HOUSE   75587-4/$4.50 US/$5.95 Can
Clare McNally

THE ARCHITECTURE OF FEAR
                       70553-2/$3.95 US/$4.95 Can
edited by Kathryn Cramer & Peter D. Pautz

...unspeakable evil

HAUNTING WOMEN   89881-0/$3.95 US/$4.95 Can
edited by Alan Ryan

TROPICAL CHILLS   75500-9/$3.95 US/$4.95 Can
edited by Tim Sullivan

...blood lust

THE HUNGER   70441-2/$4.50 US/$5.95 Can
THE WOLFEN   70440-4/$4.50 US/$5.95 Can
Whitley Strieber